GW00455262

His Mighty Hand

Volume Three: The Light

Keelan LaForge

ISBN: 9781791879723
Printed in Belfast, United Kingdom.
Cover Design by James, GoOnWrite.com
Proofread by/Blurb by Pauline Hanna.

Dedication

For Sylvia and Sadie, my two little rocks.

Chapter One

I had five hundred thoughts in my mind, but I couldn't put a voice to one of them. I couldn't differentiate between Gene's thoughts and mine, between Gene's needs and mine. My dad glanced away from the road as we sat at that red light and looked me in the face.

"You're doing the right thing, love, for Hope."

The light changed to amber and then to green and we were hurtling towards the entrance of the refuge, even at thirty miles per hour. I couldn't think of anything to counter him with, so I sat, frozen to my seat, watching the buildings pass us by. The view didn't hold any associations for me. I'd been there a handful of times during the Summer holidays, to get ice cream and walk along the seafront when I was little. I had no idea about the layout of the town; I was lost in this little land. Everything was fresh and new, and I could look at it without feeling afraid. It was like a bloodied sheet being stripped away and replaced with a pressed white cotton one.

We arrived at what I thought was the door to the women's shelter. I double-checked the door number that I had typed into my phone. Nothing marked it out from any other building in the street; that was the whole idea. No one was allowed to know where it was, and no one was allowed to visit. Everything was moving so quickly I didn't have time to consider the gravity of what I was doing. I was just putting one foot in front of the other, like a toddler's tentative steps, focusing on staying upright more than on where I was going to. I had no expectations about living in a hostel; I was too distracted by hoping to make it there alive. My phone was in my bag. I felt the urge to check it as we got out of the car. That half hour was the longest I'd gone without looking at it in years. But I didn't have to; there would be no consequences later. I walked up to the door and pressed the buzzer.

"Hello?"

"It's Aoife, I'm here."

"Coming down now, Aoife."

It was weird being addressed as something other than a pet name or a profanity.

Two women flung the door open and gave me their best smiles; welcoming without being insensitive.

I could barely speak, but they seemed to expect that.

"We'll help you bring in everything from the car. Are these your parents?" asked the dark-haired worker.

I nodded.

Everyone carried my possessions in and laid them in the hallway. Then it was time for my parents to leave. They hugged me and then, they were locked out of the building; they weren't allowed inside either. I followed the workers through a door with a glass panel in it. It reminded me of university halls a little, but without the light atmosphere or amusement.

The two workers introduced me to the child-workers in the creche. I sat down on one of the children's chairs and began to cry. One of the workers passed me a packet of tissues and I blotted my eye make-up. I was crying with sadness and crying with relief, but I wasn't crying the way I did in the house with Gene. That type of crying was reserved especially for him. Those were the cries of bitter despair. Cries of sadness were nothing in comparison.

A check-list was completed, the details of which I couldn't have remembered even at the time. I left Hope in the care of the workers and they took me upstairs to have a private chat. One of the counsellors got her clipboard and led me into a counselling room that looked just like a living room in somebody else's house. The sofa cushions gave the illusion of comfort and everything was tidy and cared for. It struck me as odd that the interior of the hostel made my own home look unhomely. It was strange to sit in a room with space around me, no clutter that shouldn't be there, no litter concealing the floor.

She asked me what felt like a hundred questions, few of which I answered truthfully. I had to do all I could to protect Gene, to ensure that getting back together was an option for us. I was just there for a little break and then I'd go back. I let the worker tick her boxes, forming a picture of my level of safety with her risk assessment. I could hear Gene inside my head telling me it was all bullshit and to make sure I told the fucking truth. So, I told a combination of his truth and my truth.

"Did he ever hurt you?"

"No."

"Did he ever call you names?"

"A few times."

"Did he stop you seeing your family?"

"No, but I was seeing them less and less. It might have just been a coincidence."

I wondered if the walls had ears: Gene's ears. I was delusional. How could I have invented a whole story out of nothing? Gene was the only person who loved me and the only person who protected me, and here I was "ratting him out," as he would have said.

"When did the abuse start?"

"It's more complicated than that. He said I was doing it too. I've hit him before. He has never hit me."

I burst into tears and pulled the last tissue from the plastic packet on my knee.

The worker regarded me with empathetic eyes.

"Would you like a cup of tea?"

"Yes please."

It was nice to be offered a cup of tea, knowing I wouldn't suffer the consequences of it later. I recalled the last time Gene had made me a cup of tea in the teapot he bought me and felt ill. I'd left that teapot sitting on top of the kitchen counter. I hoped he wouldn't break it when he got home that day. I'd left my orchid there too. It was a plant Gene had got me just after I'd had Hope. It had bright blue petals and I'd done a painting of it in my sketchpad one day. That was at home too. Everything I cared about was at home. I'd left the most important parts of my life behind; especially Gene. I wondered what he was doing in work and how many times he'd rung me. My phone was still on its silent setting, deep at the bottom of my bag. I hadn't had time to unpack my things yet; they were waiting for me in my new bedroom.

The worker seemed to sense my mind was elsewhere. She finished up the questions and got me to initial everything. I felt suspicious doing it. What were they getting me to sign? Gene always told me not to sign anything; not without checking with him first. People always used your signature against you as evidence in court. I worried they'd reproduce that file as I fought to keep custody of Hope. I hoped I hadn't said enough to strengthen their case against me.

"Do you know your way around the town?" the worker asked. Her name was Lisa, and it transpired that she was the manager there.

"No, I've never really been before."

"I have a map here."

Lisa proceeded to make little crosses on the page on the main facilities I would need: the post office, the library, the doctor's surgery, the supermarket. I hadn't even thought that far ahead. I would have to pull myself together enough that day to complete a food shop; it seemed like more than I could bear.

"Thanks for that, Aoife. I'll let you collect Hope from the creche now and let you get settled in your room."

She gave me a small smile and held the door open for me as we exited the room.

"I don't remember where I'm going," I said. My head was swirling, and I couldn't make sense of how I'd got there. I couldn't even remember ascending the staircase.

"That's ok. It's a lot to take in."

I followed her downstairs and saw Hope happily playing in the playroom. That reassured me a little; if life went on for her, maybe it could for me too. It struck me how shiny and new the toys looked, even though they'd probably been played with by hundreds of pairs of tiny hands. I hadn't realised until I saw them how grimy Hope's toys looked at home. They seemed to be perpetually coated in dust. We'd burnt so many candles to heat the place when the heating was broken that it had left soot over everything we owned. I'd spent days scrubbing it off, but they still somehow always looked dirty.

I picked Hope up and carried her with me, following Lisa back through the doors.

"Oh, before we go upstairs, I'll give you the tour."

We walked into the kitchen: four compact kitchens squeezed into one large one. There was a dining table and a TV corner with a sofa in it. There were a couple of women sitting in the room, but I couldn't bring myself to look at them, never mind make conversation. An older blonde lady approached me and smiled.

"Hello, I'm Sarah. What's your name?"

"Hi, I'm Aoife."

It seemed odd that someone cared enough to want to know my name. She seemed friendly, but I still couldn't bring myself to look her in the eye. I stared at the floor tiles instead; at least they couldn't do me harm.

"There is a fire exit here and a smoking area in case you need it."

The worker seemed to understand that pregnancy wasn't enough reason to keep women off cigarettes in such circumstances.

"We have a rota, and everyone has a weekly chore. But you won't have to worry about that this week - not until you're settled in. There is a toilet at the back. I'll show you upstairs."

I trudged upstairs behind her. I felt odd: relieved yet verging on despair. I'd left my home, by choice, to stay in this strange place and I couldn't understand why. I had no right to be there. This was a home for abused women; that wasn't a category I fitted into. I felt like a traitor walking along the hallway. The workers were probably laughing at me in private, telling each other how ridiculous it was that I was there.

Lisa showed me the bathrooms, the laundry room and finally, my room.

"Here's your key. We've given you a family room."

"Thanks."

She unlocked the door and opened it for me. She seemed to understand that doing such basic tasks was more than I could handle. She held the fire door open and I surveyed my surroundings. It looked like a dormitory; somewhere I might have gone to on an overnight school trip. There were bunkbeds, a sink and a single bed. On top of a chest of drawers, there was a basket of essentials.

"There are toiletries in here in case you need them; towels, a toothbrush and anything else you might have forgotten."

I peered into the basket and saw a bottle of nail polish and some lip balm. It almost felt like I was staying in a luxury hotel. The workers were more thoughtful about what practical items I needed than Gene had been in the past year. I'd agonised just a day before over whether I was able to afford to buy myself a plain lip balm. I'd hoped all evening that he wouldn't notice it and comment on it. The kindness of strangers was something I no longer believed in. What could they want from me? Why were they helping me? What would they trick me into doing that I hadn't agreed to? Time would tell, except I had no plans on staying to find out.

Lisa left me to get settled in. She'd told me her name when I'd arrived, but I couldn't piece together much of what had happened that day, and at that moment, I couldn't remember any of the staff's names. Hope scaled her way along the bed, investigating her new room. There was a travel cot the workers had set up for her. I looked at the grand windows. They were covered in thin veils that blew in the breeze travelling through the open window. I sat down on the bed, not sure where to start with unpacking, or if there was any point. Was I staying that night? I very much doubted it. All I wanted was to go home before Gene got home from work and act like none of this had happened. Maybe he hadn't even noticed yet. I still hadn't checked my phone; I was afraid to. I hadn't spoken to Gene in three hours and his mind would be inventing the worst. He might not even be in work; he'd probably left early and found the house empty by now. I imagined him shaking his head as he picked the ten pound note up off the kitchen counter. "That's all she left me with? Selfish fucking bitch." I'd left him one of the laptops, so he could at least listen to music and watch his boxsets that night. Maybe that was all Gene needed to be happy; I was only something superfluous. He could smoke his weed in the house, throw his clothes all over the floor and order pizza for dinner every night if he so wished. He still had access to our shared bank account, but there wasn't much left in it. Any money I had been saving was in my personal savings account. I wondered if I should split it with him. Maybe that was what he deserved. I'd suggest it to the workers when they next called by and see what they advised.

I hung up the few items of clothing I'd brought with me in the wardrobe. The room looked bare apart from Hope's toys. It felt freeing in a way, to not be tripping over clutter, to not be forbidden to put rubbish into the nearest bin, to not feel encumbered by things. There was a knock on the door. It was gentle, but it still made me flinch. I was like an animal with all its hairs on end: a caged one, brutalised by its owner, not one running free from dangers in the wild.

The door didn't burst open; even that unnerved me.

"Come in," I said. It didn't come out any louder than a whisper. I turned the door handle and looked up at the worker. She was the other worker who had let me into the building; a girl with red hair and a fearless smile: Claire.

"I found a few things for you."

I looked at her, puzzled. Why did she want to help us? What would the backlash be?

"Thanks."

"I was looking in storage and found a couple of toys for Hope and a blanket."

She handed a stuffed dog to me and a procession of quacking ducks.

"Thank you," I said, trying to smile. I couldn't tell if I was or not.

"We'll help you set up your benefits tomorrow. Just get unpacked today."

"I might have to go and get food soon."

"Do you need a food parcel?"

"What's that?"

"When women don't have enough money for food, we can order them in from the food bank."

"Oh, no, thanks. I have money."

I wasn't penniless, homeless or in need. I had a warm house to go back to if I wanted. I was only there by my own stubborn choice. It was a choice I was questioning more with each advancing minute. Was it too late to change my mind? Maybe I could pack up and sneak out without anyone noticing. I'd have to leave all personal effects behind, but I'd already done that once today. They were only material things; family was more important. I thought about filling my handbag with as much as I could and pretending to go to the shop, but I was frozen with fear. I was scared to walk down the street to the shop in case Gene somehow psychically knew where I was. We were soulmates after all; he could sense everything I felt, everything I thought, and he was quick at figuring things out. I was being silly. I needed to get lunch for Hope. I'd lost all track of time. I glanced at my phone. It was 2pm. Gene was due home in just over an hour, if he hadn't made his way there already. I could see there was a catalogue of missed calls and messages, but I couldn't bring myself to read any of them. I'd look at them later when I was feeling a little less emotionally labile. I'd get Hope something to eat and once we were fed and I was thinking more clearly, I'd decide what I was going to do; I'd decide how I was going to explain myself to Gene. Presumably, he didn't know where I was yet. But once he saw the ransacked interior of our house, he would know I'd left. Maybe I could tell him my head had gone sideways and I'd gone to my parents, but that I'd had a change of heart once I was thinking straight again. Hopefully that story would add up. I couldn't tell him the truth, or he'd never forgive me.

I bundled Hope into her coat and hat and carried her downstairs. I tried to slip past the office without drawing attention to myself. Thankfully, the door was closed for a staff meeting. I made my way to the front hallway and strapped Hope into her pram. The staff allowed me to keep it there without folding it up and storing it out of the way. No one seemed to think I was occupying more space than I deserved. It was a strange feeling: not feeling driven out of a place.

I opened the door and it slammed behind me. I'd have to ask the staff to allow me access to the building again. I didn't have a key to my own home; I wasn't allowed one. I wished I never had to see their friendly faces again. I'd rather be greeted by Gene's scowl any day. That was what symbolised home. Anything other than that was fakery; none of those strangers knew me well enough to care about my destiny, certainly not as much as Gene did. I felt a strong urge to phone Gene and have him console me. I needed him to tell me that everything would be alright and that he'd keep me safe. I left my phone in the back pocket of my bag and tried to direct my focus into finding the nearest shop. I couldn't remember where I was going and drew the map out of my coat pocket, searching for the "x" marking "Main Street." My whole world had been upended. I couldn't tell which end of the map was up, neither could I bear to ask a stranger for directions. I didn't have the courage to look them in the face, never mind interrupt their day. I stood there for long enough that Hope began to fuss. All routine had been cast aside and we hadn't had anything to eat since a rushed breakfast that morning.

I had savings, but I had no idea how long I'd need to make them last. I tried to buy the cheapest foods I could find. I had no desire to spend time cooking in the communal area, but Hope's needs had to come before mine. I piled basic ingredients into a basket. I had one narrow cupboard in which to fit dried goods. I was sharing a fridge with another lady. She had the top two shelves, I had the bottom two. I'd be getting my own fridge as soon as there was more space; families usually got a fridge of their own, I was told. I didn't feel like a family; Gene, Hope and I were a family. Without Gene, Hope and I were two nuts with the bolt that held us together missing. I balanced the items on the pram hood. Walking with Gene and doing all the pushing was like a trial run for my new life. But I was only toying with the idea of having a different way of life; I had no intention of it becoming permanent. There was a shelf I'd noticed in the kitchen where all occupants of the house placed unwanted items of food; like a lucky dip of food bank rejects. I could always add my shopping to the pile if I decided I wanted to go home once I got back. The women in that house were leading a much sadder existence than I was. I felt like a fraud walking amongst them. Once the workers realised how mild my circumstances were compared to theirs, they would probably encourage me to return home anyway. I walked back to the house, so I could get Hope's lunch on the table. I hoped no one was around so I didn't have to make conversation with them. I just wanted to be left to quietly suffer in my own internal torture chamber.

I made some soup and the passing workers peered into the pan, smelling the sautéed vegetables.

"Smells good," said a lady who'd just come on shift. "Your mummy is a good cook," she smiled at Hope.

I did a quiet laugh. She had no idea what she was talking about; I was one of the world's worst cooks. I served up our lunch and dragged Hope's highchair over to the dining table. She had to stay in it while I cooked, as well as when we ate and did the dishes. I could see that proving problematic. I hoped it was true that kids adapted to whatever was sent their way. Hope ate her soup, hitting the spoon against the bowl as she ate, and drawing in the mess she made on her tray table.

"What age is she?" asked the friendly lady, Sarah, who was sitting watching TV. She was the one who had introduced herself to me earlier.

"She's 11 months."

I didn't look up from the table and tried to make my voice and my existence disappear. I hadn't earned the right to look her in the eye. If I did, she might get angry. Who knew what might kick off? If I didn't make eye contact, no one could misinterpret a look I'd given them and fire off.

"How many months pregnant are you?"

"Four months. How long have you been here for?"

"Just a couple of weeks."

"Do you like it here?"

"It's fine. Better than where we were before."

I nodded but was unsure of whether I agreed with her. I knew I could never consider the building we were in to be home. Gene was what made a place home and if he was missing, it was just a hollow structure with no heart. A group of other women piled into the kitchen. They were extroverted and there was a lot of laughter. Two workers cracked jokes with them and they led them into one of the kitchens. Maybe it was time to run through the rules again. No – they were gathering in the kitchen to bake together.

"You do activities?" I asked, perplexed.

"Yeah, every week we do baking and cooking. Then we all get to eat it - that's the best bit. Want to join in?"

"Ok," I said, approaching the group, tentatively.

Maybe they didn't want me there. I didn't like to intrude on what they were doing. Jocularity was in the air, and I didn't want to spoil it with my lack of humour. I watched from the side lines as they made pancakes. There were a couple of children in the group. I felt like less of an oddity knowing I wasn't the only mother in the building. Maybe it was an acceptable place to bring your children to, after all.

"Hey, Sarah, want to do the flipping? Get your arse over here, love. Are you planning on watching telly while we do all the hard work?"

"Fuck off, I'm not getting paid to make them like you are," she laughed at Claire.

I waited for an argument to break out, but the worker just snorted with laughter and flung the spatula at her. She approached the pan and started flipping the pancakes, shuffling her bottom as she did it. Someone turned on the radio and everyone laughed at her performance. I hadn't worked out everyone's place in the refuge yet, but she seemed to be the clown of the group. I smiled at them and my gut relaxed a little for the first time in months.

Chapter Two

Late afternoon, when Hope was having her nap, the emptiness hit me full force. I opened the messages on my phone.

"Why aren't you answering your phone? I'm freaking the fuck out."

"Where the fuck are you? I'm coming home."

"I'm worried fucking sick. What the fuck?"

Once Gene arrived home, there were no further updates. I had to phone him to make sure he was ok. The phone rang a couple of times and the sickness returned to my gut. It was clenching so hard it was like an irate fist. Gene picked up.

"Yeah?"

His voice sounded fainter than usual, less angry than I'd expected, like the voice of a bully who'd surrendered.

"Are you ok?"

"Does it matter?"

"Yes. I'm so worried about you."

"Where are you at? Your ma's?"

"No."

"Where are you?"

"I can't tell you."

"What the fuck do you mean, you can't tell me?" Gene's faded voice found a little of its fury again.

"I'm in a hostel."

"Like a women's shelter?"

"Yeah."

"Right." Gene said it with a marked lack of disinterest, like I'd just told him I'd bought an unnecessary pair of shoes, but he wasn't going to make me return them.

"I got to go."

"Please don't," I cried, pressing my lids together to force back the tears. Gene sounded like he was weakening, and I needed to be the strong one.

"I got to go," he said. His voice broke and raised in pitch as he disconnected the call.

I rang back but he didn't answer. I hoped he hadn't cut me off for good.

■■

That night, after Hope was asleep, I resumed my frantic attempts to phone Gene. I was ringing him with the same frequency he had phoned me while I was in the house. I was experiencing the feeling of panic that had likely prompted him to do the same. I could now empathise with the evil stranger. He wasn't bad; he was just insecure, feeling like I wasn't attentive enough to his needs. It was all my fault; Gene had told me to set up marriage counselling, but instead of doing it, I had done the unspeakable. I knew I had already put excessive demands on Gene's capacity for forgiveness and moving out without telling him was likely a step too far. Gene's phone went straight to voicemail. He must have turned it off, but I didn't stop trying to reach him anyway. I had to, to make sure he was ok.

By 10pm, he still hadn't turned it on again and my brain had gone into overdrive, imagining every horrific potential outcome. I had to find out if he was ok, and since I couldn't go there myself or ask my parents to, I'd have to come up with an alternative. So, I phoned the police helpline.

"I'm worried about my husband."

"What's wrong?"

"His phone is off, and I'm worried he might have committed suicide. Is there any way you could check on him?"

"Are you not with him?"

"No, I'm in a refuge."

"Oh – I'll check on him for you."

I was surprised they agreed to do it, but also indescribably relieved. I'd probably have to wait a couple of hours envisaging them finding Gene in the position I'd always feared I would. How could I abandon him like that? How could I leave him alone to struggle with his own mind? He'd never left me alone to deal with mine, apart from that day in New York and that day in the refuge. Both times he had had good reason to cut me off. I didn't have good reason to cut him off.

I held my phone in my hand, my finger poised above the answer button for two hours. Finally, the withheld number popped up on my screen.

"Hello?"

"Is that Mrs Savoyard?"

"Yes."

"We checked on him. He's fine. Says he was just sleeping."

Every muscle in my body relaxed. I might have been in a refuge, but Gene was alive, and that was all that mattered.

■■

The next day the refuge workers supported me while I made phone calls to update my benefit details. It was only temporary. Once Gene and I resolved things, I'd be going home. I could tell from the worried look in their eyes that they thought I'd be best off at home too. I didn't want to transfer my housing benefit, but it was in my name, so I had to. I didn't want to leave Gene in the lurch; the rent payment was due to leave my account the following day. I'd decided to pay it for him. I knew he wouldn't even have a fraction of the amount owed. I had all our savings after all; it was only fair. Housing benefit would cover my rent in the refuge and savings would cover Gene's until I returned home. I hoped Gene would still go to work if I wasn't there. I doubted I'd make it to work in such circumstances.

I phoned Gene and he surprised me when he picked up.

"Yeah?"

"Are you ok?"

"Does it fucking matter?"

"Yes."

"Did you have to send the fucking cops round?"

"I was worried about you. Your phone was off."

"I was fucking sleeping."

"I didn't know that."

There was a heavy silence that hung between us like a thick wall.

"Do you know I cried myself to sleep last night?" asked Gene.

"I'm sorry."

"I slept on the floor next to my daughter's crib, because you took her away."

"I didn't take her away. I didn't have a choice."

"Yes, you fucking did."

"I just want to sort things out. I'll pay your rent this month, so we can work things out."

"Just come fucking home."

"I can't."

"Why fucking not?"

"I'm scared you'll punish me. I need to know things will be different."

"None of this is my fucking fault. You got no one to blame but yourself for this shit."

My gut tightened. I'd hoped Gene would say he'd realised the error of his ways, that he'd stop scaring me and our romance would return to what it had been in its first days. I was still scared. I couldn't go home while I feared for my life. I knew it was an unreasonable worry to have, but I couldn't dismiss the twisting sensation in my gut that told me I was unsafe. Once that died down, I'd go home and hopefully Gene would treat me like none of this had ever occurred. He was right about one thing: I was responsible for the destruction of our dream; the one we had surmounted innumerable obstacles to achieve. One spur of the moment decision, and I'd changed the entire family dynamic. But it wasn't too late to remedy that. I had to repeat that to myself, or I wouldn't survive to the end of the day. There was a knock at the door, I hung up and I dropped my phone down the back of my pillow like I was hiding a stash of drugs from a warden.

"Yeah?"

The door opened gently. I wasn't used to anything but abrupt openings anymore; of doors, of sentences, of phone calls.

"Are you ready for your meeting?"

"I have a meeting?"

"Yeah, you just need to leave Hope into the creche."

"Oh, I'm sorry - I forgot."

"It's ok."

"No, I'm really sorry."

"Aoife, it's ok."

She gave me a compassionate look and I couldn't comprehend why. I took Hope downstairs to the creche and walked into the room apologetically. Hope was my responsibility; no one else's. I couldn't accept help from Gene, never mind anyone else. I felt like I owed them something.

"I'm sorry, I won't be long."

"Take your time. We've got hundreds of toys here," Ciara beamed at Hope. Alyssa and Ciara were the only two child-workers who worked there, and I felt bad stretching their resources to accommodate us.

"Are you sure? …you do have a lot of toys,"

I took a proper look at the room. I hadn't taken in any of the details the previous day.

"Where do you get them from?"

"They're donations."

"Really?"

"Yeah, we've got so many we don't know where to put them all. We'll need to rearrange the room soon. Won't we?" Ciara said to Alyssa.

Ciara included Hope in the conversation like she was on our level. Maybe Gene wasn't the only person in the world capable of that. Hope walked over to a three storey dolls house and lifted the figures like she was as familiar with them as the toys in her own home. I thought about the individual ones we'd had to leave behind and felt a pang of guilt. Hope didn't seem to mind. Self-imposed guilt was the only thing making me believe I was an inadequate mother; that and Gene's words that still circulated in my mind.

I went upstairs for my meeting. I was getting to know the layout of the house. The blurred vision I'd had of it when I'd arrived had cleared up a little. I almost felt welcome in the hostel, like I didn't have to watch the volume of the tread of my shoes on the floors, like I didn't have to avoid looking anyone in the eye for fear they might react badly.

"Hi," smiled a new worker I hadn't met before. "I'm Brenda, welcome to the house."

She was my key worker. I was told there were about ten workers in the house. There was a blackboard where they marked in who was on duty, so there weren't any surprises. They seemed to know surprises didn't sit well with the women in the house. After leaving such a fraught atmosphere, the first thing you needed was predictability and routine. At least, that's what I was told. Who was I to pass comment on the feelings of abused women? I still hadn't earned the right to be there. I could hear Gene's voice inside my head repeating that to me. I'd better check my phone as soon as my meeting ended. I knew I likely had double-digits of missed calls and the thought of them ringing and ringing behind the door of my room filled me with terror.

"I know it's the last thing on your mind, but we need to discuss a few practical things."

"Ok."

"Do you and Gene have any shared bills?"

"Yeah, the rent, and I pay his phone bill every month."

"Maybe you need to think about cancelling the direct debits?"

"Why?"

I got defensive the second she said it.

"You aren't responsible for him. He needs to pay his own bills."

"He can't afford to."

"Well, you aren't responsible for that."

"Yes, I am."

"Why do you think that?"

"Because without me, the bills wouldn't get paid. Gene doesn't know how to do that."

"What age is he?"

"41."

"A 41-year old man doesn't know how to look after himself?"

"It's different. He's from America. He just moved here a few months ago. His visa depends on the bills getting paid."

"And whose responsibility is that?"

"Mine."

The worker shook her head regretfully.

"I'm just going to pay his rent this month until he gets on his feet."

"Only you can make that decision, but you can't keep taking responsibility for him. He's responsible for himself. You're only responsible for yourself and your baby."

If I wasn't responsible for Gene's wellbeing, why did I feel like I was? Wasn't that the role of a wife?

"How long is left to pay on Gene's phone contract?"

"A year and a half."

"Would you consider cancelling it?"

"And leave him with no phone?"

"He can get a phone. He can get a cheap model with pay as you go if he can't afford anything else."

What she was suggesting to me sounded cold and disconnected. How could I cut Gene off financially and leave him to fend for himself in an unfamiliar country? He would never do that to me. However, the thought of continuing to pay all the household bills whilst staying in a hostel seemed like too much to take on. I'd pay Gene's rent one last time, just to keep a roof over his head until I could get home.

"You're doing him no favours by paying for everything. If he doesn't learn how to look after himself, nothing will ever improve in your relationship."

I nodded but didn't really take what she said on board. It was like listening to a tune you didn't like and planning to forget the moment it ended.

After I'd collected Hope from the creche, I returned to my room. There was a feeling of injustice sounding off in my mind. Why was I paying mine and Gene's phone bills? Why was I funding all bills when Gene was the one working? Gene's wages had covered all the weekly expenses, but none of the monthly ones. I needed to take a stand, however small. Maybe if he was forced upon his own resources, he'd rise to the challenge and our relationship would flourish as a result.

I rang the phone company. They allowed me to pay off Gene's handset without paying any future airtime bills. Maybe that was a fair compromise: I paid a couple of hundred pounds for a phone that Gene could keep, and he could pay the monthly cost of using it. As on every other occasion, I was wrong. Gene was "salty" when I told him.

"So, now you're telling me I ain't got no fucking phone?"

"The phone is yours, you just have to pay the bill."

"How the fuck am I going to afford that on what I earn?"

"You could get a pay as you go deal for a tenner a month."

"Fuck that. Thanks for nothing, I guess."

"I feel terrible."

"Sure you fucking do."

"I paid the rent today, Gene."

Gene laughed at me, like what I'd done was a measly droplet in an immense ocean.

I was nine hundred pounds poorer, but that didn't compensate for how badly betrayed Gene felt.

"When do I get to see my fucking daughter?"

"I'll meet you when you're less angry."

"What?"

"I'll meet up with you when you aren't angry."

"You don't get to decide that. She's my fucking daughter."

There was a knock on the door and I cut off the call and turned my phone screen to face the bed sheet in case Gene's name flashed up on it while the worker was in the room. I got the sense that not many women remained in contact with their exes once they were in the refuge. I was the only one in almost constant contact with mine. But the difference was that I hadn't left for good; everyone else was severing all ties and moving onto their new life. I was just trying to remould the old one. Once I'd knocked out a few kinks, things would be as blissful as in the beginning.

"Yeah?"

Claire opened the door softly.

"I have something for you."

"What is it?"

"A baby monitor, so when Hope is asleep you don't have to stay in the room."

"I can leave the room?"

"Yes. Maybe it'll give you a chance to get some time to yourself and chat to the other women, if you like. You could go down and make yourself a cup of tea and sit in the TV room."

"Thank you," I smiled.

I could tell they were trying to make me feel at home, but they still didn't realise I was only passing through.

"I might go home tomorrow."

"If you do, I'll have to put in a referral to social services."

"What? Why? You said it was my choice."

"It isn't really, not when you have Hope with you."

"But you said if I wanted to go home, I could leave whenever I wanted."

"You can, but we have an obligation to notify social services and we don't know what they'll do when they visit you."

Gene was right: no one was trustworthy. No one kept their word. Everyone was out to get us.

Chapter Three

For days, I wrestled with the two worst options of my life: never return home and lose Gene for good, or risk losing Hope if social services weren't on our side. I sat on the mattress in my room, paralysed, watching Hope playing with her toys and waiting to talk to Gene. He'd gone to work every day that week. He was working on self-improvement. Perhaps he had realised the importance of fulfilling his visa obligations. He had to prove to me that things could be different, or I'd never be able to go back.

"Baby, just come home."

"I can't."

"Why the fuck not?"

"I was told if I go home, they'll send social services out."

"So fucking what? Stop being so fucking scared of everyone. They can't do shit."

"What if they take Hope away?"

"They can't fucking do that."

"How do you know?"

"They ain't got no reason to."

"They think our relationship is abusive."

"It's not like I was fucking beating the shit out of you every day."

"What about emotional abuse?"

"It was both of us. You're as much to blame as I am."

"So, you think our relationship is abusive?"

"Yeah, probably, but mostly I just think we rile each other. Call social services and talk to them directly. Tell them you're going home and there ain't nothing they can do about it."

"I can't talk to them like that."

"Yes, you can. You're just too afraid. Stop being a fucking coward."

"I'm not." I started to cry and hung up.

I was starting to get the feeling back that I'd had in the house. The one that had made me first lift the phone to the helpline: a dizzy effect inside my brain, like everything I'd once known about myself had been rewritten and I was losing my sense of self. I had to speak to one of the workers; properly, to find out what was going on. Why was I so unstable? Why did I feel so worthless? Why could I never do the right thing?

I opened my bedroom door and knocked, just audibly, on the office door.

There was a shriek of laughter and then someone called "come in." They always had a bright quality about their voices, like a cheery air stewardess who wants to welcome you on board and ensure your safety. They were my adversaries; they wanted to bring about the demise of my precious relationship, but I also couldn't deny the fact I felt safe around them. My gut unclenched itself when we spoke, and I didn't feel like I'd be punished for speaking my truth. A tear trickled down my cheek and I wiped it away, hoping no one saw how weak I was.

"Could I talk to someone when you get a minute?"

"Of course," said one of the workers, jumping up from her seat. It was a strange feeling: someone wanting to hear what I had to say. Gene used to too, and still sometimes did, when he was in good humour, but mostly, he cut me off before I managed to finish the first of my sentences.

One of the childcare workers whisked Hope away before she saw me crying and I followed Brenda into the living room. She was middle-aged lady. She almost seemed a bit stern when you met her, in a teacherly way, not in a bullying manner. But she took everything you said with the utmost seriousness and had limitless time to listen to you.

She plumped the cushion behind her back and sat back into it, like she was getting comfortable for a long chat. I had no idea what to say, or where to start. I couldn't even pinpoint the exact thing that was wrong; I just knew everything was.

"Well, what would you like to talk about?"

"I don't know," I said, pressing a tissue against my cheek like I was applying pressure to a bleeding wound.

"How are you feeling?"

"Confused."

Brenda nodded her head, knowingly.

"We hear this a lot. Would you like me to go through the wheel with you?"

"What's the wheel?"

"The power and control wheel."

"Ok."

She handed me a piece of paper and I wetted it with a few tears as I tried to read it. My mind was spinning too much to make sense of it.

"Let's break it down."

"Ok."

"I'll run through the categories and you can decide it you can relate to any of them."

"Ok, thanks."

"Money – withholding money, not allowing you to work, making all the decisions."

"I was doing that."

"What do you mean?"

"Gene worked but I managed the money. He wanted me to take care of the bills. But then he stopped going in and I was stressed all the time, trying to make ends meet."

"That's still financial abuse."

"Is it?"

Brenda nodded.

"What about threats and intimidation?"

"Yeah, but he never really hurt me."

"What do you mean?"

He just grabbed me by the throat a couple of times.

"Just?"

"Yeah, he never hit me or anything."

Brenda nodded and made a mark on the page on her clipboard.

"What about isolation?"

"He didn't stop me seeing my family. He just didn't like me going out for long without him. He rang me the whole time."

"That's control."

I shrugged. "I think he was worried I would cheat on him."

"That doesn't mean he can control everything you do. That's his issue. He needs to work through that."

The workers didn't seem to want me to take responsibility for any of Gene's behaviour. It was a new concept to me, considering I'd got into the way of doing that for years. Wasn't that what you did for your spouse?" You tried to keep them happy, tried not to make them angry, tried to manage your own level of fear. That was what marriage was about to me: taking care of someone, putting them first, self-sacrificing to make them happy. The type of healthy love I was learning about sounded rather self-serving to me. How could you create a harmonious relationship when all you did was look after your own needs and allow your partner to look after their own? That wasn't a partnership, that was two individuals living alongside each other, occupying the same house, but never encroaching on each other's territory.

"What about friendships? Did he prevent you having them?"

"No, he just didn't like my friends. Apart from one. He liked my best friend."

"Did you get to see her often?"

"She lives in England."

"Ah," she said, nodding her head like "that explains it."

"What about breaking objects?"

"Sometimes, but I did that too."

"What do you mean?"

"I felt like he was trying to make me lose my mind. Then he called me crazy, I told him I hated him, and I broke things."

I lowered my head, looking at the ground in shame. I was waiting for her to label me abusive.

"I hit him before too, lots of times."

"Why?"

"I panicked, he liked to keep me in a room and stop me leaving. Sometimes I hit him if he pushed me too far. Doesn't that mean I'm abusive?"

The worker shook her head. "I don't think it's that simple. It sounds to me like he was abusing you and you were reactive."

"But I hit him."

I'd never forgive myself for doing that, no matter how much the workers sought to absolve me of my guilt. To me, that made it clear-cut: I was the abuser and Gene was a victim of domestic violence.

"Did he ever name-call?"

"Yeah."

"Did he ever use Hope against you?"

"I don't know. He tried to take her a few times."

"What do you mean?"

"He told me he was taking her. I felt like he meant for good, but then he told me it was just for a walk. He took her away from me in town a few times. I had to chase after him to get her back."

"He was trying to get a reaction out of you."

I shook my head, doubtfully.

"I think he thought I wasn't well enough to look after her."

"Were you?"

"I don't know."

"That doesn't excuse what he did. If you needed help, he should have gone with you to the doctor's, not taken your daughter off you."

"He did that too."

That was what made Gene's behaviour towards me so open to interpretation. He was kind, he was cruel, he calmed me down, he set me off, he loved me, he loathed me. Nothing was as simple as their checklist aimed to make it. We couldn't be slotted into a box and told our relationship was abusive. It was much more complex than the average abusive relationship; we both suffered from mental illness and we'd had more practical problems than any couple I'd ever met. It was incomparable to a couple where one partner simply exerted power over the other.

I was getting annoyed with the workers again. How dare they label our relationship unhealthy? How dare they draw a question mark over Gene's love for me? How dare they imply he was a bully? The balance of our relationship was more complex than they had the capacity to understand. That's what Gene had always told me: we were special. Not many people had experienced what we had, so they reserved the right to pass judgement on it. He was the only person who got me, and I was the only person who got him. I would defend our love to the death, even if it meant batting away "help" that was extended to me.

I didn't have anything else to say to Brenda. I wished I hadn't told her as much as I had and wished there was some way to retract it. She had a duty of confidentiality, but she was still allowed to share what I had discussed with the other workers in the office, to keep them abreast of important disclosures. Confidentiality could be broken if there was a risk to myself or a risk to Hope, so I'd have to watch what I said. Gene was right; you never knew who might be recording you, who might misinterpret what you said on paper and what the onslaught would be. I'd been foolish to trust anyone other than him.

As soon as I picked Hope up from the creche, I phoned Gene.

"What are you doing, baby?"

"I'm about to make Hope lunch."

"What were you doing? I called you several times, but you didn't answer your phone."

"I was in a meeting."

25

"Oh, what sort of a meeting?"

"We have to go to meetings here."

"Why ain't you telling me shit?"

"I'm not meant to."

"This is me, babe. You can tell me."

"We were just talking about our relationship."

"What about it?"

"The abuse."

"I hope you made sure to tell them what you did to me too. Don't portray yourself in a good light and blame me for everything. You're equally at fault."

"I know. I told them I hit you."

"What'd they say?"

"That it was provoked."

"Fucking bullshit, man. So, if I hit you it's abuse, but if you hit me, I provoked you?"

"I don't know."

"Don't fucking listen to them people. They're trying to get inside your head and destroy our relationship."

"I won't."

"Hey, baby?"

"Yeah?"

"Want to meet me in town on Saturday?"

"I can't."

"Why the fuck not? I want to see my fucking daughter."

"I don't know. I'm scared."

"You don't got nothing to be scared of. Ha! What do you think I'm going to do to you? Don't be so fucking retarded."

"I have to go and make Hope lunch."

"Ok, baby, I got to get back to work. Hey?"

"Yeah?"

"Call me later, and if I phone, next time, answer your fucking phone."

I hung up, keeping my phone in my palm. I turned the volume up and took it downstairs with me to make lunch in the communal area. Hopefully if it rang, no one would know who it was I was talking to. I'd have to be careful what I said.

Chapter Four

I buttered one slice of bread and the phone rang.

"Yeah?" I answered as quietly as I could. I seemed to have the kitchen to myself, but that could change any second.

"What you doing, babe?"

"Making lunch."

"What you doing after that?"

"I might go for a walk."

I had immediate exposure to fresh sea air whenever I liked. It was hard to stop to appreciate that luxury in light of life's latest developments. Maybe if I got out of the building and walked along the shoreline, I'd be able to think more clearly and plan my escape. I had to get home in whatever way minimised drama. I wanted to sneak out, but if I did that, the workers would raise the alarm bell to social services. I had to appear as cooperative as possible, whilst conveying the fact that the whole thing had just been a terrible misunderstanding. I was no more abused than the workers in the refuge. I was able to look in on the other women's lives and what I knew of them with deep pity. They hadn't been loved adequately. I had been loved more than every healthy couple I knew combined. With that intensity of feeling, there was bound to be conflict between us. It was only normal.

"What are you doing?"

"I'm just drinking coffee, on my lunch break. Baby?"

"Yeah?"

"Just come home. What are you doing in there?"

"I don't know."

I began to cry. I just wanted to fall into Gene's arms and let him comfort me. Why was I living like this by choice? Why was I allowing fear to keep me stuck? I looked around at the kitchen. Whoever had last eaten at the table hadn't bothered to wipe it. The lady I shared a kitchen with had washed her dishes and left them to dry on a mat she'd made with paper towels. Why was I putting up with other people's idiosyncrasies, but not my own husband's? There were locks on the cupboards to stop other residents stealing your food. No bleach was allowed for health and safety reasons, so the tiles looked like they needed a good scrub. There were signs posted everywhere, instructing you on all the rules and regulations, fire exits, reminding you of your slot on the cleaning rota. It was hard to relax and make yourself at home when everything was so rigid. When I thought about it, it wasn't too far removed from what I'd been living with prior to arriving, but in a different way.

"Baby, come home. I fucking miss you and my daughter."

"Ok, just let me get my stuff packed."

"Do it today baby. I want to see you later. I fucking miss you laying next to me."

"I miss you too."

"Goodbye, baby."

"Bye."

I let out a loud sob and hoped no one had heard. I always wondered if there were cameras in the kitchen area, if the workers were learning a hundred things about you without you even knowing they were watching. Maybe my paranoia was just taking hold again. But what were they doing when they closed their office door? They probably gathered around a TV screen, watching the women on CCTV and getting their entertainment from our sad lives. That was what people were like: they derived pleasure from seeing others writhe in pain. They recorded what you were saying so they could use it against you later. It was all a conspiracy to bring you down. I knew they wanted my relationship with Gene to fail. I knew they laughed about my stupidity for willing it to work when I wasn't listening. I'd prove them all wrong.

I went upstairs after lunch with renewed determination. I was getting out of this hellhole. No more cleaning rota, no more grime-coated baths, no more scheduled meetings. The workers could all leave me alone and attend to women who needed their help. I was fine. More than fine; I was in the relationship of my dreams and I was going to return to my marital bliss. Gene wouldn't be in a bad mood anymore, at least not towards me. He'd had a taste of what losing Hope and me felt like and he would never take us for granted again. I knew it, like you know the detailed plan of a goal you've yet to put into practice.

I unlocked the door to my room, letting it swing closed behind me. I was already sick of carrying Hope up and down that staircase. Life didn't have to be so hard. I was empowered. I was choosing my own freedom. I pulled my clothes off their hangers and forced them into my suitcase. I bagged up all of Hope's toys. The whole procedure only took about ten minutes. I didn't have many possessions left. I lifted Hope and stepped out of the room, locking the door behind me and knocking on the office door.

"Come in," a voice called.

I poked my head around the door.

"I'm going to go home today."

I was taking decisive action. If I didn't use any words of doubt, no one would question my choice.

"Ok. You know if you go home, we have to contact social services?" said Lisa.

I hesitated. "What do you think they'll do?"

"We don't know. That's up to whoever receives the referral."

"I need to know I'm not going to lose Hope if I go home."

"We can't promise you that," said Claire.

I was angry with her. I felt like resorting to Gene's tactics to get myself out of there: threatening, manipulating, swearing. Why did they have to interfere with my beautiful vision of family life? It was waiting for me at home and they were standing in my way. I loathed them for allowing me to come to the refuge without knowing the choice to leave would be taken out of my hands once I arrived. I was trapped; as trapped as I had been at home, as close to losing custody of my child as I'd been at home. Everywhere I turned, I was surrounded.

"I thought it was my decision to make."

"It is, but we have to notify social services. We're duty-bound."

I walked away and locked myself in my room, sitting on my mattress with its plastic cover. It was uncomfortable, but it was my bed now. I wasn't leaving the hostel until I decided the risk of losing Gene outweighed the risk of losing Hope. I cried desperate tears and cursed myself for picking up the phone to the helpline. Why didn't I just keep my mouth shut? I could hear Gene ranting in my mind. I dreaded phoning him and telling him I hadn't had the courage to leave. I knew he'd berate me as much as I was already berating myself for what I'd done. It was all my fault. Everything always was.

Chapter Five

It was Hope's first birthday. I didn't know if Gene remembered. I'd
sent him a message as a reminder. I knew sending it would result in
him wanting to see her, but I couldn't let the day pass by without
him knowing about it. I'd thought about meeting Gene in town for
Hope's birthday, but he'd been so volatile lately I was hesitant to
meet him in a public place. I wasn't allowed to meet him at our
house, or even return to it to collect my things if he was there, so we
weren't left with many alternatives.

My phone rang. "Yeah?"

"Let me see my fucking daughter, it's her fucking birthday."

"You didn't even know it was her birthday until I told you."

"That ain't right. I got a toy for her. You better make sure she
fucking gets it."

"I can't meet you today."

"It's our daughter's birthday. You're going to fucking ruin it too?"

"I can't meet you while you're acting like this."

"I'm being fucking nice. You're creating stuff in your head again."

"I'm not." I doubted myself the moment I said it.

"Today is not about you and your head. It's our daughter's fucking
birthday."

I disconnected the call and tried to resume Hope's birthday breakfast
like everything in our lives was normal, like we weren't alone, like
we weren't homeless, like I wasn't suicidal. We went for a walk
around the town and I took Hope to the park swings. I'd been told
that sea air was healing, but I'd so many wounds it was going to take
a lot more than a few fresh puffs of air to cure them. I pushed Hope
on the swing rhythmically and tried to feel joyous about the
occasion, but I couldn't feel a thing. Gene was right. I was selfish,
cold and heartless. I wasn't even moved by my own daughter's
birthday. The cold wind was whipping my hair and Hope's hands
were getting cold. I put her gloves on and strapped her back into the
pram. I looked at the ground as I walked. I didn't have the ability to
enjoy a view or take interest in what was happening around me. I
was too miserable to do anything other than keep walking robotically

and complete whatever tasks our routine demanded of me.

I stopped at the grocery shop and bought some party food and a princess cake. If Hope's first birthday was going to be at all memorable, I would be responsible for creating the memories. I'd throw a small party in the communal area and invite any of the women and staff who happened to be there to join us.

I buzzed the door and waited for the voice on the intercom.

"Hello?"

"It's Aoife." They let me into the building. One of the workers, Anne, was waiting for me in the hall.

"Happy birthday, wee woman," she smiled at Hope.

Hope didn't react. She always looked a bit frozen, like smiling was a strain for her. Maybe she was just too young to understand birthdays.

"We have something for you in the office."

I unbuckled Hope from the pram and followed Anne upstairs.

"Happy birthday," the staff called in chorus.

They presented Hope with two birthday presents and I tried my hardest to smile at them. I took them into the bedroom and helped her open them. We added them to my small pile of presents and she looked at them inquisitively. She grabbed some of the wrapping paper and tore it up, tossing bits of it onto the floor.

It suddenly occurred to me how little cleaning I'd been doing since my arrival in the refuge. I still had to cook, wash dishes, do laundry, clean our room and complete my task on the rota, but housework was taking up very little of my time compared to when I'd been at home. I didn't need to vacuum every day, the volume of laundry had more than halved and I only had to wash one set of dinner dishes. No burnt butter on popcorn pans, no clothes twisted inside-out, no litter everywhere I turned. Maybe motherhood didn't account for all my hard work. I was in temporary accommodation, and yet, life felt easier to manage. I tried to hold onto that small amount of positivity and took Hope downstairs for her party.

Sarah and another resident, Louise, were lying watching TV and chatting.

"Happy birthday, Hope," they chimed as I walked in the door. It seemed strange that people I didn't know beyond their first names had remembered my daughter's birthday more quickly than her father had. Sarah passed me an envelope.

"Just got her a wee card."

"Thanks," I smiled. "I'm making some party food if you want to join us."

"Yummy, I wouldn't say no to that."

I walked to the kitchen and heated up all the food I'd got for Hope. Even in that room with its ugly green tiles, locked cupboards and strict safety notices, our little party felt more jovial than any celebration we'd ever had at home. I laid the food out on the table and Louise went upstairs to gather the on-duty workers to help sing "Happy Birthday" when I brought in the cake.

"Your mummy has gone to a lot of trouble," said Anne. I looked at the spread doubtfully, knowing if Gene was there, he'd tell me I hadn't made any of it myself. But maybe that wasn't what mattered; maybe it was the thoughtfulness, rather than the details that mattered. That was the first thought that made me think I still had my own thoughts somewhere in my mind, buried deep, but there, nonetheless.

Chapter Six

Life was stagnant; the same routine day in, day out. I'd been in the refuge for a month and I hadn't been offered a house yet. That was my back-up plan: wait for my name to reach the top of the housing list, move into my new home and then Gene could join me. Once I was out of the refuge, it was no one's business what I did. I was classed homeless, which gave me good points, and my mental illness increased them even more. I mustn't have been far away from receiving my first offer. You got three offers. If you didn't like the first, you could wait for the second. If you didn't like the second, you could wait for the third. If you didn't like the third, you were on your own. No matter what I was offered, I'd make it work. Anything was better than living in the refuge. Other women in the hostel had told me about their housing offers. I didn't have high hopes for mine. You were offered a concrete shell and had to come up with the money to decorate it and furnish it yourself. That sounded like more than I could cope with in my current predicament, but I didn't have the option to be picky about what I took on.

The workers tried to put a positive spin on it: it would be a chance to have your very own house. It was owned by the Housing Executive, but no one could kick you out. You could decorate it however you liked, with no one's input, or orders. Getting your housing offer was your key to freedom. When one of the brown letters with a clear window and the Housing Executive stamp on it arrived for one of the women, everyone was in a fit of excitement, like it was a God-given gift. My idea of a gift from God would have been if someone granted me permission to return home with no interference from social services.

I still attended my weekly meetings. Sometimes I got a bit too relaxed and said more than I should. My mental health social worker called out to visit me. Medical professionals and social workers were the only exceptions to the no visitors-rule. We sat down together in the living room.

"How are you?"

"I'm ok."

"How are you finding living here?"
Professionals always posed that question like they were looking for a five-star review and the go ahead to book a room for themselves for the holidays.
"It's ok. I don't mind it."
"Are the other women nice?"
"Most of them are."
"I need to run through some safeguarding paperwork with you."
"What's that?"
"It's just a procedure I have to do, to make sure we're doing all we can to safeguard vulnerable adults."
"Am I a vulnerable adult?"
"You have a mental illness, so yes."
We went through a list of questions that resembled what the refuge had already asked me. It was just another box-ticking exercise.
"Was Gene ever physical with you?"
"Not really."
"What do you mean, not really?"
"He grabbed my throat a couple of times, but he never hit me or anything."
"Ok. I need to write that in the report."
"What is the report? Is it just for you?"
"No, I have to pass it onto the police."
"Why?"
"For your protection. We have to alert them to incidences of physical abuse."
"I don't want you to."
"Well, I have to."
I went as quiet as one of Gene's bad moods. My mind went completely empty and I couldn't think of what to say. I just needed to get out of that room. All I wanted was to go home, and everything I said was just inalterably cementing my fate.
I clammed up and made as quick an exit from the room as I could. I couldn't trust anyone. I wouldn't allow any more leaks to happen. Leaking information that was documented and then distributed wasn't something I could afford to do; not if I wanted my marriage to last. I had to ring Gene to confess what I'd done. Better he found out by my own admission than by the lips of a stranger.
"I fucked up."
  "Ah," sighed Gene, like he knew it was inevitable. "What'd you do,

babe?"

"I told my social worker you grabbed me by the throat."

"Wait, you did what?"

"I didn't mean to. It just slipped out."

I gritted my teeth and cursed myself for opening my big mouth. I was meant to be on Gene's side and I was betraying him at every turn. I'd managed to keep everything to myself since that first day Gene had grabbed me, and for what? Now I'd disclosed it to someone I barely knew who wasn't going to keep the information between us anyway. I hadn't made a conscious choice to reveal it. The words had forced their way out of my mouth. I was fighting the urge to open the floodgates, and a few droplets were seeping through. But my desire to reconcile with Gene was stronger than my desire to tell all. I wouldn't make the same mistake twice.

"I hope you fucking told them how often you hit me."

"No." I could feel myself reddening and the vein in my temple tensed; my body was readying itself for attack. "I'm sorry, the conversation didn't last long. I didn't expect that to happen."

"You didn't tell her because you're fucking afraid. You know what she'd say if you did."

"What?"

"That you're the one who's violent, who fucking beats me. You're trying to make yourself look like the fucking victim, but you're not."

"I'm not trying to do that."

"You better fucking set them people straight. Tell them the fucking truth."

I nodded. He was right; I had to tell them I was the source of all our problems. I had to tell them Gene's version of events. My version of the truth wasn't reliable. I had misinterpreted too many things for it to be truthful. I didn't feel quite ready to tell anyone yet; it was hard to admit to having an abusive personality.

"I'll tell them."

Gene held a grudge until the following morning and then he phoned me again.

"Meet me in the center, babe."

"I can't."

"What the fuck do you mean, you can't? I'm your fucking husband. Stop being a fucking coward."

"I'm afraid."

"Afraid of what? That is a ridiculous statement."

"I'm afraid you'll take Hope."

"Babe, if I was going to take Hope, I'd have done it already."

"What do you mean?"

"I've got all the videos, the pictures, all the fucking recordings. I got every phone call recorded. All I got to do is call social services and they'll take Hope from you. But I ain't done that, have I?"

"Why not?"

"Because I don't want to. I want us to be a fucking family again. I told that to the guys in work."

"What'd you tell them?"

"I fucking told them what you did to me. They thought it was terrible. They told me I should call social services and get Hope taken away from you. I told them I can't. You're a good mom."

I was as edgy as when I'd been in the house. I wasn't safe from Gene just because I wasn't in the same house and he didn't know where I was. As long as Gene knew my name and had a working phone, there was always the possibility that I could lose my child. I felt haunted, like when you wake from a nightmare that unsettles you for the rest of the day. Just because it's over doesn't mean the trauma is, or the threat of it happening again. I'd meet Gene in town. I had to, to keep him on my side.

Chapter Seven

That Saturday, I stepped off the train in Belfast for the first time since setting foot in the refuge. Gene would call me when he arrived, and he'd meet us wherever we were by that time. I wasn't used to approaching town from that perspective. It was strange seeing town from a new angle. Gene and I always walked the same walks, in the same sequence, starting from the same point. Maybe life could be broader than I realised. I equally felt fearful about stepping outside the tight confines of our relationship. I still hadn't told Gene what town I was residing in, so I'd asked to meet in the centre of Belfast rather than at my train stop. I would trust him enough to meet up with him, but not to tell him where I was living.

I pushed the pram around the familiar shops. I didn't know how to deviate from our patterns, so engrained were they in my psyche. I might have had a pass to freedom, but I didn't know how to use it. I was scared to try. I couldn't exist without Gene. Even in the refuge I couldn't survive without him. Had I not spoken to him every single day since my arrival, I never would have lasted for as long as I had living inside those walls. Gene was my rock and he'd help me through the most trying periods of my life, even if he was the one that had created the circumstances in the first place.

Gene was running late. He'd left his phone in the house and had to get back off the bus to get it. He was "salty." The "motherfucking" bus hadn't shown up for nearly a "half-hour" after he returned to the stop. I predicted the rant that would come when I met him. I could hear Gene's exact words before he even spoke them. They spun maddeningly in my mind.

It was approaching lunchtime and Hope and I were in *Victoria Square*. I was thinking about pushing myself outside my comfort zone and going somewhere different for lunch. But Gene would never allow that. He liked *Burger King* or the rare Chinese buffet. He'd never agree to go somewhere different; at least not without kicking up a fuss. The food would be wrong, the service would be wrong, the layout would be wrong, and it would be all my fault. I couldn't risk putting myself through that. We'd stick to an option I knew was safe. We hadn't seen each other in a month and I didn't want our first meeting to be traumatic. I needed to ease myself back into the relationship. Gene and I were still together, by phone, at least. But with phone calls, there was always the option to hang up when Gene became overbearing. In person, I couldn't walk out. If I tried, there would be an enormous scene, or Gene would abduct Hope. Once I met him, I'd committed myself to staying for the full length of time Gene wished to spend together, no matter what was said and no matter what happened.

My phone rang, and I jumped. I knew it meant that Gene was nearby. He was probably near the City Hall if he'd just got off the bus. But if he had tried to guess where I was and begun walking, I could cross him at any corner. That thought terrified me. My phone shook in my trembling hand and I felt a lurch in my stomach, like the final violent wretches that come after sickness: the ones that expel the last of it with the most force. I struggled to press the right button to answer the call. Why was my body physically reacting against seeing Gene? My mind was telling me that I should, but my body was protesting so strongly it was undeniable.

"Yeah?"

"I'm in town. Where the fuck are you?"

"Why do you sound angry?"

"What the fuck are you talking about? Where the fuck are you and my fucking daughter?"

"I can't meet you if you're going to act like this."

I shook uncontrollably, and I stood paralysed in the shopping centre, holding onto the balustrade to keep myself upright. My legs felt like they were crumbling away beneath me. I couldn't find any volume in my voice.

"Tell me where the fuck you are right now."

"I can't."

"Stop being a fucking asshole. I came all the way to town to meet you and now you're going to refuse to meet me? Fucking bullshit."

"I'm sorry. I can't, I'm scared."

I hung up and my body untensed itself a little, but I kept alert, like a cat with its hairs on end. Attack was still imminent. Belfast wasn't a big city, and if Gene decided to, he could find me. It just depended on whether he could be bothered expending the energy hunting me down. If he was angry, I knew that was likely. Gene angry was like a starved cheetah hunting its prey. Neither distance nor time was an obstacle when it came to ensnaring dinner.

I couldn't walk back to the train station yet. If I did, I might pass Gene no matter which street I chose. I needed to go somewhere Gene would never think to look for me. I took the lift to the top floor of *Victoria Square.* You had to get a separate lift to reach *Pizza Express* at the shopping centre's summit. Gene would never think to look there. I doubted he even knew it existed. I pushed the pram inside and felt safer amidst the diners and waiters. They looked attentive, like they'd notice if something was afoot and call in emergency aid. That consoled me a little.

"Could I get a table for one and a highchair, please?"

I tried to look normal, to hide the shakes that made me look like I was in the worst kind of a comedown; and I was.

"Of course."

The waiter was kindly and amenable to whatever I needed. I was immensely grateful for that. It was a feeling that was foreign to me. I needed to get back to the refuge as soon as I knew the coast was clear. Behind its locked doors, I knew I was in a place of safety. I wished for a moment that I could employ a bodyguard to accompany me everywhere, just in case. Then I realised how ridiculous a thought that was to have. Gene was my husband, not my assailant. How could I view him so fearfully? Why couldn't I get a better handle on my mental illness and let him see his daughter? The reasons behind the irrational feelings didn't matter. I sat stationary; immobilised by fear.

I ordered a pizza for Hope and myself to share. I knew it was extravagant - eating out, but I hadn't planned out the day's food. I hadn't planned much beyond meeting Gene. When Gene was involved in a day, Gene was all that existed in that day. I needed to try to readjust my focus to myself and Hope and our survival. I cut up Hope's pizza and smiled at her enjoying it. She seemed content for the first time in so long I couldn't remember. I thought she must secretly resent me for dividing our family. Gene told me she would, but she seemed less tense than usual. Maybe I was imagining it.

I drew out our meal as long as I could, just to be on the safe side. I checked my phone for missed calls and messages from Gene; nothing. Again, I hoped he hadn't cut me off for good. What I'd done to him was unforgiveable. I'd encouraged him to meet me in town, got him to make two bus journeys for the sake of it and then changed my mind on a whim. He was right: I was a terrible person, a lunatic. I packed all Hope's things into the nappy bag, got her ready and we left the restaurant. The cool air hit me like a warning when I opened the door. I was exposed again, back in the same world as Gene and there was the potential for anything to happen. Being stalked, having my child removed, being abducted; they all felt like conceivable outcomes to the day. I really was losing my mind.

I walked as quickly as my feet would carry me. I wished I could hitchhike to the station. Everywhere I looked, I saw men who resembled Gene: leather jackets, black and white Converse, long, dark, flyaway hair. They turned around and their faces were different each time, but they could have been him. He could be anywhere. I didn't like not knowing where Gene was, or rather, where he wasn't. The walk from *Victoria Square* to the *Europa* took ten minutes at my quickest pace. It felt like fifty with fear. I ran along with the pram, power-walking as fast as I could without drawing unwanted attention to myself. I hoped no one would pass comment on me. People had a knack for commenting on your weakness at the worst moment. Everyone around me was leading a normal day; from what I could see anyway. You never know what is hidden behind the semblance of normality. Office workers were picking up takeaway sandwiches for a quick lunch, drivers were beeping at each other for sleeping through the light changes, other mothers were unhurriedly pushing prams along the pavement. I envied their lives. I didn't know what their lives were like, but they looked more vivacious than I felt.

I made it to the train station in one piece. Well, the number of pieces I'd been in before I arrived there anyway. The train was waiting for me on the platform and I stepped on board. The doors clapped shut and I scanned the carriage for Gene's form. Had he been following me? Did he know where I lived? Gene was all-knowing. Even when you didn't tell him something, he seemed to somehow figure out the details anyway. He'd known I would leave before I even knew it myself. He was good at being in the know, at meeting the most streetwise characters who could source any information he needed to know. I knew it was likely he knew where I was, right down to the room number.

I shook in my seat and checked my phone again for missed calls. If it rang, I'd better answer. I was as fearful of the phone ringing as I was of it not ringing. If it wasn't ringing, I didn't know what Gene was doing, when he might hunt me down, when he might destroy the final parts of me that remained. I knew there would be payback for what I'd done to him. I'd refused to meet him purely out of fear, but he would decide it was a campaign to take him down, to make a mockery of him by controlling his behaviour. I knew that Gene would believe I'd coerced him into meeting me in town, never having any intention of meeting him. He thought I did things on purpose to humiliate him, to make him look like less of a man. I didn't know anyone who was more of a man than Gene. Gene's masculine energy was so concentrated it was like the rage of fifty incensed males combined. I couldn't think of any long-term outcomes of my behaviour. All I was able to do was worry about making it back to the refuge alive that day. When you're in danger, all you can do is focus on the present. I felt in danger, but maybe I was just creating danger in my mind where none had ever existed.

I sat, willing the train to reach its final stop. It was a long journey and I was struggling to keep my tears back. I turned my head down, looking at my lap and cried with as much subtlety as you can under bright tube lighting and the eyes of a row of observers. I couldn't look them in the face. I was ashamed to be alive, ashamed to occupy a seat that could have been given to a worthier person than me.

The journey felt the distance of the journey I'd made to Chicago to first meet Gene, but no excitement was bubbling up in my gut; the only stomach sensation I had was the downward drag of dread. It was late afternoon and already falling dark, like life was closing in on itself. Mentally, I felt enclosed in a cupboard. I needed to talk to someone, urgently. If I didn't, I'd ring Gene and beg his forgiveness for my actions that day. I already knew there was nothing I could do that would restore his respect for me. Gene hated when he thought you were playing games with him. Gene was too honest for games. I'd never played a game with him, but he believed I had. He believed everything I did was fuelled by manipulation, and everything I did out of fear only served to strengthen that belief of his.

I pushed the pram off the train and hurried back to the refuge. Buzzing the doorbell, I moved around with agitation, praying it would open before something happened to me. Every shadow looked to me like Gene's outline. I kept looking back over my shoulder to check, double-check and triple-check he wasn't standing behind me. I looked at the face of my phone; still nothing.

One of the other women opened the door for me. I felt like falling into her arms and imploring her to keep me safe. I couldn't show my vulnerability to a stranger. Vulnerability was something that should be only be reserved for my husband. If Gene and I were back on speaking terms later, maybe I could talk openly to him about it; he'd be my shoulder to cry on, like he always was. No one was as good at consoling me over Gene's behaviour as Gene himself. He was the only person who knew how to say the words that undid his earlier ones. No one else could make it right for me.

That night, after Hope was asleep, I tapped on the office door anyway. I needed to have a word with someone, even if that someone wasn't Gene. If I couldn't have God himself, one of the angels would have to do.

"Could I have a chat with someone?"

"Of course. Give me one minute and I'll meet you in the living room."

I walked in and sat down on the hard leather sofa. It wasn't comfortable, but it wasn't somewhere I wanted to make myself comfortable for long anyway. Everything about the situation screamed discomfort.

Another worker, Lana, came into the room and sat down with her file in front of her.

"I hate these things," she said, flipping it open. She loathed bureaucracy as much as I did. That was a good starting point for an honest conversation.

"We'll fill it out later. Want to tell me what's wrong?"

She looked concerned, watching me padding my eyes with a balled-up tissue. The tears kept flowing, like the pipe had finally burst.

"I went to meet Gene today."

"Ok," she said.

She gave me a small smile, like she understood but wasn't allowed to be overtly supportive of that in her role. I didn't sense she was judging me, and it felt strange. It must have been something she heard all the time.

"What happened?"

"When I got there, I didn't meet him."

"Ok."

"He phoned me to tell me he'd arrived in town, but his voice sounded threatening on the phone, so I freaked out and refused to meet him."

"That's understandable."

"Isn't that awful? That I got him to come into town and then refused to tell him where I was?"

"No, it was because of his behaviour."

"So, you don't think it was my fault?"

"Not at all."

The thought that something might not be my fault was a novel idea. I was so used to being told that everything was my fault. If something wasn't my fault, it was still half my fault; I never heard the expression "not at all," when Gene was assigning blame. I couldn't grasp what she was saying. I had to convince her otherwise. I couldn't insinuate that Gene was at fault; that was a cardinal sin. I had to spare him her judgement. I had to efface myself to raise him back onto his pedestal.

"I promised Gene I'd meet him. He even got two buses because he forgot his phone the first time."

"So?"

"Well, isn't that my fault?"

"No, it's his responsibility to remember his own belongings."

I shook my head. She was rattling the cage that held my entire reality.

"The only people you are responsible for are you and your daughter. He is a grown man. He can look after himself."

"Isn't that selfish?"

"No."

"He needs me to support him."

"There's a difference between supporting someone and doing everything for them."

I kept crying. It felt like I was releasing some of the pent-up feelings of responsibility I'd carried for the last couple of years. I still couldn't believe what she was saying. It couldn't be true. If what she was saying was true, the groundwork of my beliefs was being ripped up. It was safer to stick with a false truth than adopt a new one that was unfamiliar to me.

"Well, why did you decide not to meet him? What were you worried about?"

None of her questions were prompting me to answer one way or the other; they were completely open-ended. Maybe she hadn't decided the answers for me before I'd had a chance to give them. Maybe I wouldn't be punished later for my response. That building wasn't home; it was nothing like it, but it was the first time in a long while I felt safe, and for a moment, that felt important.

Lana reached across and grabbed the tissue box, extending it in my direction. I pulled a couple more from it.

"Maybe I should just keep the whole box," I laughed.

"We've got a store room full of them. Work away."

I smiled at her. She smiled back at me, not with the conditional approval I'd got used to seeking, but with acceptance for the state I was in.

"So, what were you worried might happen if you met him?"

"That he'd take Hope, that he'd ask me for money, that he'd get angry about something."

"Those fears don't sound unreasonable to me. Why did you agree to meet him?"

"I told him I would, so he could see Hope. He missed her birthday because of me."

"Because of you or because of his behaviour?"

"I don't know."

"If he wasn't behaving the way he was, you wouldn't have had to leave, and you would have taken Hope to see him on her birthday."

What she was saying eased my feelings of guilt a little, but I couldn't believe it was true. What I'd done to Gene was utterly unforgiveable.

"Why don't you have a hot bath now Hope is asleep and go downstairs and watch TV for a while?"

I nodded at her.

"You can't take responsibility for other people's actions."

Everything she was saying was turning my typical thought process upside down. I was responsible for every shift in Gene's moods, every change in facial expression, every hint of anger in his voice.

"Thanks," I said, getting up. "I'm sorry for wasting your time."

"Don't be silly. I'd much rather do this than sit alone in the office," she smiled. "Here, initial these for me, would you?"

My folder was filled with paperwork already. I couldn't understand how a month of refuge-living could produce a ring binder filled with every one of my issues. Gene wasn't abusive, and yet the material in my folder suggested otherwise.

I made a few pen marks on her page and she smiled at me.

"Thanks," I said.

"You don't have to thank me."

I waited for her to grow angry, correcting my choice of wording. Her smile didn't change. My entire reality was being overturned and I didn't like it. If these women were my allies, that meant Gene was my enemy; and that couldn't be right. I needed to treat them with greater suspicion and not disclose the secrets of our relationship as readily.

I went to the room and checked my phone. There still wasn't so much as a message from Gene. I'd expected him to make his furious return by now. He must have been especially wounded if he hadn't doled out my punishment yet. I dialled his number, my whole body shaking. I was worried he wouldn't answer and worried he would. There was no winning; no matter what course of action I chose.

"What the fuck do you want?"

"I want to talk to you."

"I don't give a shit what you got to say."

"I'm sorry."

"You got me to go all the way to the center and then refused to meet me. You like fucking with me. I'm sure you got a lot of enjoyment out of that."

"Why would I enjoy that? I was going to meet you and then I got scared because you sounded so angry on the phone."

"No, I fucking didn't. Stop trying to blame me for this shit. This is all on you."

"I was going to meet you."

"I don't believe that."

"You never believe me."

"All I wanted was to see my fucking daughter and you wouldn't let me. I should just kill my fucking self."

"No, please, don't."

"You'd be happy if I did."

"That isn't true. I love you."

"Then why don't you come home?"

"I can't yet. Nothing has changed."

"You're as much to blame for this as I am."

I didn't know what to say to that.

"I'm giving you one more fucking chance. Meet me in the center tomorrow so I can see my fucking daughter."

"Ok."

I knew I couldn't refuse. I'd pushed it too far. If I wasted any more of Gene's time, I'd never see him again. If he committed suicide, it would be too late to reverse my bad behaviour. I had to treat him with the respect he deserved.

"Meet me tomorrow."

"Ok."

I'd lost the use of my vocabulary, and it was for the best. Submissiveness was the key to keeping Gene happy. If I kept Gene happy, he wouldn't end his life and there was still a chance we would get back together. My existence hinged upon that happening. Gene and I hadn't separated; I was just waiting until I'd gathered enough courage to face him down under our roof again.

"Don't fucking mess me around again, Aoife."

"I won't."

I ended the call and decided to follow Lana's advice and take a bath. I needed to keep my mind occupied so it didn't reach for unhealthier modes of entertainment. I gathered my toiletries, my towel and a change of clothes. My arms were laden, but we weren't allowed to keep personal effects in the bathroom. I checked on Hope. She was still sleeping the peaceful sleep of childly unawareness. I picked up the baby monitor and locked the bedroom door. I felt safer leaving Hope unattended in that building of strangers than in my own home. That thought struck me as bizarre, and I put it to the back of my mind.

I walked down the stairs to the bathroom. The refuge was filled with flights of stairs, and you had to use them to reach every one of your basic needs. At least that night I had only my possessions to carry, without having to balance Hope on an arm as well.

I shut the bathroom door and picked up the cloth and the cleaner. There was scum on the tub, left over from the last user. Some residents cleaned up after themselves, some didn't. You just had to live with people's habits. I was used to doing that. No big deal. I scrubbed the porcelain as hard as I could. It didn't do much to lift the residue, but at least I knew it was hygienic. My pregnant belly was growing and making everything more cumbersome. I filled the tub and slid into the warm water. I hoped it would wash away a few of my worries. I was as tense as before I'd left home, but I wasn't in imminent danger. Relaxation still didn't come easily to me; my body was on high alert. Footsteps, the sound of a door opening, the tone of a voice: they all signalled danger to me.

I lay for twenty minutes, feeling no less fearful. I needed the distraction of conversation. The ones that played out in my mind were too maddening to listen to for any length of time. I got dried off and changed into my pyjamas and slippers. Time to go downstairs. Thankfully Hope hadn't stirred. That was one bit of pressure I didn't need: Hope keeping me confined to the room. If she woke up, I wasn't allowed to leave it.

I dropped my belongings back to the room. She was still in a deep slumber. She seemed more relaxed in the refuge, or was that another one of my crazed imaginings? Why would she be more content to live in a hostel than in her own home? My mind was playing tricks on itself again. Maybe I should have spent the evening talking to Gene. Whenever I went without speaking to him, I always became less grounded. Gene was my mood stabiliser and my thought-controller. Without him restricting me, I was lost in the bottomless pit of the abyss.

I walked into the kitchen area. Sarah was sitting on the sofa watching something benign on TV: celebrity chefs, interviewers, not a horror scene in sight. My stomach unclenched itself a little and I sat down across from her.

"Hey."

"Hello, preggers, how's you?"

"I'm ok. You?"

"I'm just watching this. Was going to make a cup of tea. You want one?"

"Yes please."

I lay back as she made me a drink. I felt like I owed her something, but when I looked at her, she just smiled.

"What were you doing today?"

"I went into town to meet my husband."

"Yeah? Are you sure that's a good idea?"

"I don't know. I left without seeing him. I might meet him tomorrow instead."

"Be careful. I don't trust him."

"What do you mean?"

"Just please be careful. Don't follow him down any entries or anything if you do go. Stay safe."

The thought that I wasn't safe with my own husband was an absurd one, but maybe her warning wasn't without cause. I'd bring the personal alarm I'd been given in my handbag, just in case.

"You know, I moved here from England," she said.

"Really?"

"Yeah, with 50p in my pocket."

"What'd you do?"

"I had to get an emergency loan and a food parcel. Talk about losing your dignity over a man. Don't repeat my mistakes."

"I feel like I should never have left."

"Honey, if you'd stayed, you'd be buried under the patio by now."

It seemed like a preposterous notion: that you could be killed by your own husband. Sometimes I felt like it was a real risk I ran, but then Gene talked sense into me. It was just my mental illness taking over.

"I don't feel like I've earned the right to be here."

"That's the brainwashing. That's what he has conditioned you into believing."

"But why would he do that?"

"Because it makes it easier to blame and control you. That's what these manipulators do. It's one of their tactics."

I wasn't sure if what she was saying applied to my situation, but hearing it somehow made me feel relieved and validated.

"At least now we're here we know things can't get any worse," said Sarah, with a snort of laughter.

"Yeah," I laughed. "Talk about rock bottom... Gene says it's my fault I'm here."

"What a load of horse shit. Where does he think you are exactly? A five-star hotel? It's not exactly high-count cotton sheets here, is it? Every time I roll over in bed the fitted sheet comes off and I'm wrapped inside it like a bloody caterpillar in a chrysalis. The plastic cover makes it sound like I've got chronic wind."

I did a hearty laugh.

"You're getting better since you've been here, honey. I know you don't see it, but you wouldn't have laughed this freely the day you arrived. You looked like a deer in headlights. I'll never forget that look on your face."

"Really?"

"Yeah, I was scared to approach you. You look shell-shocked. Look at you, leaning back on the sofa. You'd have been scared to perch on the edge of it when you got here."

"I still worry I'm taking somebody's seat."

"That's the conditioning."

"I might make some hot chocolate. Would you like a cup?"

I peered into her tea cup to see if she was finished with her tea.

"Fuck, yeah. I haven't had hot chocolate in so long."

"Cool, would like you like marshmallows?"

"Yum. Yes please. You're spoiling me now," she said.

She smiled, pulling her slippered feet up onto the sofa cushion next to her. It felt like a girls' night in and I almost forgot where I was for a while.

I handed Sarah her cup of hot chocolate and sank back into the sofa padding. No one was on my back and it was an odd feeling. I waited for a complaint about my hot chocolate, but none came. The noose I constantly felt constricting my throat slackened a little. It was still there, but it stopped choking me for a change.

"This might be the longest you've sat for without Flossy Doodle calling you," Sarah said, nodding at the baby monitor.

I laughed. "I know, she was in a deep sleep."

"She's been chattier this week. She's coming out of herself."

"I guess the place is less strange to her now."

"She looked terrified to make a sound when you got here. She wasn't used to having people around her – you could tell."

"I guess she only really saw Gene and my parents."

"He was isolating you, honey."

There was something about her warm way of wording things that didn't cause offense. Even when she pointed out Gene's deficiencies, they sounded more like objective observations than condemnations. I needed gentle hints about the truth of what was happening; no grand pronouncements. I wasn't ready to label Gene an abuser and I certainly wasn't a victim. I'd been too much of an active participant in our disputes to be the victim.

"Your eyes are getting heavy, honey."

"I think my medication is kicking in."

"I can tell. Your eyes get glazed and you look bored by everything I'm saying."

"I'm not," I laughed. "Sorry."

"I know, honey. Get some sleep. Let's do this again."

"Any time."

"If you meet him tomorrow, promise me something."

"What?"

"Don't go anywhere alone with him."

"I won't."

Fear hung in the air and I consciously realised for the first time that I was petrified of my own husband.

Chapter Eight

I stepped off the train for town and walked to the City Hall to meet Gene. I had three blocks to think through my decision. Every nerve end was screaming at me to turn back. I fought through my physical reaction. I needed my mind to overrule my body, or I'd lose Gene for good. That was too terrifying a thought to contemplate, even more terrifying than the thought of seeing him. I checked inside my handbag to make sure my alarm was still there, just in case. I saw its red thread tucked down the side of my purse and felt slightly safer. Walking along the footpaths that were as populated by pigeons as people, it scared me not being able to see my way through the crowd. I looked up at the buildings that stood over me, like a human foot to a tick. That's what my value was reduced to in the presence of Gene. He was a god and I was the smallest being under his power. My heart rattled in my ribcage and my palms were so clammy the pram handle slipped from my grip. I turned the last corner, and Gene's eyes met mine. Now he'd seen me, there was no way of undoing it. I was his prisoner until he decided I was ready for release.

He strode towards me, pummelling the pavement with his shoe soles. His hair flapped madly behind him and the air felt charged with murderous rage. Gene unbuckled Hope from the pram and lifted her out of it by the scruff of her coat. I grimaced, but Gene wasn't being aggressive, he was merely being playful. He was desperate to see his daughter after a month apart.

I was still worried. "Careful," I whispered.

"She's my fucking daughter," Gene shouted. "Even though you took her from me."

"I didn't want to."

"You still did it, didn't you?"

"Stop shouting, please."

"I'm not fucking shouting; I'm just talking."

Everyone was looking at us.

"Give me a fucking kiss."

I pressed my lips against Gene's and felt something like a spark.

Fear and love had become so entwined I couldn't separate one from the other. I had no idea at the time that the spark could have been produced by the former. I tasted Gene's *Winston Reds* on his breath and felt the urge to gag, not because I was pregnant, and not because of the odour itself, but because of the negative associations it brought up. He gave me a bear hug and I smelt his scent; it frightened me but comforted me more. That smell signified home and I was home sick for the place I hadn't seen in over a month. It was only two miles from where we stood, but I couldn't go there even if I wanted to. If I did, the workers would be straight onto social services and we'd be flagged on their system. If I wanted to move back in with Gene, I had to do it in a more measured way. I needed to reign in my passionate impulses and arrange it in a deliberate way, planning my every move with all involved agencies. I felt like begging Gene to take me home, allowing him to take me onto the bus, to let me lie in my own bed, smelling the scent of home on the sheets. He could protect me from all outside involvement. I knew it was an unrealistic fantasy, and that only increased my sense of longing. We could flee the country, but I wanted to go home to that house. Once again, our future wasn't in our own hands.

"Let's get coffee, babe," said Gene, pressing his hand on top of mine. I was back in my place, at the bottom again. I remembered how that felt and my mind spun with the yearning to go home battling the urge to bolt back to the refuge.

"You get it. I'll wait with Hope."

Gene sat at an outdoor table that faced City Hall. It was a busier place than the most bustling café, with ten public transport users passing us each second. I wondered why Gene chose it rather than going inside. Maybe he didn't want everyone to hear what we had to say to each other. We couldn't declare our love for one another inside without every listening ear hearing. Outside, our sounds vanished into the sounds of city life.

I walked into the café, pulled my purse from my bag and joined the queue. I looked back over my shoulder, checking that Gene was still sitting outside the window. He was holding Hope and I knew where she was. I loathed myself for leaving her alone with Gene, for increasing the risk of him running away with her, but now I was in Gene's company, I had to keep the peace. I had to minimise the chance of him taking Hope away by not pissing him off. I would be self-effacing, unreactive and compliant, and maybe Hope would still be by my side when we went back to the shelter at the end of our meeting. If I didn't keep Gene happy, I wouldn't have her at all. What would the workers think if they knew I'd risked that? What would social services have to say to me when I fought to get custody of my daughter? They'd tell me I'd willingly handed her into the arms of someone I knew was a danger to both of us. My mind was running away with its crazed self; Gene was my husband, not an armed gunman, not a child abductor, not a criminal. I needed to get my mind under control. Gene was right: I let it take over and I was completely at its mercy. I moved up the queue, keeping my eyes on that window. It framed Gene and Hope like a scene on a screen; a picture of a world I could only enter through my memories and my imagination. I'd better hurry up, before they were gone. I jiggled my leg more than Gene ever had in any queue and willed the baristas to speed up and stop their small chat. They were giving each customer their undivided attention, but as admirable as that may have been in any other scenario, it was a threat to my daughter's safety. The lady behind me asked to examine a panini in the display cabinet. She brushed in front of me and blocked my view of the window. I stood on tiptoes, craning my neck to see past her. She didn't know how much she was endangering my daughter. She was perfectly pleasant, but I couldn't follow what she was saying to me or even conjure up a smile.

I got to the head of the queue and raced through my order. I tapped my foot, hoping they'd take the hint and hurry things along. I knew I just looked like an impatient asshole, but they knew nothing about the life I was living. I was in a high-speed chase scene and they were in a leisurely filler scene. We might have been in the same movie, but our scenes didn't overlap, and they knew nothing of the demands of my role.

I got our cups of coffee positioned on the tray, flung my change at the tip jar and carried it outside as quickly as I could. I'd tell Gene they had no ice. The wait for ice would push me over the edge. My stomach lurched, and I felt like dropping to the footpath beneath me to stop my head spinning. But I had to act like everything was ok. Any drama, and Gene would start a scene. I was going to be anything other than myself that day, and hopefully everything would go smoothly.

I slid the tray onto the table and Gene didn't thank me. He picked his coffee up off the tray. Hope was back in her buggy. I looked at her, confused.

"I had to set her down, babe. My hand was fucking hurting me, and you were taking forever in there."

"Sorry, there was a long queue."

"The service is fucking shit. Hey, did you get me ice?"

"No, sorry, they didn't have any."

"They didn't have no fucking ice?"

I shook my head, looking at the ground so my eyes wouldn't tell him I was lying.

"What kind of a coffee place don't have ice, man? This country is fucked up."

Gene took a sip from his coffee and didn't grimace. He'd relented. I sat down with Hope on my knee.

"Did you even look in a mirror before you left this morning?" Gene said, with a smirk.

"What do you mean?"

"Your hair is fucking crazy looking, ain't it?"

I stroked my hand over it to calm the curls.

"I didn't have time to wash it. You don't have to embarrass me."

"I'm only fucking joking, babe. Jeez - it is crazy looking though."

Gene held my hand across the table and took a slurp from his cup.

"Hey," he said, leaning in.

I wondered if he was going to apologise, begging me to come back home, promising me the Earth if I just gave him a second chance.

"You know the way we used to hear about them people on the news? Them dudes that murder their spouses?"

"No, I don't remember."

"You don't remember shit, man."

"What about it?" I asked, sickness rising from my stomach to my throat.

"We said we didn't get how anyone could ever do that."

"Yeah."

"Well, yesterday when you dragged me into town and wouldn't meet me, I got how they do that. I could have fucking killed you." He said it barely audibly, spitting the words out like they had a bad taste.

I backed away a little, still holding his hand. I couldn't breathe and every muscle in my body clenched. I wasn't safe. I was going to die. I was going to lose my daughter, and not only would she not remember me - the version of events she would hear would paint a picture of me as a despicable person. She would be glad she'd never known me.

I needed to get away, but I couldn't. Gene moved closer to me, putting his arm around me.

"What you did yesterday was fucked."

"I'm sorry, I didn't mean to. I just got scared."

"For no fucking reason. Your mind was just playing tricks on you, again. I'm the only one who suffers because of your fucking head."

"That isn't true."

Gene looked enraged and I backed down. I'd be subservient and reduce the chance of causing offence. From that moment onwards, I was taking a different tack: I was to blame, and I would willingly admit full fault face to face – anything to contain his rage.

"I'm sorry I didn't meet you. I didn't mean to mess you around."

"You did though. You fucking enjoy it."

I said nothing and turned my eyes away from his, looking at the dark fluid in my cup. I imagined my soul the same colour as it: tainted, blackened, opaque. There was no light left inside it anymore, no goodness.

"You about done with your coffee?"

I was halfway through my cup, but I nodded, getting up and strapping Hope into the pram on my own. I packed up her snacks and the baby wipes and put my coat on, while Gene stood beside me lighting his cigarette.

"Want to get lunch, babe?"

I nodded. I knew I'd be paying, but I needed to make amends for the hell I'd put Gene through the previous day.

"Where do you want to go?"

"There's a burger joint on the corner. Want to just go there?"

I nodded. I didn't mind where we went, so long as Gene didn't kidnap our daughter.

We walked into the diner and the waiter led us to our table. It was the first time I remembered doing that with Gene. It must have been an occasion worth celebrating: our reunion. I knew this was the starting point from which we would attempt to repair our relationship, and this time I was going to make it work, no matter what the cost.

"Man, the prices are steep in here," said Gene. "You got to pay for French fries on the side? That's fucked up."

A waiter passed us and gave us a disapproving look. Gene didn't put on airs, even if it meant he might end up with a glob of spit in his hamburger.

"What are you getting?" I asked.

Whatever Gene was having was what I wanted too. I was tired of making my own daily decisions. I wanted a rest, and for Gene to take over, to pick up where we left off on the morning that I gave him that last kiss. I rested my head on Gene's shoulder, smelling his special scent. I was home. I wasn't allowed inside my physical home, but Gene was what made a place home. If we had shared the same sleeping bag on the street, I'd have been happy to live there. Sitting beside Gene, I feared nothing, except Gene. I pushed that thought from my mind. The whole thing had just been a huge misunderstanding: Gene had never wanted me to leave, he would never take Hope, he would never intentionally hurt me. Gene gave me a serious look, his eyes filled with love.

"Come here," he said, pulling me closer and kissing my head.

The waiter interrupted our momentary closeness. "Are you ready to order?"

I signalled to him to take Gene's order first.

"A cheeseburger, fries, a coke."

"The same, please," I said.

"What about Hope?" asked Gene.

"She can share mine."

Gene nodded. "You got her water, babe?"

"Yeah."

The waiter walked away.

"You still not letting her have juice?"

"I want her to have good teeth."

"So - I ain't allowed to give my daughter juice?"

I shook my head, not knowing what to say.

"Hey, babe. Get Hope out of the stroller."

I jumped up and lifted her out, strapping her into the highchair the staff had provided for us. Gene didn't get up. Our *Cokes* arrived, and Gene took a swig from his. I sat back down.

"Eh, babe, you might want to put a bib on her."

I got up again and dug through the nappy bag for one, putting it around her neck. I sat back down. Our food arrived, and Gene lifted the lid of his hamburger, inspecting the inside.

"Why do they got to put all this shit inside it, man?"

He pulled out a pickle and any other vegetation that masked the flavour of the meat, throwing it to the side of his plate.

"I thought you liked pickles?"

"Not on my burger, man."

Gene approval was dipping, but not getting anywhere near annoyance yet. I was still safe to relax. Hopefully the rest of the meal would go smoothly and there would be no other slip-ups. Gene devoured his burger in minutes. He really must have been starving. I felt terrible, not knowing when he'd had his last meal. How could I do what I'd done to him? He looked noticeably leaner. His belly was trim and any extra weight he'd gained from the regular meals we'd eaten together had gone. How could I allow the one I loved to go without his needs? How could I abandon him in our family home? How could I take the only two people in the world he loved away from him? I must have been a cold-hearted, callous person. I had to correct my errors, even if it meant losing what remained of myself. Love was about self-sacrifice, and I had chosen the selfish path of survival. I had to make it right.

I went to settle the bill, but Gene insisted on paying. "Let me get this, babe. I got some money I put aside from work, so I could treat you and Hope."

Things were changing. In fact - they had already changed.

Chapter Nine

"Hey, babe," said Gene, as we arrived at the City Hall.

"Yeah?"

"Call me when you get home."

"I will."

"Where do you get your bus?"

I hesitated.

"You don't want me to know where you're going?" Gene's eyes looked angry again.

"I'm not allowed to tell anyone where it is."

Gene got his anger in check.

"Oh, ok. Call me," he said, turning around to give me a last look before we parted ways at his bus stop.

I had made it through one outing with Gene without him taking Hope. My worries had been for nothing. Now I knew I could safely take Hope to visit Gene regularly. I wasn't going to wait for social services to get in touch with me, I'd decided; I was going to contact them. I'd ask them to agree to the terms on which I could return home. All I had to do was convince them that things had changed and that it had all been a gross misunderstanding and they'd be fine with us cohabiting again. I thought about the phrasing of what I planned to say to them on the phone the whole train journey home. It was no more time-consuming than the mental rehearsals I had for every subject I discussed with Gene. I just had to say the right words and they'd produce the right effect. Our rent was due in a few days and I couldn't afford to pay rent in two places, especially with my housing benefit redirected to the refuge. I got off the train, struggling to get the pram down the steps. If only Gene was with me, he would have offered a helping hand. That's what I told myself, at least. I was in honeymoon mode; I'd mentally erased every problem in our relationship. Gene and I were perfect for each other again. I just needed to turn a blind eye to a few minor details and they'd cease to exist.

I arrived at the door to the refuge and Lana let me in. She must have seen me coming on the video camera. I was always under someone's watchful eye.

"Good day?" she asked.

"Yeah," I smirked.

"You saw Gene, didn't you?" she smiled, knowingly.

"How did you know?"

"You look like you're back in the honeymoon period."

"What do you mean?"

"Just remember it's temporary, ok? He's trying to win you back."

That wasn't what I wanted to hear so I ignored her comment and breezed past her.

"Can we have a chat later when Hope is asleep?"

"Of course."

She tucked the stray ends that had escaped her ponytail back in.

"You're getting bigger by the day, missus."

"I know, I feel pregnant now."

"Well, you are five months pregnant. Did Gene meet you near here?"

"No, I met him in town."

"Isn't that a bit of a trek for you?"

I shrugged. It felt like nothing compared to the miles I'd walked for Gene's tablets before I'd arrived. I remembered what that had felt like and my stress levels surged again. That memory didn't fit with the future life I wanted with Gene, so I decided to remove it from my memory bank. Come to think of it, I hadn't seen Gene take one pill in town. So, I decided, it mustn't have been a problem anymore.

"I'm going to make dinner," I said.

"What are you making?"

"Risotto I think."

"Yum, can I have some?" she laughed. "Only joking, your cooking always smells good though."

She must have imagined it; Gene never thought my cooking smelled good.

"What are you having?"

"Sweet chilli chicken wrap."

"That sounds good too."

"I can stick it in the oven and I don't have to do anything. Is Hope ok? She seems quiet."

I felt Hope's head, and sure enough, she had a bit of a temperature.

"Maybe she's getting a cold, she's a bit warm."

"Just keep an eye on her. I'll log it in the book."

"Do you have to log everything in the book?"

"Yeah, just so when we get into work, we haven't missed anything important."

"You just want to catch up on the gossip."

She laughed.

A joke without a look of disapproval, or a refusal to laugh; that was the first time I'd relaxed enough to allow something unplanned to slip out of my mouth. Seeing Gene must have done me some good. I felt more like myself again, but safe in the refuge; safe to be myself, whoever that was. I was suddenly feeling a lot livelier; there was a chink of light and Gene was standing at the opening of the tunnel.

■■■

I walked into the kitchen at the same time I did every night. I always cooked dinner early, so Hope could eat at 5pm. Barbara, the lady with whom I shared a kitchen, had beaten me there. It was more of a kitchenette than a kitchen. It could only accommodate one user at a time. She gave me a snide look and I wondered if I'd imagined it. Families were meant to be given priority for cooking times. She knew the rules and knew when we ate, but she was choosing to intrude on my space. There was nothing I could say, so I sat down at the table and while I waited, Sarah approached me.

"Does Flossy Doodle want a biscuit?"

"Yes please."

She nodded her head in the direction of my kitchen.

"What's she at now?"

I shrugged and gave her a look of frustration. Working around fourteen other women, workers included, in the communal areas, was getting old. I just wanted to pack up my case and go back home where I only had to work around one other person's living habits. Some of Gene's habits were hard to circumnavigate, but surely one person's quirks were easier to manage than a dozen people in one cramped kitchen?

Sarah set a cup of tea in front of me and handed Hope a biscuit.

"Thanks," I smiled. At least her manner was gentle. She offered me a reassuring word, a laugh and shoulder to cry on; all those things with no payback later. Maybe that was worth a lot. I'd talk to her about my idea to go home and see what she thought. She could be relied upon to give it to me straight. I'd wait until a quieter moment when Barbara wasn't lurking in the corner of the room, listening to our every word. I was beginning to learn who could be trusted in the refuge and who couldn't. I knew that Sarah had my back and that she'd never steer me wrong. And yet, I looked across the room at Barbara and realised that bullies were everywhere. It was just the way life was. It didn't matter if you were in your own home or in a women's refuge, it was just one of life's facts you had no choice but to accept. An hour later, Barbara vacated our kitchen. She'd left the remnants of her meal in the sink and the dishes to drip dry on paper towels. The grilling machine sat on the counter, encrusted with burnt meat, and the stench was terrible. I had no alternative but to work around it. I served Hope's dinner an hour later than usual, but at least she had had a large lunch, thanks to Gene. Hope still devoured her risotto. She'd been eating better lately, but maybe that could be attributed to her age. The phone rang the second I sat down to eat. It was Gene.

"What the fuck are you doing?"

"Eating dinner."

"Why didn't you fucking call me when you got home?"

"Sorry, I forgot."

"You forgot? What you been doing that's more important?"

"Nothing. I was just cooking."

"Right -"

"What are you doing?"

"Drinking fucking coffee. Hey, babe, when is the rent due?"

"In two days."

"Are you fucking coming home or what?"

"Yeah, I just need to talk to social services first."

"Well, get on with that shit. Babe, I got to ask you a favour."

"Yeah?"

"Can you pay the rent this month?"

I hesitated. "I thought you were working."

"Are you being fucking serious? You do know the rent is 695?"

"Yeah, I know, I've been paying it."

"How the fuck am I supposed to pay that on what I earn? You know whose fault this is, right?"

I didn't say anything, but I could make a few guesses as to whom the culprit was; none of them Gene.

"Your fucking dad."

"Why?"

"What the fuck do you mean - why? I told him this place was too expensive, but he wouldn't listen to us. Now look where we're at. You've got no one to blame for that but your fucking parents. They talked you into leaving."

"They didn't."

"Baby, you told me that. When you come home, I don't want nothing to do with them fucking people no more. They're toxic."

"So, I can't see them?"

"Did I fucking say that? I just ain't going near them. Do what the fuck you want."

My muscles tensed as I thought of all the familial problems that would ensue. I'd be forced to pick: my family or Gene. I had to remain loyal to Gene even if it meant cutting my family off for good. I knew he was right about the rent; it was too much to expect him to pay on his salary. Gene was making nine hundred quid a month, and that was on a good month, when his shoulder wasn't playing up.

"I have to go," I said, "I'm not alone."

I had to buy myself some time to figure out what I was going to do about the rent.

"Hey?"

"Yeah?"

"Call me when Hope's asleep. Don't fucking forget this time."

"I won't."

I'd run the idea of paying Gene's rent for one last month past Lana and see what she suggested. I needed some perspective on the situation; I was too immersed in it to see anything clearly.

After I got Hope to sleep, I stopped at the office door. It was propped open and Lana gave me a wave to say she'd join me in a minute. She was on the phone.

I walked into the empty room and smelled the fresh furniture polish. It was my chore that week: dusting one room. The workers gave me light housework, taking my pregnancy into account. It was strange to have someone do that. Shopping, cooking, laundry and a bit of dusting; it was nothing compared to what running a house had entailed. Maybe life was easier in certain ways in the refuge and I hadn't even realised it. But what was the use of easier living when you were left with nothing but your own loneliness once you'd finished cleaning up? Being with Gene was back-breaking work, but he kept my mind busy; too busy to think. Too much time to think was the greatest curse to someone with my illness.

I sat on the stiff-backed sofa and thought of my own sofa at home. It was over-used and filthy, but it sank down when you sat on it. You could really relax there, unless Gene was in bad form, that was. I missed home terribly. It sickened me thinking of it. I tormented myself tracing over every detail of the house in my mind. So much had happened in that house; it was my place of peace and my torture chamber. I couldn't get it out of my head. It would forever leave a home-shaped imprint on my mind, whether I returned to it or not. Nowhere else could be the site of so many strong feelings as that place.

Lana joined me in the room. She dug the stopper out from under the door and closed it firmly behind her. I knew whatever I said to her was truly confidential. I could ask things off the record and she'd give me the reassurance I needed. Maybe she was the first person since Gene that I'd been able to trust.

"Well," she said, sitting on the sofa facing me. "What did you want to talk about?"

"I wanted to talk to you about Gene's rent."

"Ok," she said. She drew the word out, so it sounded like a loaded question.

"I think I'm going to pay it this month and then go back."

"Well, that's your decision. You know we can't tell you what to do. But do you think this will be the end of it?"

"The end of what?"

"You paying for everything."

There was a tug in my gut, like my unconscious mind was yelling in agreement with what she said.

"I don't know. If I go home, I won't have to pay rent in two places anymore."

"You don't have to now."

"I do."

"Gene has convinced you that you do, but you aren't responsible for him."

"I feel like I am."

"He's a fully-grown man."

"If I don't pay his rent, he'll have nowhere else to live. He'll lose his visa."

"And whose responsibility is that? He is responsible for his own behaviour. If you don't pay his rent, you're really doing him a favour."

"How?"

"He needs to learn to look after himself. If you keep doing it for him, he never will. You're looking after yourself, your daughter and him."

"It's not his fault. The rent is really high."

"But why is that your responsibility? Why can't he move if it's too much?"

"He thinks I'm coming home."

"What age is he?"

"41."

"And you're 27. He needs to learn to grow up and he's never going to do that if you keep doing everything for him."

She was right: if I kept carrying Gene, our relationship would never be equal. I was doing us both a favour by forcing him onto his own resources. It would take real resolve to refuse him the money, but he would thank me for it in the long run. I still dreaded breaking the news to him; I knew it wouldn't be well received.

"Lana?"

"Yeah?"

"If I go home, will social services take Hope? Tell me the truth."

"No, they'll be involved. We can't tell you exactly what they will do – that's up to them, but if they were going to take Hope, they'd have to discuss it with you first."

"So, what will happen?"

"They'll put together a protection plan and if Gene breaches it, then they'll give you an ultimatum: leave Gene or they'll remove Hope."

"So, it wouldn't happen straight away?"

"No, they can't do that."

Hearing those words was the greatest gift I'd ever been given. They brought hope back to life in my heart. There was real hope for Gene and me, and that was all I needed to survive in the refuge.

Chapter Ten

When I returned to my room, I had twenty-two missed calls and five messages. Gene was going to be "salty as fuck." I'd promised to ring him as soon as Hope was asleep. He knew she went down at 8pm and it was now 9.15pm. How was I going to account for those seventy-five minutes? I could say there had been a house meeting. They happened on Sunday nights, but how was Gene to know how frequent they were? I couldn't lie to Gene, but I couldn't face the consequences of honesty either. If I told Gene one white lie, it would protect me from an outburst and him from the feeling of upset that he was coming second. He was right; I'd put him second on that occasion, but I needed advice about him and he wasn't the person I could ask. I picked up my phone, not bothering to read the messages. I knew what they'd say: threats and accusations. Who was I with or what had I been doing that was more important? Why did Gene always come last on my list? I loved Gene intensely, enough to cut out all other influences in my life. But how could I prioritise him over a crying baby, a bill that needed paid or a scheduled meeting? Gene didn't understand that. He put his own life on hold for me. He had no other commitments; he came and went from work as freely as he pleased, he never paid a bill and the only doctor's appointments he attended were his own, usually with me by his side.

I was about to piss Gene off well beyond any time I had before. I dialled his number, my body stiffening as the phone rang. I sat on the edge of the bed for support.

"Hi, sorry –

"What the fuck were you doing? You said you were going to call me when you got Hope to sleep."

"Sorry –

"Fuck your sorrys. Everything else is always more fucking important. What the fuck were you doing?"

"I had a house meeting."

I tried not to let my voice falter. If it did, Gene would know I was lying, and the consequences would be unimaginable.

"What for?"

"To discuss chores and things."

"What things?"

"Just stuff in the house."

"You ain't going to tell me?"

"It's confidential."

"This is me you're talking to."

"I'm sorry."

"Ok, I guess if we're keeping secrets now, I will too."

"What kind of secrets?"

"You're the secretive one, sneaking around, acting shady as fuck."

"I'm not."

"Meet me tomorrow in the center."

"I can't."

"What the fuck do you mean, you can't? What else you got to do?"

"Hope seems like she's getting a cold."

"Alright, don't drag her into the center if she's sick, babe."

"I love you."

"And I love you, my girl. Hey?"

"Yeah?"

"Thanks."

"What for?"

"For today."

I smiled. Gene and I were back in our bubble again. No one could touch our happiness.

"Babe, do I got to do the bank transfer to the agency or are you going to do it?"

"I'm sorry, I can't."

My stomach churned, and my palms moistened.

"What?"

"I can't send the money."

"So, let me get this straight – You're going to let me live on the fucking street?"

"No. Can you just ask the agency for an extension on the date it's due?"

"You know I can't do that. They ain't going to agree to that shit; they're fucking assholes."

I knew Gene was right. Should I pay it just this once? If Gene didn't, he'd get an eviction notice. An eviction notice wouldn't do his visa any favours. I still had a little time to think about it. As soon as I got off the phone, I'd transfer the money for the electricity bill to keep

Gene sweet. I couldn't cut him off from everything at once. I had to ease him into fending for himself. What kind of a heartless person would do what I had done? I'd left my husband, taking our daughter with me, I'd cancelled his phone contract, and now I was considering cutting off his rent money too. He was right; I was a controlling, crazy bitch. The irony of it was that I'd been the one to combat Gene's past money problems and here I was, allowing them to amass again.

I moved money into our joint account to cover the electricity. It had three pounds in it and I hoped Gene's personal account was further from being in the red. I went to bed and put our money troubles behind me for a while. Sleep was the only escape that I had from the life I was leading.

That night, I had a nightmare. I was back in the house with Gene. The doors and windows were locked, and Gene had pocketed the key. Hope was asleep, and I was still sitting in her bedroom, pretending I was occupied with bedtime stories, so I didn't have to go downstairs. I stared out her small bedroom window at the night sky. It was like a blanket of black, not one visible star. I guess the moon was on one of the windowless sides of the house. Wherever it was, I couldn't see it. I could just about make out the forms of the neighbouring buildings, but there was no sign of life about them. The only life was the metal music I could feel vibrating through the floor. I opened the door, taking light steps on the stairs. If I entirely effaced myself, maybe there would be no cause for conflict.

I woke up in my single bed at 3am, the fitted sheet wrapped around me, my leg stuck with cold sweat to the plastic cover. I felt sick to my stomach and relieved to have awoken in the refuge. But dreams bore little resemblance to reality, I told myself. My fears were unfounded. I went downstairs to get a glass of water and one of the workers was moving around in the kitchen. They usually left at 10pm.

"How come you're here?" I asked.

"We've got a new intake."

Her wording was quite dehumanising, like we were all just faceless numbers in a heap of box files. Gene terrified me at times, but at least he made me feel special enough to have more than an assigned number. I was number one in his life and no other numbers existed on the page. Would anyone even notice if I left the refuge beyond making a social services referral and filling out the discharge forms?

I was no one in this big world; just one of the specks of which the dust on the ground was composed.

New arrivals weren't a major event; there had been more than I could remember since my arrival, most of them returning to their partners within the first twenty-four hours. I always envied those that went home. If only I'd had the same courage to do that on my first day. I'd never intended to stay, and yet, I'd become part of the wallpaper.

I went back to the room and found Hope in a similar state of wakefulness. Her temperature was still elevated, and she was restless on her own substitute bed. It didn't feel right having her there when she was unwell; she deserved to be in the comfort of her own home. But my dream's warning was still ringing in my ears. I'd take her to the doctor's in the morning in case she needed an antibiotic. Hope and I slept on and off, with night reaching for the morning and never quite making it there.

In the morning, I knew Hope had more than just a cold. She refused her breakfast and was turning down all the fluids I was trying to give her. She was weak and worryingly quiet. I phoned the doctor's surgery to make an emergency appointment. I'd tell Gene what the outcome was afterwards.

I bundled Hope into the pram and walked the mile to the clinic. If only I hadn't brought her to the refuge. Maybe I'd exposed her to germs she wouldn't have encountered at home. If I'd been at home, Gene would have been there to accompany me to her appointment, holding my hand through the process. I was officially alone, and it was no one's fault but mine.

Hope was dehydrated. The doctor suggested I take her straight to hospital. They could connect her to a drip and get fluids into her body by that means. It was likely a viral infection, but they were concerned about her refusal to drink. The hospital was in Belfast. How was I going to get there? How long would we be staying there for? How would I manage my interactions with Gene? I just wanted to phone him and tell him to meet us there and stay until she was discharged, but what if social services prevented that? I didn't want to flag up any concerns on their system that were currently lying unaddressed. Gene and I were at the bottom of their administrative pile. I hadn't been assigned a social worker like most other residents of the refuge, likely because we had been forgotten about. I hoped things would stay that way.

I phoned Gene as soon as I exited the surgery.

"Yeah?"

"Hope isn't well. She's going into hospital."

"What's wrong with her?"

"Just a bug, but she's dehydrated."

"Call me when you get there, and I'll meet you there."

"Are we allowed to do that?"

"Who gives a fuck? My fucking daughter is sick. They can't keep me away from her."

I wondered if he was right, but Gene was so confident of the fact, it made me doubt my own doubts.

"You got to stop allowing other people to dictate your decisions. You're a coward."

I emotionally recoiled from his words. I knew they were right and if I let them touch me, they'd define me forever. Gene was good at influencing my impression of myself. He confirmed most of the beliefs that whispered inside me about my inadequacies, turning them into a yelling critic.

"I'll ring you when we're on our way to the hospital."

"Ok, baby. I'm in work but it's nearby anyway."

I hurried back to the refuge to book a taxi. It was one of those times I would have killed to have my own transportation. Carrying a car seat for Hope, along with the baby supplies required for a couple of days sounded like more than my pregnant body could withstand. But it was proving its own strength to me every day. I pushed the pram all over my new town, running errands and buying food shopping, I carried Hope up and down the flights of stairs of the hostel as well as all our toiletries and towels every time we needed to have a bath. I was becoming sturdier, more able to manage things physically, and yet, emotionally, I was like a tent cover without the poles.

The refuge workers were waiting for us at the front door. They looked as concerned as if they'd been female relatives of mine. They wanted the best for Hope and me; I could see it clearly that morning. How long that state of clarity would last before it shifted to them becoming untrustworthy figures again, I couldn't say.

"You get Hope ready and we'll book you a taxi," said Lisa.

"Thanks," I tried to smile.

"She really doesn't look well, does she?"

I shook my head. Guilt stirred inside me. Hope's ill health was because of my ill-advised choices. I'd exposed her to a world she should never have seen. Her pale complexion could have been due to physical illness, but equally, I wondered if it was a bodily response to her unnatural surroundings. Maybe anxiety was making her as unwell as it was me. I felt judged by everyone; I knew they thought I was a bad mother. I couldn't wait to see Gene, so he could reassure me that I wasn't. Excitement was filling me up. That bright yellow feeling of sunlight that only Gene could produce was coming back to life. I couldn't go home with Gene, but I could see him in the flesh, kiss and hug him and talk to him, and that alone made me happy.

"Make sure you tell the nurse you're in a refuge when you arrive," said Lisa.

"Do I have to?"

"If Gene's meeting you there, you'll have to do that."

I felt sick. I'd wanted to just enjoy my time with Gene, without tainting it with questioning from nosy nurses and the blank boxes awaiting ticks on their clipboards.

The taxi arrived, and the workers helped me into it. I didn't know what I'd do at the other end, but I'd figure it out, one way or another. I knew by that stage that planning was pointless; nothing in life ever unfolded in a predictable way. I watched familiar scenery out the taxi window: scenery that I hadn't seen since I left home, and it felt like part of a land from a fairytale. It was a land I could no longer access, but that held my happiest moments. If I said the right things, took the right actions and undid my mistakes, I knew I'd get back there some day.

The hospital's many windows were like monstrous eyes, watching my every misstep. That whole building symbolised fear. I couldn't look at it without feeling severely sick. The day of Hope's birth and the days that followed it returned to me with the hurt that had accompanied them. Looking at something I hadn't thought about since that day unearthed all the memories I wanted to forget. I hoped we wouldn't make any more of them that day.

I struggled out of the taxi with all our belongings and hoped that Gene would walk up behind me and lighten the load, but he didn't. He might have still been in transit. I'd texted him from the car to tell him we were on our way. I got Hope inside and took the lift to the children's department. The walls were painted with toys and teddy bears, which somehow gave the place a feel of threatening benevolence. It was like a pat on the shoulder after you've just lost a limb.

"Hello," boomed a bossy nurse.

She had a friendly way of taking over and making sure you didn't block her role. She whisked Hope away into a side room and I followed timidly, not sure if I was meant to be there or not. Hope was stripped off and placed in a bed with four metal sides raised around her, to make sure she didn't fall out. The nurse hooked her up to a drip and Hope crawled around her cot. Gene walked into the room and I could feel it on my skin: that addictive blend of joy and fear.

"Alright, baby, what's happening?"

"They put Hope on a drip. She's dehydrated."

"Did they say what's wrong with her?"

"No, I'm waiting for the doctor to call in now."

"Right."

Gene sat down at the bedside and lowered his work bag to the floor.

"Can I pick her up, babe?"

"I don't think so, not while she's on the drip."

"Right. Don't make no difference. I don't get to see her anyway."

"Why are you being like this now?"

"I ain't being like nothing. I'm just stating facts."

"It isn't true."

"Babe, I ain't seen my daughter for fucking weeks."

"That's not my fault."

"Well, whose fucking fault is it? Come on, tell me it's mine."

"Why?"

"I want to hear you say it. Then I'm going to get up and walk out the fucking door."

Gene's voice was growing louder and louder. If anyone heard his tone, they might think it was a confrontation and send him out of the hospital. I'd better do something to bring the volume down.

"I didn't say it was your fault."

"But it ain't yours, right?" Gene did a disbelieving laugh.

"I don't want to talk about this now. Our daughter is sick, and I'm worried about her."

I remembered I'd better go and tell the nurse on duty that I was staying in a refuge. If I didn't, and the workers found out, I didn't know what might happen. I had to make sure I was seen to protect Hope, even though it was a laughable notion that she'd need protected from her own father. 2015 was nothing but an age of professionals covering themselves, documenting every fact about your life so it couldn't come back to haunt them if they missed something essential. If Gene and I capitulated and filled in whatever forms we needed to, there was a better chance of getting their blessing when we got back together. I was thinking in long term goals and I hoped Gene would have the foresight to do the same. Gene loathed authority and I doubted his ability to go along with being bossed around without an outburst occurring.

"I'm just going to the toilet," I said. I felt sick lying to him but telling him the truth wasn't an option. I needed Gene in the room with me and if I was honest with him, he'd be removed from the building and barred from returning.

"Ok, baby."

I was a traitor; I loathed myself for siding with the enemy. Updating the nurse on my living circumstances was a betrayal of Gene. How could I portray him so badly to others? How could I allow myself to be viewed as the sole victim when Gene was as much of a victim as I was? I approached the nurse at the desk diffidently. I'd got used to the reactions I got from professionals when I owned up to living in a refuge. They always gave you a look of pity and then tried to call in the forces to keep you safe. I didn't want to be kept safe from Gene; I wanted to be safe with Gene. I'd downplay it all; that was the best I could do with the miserable situation. I had to be truthful. The abuse was already recorded, but I could slowly reduce it to nothing in their minds. I wouldn't admit to anything too damning about Gene; I'd stick to the basics.

"Excuse me," I whispered, barely audibly.

"Yes?"

"I'm staying in a refuge and I was told I had to let you know."

"Ok. Is that your husband that's just arrived?"

"Yeah."

"Is he the reason you're in the refuge?"

"Yes, but I'm fine with him being here."

"Well, as long as you're comfortable with having him here - that's your decision. I'll need to update the hospital social worker though. They'll call you in to complete a report."

I felt the hopeful surge in my heart physically slump. Nothing was ever simple regarding Gene, and I had no one to blame for that but myself. Why couldn't I have continued to keep the secrets of our relationship? Why had I let other people in on our private life? I couldn't even meet my own husband without being watched like a hawk by everyone in our vicinity. I just wanted to be alone with Gene behind a locked door, but the thought of that simultaneously brought sickness to my stomach.

I walked apologetically back to the room. I'd have to own up to Gene or his anger would come more loudly when I was called into the side room. I knew he'd want to join us, but there was no chance of that happening. Hopefully I'd have enough time to pacify him before the staff arrived.

"You were gone a long fucking time at the bathroom. Who were you talking to?"

"The nurse."

"What was she saying?"

"She said I have to meet the hospital social worker."

"What the fuck for?"

I thought about hushing Gene but knew that would only result in amplifying his voice. It almost seemed like he enjoyed testing authority to see how much he could get away with. But he was just a confident person, who didn't like being talked down to like a child.

"They said they have to fill out a form because I'm in a refuge."

"How the fuck did they know that?" Gene looked at me like he knew I was the source of their information; like I'd broken our code of silence all over again.

"I had to give them our address and say where it was."

Gene looked at me like I was spinning more elaborate stories than a Northern Irish person in a power cut.

I lowered the tension by turning my focus to Hope. She was crawling around in her cot, looking ill but in perpetual movement. I'd been so worried about her, but Gene was good at distracting me from that, by redirecting my energy to him. I felt guilty for becoming consumed by things that were trivial in comparison to our sick child. We'd work it out; we had to, for Hope.

The nurse popped her head around the door.

"Can you come with me for a minute Mrs Savoyard?"

"You ain't changed your name yet," muttered Gene. "That surprises me."

I shook my head and looked at him as lovingly as I could in such a manufactured moment.

The nurse ushered me into a room with a lady I'd never seen before. I was relieved she wasn't the social worker I'd met with before. I knew that, with her, I'd be damned before I spoke. The lady got up from her seat to shake my hand. She smiled in a way that almost put me at ease.

"I just need to ask you a few questions and then I'll let you get back to your daughter."

"Thanks."

"The sister on the ward tells me you're staying in a refuge."

"Yeah," I said, reddening and staring at the floor tiles.

"Is that because of your husband?"

"Yeah, we weren't getting along."

"Would you like to get back together?"

She was the first professional to pose that question to me, to make it seem like a workable option.

"I would love to."

"Do you know when you will?"

"I'm just waiting to see if social services agree to it."

"I don't see why they wouldn't if you just weren't getting along."

I knew she didn't see the full picture and was lacking the information the refuge workers had collated in their file. But I preferred her response to anything else I'd heard to date; it made it sound like my dream of being a family was still fully achievable.

"I'm sure you'd love to reconcile before the baby comes," she said, nodding at my growing bump. Only four months remained to resolve our problems and move back in together, getting social services on board. It suddenly felt like time was running out. Was it possible I would give birth whilst I was staying in the refuge? I couldn't imagine anything worse. All I wanted was to return to the cosiness of my own home, to feel the comfort of my own sheets, to live with the protective presence of my husband when I was in my most vulnerable physical state. But fear prevented me impulsively correcting the situation. Getting back together had to be something we did in a logical way, so we wouldn't lose Hope.

"Well, I won't keep you. I'm sure you want to see how your daughter is. Good luck," smiled the social worker. It felt like receiving the blessing of social services to repair our fractured family.

I walked back into the room and tried to meet Gene's eye. He refused to connect his gaze with mine.

"I got to go, babe."

"What? Now?"

"Yeah, I got to go to work."

"But Hope is really sick."

"I know, but I got to find the money to pay the full rent or I'm going to be on the street."

I hesitated, not knowing what to say.

"I wish you could stay longer."

"Well, whose fucking fault is that?"

I shook my head. "I didn't want things to be like this."

"Then why the fuck did you make them like this? You should have just come home."

"It isn't too late to fix it."

"Well, get to it. Call social services when you get back to the shelter. Tell them you're coming home."

Gene pushed past me to reach for his workbag and threw it over his shoulder, like a load he gladly would have rid himself of, given the chance.

"Goodbye, my baby," he sang to Hope, picking her up.

She looked too lethargic to fully recognise him, or me, for that matter.

"She don't even fucking recognise me," Gene shouted. "That's your fucking fault."

"Here," he shouted, forcing her into my arms.

Before I could justify myself, he stormed out the door. The air felt still in his absence, and I looked at Hope's tubed-up body and her little off-colour face, feeling like we were the last two people in the world.

Chapter Eleven

I sat up all night, in a chair at Hope's bedside, alone. Gene didn't come back after work. He said he was too tired and that he'd swing by tomorrow. He had worked a long shift; I hadn't. Who was I to protest? My whole body cramped with the weight of the baby and the severe shape of the chair. I was getting sick too; I'd caught whatever Hope was suffering from and I wanted nothing more than to climb into my own bed and find health in sleep, but that wasn't an option. I hadn't slept well since I'd vacated my side of the marital bed and I was in a perpetual state of exhaustion. I was rapidly approaching burn-out, but there was no sign of a resting spot, so I had no choice but to keep going: keep stressing, keep suffering, keep mothering. Once Gene was a fixed feature in our lives again, all of that would change.

I sat up, messaging Gene throughout the night. He had got back to the house at tea time, but he'd been too worn out from work to make a second trip to the hospital. He promised me he'd call by in the morning. I craved his presence; I wanted to burrow my head into his chest and let him receive the strength of my sobs. But there was nowhere to release them, so I kept them stored up inside instead. The night duty nurse called in, checked Hope's vitals and left. She offered me a pillow and I felt like asking her for her shoulder too, but she was busy with other things. Everyone was busy living their own lives; too busy to fill the Gene shaped void. How could I have ever believed I could survive without him? Why hadn't I factored in emergency situations: deaths, hospital visits, illness. I hadn't adequately considered my decision before making it; I had just leapt without looking. And there was no net to catch me outside the walls of 2 Belmont Place.

Gene went to bed and I was the one waiting up for once: waiting for him to wake up, waiting for him to call me, waiting for him to sit in the empty seat beside me and hold my hand. It didn't feel good being on the waiting end of the phone; I was getting a taste of my own medicine and I realised I had treated Gene terribly.

I dozed on and off, roused at intervals by the snores of parents in neighbouring cubicles, the heel clicks of the sister, the swish of hospital bed curtains. I had never been gladder of Hope's fussing at her waking hour. I jumped up and felt her head. Her temperature had lowered, her eyes looked moist and alert. I knew she was getting better. She shifted around in her cot bed, ready for play time and to go home. I was desperate to get home, but no more eager to return to the refuge than to stay in the ward. One was the same as the other; neither was home to me.

I felt tingles travelling up my back: Gene. I knew he was in the room; I could feel his energy agitating the atoms in the air. He pulled the privacy curtain back.

"Hey baby," he smiled.

I'd never been so happy to see him before; not in the airport, not getting out of the taxi post-New York, not on his return from his longest work day. I fell against his chest, weeping.

"It'll be ok, baby. I promise you that. Tell me what's wrong."

"Everything is so messed up."

"I know baby, but we can fix it. Hey?"

"Yeah."

"Do you love me?"

"Yes."

"Well, I love you. That's all that matters. We can fix anything else."

I pressed my lips against his and felt the loving touch of his kiss that could comfort me in any catastrophe. Gene and I were still together; nothing could separate us.

He reached into the plastic bag he gripped in his hand. Gene never held a bag by the handles; he always held it like he was grabbing an animal by the scruff of the neck. I looked at his fist; Gene wasn't violent, he was just a bit clumsy and coarse in the way he did things. I had misinterpreted every one of his negative actions. When we reunited under the one roof, everything would be different.

Gene pulled a stuffed animal from the bag and thrust it into my hand.

"I got you a present, baby."

"What is it?"

"I looked at the deer and read the caption on its tummy; "World's Best Mum."

"I love it," I said, bursting into tears.

It was the most thoughtful present anyone had ever got me. I had thought that Gene had left the hospital early to work and watch TV, but he was much more kind-hearted than I'd given him credit for. I was madly in love with him again.

He reached into the bag a second time and produced a stuffed rabbit, placing it in Hope's bed.

"Don't worry – Daddy didn't forget about you. Do you love him?" he beamed.

Hope reached for the striped rabbit and put it into her mouth.

"Does he taste good too?" laughed Gene. "Daddy's glad you like him, beautiful."

Gene stayed for a couple of hours until he had to leave for work. He walked to the canteen to get me some coffee and breakfast, asked the nurse about Hope and rubbed my strained shoulders.

"I just want to go home," I said, with tears accumulating in my eyes. Gene enclosed me in a bear hug.

"I know baby, you will be soon. As soon as you get back, call social services – we'll get this shit sorted."

"Ok."

"I mean – we could have had it sorted already, but you're too afraid of everyone."

"I'm scared of losing Hope."

"They can't take her. You're worrying for no reason. It's not like I was beating you black and blue every day."

"I know," I said, embarrassed.

I felt ashamed again that I'd gone to the refuge and created such a commotion out of nothing. I'd painted a bad picture of Gene, wasted the workers' time and only exhausted myself in the process.

"I'm sorry," I said, kissing Gene.

"We'll make it right, babe. You're made for me."

Gene stayed until the rush hour hit and then made his way to the bus stop. I expected they would discharge Hope before he made his return journey.

The nurse called in to check Hope's progress. She was still ill, but much more vivacious than the previous day. Her hydration levels had improved, but they still weren't willing to take any chances. They'd keep her in until later that day and then get the doctor to perform a final check. I was tired of sitting in the ward, but hopeful I'd get to see Gene again. The hospital curtain afforded us more privacy than we would have got anywhere else we were allowed to meet. I craved Gene's company again. Once you got a fix, you were dying for the next one. I hadn't managed to wean myself off him since staying in the refuge, but now that I'd seen him again, it only intensified my desire to be together all the time. My mind was too occupied with our troubled romance to focus on the emergency at hand. Once Gene walked in, he moved my attention from my baby back to himself again. It wasn't Gene's fault; our circumstances were just abnormal. Once we were living together again, we'd be the happy family I knew we had the potential to be.

My mum called up to the hospital with some essentials. I hadn't had a chance to have a shower, change my clothes or remove yesterday's make-up. She arrived in the ward with a bag filled with every item I could have needed for a week-long stay. Gene's gift still meant more to me than if someone had donated a year of their night's sleep in exchange for my sleepless nights. My mum took my place in the bedside seat and I went to find the shower room to freshen myself up. My developing cold had turned into a flu-like virus, but I hadn't had time to think about that. The hot water on my body relieved some of my aches and brought me back from the brink of burn-out. I returned to the bed and leant over Hope, holding her little hand and smiling into her bright eyes. My baby's health had returned, and I knew I could relax, about that aspect of life, at least. The nurse had called over during my fifteen-minute absence to announce that she had requested a doctor complete the discharge papers with us and allow me to go home. I was desperate to go back there. The sooner I dealt with the logistics, the sooner I could go back to Belmont Place and the last month would be nothing but a blip in our relationship. Gene and I were perfectly suited to each other; I couldn't understand how I had ever believed that my leaving was the solution. I mustn't have been in my right mind to think like that.

Chapter Twelve

"I need to talk to a social worker about my relationship." I'd practised the sentence hundreds of times, trying to sound as nonchalant as possible when I said it. My voice still broke when it came to the real deal. So much was at stake, and it all pivoted on my ability to convince the listener that my relationship was no longer abusive. If I could convince them of that, I'd be permitted to return home without an ambush the minute I crossed the threshold.

"Please hold. I think Peter is on duty. I'll put you through to him now."

I waited on the phone, trying to hold my breath so my pants of panic didn't sound in his ear.

"Hello?"

"Hi, I'm staying in a refuge and I was just ringing to find out what the process would be if I returned home?"

If I stuck to official wording, maybe they'd take me more seriously. Maybe they'd think I was the logical type: someone who wasn't driven to decisions by their untamed emotions. I wanted to exude confidence, to emit a knowing kind of calm, like I'd carefully considered every eventuality before returning home.

"Ok, what are your circumstances? Do you still see your partner?"

"Yes, we meet up, so he can see our daughter."

"And does it always go well?"

No time for hesitation.

"Yes."

"So, what were the issues before you left? Was he violent?"

"A couple of times. Our arguments just got out of hand, but we have learnt how to communicate much better since then. I think there were just a lot of misunderstandings."

"I don't see why anyone would prevent reconciliation in that case."

"So, what would happen?"

"We'd call out to do an assessment, but it doesn't sound like you'd need intervention."

"Oh, that's great, thanks for your help."

"No problem, call any time you have a question."

"I will."

I hung up. The phone call had gone much more affably than I could ever have predicted. My worries about reuniting with Gene were silenced. I tapped my recent calls button to phone Gene. He was still always positioned at the top of the list.

I lowered my voice as soon as he answered. I wasn't sure if our conversations were private, even behind my locked door. It felt like the room could be bugged. There were regular room checks, where the workers went through every cupboard, looking for unpermitted items. One resident had been forced to get rid of her craft supplies; they were a health and safety risk. I didn't trust that they weren't listening. The office was situated next door to my room and I knew the walls were paper-thin. They probably heard every word of our phone calls, and I had no plans to let them in on the latest developments in our romance.

"Gene?"

"Yeah, babe?"

"I phoned social services."

"And?"

"They said they wouldn't stop us getting back together and would just do an assessment."

"Why are you whispering?"

"In case they hear us."

"Who's they?"

"The staff."

"Fuck them, they can't stop us doing what is right for our family."

"They can."

"No, they fucking can't. Stop being fucking afraid."

"I just didn't want to risk losing Hope."

"And your fear has stopped us getting back together for the last month. I told you they couldn't stop us, but you never believe me. Why do you always believe what everyone else tells you, but not me?"

"I don't."

"Yes, you fucking do."

"Well, can we not be happy?"

Gene's tone didn't lighten a bit.

"When are you coming home?"

He said it in the timbre with which a bully would say "you better fucking –

But I was just imagining things. I knew my illness made me over-analyse everything. I found negative meaning where there was none to be found. Gene just wanted to know a timeframe for how long it would be until our family unit was reunified.

My gut still tightened like it was in a vice. Why did that question create anxiety in me? I had longed for that answer from social services since the day I set foot in the refuge. We had got the answer we wanted, and I still had reservations. Gene was right: I needed to forget my fears, including those that were directly related to him. He was my husband; he wanted nothing other than happiness for both of us, and a loving environment for our child.

"I'll talk to the workers when we get off the phone and tell them I'm going home."

"Go do that now, babe, and hey?"

"Yeah?"

"Would you call the agency and pay the rent? We got to buy some time in this place – until we find some place else to live."

"Ok."

Paying the rent would cost me the last of the money I had managed to save in the last three years, but I'd pay any amount to rebuild the relationship. I remembered about the electricity bill and wondered if it had been paid. I'd check when I got off the phone and make sure everything was financially in order before I stepped out of the supposed safety of the refuge. Once I was back in Gene's grasp, everything would be ok.

Chapter Thirteen

The bill hadn't been paid; Gene had withdrawn the money from our account the day I transferred it. Maybe he didn't know what it was for. I was sure I had advised him of its purpose, but maybe I had forgotten, like I forgot so many other things. The money wasn't in the account and the direct debit had bounced. Gene hadn't mentioned it to me. Maybe something crucial had cropped up and he had been too ashamed to say.

"Gene, did you withdraw money the other day?"

"I might have done, why?"

"I transferred money to our account to pay the electric bill, but the account was empty when they requested it."

"Oh, was that what that was for? I used it for smokes."

"You used it for cigarettes?"

"Yeah, how was I supposed to know what it was fucking for?"

"I thought I told you."

"You didn't."

"Well, why did you use it when you didn't know what it was for?" Rage was growing inside me. Years of being the only partner responsible for our finances was building into resentment. People always said love was work, but I hadn't known it was one-sided work.

"I'm not fucking psychic. Not like you -"

"Why am I the only one responsible for our finances? Nothing has changed."

As I pronounced the final statement, I knew it was true: nothing had changed. I had to delay my planned return home, until Gene was ready to carry his half of the relationship. The workers' words were moving around in my mind like pennies deposited in a piggy bank that suddenly added up to a considerable amount. Gene wasn't pulling his weight, but any anger I felt about that was overridden by my worries about his financial ruin. If I didn't bail Gene out, he'd be evicted from our house, he'd run out of oil, he'd run into the red on our electric bill, and all those points would make it that bit harder for me to go home. I wasn't just paying to rescue Gene from homelessness; I was paying to preserve my only dream. Without it, there was no reason left to hold onto life. If I didn't keep hoping, I'd have to face the fact that I was living in a women's refuge without the incentive to keep putting one foot in front of the other. I was a pregnant, separated mother: a figure of failure. I came from a traditional society. Everyone used to warn me against such failings when I was in secondary school. Having a baby without a career in place or a reliable partner made you fearfully foolish. I couldn't allow myself to fulfil that role. Our marriage would work out; I would make sure of it.

"It's ok – I'll ring them and pay it."

"Thank you, baby. Hey, did you pay the rent yet?"

"Not yet. I will soon."

My mind wrestled with itself. Two opposing options were hollering so loudly I couldn't make out which of the two was the more sensible choice. I had to talk to someone, to clear that up. But who could I talk to that was reliable? Gene was fighting on Gene's side and the workers were doing battle on the other side. There was no one with a balanced view of the situation. There was no one I could trust to tell me the truth.

"I have to go. I'll ring you soon."

I hung up before Gene had time to interrogate me about where I was going, what I was doing and why everything was always more important than him. I walked past the office and the door stopper was in. One of the workers, Anne, gave me a smile.

"How is Hope now?"

"She's better, thanks."

"How about you?"

"I'm tired."

"Get a good rest tonight."

"I think I need to talk to someone."

"Sure, I'm free now. Come on in."

I sat down on the swivel chair on the other side of the desk. Anne was a soft, mumsy type who made you feel like she could take care of whatever ill came your way. She played with the badge on the lanyard round her neck.

"What can I do for you?" she asked, nudging her chair closer.

"I'm just really confused."

"Ok, well, let's try and unpick it for you."

"I want to go home."

Anne drew in a breath through her nose, which was enough to tell me she thought it was a bad idea.

"Ok. We can't tell you what to do. Just give it some thought first. Has anything changed?"

"That's why I'm confused. Gene came to the hospital and he gave me a teddy bear as a Mother's Day gift. He asked me to pay the rent before I move back."

"So, he gave you a teddy bear and now he wants you to give him hundreds of pounds?"

"I know, but I think he's trying to make things better."

"He has had a month to sort out his finances and prove to you that he is a responsible adult, but he hasn't done it."

"He can't with the job he has. The rent is too dear."

"Well, he could have moved to a smaller house and got it ready for you to come home. Or he could have got a second job to show you he's taking responsibility for himself. Has he tried to pay for anything?"

I racked my brain for a suitable answer to that question, but all I could come up with was the teddy bear and the day we'd gone for burgers. Neither of those were practical items, even if they were given with goodwill. I didn't like her question; it was prodding at a wound I wanted to leave well alone.

"I don't know if I should pay it. The rent is due tomorrow. If Gene doesn't pay it, he'll get evicted."

"And whose responsibility is that?"

"It's my home too."

"But he isn't paying half – he isn't even contributing, is he?"

I shook my head and looked at the carpet tiles. I'd become familiar with their textured shapes, spending much of the time I talked about Gene with my eyes to the floor.

"Well, what if you wait a while and see if he offers to pay? You could delay paying the rent for a few days and see what happens. You'd be doing him a favour in the long run."

I failed to see how I could be doing Gene a favour; what Anne was suggesting ran against all my morals. Gene was my partner; I was responsible for his wellbeing and my money was his; it had been since day one. Not paying the rent would be an act of utter selfishness. How would I ever admit it to Gene? He'd be livid once he knew I'd given him false hope.

"What should I tell Gene?"

"You don't have to tell him anything. You don't have to talk to him if you don't want to."

That phrase made me realise she didn't understand me after all. Not speaking to Gene on the phone for an hour was the emotional equivalent to holding my breath for two minutes. Whether I spoke to Gene or not wasn't a choice. It was something I was programmed to do. I hadn't gone more than a few hours without talking to him since the day he'd faked his suicide in New York, and that day had nearly killed me. I'd have to phone Gene as soon as I returned to my room and break the news to him gently. If I told him I couldn't afford to pay the rent until a couple of days later, hopefully he'd understand. Gene knew what it was like not being able to make ends meet, so, I thought he couldn't castigate me for having the same struggles. He knew I was living in a shelter, so he must have known that I wasn't living in luxury.

"Why is he asking you for money anyway?" asked Anne. "Doesn't he know you're in a refuge? It's not like you're staying in a five-star hotel."

Could she read my thoughts? Was Gene right? Was everyone watching me, spying on me, dissecting me? I was too transparent; I needed to retreat to my room and put a barrier up between myself and the staff. Only Gene was allowed to rent a space in my head; I couldn't afford to let anyone else inside it, or we'd never get what we wanted.

I excused myself and returned to the bedroom. Tiredness was the only excuse I could come up with. I hoped she wouldn't overhear me talking to Gene on the phone until her shift ended at ten. She'd think I was lying. Gene was right: I was a master of manipulation. My mind was hazy with so many unfinished thoughts. I began to have one of my own, but each time it was interrupted by Gene's voice. His sayings were so often repeated they became like incantations in my head. Gene was my soulmate; we were connected on the deepest level. No one could understand the level of closeness we had, and try as they might, no one could sever our bond, least of all me.

Chapter Fourteen

Gene wasn't happy when I told him I was delaying paying the rent. He accused me of having money stashed away. He knew I was careful with money and that I'd never let my bank balance drain away to nothing. I could hear his tone becoming shaded with suspicion, like he thought I'd gone back to the other side: the one where everyone was his opponent.

"So, you're going to let me live on the fucking street?"

"No, Gene, that's not how it works."

"Well, that's what you're doing right – getting me evicted? That's what you want."

"No – I want to come home."

"Aoife, if you wanted to come home, you'd have come fucking home. You've been gone for over a fucking month. All you do is lie to me – telling me we're still together. You ain't got no intention of coming back."

"That's not true. I just need to know things have changed before I do."

"You ain't going to know if things have changed unless you come back."

"That's what scares me."

"Stop being such a fucking coward. You let fear make all your decisions for you."

"Well, are you going to treat me differently if I come home?"

"What the fuck are you talking about? I treat you good."

"Yeah, but will you all the time? I'm scared you'll punish me forever for leaving."

"Well – you shouldn't have fucking left."

"So, you will punish me forever?"

"I didn't fucking say that."

"You think it's all my fault."

"It is your fault – I told you to set up marriage counselling months ago and you refused."

"Marriage counselling doesn't work with abuse."

"You're the one who's fucking abusive – hitting me, telling me you hate me. What the fuck are you talking about? I could have Hope taken off you, you know. One fucking phone call – that's all I got to make. I have all the recordings Aoife, all the pictures. I can prove that you're crazy."

"I'm not crazy," I began to cry.

I'd never felt less convinced of that statement than I was the moment I said it.

"Yeah – you're not crazy. You let your head fuck everything up – you believe your own delusions and that's why you left."

"I wasn't imagining it."

I desperately clung to that point, but it was slipping from my grip and I was struggling to believe it myself. I had no hope of convincing Gene of an argument I couldn't substantiate. He was right, and I was wrong. Submitting to his will was the only way I'd ever be right, and I was tiring enough to lose that war.

"You listen too much to other people, man. You let your family convince you that leaving was the right thing to do. When we get back together, I ain't talking to them fucking people again."

My gut twisted. For a moment, I knew that it wasn't safe to go home and that I wouldn't be allowed to contact my family if I did. Could I sacrifice any connection with my family for the sake of Gene and me? It was hard to know while it remained something theoretical. Living in the refuge was anything but desirable, but I had choices there: the choice to stay where I was, the choice to go back, the choice to pay bills, the choice to withhold payment, the choice to have family and friends. Once I returned to 2 Belmont Place, my choices would be whittled down to nothing. I knew that, but the lure of home was still calling me.

"I'm sorry. I don't mean to."

"You don't mean to – but you still fucking do it. You got to stop letting people get inside your fucking head."

I knew I was guilty of that; the more I let others influence my thoughts, the less of a hold on them Gene would have. He didn't like his position as thought-director to be taken up by anyone else. He knew nothing about the staff in the refuge; anything he surmised came only from his own hypotheses. Gene wasn't unfamiliar with the concept of women's shelters. I hadn't known a thing about them until I'd gained entry to one. Gene didn't think they were a big deal. He thought most of the women that stayed in them were using their feminine guiles to convince professionals that they were at risk, when all they were at risk of was hypochondria and manipulation. Men didn't typically hit women without good reason; that's what Gene told me. He admitted to hitting his exes, but he'd never done it unprompted. He tended to end up with tempestuous types who usually threw the first punch. What he did was only in self-defence. Gene would never intentionally hurt someone. Overall, he was a good guy.

"Do you think you're a good person?" I asked him once.

"What kind of a fucking question is that?"

"I was just curious. Do you think everyone thinks they're a bad person?"

"I don't think I'm a bad person, don't think I'm a good one – I ain't the worst there is. Everybody has good and bad in them – nobody is all good or all bad."

He was right: life wasn't simple enough to assign blame to one person and innocence to another. We were all equally guilty and when things went wrong in our relationships, we were all culpable. And it was that way of thinking that almost brought about my demise.

Chapter Fifteen

"Meet me in town tomorrow, babe."

"Ok, are you going to be angry?"

"I want to see my daughter."

"Promise you won't be angry?"

"I ain't going to be fucking angry, I ain't never angry – you're just imagining shit. I just want to see my fucking daughter. I've barely seen her in two months thanks to you."

"I'm sorry – I just get scared in case something bad happens when we meet up."

"Stop being fucking retarded – nothing bad is going to happen. We're going for a fucking cup of coffee and I'm going to visit with my daughter."

"Ok, I'll meet you."

"Ok – meet me tomorrow at my bus stop. Uh – at 12pm."

"Ok –

I'd have to explain to the workers where I was going, and I knew they wouldn't be happy. It had been almost a month since the rent was owed, and I still hadn't paid it. Gene was salty, and I knew meeting up with him brought a whole new range of risks it hadn't before. What if he robbed me? What if he took Hope away as revenge? What if he kidnapped me? Those were all irrational fears to have, but they still continuously popped up as possibilities in my brain.

I tucked Hope into bed and sat, almost enjoying the tranquillity in the room. For a house filled with so many different characters, the peace that was to be found there was surprising. Of course, there were disagreements: disputes over cleaning and the use of the shared spaces, personality clashes, habits that weren't conducive to harmonious living, but they were nothing compared to the issues at home. I still felt a pang every time I thought of that building that held my whole material world. Every book I'd collected over the years was stored in the bookcases in the library, my artwork from my university years filed away, some of my favourite dresses still hung in the wardrobe, as far as I knew. I'd expected Gene to do something extreme with my belongings as soon as he'd arrived back at the empty house. You'd be surprised in an emergency the possessions you forget. I'd left behind too many items to enumerate. Now and again, something would pop into my head; a picture of where I'd seen it last, but mostly, I didn't miss it as much as I should have. There was something freeing about living with very little. I'd grown accustomed to my new way of life. I could fit most of it into a single suitcase and come and go as I pleased. The house and its contents had become almost fictional in my mind: a part of the familial fantasy I cherished. I was in denial, and I didn't know it. The only break I had from my imaginings were when I went downstairs for a bit of light conversation with the other members of the house. That was one thing I'd come to enjoy: the laughter that rang out in the corridors like a series of cheerful chimes. Dire circumstances made for good humour and I went in search of some. I walked into the communal area and sat on the sofa next to Sarah, Lana and Louise. They were watching an amateur cookery programme and passing comment on every lopsided cake that made its way out of the oven.

"Fuck, look at that, I could do better myself."

"Well, get into the kitchen and get to it. We're waiting," smirked Louise.

Lana nodded at me and pointed to Sarah. "See, she's all talk."

"What are you on about? I've never seen you do more than stick chicken nuggets in the oven."

"Don't knock chicken nuggets, they're better than what they're serving up."

"You're so professional, Lana."

"I know, you're all lucky to have me," she laughed.

"I'm going for a cigarette," said Louise, pulling her jumper back on. She walked away laughing, her slippers shuffling on the floor.

"Here, there's a letter waiting for you upstairs," Lana turned to face me.

"Shit, I hope it's not an offer."

"Most of the women in here are counting down until their offer comes through and you're sitting hoping it never does – what are you like?!"

"I can't help it – I don't want my own house."

"It'd be lovely - you could decorate it exactly as you like. You could get whatever furniture you want, paint it the colours you like – you wouldn't have anyone telling you what to do."

My stomach sank at the thought of it. Freedom of self-expression no longer struck me as something covetable; being told what to do and how to do it was what I'd grown used to. Too much autonomy made me feel like small fry that had fallen away from its shoal. The world was too vast a place to survive alone, and I didn't trust myself enough to attempt it.

"Well, I better get my bum upstairs and make a few phone calls."

"Aye, what do you think this is? A free for all? Get back to work," laughed Sarah, draining her tea cup and setting it on the corner table. Lana cackled and jumped up from the sofa, walking out the fire door. The slam of it sounded for several seconds and intensified the silence left behind.

"How are you, honey?" asked Sarah.

"I'm ok. Want some hot chocolate?"

"I'd love some," she smiled.

I made us hot chocolates topped with marshmallows and joined her in the TV cove.

"What were you doing today?" I asked.

"Just lazing about, I'm skint – nothing to do. Did you see they put up a sign about that Easter dinner?"

"No, what's that?"

"They found a turkey in the freezer, suggested we all cook together and have a house dinner."

"Sounds good. This week?"

"Sunday."

I hoped Gene wouldn't ask me to meet up on Sunday; that would be another thing to fight about.

"I'm thinking about meeting Gene tomorrow."

"When did you last see him?"

"A month ago."

"Where are you meeting him?"

"In town."

"Belfast?"

"Yeah."

"Good, don't let him come here. Does he know where you're staying?"

"No."

"That's good, I wouldn't tell him."

I got the sense that I shouldn't either.

"Just be careful if you're meeting up with him – I worry about you."
"Why?"
"He's dangerous. I don't trust him. I saw a picture of him on your Facebook."
"Yeah?"
"I'm sorry to say this, but he has evil eyes. You know when people say the eyes are the window to the soul? Well, his are like something demonic."
"I never noticed."
"That picture of the two of you together – you remind me of a scared bird trapped in a cage."
I shook my head; I couldn't see what she meant. I'd seen that picture thousands of times. It was the one we had taken before I'd left Flint the first time. All I saw when I looked at it was my own sadness about my upcoming separation from Gene. The fear she saw in my eyes must have been due to that.
"Promise me something."
"Yeah?"
"Don't follow him into any entries."
"Why?"
"I just have a bad feeling – I don't know what he's capable of."
"Do you really think he's dangerous?"
"Yes. He could have killed you. If you'd gone back there, I believe I'd be at your funeral now."
That notion sounded like an implausible storyline from a badly plotted play. Gene wasn't a criminal; he was just Gene.
"Ok, I won't. You don't need to worry. I don't feel like I should even be here."
"Why?"
"I always feel like I don't deserve to be here – like everyone thinks it wasn't abuse. Maybe I was as responsible for our problems as he was."
Sarah shook her head resolutely.
"If anyone needs to be here, it's you. There are some people who live here, and you would wonder if they were abused or not, but you aren't one of those people."
I couldn't understand what she was talking about; I was just someone who overplayed the bad situations in their life. I couldn't help doing it; it was symptomatic of my illness.
"Take the personal alarm the refuge gave you in your bag and if

anything kicks off – just pull it and run."

"Ok."

I knew I was still going to go, but I'd vaguely take Sarah's concerns into consideration. She hadn't met Gene. She didn't know him like I did; she had only heard the bad stories, she hadn't seen his soft side. It was that side of him I was looking forward to seeing the following day; that was why I went to meet him.

I stood at the bus stop with sick fear building inside me. Every bus that pulled in to the bus bays made me nauseous. I felt the urge to run while I still could, but I was just being melodramatic. Gene was looking forward to seeing us and I was looking forward to seeing him too. The feelings I had for Gene were multi-layered and the layer of terror strengthened the excitement I felt about seeing him. When strong positive and negative emotions blend together, they make an intoxicating mixture. I couldn't help myself; sipping from that mixture was something I needed for my survival. When I tried to skip a sip, the withdrawal I experienced was so powerful I'd sacrifice anything for a few words from Gene: my family, my freedom, my life.

Gene was the last to get off the bus. Strangely, although Gene detested social graces, he always let everyone off the bus before him. Maybe that was more to do with feeling harassed by the crowd than it was to do with looking out for humankind.

Gene jumped off the bus in his usual way: a quick skip without appearing to lift his feet as he did it. He spotted me and hypnotised me with his eyes as he took slow strides towards me. I was under the warm beam of Gene's attention once more. The joy it brought me felt enhanced after a month of its absence.

"Hey, baby," he said, pulling me towards him to kiss me on the lips. "I brought some stuff for you."

He handed me a bag filled with some the jewellery I had left behind and my favourite white boots. I peeked inside and smelled the heavy perfume of cigarette smoke issuing from the bag. I knew Gene had been smoking in the house. I thought about asking him what else he did in the house, but that was his business, not mine. It had ceased to be my business when I'd made the decision to leave. I thought about what state the house must be in without the constant cleaning service I had provided. I imagined if our roles had been reversed; if Gene had walked out on me with Hope and how I'd have felt returning to not so much as a note of explanation. I was a terrible wife. How could I betray my own husband to such a degree? If Gene had done the same to me, I never would have survived it. I'd have to make it up to him somehow. I knew it would take a lifetime for him to forgive me for it, but I was prepared to work for that long to make it right.

"Thanks, you didn't have to do that," I smiled.

"I didn't want you not to have them. I know they're important to you, baby."

"I love you."

"I love you too, baby."

"Where are we going?"

"Wherever you want? A coffee house? Somewhere not too busy."

I followed Gene with the pram. He always knew exactly where he was going, even if he led you to believe he didn't.

"Hey, babe, let's call into B&M, have a look while we're here."

"Ok."

I knew it was a bad idea, but I'd do anything to minimise the number of potential public blow-ups. I saw some sweets I knew Gene loved. I wanted to treat him; he'd had such a rough time, so I paid for them and handed him the bag.

"What's this?"

"I just saw those sweets you like."

"Oh, thanks babe."

I hoped it showed him I thought about the little things and that he was the main feature in my world; all other aspects of life merely side acts to him.

"Want to call into the pound store, have a look around?"

"Yeah, I wanted to look at the jewellery there. Someone I know had a nice ring from there and told me their jewellery is really good."

"Alright babe. I'll come with you."

We walked through the sliding doors and Gene reached straight for a bottle of juice in the door-side fridge.

"Here, get me this."

His order bothered me, especially since I had just got him a gift.

"Gene, you could ask first."

I knew as soon as I said it, I'd created a scene, but it was too late to take it back. If looks could kill, Gene's face would have been responsible for bloody slaughter.

"I'm waiting outside. Hurry the fuck up."

He spun around and stormed out of the shop with half the customers present watching him, a mixture of intrigue and fright on their faces. I was determined to not give in; I didn't believe I'd done anything wrong. Why did Gene think it was ok to demand money from me without so much as a please or thank you? Why did he always expect to get something to show for our meet-ups, no matter how small? I knew I'd over-reacted to him asking me for a drink, but his manner was what had set me off most of all. He had no respect for me, and in that moment, I could see it. If I had handed Gene my purse, I felt like he would have had the relationship he wanted; one much improved on the version that existed. I was the keeper of coins, and he just had to work me in order to release them.

I stood at the jewellery shelves and couldn't focus enough to look. I kept looking back over my shoulder at Gene. He was waiting outside the shop with his back facing me. I knew what his face looked like without him having to turn around. He was irate, and I could either face up to it now or delay it for another few moments. Either way, I knew that the reaction was coming; not just his – mine.

I unthinkingly grabbed a couple of items. I neither liked nor disliked them; I just needed an excuse for taking up Gene's valuable time while I was in the shop. I knew he would resent me for treating myself when I hadn't bought his drink, but if I emerged without an item, he'd quiz me for hours on what had taken me so long, and that was worse.

I stepped away from the till, my gaze lingering on the kind smile of the cashier. I wanted them to hold my hand and protect me from whatever I was about to experience. Gene was right: I was a coward.

"Gene," I said, approaching him with caution.

Gene wouldn't look me in the face or answer me.

"Daddy missed you," he cooed at Hope. There was an undertone of sarcasm in his voice, or maybe I was just imagining things again.

"Daddy's going to get you out."

My heart seized, like it had forgotten how to beat.

"You're getting her out of the pram?"

Gene ignored me and unstrapped Hope, carrying her away.

"Wait for me, Gene," I shouted after him.

He didn't turn around or slow down. I ran along behind him with the pram, trying to keep up. What was he going to do? I waited for him to bolt with our baby. I had to keep up, no matter who was looking. Gene took large, violent strides. He was talking animatedly to Hope, but not in a pleasant way. She mightn't have picked up on that, but I did.

"Daddy just wants to hold you because Mama won't let him. Daddy never gets to see you because Mama is crazy. When you grow up, you'll understand everything. Daddy will make sure of that."

I jogged along behind Gene for block after block. I had no idea where he was going or if or when he would stop. I chased him down the street in front of hundreds of strangers, like a clingy girlfriend who couldn't take a hint. He turned around to give me a scathing look and then continued walking, upping the pace.

"Gene," I called.

I could barely hear my own voice and wondered if anyone else could. If Gene did, he didn't acknowledge it in the slightest.

"Don't worry, Daddy's going to look after you."

"Gene, where are you taking her to?"

Nothing.

I started crying. I felt gagged. No matter how loudly I cried, Gene wouldn't respond. He didn't even raise an eyebrow or display the smallest emotion when I called him. I raced up to him, crying uncontrollably and grabbing his arm.

"Gene."

"Stop fucking grabbing me. What the fuck do you want?"

"I just want my baby back."

"She ain't just yours."

"Please - I just want to hold her."

Hope looked unsettled; like she knew something was going on, but she didn't have enough years to enable her to process what it was.

"Please, just let me hold her."

"You can't hold her, you silly asshole. Look at how you're acting."

"Can we just go in here," I said, pointing to the bar we were passing. It was quiet in the afternoons and sold coffee: two factors that increased my chances of placating Gene.

"Fine, but you're getting it."

Gene claimed a table and sat down with Hope, still holding her out of my reach.

"Get me a coffee. Don't forget the ice."

I wanted to shout at Gene for dishing out orders again, but I couldn't risk pissing him off more than I already had. I'd keep quiet, no matter what it cost me, no matter what behaviour it meant I had to accept. I had to, to get my daughter back.

I hoped once I carried Gene's coffee to him, he'd love me again and that would be the end of it. I couldn't even recall what had started the argument. My emotions were too far out of range for me to make sense of them or think rationally. I just knew that I was going crazy again. Why did my mental health always seem to deteriorate around Gene? He was the only person who could save me from my own mind, and yet, I spent more time toiling with it when we were together than when I was alone.

I set Gene's coffee down on the table and he took it without saying thanks.

"Did you put ice in this?"

I nodded.

"It's still hot as shit."

I started crying again; so many tears had built up inside me they had to go somewhere, and unfortunately, that somewhere was visible to Gene and everyone around us.

"Stop acting crazy, everyone is looking at us."

"I don't know why you do this."

"I don't do shit. This is all on you – all I did was ask you for a fucking drink, and you couldn't even get me one without being an asshole about it."

"I already got you sweets. It was the way you said it – it sounded demanding."

"You're wrong. I just asked you for a drink – but you always got to be like this about money, man."

"I'm not – when do you ever give me anything? You're always the one asking."

My emotions were so amplified, I couldn't control what I was saying. I couldn't even remember what I'd said the second it came out of my mouth. That was the most dangerous position to be in with Gene; then he could rehash the argument later and I wouldn't remember any of the details to defend my corner.

"I ain't like you about money – all you care about is fucking money. If I had it, I'd give it to you – I wouldn't say nothing."

"You never have it."

"Well, if I did, I wouldn't use it like you do."

"I don't use it, you just drain me of everything I have."

"I'm your fucking husband."

"You don't help me with anything."

"Who are you to talk to me like that? You think you're so smart. You think you're so important, all because you went to fucking university?"

"I don't know what you're talking about."

I tried to stifle my sobs, but they were audible to everyone in the room.

"You think you're so much smarter than me, all because you went to college. But you don't know shit. You ain't nobody. You're NOBODY. You ain't been through shit."

The last phrase broke me. I sat down and howled into my hands on the chair. I couldn't concern myself with how many people were watching and what they thought of me. All I wanted was to be dead. The person I loved, the only person whose opinion truly mattered, thought I was worth nothing, so I was.

Before I left, I gave Gene one hundred pounds. He didn't have anything to eat and he had to top up his phone or we wouldn't be able to talk.

Chapter Sixteen

When I got back to the refuge, I held my hand out for the brown envelope. I wasn't sure if I was going to take my offer, but I'd have a look out of curiosity anyway. I'd been offered a house in Belfast, still in East Belfast, but far enough away from our old life that it would feel like a fresh start. Even if I didn't intend to move there, it was something to think about when refuge life was getting too much for me. If I loved it, maybe Gene and I could move there instead. The Housing Executive would cover almost all our rent, so it would be a huge weight off us. I wondered if that counted as increasing the burden on the state, but I couldn't afford to worry about the particulars of visa rules anymore. Getting back together was a feat on its own.

I took my dad along with me for a second opinion. I was unable to make decisions alone anyway. If someone didn't direct me, I'd have stood there tussling with my decision until the house was offered to the next person on the list. I had no sense of what the right or wrong thing to do was anymore, so much had my brain been tinkered with. We pulled up in the street. It was a side street next to a main road, the paint chipped, murals on the gable walls. Once a charming little house, it had become grotty with too little upkeep. My dad and I stepped inside the gate and stood on the doorstep. The day was as grey as granite and didn't exactly inspire faith in me. An employee arrived late and let us into the bleak hallway. It hadn't been painted and the walls were a patchwork of paint and wallpaper. The place was so cold it felt like it had never been heated and there was a heady damp smell in the entrance.

It was the kind of place where you could picture yourself dying of hypothermia, or by the hand of an armed intruder. It would take a hell of a lot of work to make it look half like home. But was any place of my own preferable to sharing a house with a dozen strangers? It was hard to say, but I had survived in similar dwellings in Flint. Ok, things were different now I had a baby, but life would have been no different for us had I moved to America instead. There was a small living room and kitchen, a downstairs bathroom and two bedrooms upstairs. A yard at the back was dominated by bins and abandoned tools. I had some savings left, but not enough to do a complete overhaul of the place. Maybe I could squat in it while I fixed it up and I could sort Hope's room out first. It didn't sound like a pleasant way to spend the last months of my pregnancy, but I wasn't drowning in options.

I followed my dad upstairs to the bedrooms. He looked so unimpressed I knew there was little chance I'd talk him round. He had no knowledge of my intention to move Gene in either. If he did, he likely would have refused to view the place with me in the first place. In the upstairs of the house there were wires hanging loose and a roof-space that was an uncovered, gaping hole. Enough was enough for my dad.

"You'd think they would have fixed this place up before showing it to you. You can't live here with kids."

"Maybe I could work on it?"

"It would cost more to make it liveable than it would to just rent somewhere."

I knew he was right, and I had to turn the place down. It was only number one of three anyway. I had two housing offers remaining. I decided I'd better like one of them, or I'd be off the list and back to square one.

Chapter Seventeen

The next time I saw Gene, he met me in the same spot: right beside his bus stop. He was waiting for me when I got there, his arms hanging at his sides, music in his ears.

"Hey, baby," he said, pulling one earphone out. He finished the song and then turned the music player on his phone off. Gene had all my music; he had moved it all to his external hard drive to free up memory on my computer. I hadn't realised until after I'd left that I'd lost all the albums I loved.

"Gene, I forgot my music."

"What do you mean?"

"It's on your external."

"Ok, tell you what – next time, I'll bring it, you can bring your computer and I'll transfer it all to you."

I hoped we would continue getting along until then, or I knew I'd never get it back. Music was such an enormous part of my identity, without it I almost felt as hollow as I did without Gene. I barely listened to my own music anymore; I only listened to music that reminded me of Gene. I played it and it soothed my sores.

Gene started to walk into an entryway and I followed him.

"Where are you going?"

Gene looked at me with the utmost seriousness. "I was going to knock you over the head and take Hope."

He paused for a moment and then did a cruel cackle.

"I'm just fucking with you, you silly asshole. Don't look at me like that."

Sarah's words replayed in my head: "don't follow him into any dark entries."

Her warning suddenly seemed a little less absurd. Maybe I took a few too many risks because Gene was my husband, or maybe I was just humourless. I could never take a joke: Gene's jokes.

"Let's get a fucking cup of coffee so I can hold my daughter," said Gene.

"Ok."

I followed Gene into a coffee shop and went to queue at the counter while he installed himself and Hope at a table.

"Hey, babe," he called, "get Hope something to munch on."

"Ok. Do you want anything to eat?"

"No, I don't want nothing."

I scowled as I turned away from him. I had no forum in which I could express my disgruntlement. "Please" would have cost little, but it was too great a favour to expect from Gene. When I thought about it, everyone else I spoke to used "please" and "thank you" – all but Gene. He made out it was an outdated social practice, but maybe he just couldn't be bothered saying it. He sometimes showed an attitude of entitlement, like he was exempt from utilising all social rules that applied to everyone else. Maybe he was just a confident guy who knew his own mind and wasn't easily swayed; certainly not as easily swayed as I was.

I sat down at the table with our coffees, Gene's ice and Hope's snack. I set the cup in front of Gene and he didn't say anything. He just lazily rolled his eyes upwards to meet mine, looking irritated, or what I perceived as irritated. I lost it.

"Why can you never say please and thanks? Other people always say it to me."

"Why do you always got to worry about what other people are doing? You don't know your own mind. You can't make no decisions for yourself – you always got to do what other people tell you to. Stop being so weak-minded."

"I don't mean to be. It just upsets me when you don't say it – I feel like you just expect it."

"You're wrong – you always got to make me look like a fucking dick, don't you? Put crazy away."

"I'm not trying to act crazily. I hate the way you order me around and don't say thanks."

"I don't do that. You're imagining shit again."

Was I? Had I imagined a sense of expectation emanating from Gene where there wasn't one? Had he given me a loving look instead of one of dull boredom when I'd set his cup in front of him? Did Gene just have a neutral facial expression and I dreamed up negative emotion where there was none? I couldn't tell the difference between my reality and Gene's. But Gene's must have been more reliable than mine. He was so confident about every pronouncement he made. I struggled to make basic decisions for myself, changing my mind just as I was about to make it up.

"Hand me my daughter."

"Ok."

Hope was still strapped into the buggy; Gene hadn't bothered to get her out.

"Did you get a highchair?"

"No, babe, this fucking hand is killing me."

Gene clenched and unclenched it multiple times, grimacing as he did it. I looked out the window at the city streets. They looked grey and bleak; all colour had left them, like a faded photograph. I wasn't part of the real world again; I was in my alternate universe with Gene, and no one else could reach me, or rescue me.

"Babe, when we leave here, I need you to go into the store for me. I'll wait with Hope."

"What for?"

"I need you to get me Co-codamol."

"Are you still taking it all the time?"

Gene gave me a look that cut me off.

"I'm in fucking agony and you can't even go to the fucking store for me?"

"Ok, I'll go."

I felt guilty for hesitating over such a small favour, but I was still reluctant to leave Hope alone with Gene. If she was out of my line of view, he could take her away and I wouldn't even know she was gone until I'd left the shop. I wanted to raise that point with him, but I knew that doing so would make an abduction more likely, not less. Not pissing Gene off was my aim of the day, and I'd do anything to keep him calm.

"I'll go. Sorry, I was just worried about you."

"You don't got to worry about me – I've taken much stronger stuff than Codeine, babe. It's the only thing that helps this hand."

"I know that."

Gene's gaze warmed up towards me. He held Hope securely on his knee and I knew that if I tried to reach for her, he'd pull her away. I wasn't getting her out of his grasp until the box of tablets was in his hand: one prize in exchange for another.

I shut up and took a sip of my coffee.

"You about done, babe?" Gene stared at my half-filled cup impatiently.

"Hope is still eating."

"Why did you get her a croissant, man? That shit takes forever to eat."

We sat in a silence that was anything but placid. Gene's knee jiggled at two hundred beats per minute. I was on edge and desperate for Hope to finish up. I took a bite of her croissant and picked up the pastry from her tray, encouraging her to open her mouth for it.

"She ain't going to eat all that, babe, you're wasting your time. You're just playing Mama, ain't you?" he said affectionately.

I wondered if there was a touch of transference in his comment. Was he the one doing that?

"Let's go, babe."

"Ok."

I wiped Hope's highchair with a baby wipe, picking the larger crumbs up off the floor.

"You don't fucking work here, babe."

"I know but we've left a huge mess."

"That's what them people are getting paid to do."

For someone who hadn't grown up in opulence, Gene's lack of empathy for others' labours astonished me at times. Gene strapped Hope into the pram and I slung the nappy bag onto the back. I gathered our dishes onto the tray on the table.

I held the door open for Gene while he pushed the pram out. He was walking with more haste than usual, his limp having apparently abated. Maybe knowing he was en-route to painkillers worked like placebo.

"Alright, babe," said Gene, slowing to a stop at the front of the pharmacy.

He kept the pram and I worriedly moved my eyes back and forth between his face and Hope's. Gene could still always read what I was thinking.

"Would you stop? I ain't taking Hope. I just need you to get my meds."

How do I know that for sure?"

"You got to trust me. Where would I take her to? Babe – if I was going to take Hope from you, I would have done it already. Just go to the store."

"Ok," I said, backing away, unable to peel my eyes from Gene's location.

The shop he'd chosen was a three-storey chain, and I knew I'd have to go to level two to get to the drugs counter. Gene would have ample time to make a run for it. The only point that reassured me was that I suspected Gene was too selfish to take care of our baby alone. Gene shirked any responsibility that fell upon him, never mind choosing to seek out more. He wouldn't be able to work if he had Hope, and if he didn't work, he couldn't afford to live.

I walked at as nonchalant a pace as I could muster until I was behind the doors. Once I could be certain Gene couldn't see me, I started running. Other customers regarded me warily, but I couldn't afford to waste time caring about that. I had to get the tablets and get back to my daughter as soon as possible, or I might never see her again.

I took the escalator, moving at quadruple the speed it was. I could see a mile-long tailback at the tills. Everyone and their granny were stocking up on their medical supplies. I joined the end of the queue, shifting around, all my nervous energy rising to the surface. Each customer seemed to take more time than was required, just to thwart me. I felt like screaming all over the shop that I needed to jump the queue because there was an emergency, but it sounded too pathetic when I tried to arrange my sentiments into a sentence. Fifteen minutes and fifteen accompanying mental breakdowns later, I arrived at the top of the queue.

"Next!"

"Please could I get some Co-codamol?"

"Is it for yourself or someone else?"

"My husband."

"Why are you getting it?"

"He's waiting with our daughter."

"What's he taking it for?"

"Aches in his hand, shoulder and foot."

"Has he tried Paracetamol?"

"Yes."

I couldn't tell if she was being thorough or just contrary.

"Has he taken Co-codamol before?"

"I don't think so."

"He can only take these for 2-3 days and then he has to discontinue usage."

"Ok," I grabbed the box, handed over a few pound coins and made a mad dash for the door.

I prayed Gene was still standing where I left him.

As I stepped back out into the natural light, I had a moment of panic; Gene wasn't there, just like I knew he wouldn't be. I scanned the crowd for them; there were so many people and prams, it was hard to differentiate one family from another. I felt sick and stuck to the spot. I didn't know which direction to walk in; if I chose the wrong one, I'd be walking further from Gene with every step I took. That was a terrifying thought, so I stayed glued to the spot.

A man at an ATM next to the shop dreamily took his card, cash, receipt and finally stepped aside. Gene was behind him. My whole body seemed to sigh when I saw him. He was still standing, exactly as I'd left him, one hand on the handle of the pram, the other coaxing a cigarette from its pack.

"I got it," I said, holding the tablets up for Gene to see. His eyes brightened, his eyebrows raised, and he nodded, extending a hand for the box. He put it in his inner pocket, like it was more precious than the passport that had got him there.

"Let's swing by the store. I'll get a drink to take these with."

I nodded and took the pram back, thankful for once to be the one pushing again.

Chapter Eighteen

"Has he stopped taking the tablets?" asked Brenda, sitting cross-legged on the sofa.

"Yes," I said, hoping it sounded believable.

I thought about the last few times I'd met up with Gene and the tour of the pharmacies we'd done. We'd spent more time doing that than we'd ever spent in a playground together. It wasn't Gene's fault – people just didn't understand the severity of his joint pain. If I stayed optimistic, there was more chance he'd stop taking them anyway. He was adamant that he wasn't addicted, and if Gene was sure of something, so were you. He believed his stories with more conviction than any born again Christian.

"How do you know he stopped taking them?" Brenda asked.

"He hasn't taken them when I've been with him."

"He could still be taking them at home."

I was growing angry. I hated anyone accusing Gene of anything, especially if it was something he vehemently denied. I'd lie if I had to, just to protect his name. My morals had changed. I used to leak honesty all over myself and everyone else, but I needed a new strategy. Life was a more hazardous game than I'd ever imagined.

"I want to go home soon, before Gene gets kicked out of the house."

"Isn't he getting kicked out anyway? He hasn't paid the rent, has he?"

"No," I said, looking at the blank TV screen that seemed to stare me down.

I'd never seen it lit up. I wondered what its purpose was; Gene would never allow a TV to be wasted like that. My mind wandered away to my dream world of what Gene and I could become. I pictured us sitting in our beautifully furnished house, Gene drinking his coffee and watching TV while he got ready for work. There was no longer any doubt in my mind about Gene's capability to hold down the job. In my vision, he'd proved himself to be the capable worker he'd advertised himself as when we first spoke. He climbed into his work van, with his name printed on the side. He had the business of his dreams and everything had fallen into place, right down to family park days, an appreciation of my cooking and no swearing in front of Hope. I felt a warm glow spreading throughout all my limbs. The numbness I'd been feeling for so long lessened only when I had those fantasies. And they were better than most daydreamers' fantasies, because they felt achievable. All we had to do was move back under the one roof and we'd have everything we wanted, that no one believed we could have. It didn't matter what others thought. I had enough faith in the power of us to move us past any barricade.

Brenda snapped me out of my daydream.

"What makes you think anything would be any different?"

"I just hope that it will be."

"Is hope enough? Can you put yourself and your children's lives at risk because of what you hope will change?"

I didn't answer. I thought about the baby growing inside me and all I could focus on was time ticking down to the birth. I couldn't live in a refuge with a newborn, I couldn't be separated with a newborn; we would have to reconcile before then, or I didn't want to be alive. Those were the only two solutions to our disastrous circumstances: reconciliation or suicide.

I went to a black place in my mind that was so dark all I could see was my own body dropping to the ground in fifty different ways. I thought about how easy it would be: I could walk into oncoming traffic and make it look like an accident, I could jump in front of a train at the station, I could sneak out at night and drown myself in the sea. There were so many available answers to my problems that were no distance away at all. But was I ready to give up on my love for Gene? If I stayed alive, we had the option to get back together, if I didn't, we never would. Not unless our souls reunited again in some other realm, once this hellish one had passed away.

I still couldn't grasp how I had arrived in this place, not just the physical location, but so far from the dream life we had finally had the chance to have. We had fought so hard for it, it had taken every emotional ounce of me to do it. I could never give up on it. I would never let anyone convince me to do so.

"I can see changes in him. I think he is trying to make things better between us."

"Well, why hasn't he paid his rent? He could have moved out of that house and found somewhere affordable if he wanted you to come home."

"I don't know."

"Or he could have got a second job to allow him to afford the rent." The worker just sounded unreasonable to me; she was placing so many expectations on Gene that I doubted anyone could ever fulfil, no matter how ambitious they were.

"I don't know. Once we sort things out with the house, I'm going to move back."

"Or you could consider taking the house you're offered. You could fix it up however you like and then it's up to you whether Gene moves in. At least then it would be in your name and then if things hadn't changed you could have him removed?"

I knew it made no difference whether the house was in my name or not; once Gene and I moved in together again, he wouldn't be going anywhere again, whether I insisted upon on it or not. He could do anything to me and I would never report him; I would choose death first.

Chapter Nineteen

"I need to borrow some money, baby."

"How much?"

I was in town with Gene and he had pulled me aside, conveniently right next to a cash machine.

"Two hundred."

"Two hundred?" I said, incredulous.

"Well, if you can afford it, baby. I wouldn't want to leave you and Hope with nothing."

"What's it for?"

"Food, buses, my phone."

"Ok."

I resentfully punched my pin number into the keypad, withdrawing the cash. Gene took it from me before I'd had time to hesitate about it. He knew how indecisive I was. Just because I said yes one minute, it didn't mean that I wouldn't say no the next.

I ran through the bills I had to pay in my head: I had to pay my electricity bill in the refuge, keep money for laundry, keep money aside for groceries, clothes for Hope and save up an emergency deposit and first month's rent in case Gene and I had to move. I thought I had enough to cover everything, if I was careful. We were still waiting on Gene's eviction notice arriving in the post, and we knew it could come any day now. We had to be prepared for the worst. If that happened, I had to find somewhere else for us to live before Gene was removed by the police. I hoped on top of everything else, they wouldn't fine us for the state we'd left the place in; hopefully Gene had used his extra free time to fix it up while I'd been gone. In the end of the day, how much mess could one single person make?

I withdrew the two hundred pounds. Not withdrawing it would draw a response from Gene I couldn't cope with. When there was peace between us, it was glorious, and any amount was worth paying to sustain that. Gene took the money from me and tucked it into his pocket.

"Hey, baby?"

"Yeah?"

"Thank you," he said with extra emphasis.

"That's ok, I just want you to have what you need."

"We'll get all this shit sorted, baby. Soon we'll be living together and none of this will be an issue."

I smiled up at him.

"Do you think we will get back together?"

"What's that supposed to fucking mean?"

I turned my head to the ground.

"Sorry, I meant living together."

"Oh, yeah. If you would stop listening to what everyone else tells you, we could have been together months ago. But you let people get inside your head."

I wondered for a second if he meant people or Gene. I didn't have time to ponder that thought for any length of time.

"I got to ask you a favour, baby."

"Yeah?"

Gene looked so deeply into my eyes it felt like he could see what lay inside me better than I ever had.

"Start looking at houses."

"I thought you wanted me to come home?"

"I do but that place is too fucking expensive, and it's a dump. I think we should look for somewhere we can afford. It'd be cheaper to make a down-payment on a new place than to catch up on the rent in this one."

"I know. I miss that house though."

"It's just a house, babe. Four walls: that's all it is."

On a rational level, I knew that, but my heart told me otherwise. It was the last real home I'd had, and it had reached folklore status in my mind: it was the fairytale castle I dreamed of living in but to which I could never find a means of entry. But no matter how I felt about it, I knew Gene was right. He was always much more clear-sighted than I was about life.

"Ok, I'll look when I get back to the hostel."

"Good. You don't got to worry about being homeless like I do."

"I am homeless."

Gene scoffed at me. "You don't know shit about sleeping rough."

He was right about that too.

"Sorry, I just meant I don't have a home."

"You do got a home: with me. It don't matter where we live – I'm

111

home to you and you're home to me. Nothing can ever change that, baby."

I beamed at him.

"Where do you want to live?"

"I don't give a shit, so long as I'm with you."

"What about work?"

"I can always find another job – that ain't hard to do."

When I got back to the refuge, I started a house hunt online. Anywhere with two bedrooms and an affordable deposit would do. I looked at areas I'd never visited, never mind considered living in. I knew I'd be getting a second housing offer, but I had no idea when it might come, and I'd already abused the little patience I did have that last couple of months.

I looked at hundreds of houses online, making a list of ones we should view. Something in the pit of my stomach pulled me back every time I picked up my phone to arrange a viewing. It was like a lodged lump of lead I couldn't shift. I tried thinking idealistic thoughts: thoughts about everything Gene and I could be if I just took a step forward. But I was stuck in limbo; I couldn't move on from Gene, but I couldn't turn back. There was too much at stake to opt for either option.

Gene would be "salty" when he found out about my stalling. When he asked me to complete a task, there was no delay allowed. It had to be my top priority until another pressing need of Gene's crept up. I had to talk to one of the workers, to make sense of what was happening to me. Why was I frozen to the spot? Why was I miserable with my current mode of existence, yet unable to change it? How could I break so many promises to the one I loved?

I picked Hope up and walked to the office, hoping someone was working alone. If they were, there was more chance I'd have the courage to request a chat. Lana was sitting typing at her desk and she looked up when she heard my carpeted creak on the floorboards.

"Aoife," she smiled. "How are things?"

"Ok, if you have time, could I have a chat?"

"I always have time."

I smiled at her.

She nudged a swivel chair towards me and I joined her at her desk.

"What's up?"

"I'm confused."

"Ok, what about?"

"Gene. I want to go home, but I'm scared."

"What are you scared of?"

"That things won't change."

"Well, why don't you have a look at this worksheet?"

She flipped through the pockets of her folder quicker than a banker counts bank notes. She seemed to know the order of worksheets by heart. I wondered if it was possible that I was like the other women in the house. I never believed that I was. I believed that I was the only one that didn't deserve to be there, that didn't have the need to be. But the fear in my stomach fought me on that point.

"What is it?"

"It's called "signs an abuser isn't changing.""

"But how do you know that applies to me? What if Gene just struggles to manage money? What if I'm the one that's abusive?"

"What makes you think you're abusive?"

"Gene thinks I am."

"We have all lived with you for a few months now. If you were abusive, we would have seen some sign of it by now, but no one has."

"Maybe I'm only abusive with him?"

"You wouldn't be able to stop yourself being that way here either. It's all about power and control. We're in close quarters and we haven't seen one incident where you've demonstrated abusive behaviour."

I felt a little reassured by that; they were the experts on what constituted abuse after all. Was it possible that Gene was trying to get me to believe falsehoods? But why would he do that? He was the most honest human being I'd ever met; he couldn't even lie to his boss about the mundane to keep him sweet. Gene was a straight-talker. He was the one who told everyone exactly what they didn't want to hear.

"Want to have a look?"

She slid the page towards me and I took a few minutes to process what was printed in black and white. The signs listed seemed clear, but when I applied them to my own relationship, they were anything but.

"Making promises that they don't follow through on."

I could relate to that one, but there were reasons why Gene had been unable to follow through on his. The worksheet hadn't taken any of the factors that shaped Gene's behaviour into account. Gene had joint pain that meant he couldn't work, so he was practically penniless. He wanted to change, but sometimes physical pain made the final decision. He had come from an abusive home, so he had learnt unhealthy methods of resolving conflict. That wasn't Gene's fault. He was working to address them. The page didn't mention anything about mental illness as a mitigating factor. There was a difference between choosing to behave in a particular way and doing it unintentionally because you had so many stressors causing you problems. All the worksheet taught me was that its rules didn't pertain to Gene's life. He needed a set of more flexible ones.

"I don't know if these apply to Gene," I said.

"Den-i-al," said Lana, smiling to herself and pencilling something I couldn't see onto her page. "Why don't you take this with you and have a wee think about it?"

"Ok, thanks."

I lifted the page, folded it up and set it on the desk in front of me. It sat there staring at me like a truth I didn't want to acknowledge. I put it away in my pocket.

"Do you honestly think he has changed?" Lana asked, searching my eyes with her own.

"I want to think he has."

"That's the key – look for proof, not hope."

"What kind of proof?"

"He could have gone to the courts to arrange contact with Hope. He could have done supervised contact and had her at the weekend by now. He could have taken an anger management course. I can't see him doing any of that."

I shook my head so slightly I wasn't sure if it was perceptible.

"When did he last ask you for money?"

"Today."

"And did you give it to him?"

I nodded, looking away. My eyes traced the outline of every object in the room: the stationery on the desks, the wall charts of rotas, the veiled windows that shaded the place from public view. I looked anywhere other than into Lana's knowing eyes.

It suddenly occurred to me that there might have been more love within those four office walls than there had ever been within the walls of my family home.

"How much did you give him?"

"Not that much."

"Does he not worry about you and his daughter? He's taking food out of her mouth because he can't be bothered growing up."

"It's not that – we're better off than he is."

"Aoife – you're living in a women's refuge, because of him."

"We have money for food."

"If he doesn't, he's got no one to blame but himself. He's a grown man. What age is he again?"

"41."

"And you're 27?"

"Yeah."

"He had everything handed to him on a plate and he ruined it."

Part of me almost thought she was right, but the part of me programmed to defend Gene was stronger.

"It isn't his fault. It's mine – I shouldn't have left."

"You had no choice. Why would you choose to come here if you didn't have to? It's not an easy choice to make."

"I don't know."

I decided to ask the question that lingered in my mind but remained unanswered.

"Do you think I shouldn't be here?"

"What?"

"I always think I don't deserve to be here. I see women arriving with broken bones, black eyes, scars – I feel like I haven't earned the right to be here."

"Physical injuries heal quicker than emotional ones. Do you know anything about brainwashing?"

"Not really."

"He has brainwashed you into thinking all of this. If anything, I think you're at the opposite end of the spectrum. You need to be here. He is extremely controlling, and he is still playing with your mind."

"I don't know my own mind. I don't know whose thoughts are whose anymore."

"That's because he has conditioned you."

I couldn't believe that Gene would do such a thing; it was just an unintended effect of living with our mental health problems.

"How do I see my way out of this?" I asked.

"There is only one way – stop talking to him."

"I can't do that."

"Yes, you can. Even just take a break for a few weeks and see if you can see everything more clearly."

"I can't. I can't get by without him."

"You only think that."

"I don't – it's true. Without Gene, I'd be dead. I can't cope with my own head without him."

"He has just brainwashed you into thinking that."

I stubbornly shook my head.

"I can't survive without talking to him."

I knew the minute I returned to my room, I'd be on the phone to Gene. It was pointless trying to hide my dependency on him; the workers were fully aware of it. I didn't know how I could ever break my addiction to Gene. I needed him to reassure me that everything would be ok; that it wasn't too late to correct my mistakes, that my mind wouldn't kill me, that we'd be the family we should have been. I returned to my room, filing the page away in a drawer. I couldn't allow the workers to influence my opinion of Gene. They didn't know him like I did; they hadn't even met him. Everything they thought about him was merely supposition. Gene always said they were trying to divide us, and I had to agree with him. They had painted me as the helpless victim when really, we were two equals; equally flawed, equally abusive, equally loving towards one another. Everyone outside our relationship unfairly gave me a by-ball; everyone was out to get Gene.

Chapter Twenty

"You're going to have to find me somewhere else to live, babe."

"Why?"

"The eviction notice arrived – I got thirty days from today to get out."

Why hadn't I just paid the rent and spared us such issues? Gene's issues were mine; I'd known when I hadn't paid it that I could never separate myself from his problems, so why had I tried to? The bill would always catch up with me in the end.

"The motherfucking fridge is broken."

"Shit, since when?"

"A few days. I can't even call the agency out to fix it."

"Can you survive without it?"

"I'm going to have to, ain't I?"

"I'm sorry."

"You ain't sorry for shit."

"I'll help you find somewhere to live."

"I need you to sort my taxes out. I got to get that rebate, babe."

"I know."

It was the least I could do to help; the entire mess had been created by my reckless impulsivity.

"Gene, did you pay your National Insurance contributions?"

"How the fuck would I know that?"

"They go out of your account by direct debit every month."

"Uh, I don't fucking know – it's you that keeps track of that shit."

"Ok, I'll check."

I doubted it had been paid; if Gene had twenty pounds in his bank account and knew that it was there, he'd feel compelled to get it down to a zero balance again.

"Do you have a record of the weeks you've been paid since I left?"

I had been rigorous about keeping clear records of what Gene had owed and the work-related expenses he had paid since he started. I'd inevitably left the papers in the house. I could ask Gene to look for them, but I somehow already knew I'd be starting from scratch. I'd have to go through his bank statements and work out what was what.

"Gene?"

"Yeah."

"Would you be able to get me the paperwork I left in the house about your earnings and outgoings?"

"I don't know where that shit is, babe."

"It's in the spare room."

"There is so much shit in there, man. How am I meant to ever find it?"

"Ok, it doesn't matter."

"I mean, I'll look, but I can't guarantee I'll find it."

Gene didn't find it and I spent the rest of that day stressing over figures and minding Hope while I did it. It was important; I couldn't leave it until it was done.

■ ■

A few days later, I set up a viewing for Gene. It felt like I'd looked at every apartment in Northern Ireland and I had finally found one that sounded ideal: a bedsit, all bills included, well within Gene's budget if he went to work. Gene had grudgingly agreed to view it. He probably would have stayed in the house until the police removed him, had he not wanted to rebuild our family. Gene would do anything for us; I still knew at the bottom of my heart, underneath all the hurts, that he would.

"Where do I got to go for this viewing, babe?"

"It's just off the Castlereagh Road."

"Send me directions – detailed ones. I can't afford to get lost today, man."

"OK, the guy is meeting you there at 12."

I had dealt with all correspondence on Gene's behalf. The man who was renting out the room was looking for a lodger to join the four others already living in the house. I hoped it was a spacious house; I had my doubts about how well Gene could cope with communal living. Based on experience, he'd probably manage to piss someone off before his landlord handed him the key. I hoped I was wrong. The last thing Gene's visa needed was for him to be homeless. He'd never get his renewal. I tried not to think about all other damaging factors in his visa renewal: the records of us living separate lives, my reinstated claim for the benefit I had cancelled upon Gene's arrival, the agency's records of Gene's failure to vacate the property. There was so much working against us, but none of it was set in stone. If we managed to reconcile before Gene's visa was up, create a new, settled life and pay enough taxes to replace the money we'd claimed, everything would be alright. That's what I told myself every day.

"Did you send me the directions yet, babe?"

Gene was still on the other end of the phone. I typed frantically, filling an email with all the markers Gene could possibly need: all the street names, the left and right turns, the shops he'd pass along the way. I was so meticulous, there was no chance my directions could be criticised.

"I'm about to send them. Just a minute," I said, still typing, trying to talk at the same time without typing what I was saying and directing Hope away from emptying the chest of drawers.

"Babe, you got to hurry up, I got to be there in 45 minutes."

"Ok, sorry, I'm nearly done."

"I need time to read through 'em."

"I know, I'm hurrying."

Gene sighed into the phone.

"Ok, sent."

"Right, thanks babe. I'll take a look and start walking. I'll call you in a little while."

"Ok."

I picked Hope up, shoved all the belongings she'd pulled out of the drawers back inside. I'd organise them properly later when she was asleep; when I had some time to myself. I propped her on my hip. Between Hope and the weight of the baby, I felt like I was carrying a large burden; one that was almost impossible to support. I pulled the bedroom door behind us and locked it. I never failed to lock it; you never knew who was living in the house. You might get to know certain tenants on a superficial level, but you never knew for sure what they were capable of. Food was sometimes stolen from unlocked cupboards, so I wasn't taking any chances. I carried Hope down the two flights of stairs. I'd better hang up our laundry later; I'd have to wait until a clothes horse came free. There were three for the full house, and some women marked one as their territory, like tourists claim their sun loungers with beach towels. The washing machine was in perpetual use and some residents took their time emptying out their load.

I carried Hope into the kitchen, strapped her into the highchair and trailed it twenty feet to the corner that held my kitchen. She'd be sitting there until I'd cooked, fed her, washed and dried the dishes. She was used to the wait by then. There was an awful mess in the kitchen. The last lady hadn't dried her dishes and had left the soggy remnants of her plate scrapings in the sink. I washed it out and tried to look out the window instead. There wasn't much to look at: a metal fire escape and a bucket of cigarette butt soup. Everything around me seemed to be grey, but maybe my mind was turning it that colour. That's what happened when I was on a low: the colour drained out my surroundings until it looked washed out and drab. My mind was playing tricks on me; nothing was as hopeless as I believed it to be. I felt like it was, but my feelings couldn't be relied upon. They were more changeable than my circumstances were. I emptied a tin of beans into a pot and shoved a couple of slices of bread into the toaster. I wanted to spend minimal time in the kitchen, so I could get out and get a breath of sea air. The toast popped up and snapped me out of my trance and Hope chirped so cheerily it was like music in the silent room.

Sarah walked up behind me.

"Alright preggers. Look at her –

"Hiya, I know, she's noisy."

"She wouldn't have dared make a sound when you first got here. Look at her now. She must feel relaxed here."

I nodded but couldn't comprehend why that would be the case. Hope was obviously relaxed, but how could she be, living in temporary accommodation? She had never been a child who cooed. She had been unnervingly quiet in our house, but that was probably due to her younger age and her less developed sounds. I resented anyone suggesting that Hope was happier in the refuge. How could they speak so badly of my husband? How could they imply that being pregnant in a refuge was preferable to being at home? No one seemed to understand how I felt. The only one who understood my sheer misery was Gene. I knew he felt it too. I felt a painful pang of longing for him. I wondered if he had found the house. I didn't like to phone to check; if I interrupted anything essential, I'd put him under undue pressure. I waited, trying to find enough of an appetite to choke down my toast. Hope nonchalantly played with her beans, like she'd forgotten Gene and like whether he stayed in the country made little impact on her life. I sat, watching the face of my phone, willing it to ring.

It did, and I rushed to answer.

"Did you find it?"

"No, your directions are fucked."

"I double-checked them."

"Well, they're wrong. I got ten minutes to get there. You better sort this shit out."

"Where are you?"

"The corner of Castlereagh and Beersbridge."

"Ok, which direction are you walking in?"

"I don't fucking know. You're meant to know that."

"Well, which side of the road are you on?"

"What are you fucking talking about?"

"Can you see any other street names near you?"

I opened maps on my phone and zoomed in to look for recognisable street names. If I could find a shortcut, Gene would forgive me for coming up with such unreliable directions.

"Are you near Paxton street?"

"No."

"What about Frank street?"

"Are you just making this shit up? I ain't near either of those. You better fucking hurry – I'm going to miss this viewing."

I felt sick with panic. If Gene missed the viewing, he might not get another one, certainly not a place so affordable and handy for his work. I had to get him there on time.

"I'm at Templemore."

"Ok, can you see the Castlereagh Road?"

When I looked at the map, they were situated next to each other.

"No."

"Well, look at the street signs."

"It ain't here."

"Well, it's on the map."

"I'm standing here. You're wrong."

"Well, I don't know what to tell you to do."

"Fucking fix it."

"I'm trying."

I was getting hysterical and trying not to let it show in my voice, but I needed a minute or two to compose myself. If I lost control of my mind, Gene had no hope of making it there on time. I hung up and leant over the counter, breathing heavily and blotting tears with a bit of torn-off kitchen towel.

My phone buzzed, and I answered.

"Yeah?"

"Why the fuck did you hang up?"

"I was getting too upset and didn't know what to say."

"How the fuck am I supposed to find this place if you hang up on me?"

"Sorry."

"Hurry up and tell me where I got to go."

"Where are you?"

"I fucking told you already."

My mind was like a slate wiped clean of all its thoughts. Too much trauma had rid me of every one of them. I tried to come up with the name of a nearby street, but not one came to me.

"You don't remember shit."

"I'm trying…Ok, let me think for a second."

"What's there to think about?"

"Just listen for a minute."

Gene went quiet and waited. I could feel his impatience rising between us on the phoneline like the timbre of our strained voices. I went silent for a few seconds while I tried to make sense of the map. My mind was no longer functioning properly. Once there was too much pressure on me to mentally perform, my mind fell apart like an unbound book. I was groping for the pages, trying to put them back in an order that make sense. But Gene didn't have time for that.

"Why aren't you fucking talking?"

"I'm looking at the map."

"I thought you said you knew the way to this place."

"I'm trying to work out where you are in relation to it."

"I fucking told you – I'm at the corner of Templemore."

"Ok, so you turn right."

"You just told me to take a right and it was the wrong way."

"Well, I'm not there, I'm just looking at a map. That's what the map says."

My voice was growing louder, and I was losing control of myself. I was washing the dishes, while I figured out the map with one soapy hand, and Hope was losing patience in the highchair. I was nowhere near finished with my lunchtime clean-up, so I couldn't vacate the kitchen. I'd have to somehow clear up, get Gene to his viewing and occupy Hope, without drawing attention to myself. Thankfully there was no one else around, or so I thought.

"Ok, it's definitely right."

"It's not. You better fucking hurry, if I'm late for this dude, I ain't going."

"Just tell him you got lost – he'll understand."

"You got me lost."

I started to cry. I'd tried so hard to get Gene where he needed to go, but something always inevitably went wrong. The world was against us and every tiny step we took towards getting back together. I was losing faith in myself, losing faith in life's goodness and losing faith in second chances.

I tore off some green kitchen paper to blot my eye-makeup with. If one of the workers walked in, they'd instantly know I had been crying, and they'd know what about. They weren't just observant; they seemed to sense what was happening as it unfolded. I had to protect Gene. If I showed that he was still causing me distress, they would never support my decision to reunite with him.

"I typed it all out. I don't know why you didn't just use my directions."

I was running out of new suggestions and just reaching for the old ones; anything to move Gene a few feet closer to his viewing.

"They didn't make no fucking sense. Did you even read them?"

"Yeah, I was really careful about getting them right."

"Well, I'm fucking lost now, ain't I? I got to go."

Gene hung up the phone. I phoned back right away, but it went straight to voicemail; he had shut his phone off – my punishment for the day. I burst into tears again. Not only did I not know when Gene would be back in touch, I didn't know if he'd made it to his viewing or not. My heart told me he hadn't. If he had, he would have signed off much more pleasantly.

My body shook with the strength of my sobs and I tried to stifle them. I knew anyone could walk in at any moment and I wouldn't have enough time to compose myself. But I was too upset to stifle my reaction. Everything was always going wrong. Every little daily event that didn't work out just added to my belief that life was crumbling apart. I didn't know how much longer I could keep going with this life; this unwarrantedly harsh one. I was more tired, I supposed, than most humans when they reached the last days of their old age. Worry was eating me from the inside out.

The girl in the next kitchen poked her head through the counter between our two kitchens. I had no idea she'd been there. I wondered how much of the conversation she'd heard. I hadn't heard the fire door slam closed with her entrance, but my emotions were at such heights I likely wouldn't have noticed if a wrecking ball had swung through the door instead.

"Are you ok?" she asked.

Her eyes were filled with sympathy for me, and I felt repulsed by it. I didn't like the reflection of the person I saw in her eyes: someone worthy of pity, someone who needed to hear condolences about their life.

I nodded and couldn't find so much as a syllable to respond with. I turned back to my dishes, hoping I didn't look rude and that she'd brush past the incident as if it had never happened. She was the only witness, so if she did, I could pretend it hadn't too.

■■■

Gene turned his phone back on again a couple of hours later. He didn't come looking for me, he just happened to answer when I tried to call him again. I expected him to be "salty," but his voice had returned to its neutral state.

"Yeah, babe?"

"Did you get to the viewing?"

"Yeah, I made it."

"And?"

"He's going to give me the room."

"That's great."

"I guess."

"Are you not happy about it?"

"Happy about living with a bunch of dudes I don't even know? Not fucking really."

"Well, at least you won't have to worry about rent anymore."

"Yeah."

"What's your room like?"

"It's a room."

"What's in it?"

"A bed, TV."

"What about the bathroom and kitchen?"

"I got to share with four other dudes."

"Sorry."

"I was supposed to be living with my wife – why am I even here? I should have gone back to America."

"No –

That was my greatest fear: that Gene would abandon all attempts to reconcile and return to America. I couldn't even allow myself to consider it; the thought alone was enough to bring on a panic attack. I sat down on the bed, my head spinning like the world in its daily turn that brought me nothing but trouble.

"Please stay – we'll work everything out."

"That's what you've been telling me for months. I'm a fucking fool. You ain't got no intention of being with me."

"That's not true."

"I should just fucking kill myself."

"No – I love you. We'll get back together."

"I asked you to look for a house for us a month ago and you didn't."

"I did look, but I can't move in with you until I know things have changed."

Gene's salty temper returned.

"This ain't all on me – this is your fault. You're the one that left."

"I had to."

"No, you didn't. You just tell yourself that to justify what you did."

I felt hideously guilty.

"I know you talk shit about me in there."

"What?"

"To the people that run that place. I ain't stupid."

"I don't –

"You try to make yourself the victim but we both know the truth."

I doubted whether I ever knew the truth. Just like myself and Gene, truth and fiction were so intertwined I didn't have a hope in hell of separating one from the other. Gene and I were so tightly knotted to one another I couldn't breathe without his command to do so. I might have been living in a place he didn't know existed, but my heart was still right next to his, pumping from his supply when he chose to give it to me.

"I don't make you look bad. I just talk about things I need help understanding."

"We were both treating each other like shit. I don't want things to be like that no more. But you won't give it the chance to work."

"I'm scared things won't change."

"Well, there's only one way to find out."

"That's what I'm afraid of. If I move in with you and it's the same as before, it'll be too late."

"You've never had any intention of moving back in. You're just playing games with me."

"I'm not trying to."

Gene did one of his ha's. The argument felt perfectly circular with no chance of us breaking out of the loop.

"You want to get back together, you got to prove it. Find us a house."

"Why is it all down to me?"

"Because you're the one that left."

"Because of how you were treating me."

"We were both treating each other shitty. You got to face up to what you are. I can't do it for you."

What was I? A manipulative control freak? Someone who liked to play the role of martyr in the disaster that had come about by their own design? Did I really treat Gene as badly as he treated me? Something told me I didn't, but my gut was twisting with gnarls of guilt. I knew that it didn't matter how culpable I was or believed myself to be; I had to pretend I was if I wanted to salvage my relationship with Gene. Gene hated being held responsible for things. I was never going to get the apology I longed for. I had two choices: start afresh with a new life or deal with the conditions of the old one. Leaving Gene wasn't an option, so I'd have to select the second. I was in stasis, waiting for a signal from the universe to show me what to do. I knew I had to take a step in one direction, but my feet were stuck to the floor, fear disabling my legs.

Gene was due to move a week and a half later. I wanted to offer to help him, but I couldn't; I wasn't allowed back to the house without involving social services. Gene told me he could make the move in one taxi run. That reassured me a little. I hated thinking of him being expelled from his home, having to transport his belongings and being in a new and uncomfortable environment all by himself.

I was waiting for Gene to ask me for the payment for the room, but he surprised me: he didn't ask. Maybe the tides were turning, and Gene was realising what he owed in contributions to our relationship. I didn't like to ask where he got the money and I was thankful when he told me it was legal. His tax rebate had come through swiftly: a thousand pounds to spend how he saw fit. That made an enormous difference to my stress levels. A single man, living in a bedsit could make that sum last for a very long time. Gene lived on nothing but hotdogs and cigarettes, and his house was furnished with every one of his needs: a TV, a microwave, a laid-back landlord who didn't question his smoking habit nor check the state of his room.

Gene moved the belongings he believed to be important into his new house. He left me the door-key under the mat, so I could return to the house for some of the items I'd left behind. I had one day to do it; the agency was waiting for the key's return.

"I left you the key, babe. There's a toy in the living room I got for Hope."

I wondered why he hadn't brought it with him; maybe it pained him too much to do so. It was a physical reminder of the daughter that was missing from his home.

My dad accompanied me to the house; I had no idea what I might find there. It had been four months since I'd last set foot in the place and I hadn't expected to do so again. I felt a rush of good old familiarity when I turned the key in the door. But it was misleading, because I wasn't opening the door to the smell of dinner cooking, the sound of music blaring, the perfume of candles I used to combat the odours. A waft of cigarette smoke hit me. The house was cold; it hadn't been heated since Gene ran out of oil again. I'd offered to refill it, but Gene liked the cold. The windows were all open, adding to the chill. I turned the overhead light on and walked into the living room. Tears pushed their way upwards, like emotions clawing their way out of my body. Gene's computer was gone, the coffee table remained, with the toy dog on it that Gene had got for Hope. I picked it up first and added it to a box we had brought in. The room was grotty; no more than it had been when I left, but I was seeing it from an almost objective viewpoint now I wasn't living in it. There was a jar filled with water on the coffee table, full of roaches. I'd thought Gene had quit smoking weed, but he'd made no efforts to conceal his habit. It reminded me of when I'd asked him to pick up the cigarette butts off the driveway and he'd extinguished his cigarette on the bin. Pass comment on what Gene chose to do with his time and suffer the consequences of your complaints. Gene's battle jacket was gone, his external hard-drive, the contents of his shoeboxes. The boxes still sat there and the sight of them made me feel sick. I turned around to check that Gene wasn't behind me. I could still feel him in the house, like a spiritual presence. I jumped when I saw the form in the doorway, but it was just my dad, carrying extra moving boxes into the room. The fear didn't leave me; it reproduced with every item I saw that brought up bad memories. I couldn't understand how a few flattened cushions and a stained red throw could make me feel afraid.

"We'll come back tomorrow with Poppy and Pete and pack up some more," said my dad. "I'll take the cot apart and put it in the car."

I couldn't bear the thought of seeing the cot again: the one I'd cried next to on my final nights, the one where I'd struggled alone to get Hope to sleep, the one that sat right next to the closed door that concealed Gene suspended from the ceiling. But I couldn't afford to be picky; I needed items with which to furnish an entire house. The cot would have to come. I went upstairs to the bedroom. It looked the same as it did when I'd left. Gene hadn't moved any of my belongings. I remembered how much was in the house; I'd have to leave most of it behind. We simply didn't have the time nor the space to bring it all.

"Just take what you can, we can't take it all," my dad called, in unison with that thought.

I pulled dresses from their hangers, deciding which to take and which to bin. I didn't want to leave a huge mess for the agency; it would be their cleaners that would have to clear the rest. I noticed some gifts I had got Gene sitting around. Maybe he hadn't cared enough to take them with him, maybe he just didn't have the room. I thought about taking them with me and bringing them with me on one of our trips into town, but I didn't. If he didn't want them, I wasn't going to force him to keep them.

I kept bagging everything in sight; I was utterly overwhelmed. There was more stuff in the house than I'd ever imagined when I performed an imaginary clear-out in my head. I'd dreamt of all the items I would lift given a second chance, but now that I was back in the house, I couldn't remember what one of them was. I knew as soon as I left, I'd remember an item hidden away in a cranny that I'd never see again. The remaining items were likely to end up in the dump, but I couldn't allow myself to spend much time considering that. They were only material items, but they were symbols of the married life I'd tried to build with Gene, and the person who'd existed before he'd entered the picture.

"Could you help me with the cot, love?" my dad called.

He got me to hold the sides while he unscrewed the bolts. Standing in my daughters stark, toyless room was more than I could bear, but I stood there all the same, mechanically separating the cot sides and trying not to look at the keepsakes that remained behind.

"Ok, I'll put this in the car while you finish up. We'll go in about ten minutes, ok?"

It was already dark outside and there was a sense of time moving too hastily, like days bumping into one another like fallen dominos.

I grabbed as many of Hope's belongings as I could fit into a box: the container we had got for her first lost tooth, the teddy bear that my parents had got her when they were in Finland, the baby booties that were smaller than I remembered her feet ever being. I put them all in the box unpadded. It was a time for a grab and run, not careful padding and protection. I left the rest for tomorrow; hopefully with four pairs of hands I'd get closer to preserving the physical parts of my family dream.

Back in the house the next morning, everything felt more real in daylight. The rash decision I had made just a few months before hadn't been as reversible as I'd believed it to be. Our home looked less homely than when we'd first unpacked; remnants of our marriage remained behind like the belongings of a dead family member you'd loved with all your heart. There was no way I could bring it all. The items I did bring with me would be stored in my parents' garage until I found a house of my own. I didn't have anywhere left to put them in my bedroom in the refuge. I suddenly needed to get away from everyone and the hallway we all stood in felt oppressive. There was every other member of my family, leading their successful lives, all brought along to witness the mess of mine like sick entertainment. I went upstairs, hoping no one would follow me.

I sat down on the floor of what once could have been my library, or my drumming studio, but that had become nothing but a cell: a compartment in which to take cover. I didn't know where to start. There were so many items around me and when I looked at them they all seemed to mean a lot to me: a candle holder my best friend in Glasgow got me, books I'd collected over more than a decade, folders of artwork from when I used to take painting classes, mementos I'd saved since I was a child. There were scrapbooks, photos, letters from friends, jewellery; now all of it was filler for the dump. I couldn't take it all. I'd have to be so selective; choosing what I needed rather than what I wanted.

I grabbed painting tools rather than pictures, believing the tools to make more art were more valuable than the art itself. I couldn't think clearly about what item was what; I knew I'd have regrets about what I'd left behind later, but I could do nothing to change that.

Everything was a blur and time was against me like a ruthless opponent in a cruel game.

I heard my dad's voice, beckoning me to finish up. Poppy and Pete had cleared the kitchen and the living room. We all had to go; they had to get home for lunch. Not leaving a mess was more pressing than picking and choosing what I had to bring. Trying not to look, I shoved an armful of clothes I loved into a bin bag, along with a box of jewellery I knew likely contained treasures from my childhood, relics from family members, my old camera, my old kindle. What I was throwing out wasn't thought through: it was done in a moment's panic; time was almost up.

"Aoife, we're going now," yelled my dad. "Are you finished?"

I knew I had to be. I took some pictures of the carcass of our house, hoping that doing so would make me never forget it, even in such a sad state. I turned, carrying a bag of items I'd chosen to keep downstairs with me. I glanced back, seeing the teddy bear sitting on top of the wardrobe: the one that we had got Hope but put away for when she got bigger because she was afraid of it. Seeing it disappearing into the past somehow scared me more than that bear had ever induced fear in her.

"Are you already finished? That was quick." I tried to act cheery. Everyone nodded.

"There are still things left behind, but we can't take everything. You've just got to cut your losses in a situation like this."

For a moment, I wondered what my dad knew about that feeling, but then the thought passed away, with all other irrational thoughts in my mind.

"When you decide to leave, you've got to sacrifice something."

He made it sound like I had won, and Gene had lost. But I felt like both of us had lost everything.

Chapter Twenty-One

Gene didn't think too highly of his new flatmates, but the only time he spent around them was when he bumped into someone en-route to the bathroom or on his way to the microwave. I was thankful they kept their distance; had they not, we would have been presented with a new portfolio of problems. Space was what Gene needed, so the house was ideal, until we found our own, at least.

That week, my second offer came through. I told my dad I was going to look at the place; he wanted to come too to inspect it. He'd rather I found a private rental than take a house that was unliveable. The last thing I needed with a baby due in a month was a renovation project. I checked the address on the letter; it wasn't far from where Gene was staying. That filled me with fear, but I couldn't say why. My body had just got itself into a tense state, automatically reacting to things that required no reaction.

My dad drove me to the house and we sat outside it. I had a viewing the following week, but he wanted to take a look at the area and the exterior first. It wasn't a desirable location; every house on the street was in need of more than a paint touch-up. The walls were cracked, with chunks missing, weeds were thriving more than any of the street's residents were. A few unsavoury characters were hanging around, with a look of ennui on their faces.

"It's not a good area, love."

"How do you know?"

"I can just tell. I'd worry about you living on your own here."

For a moment, I considered telling my dad that I wouldn't be living alone but thought better of it. If he found out I might move Gene in, he'd have deposited me on the kerb, telling me to ruin my life unaided. Everyone was convinced my life would vastly improve once I had accommodation of my own: a sanctuary for myself and Hope, but the thought of it filled me with dread. Not only was I incapable of functioning without Gene, I had grown accustomed to the high drama lifestyle we led. Miserable as it was, I was used to living on extreme highs and extreme lows. I couldn't remember how to happily live in the middle and not feel that everything lacked meaning. When you step off a rollercoaster, stopping on still ground feels less comfortable than continuing with its flips.

"You can look at the place if you want, but I really don't think it's a good idea, love."

"Ok."

My eyes hovered on the number on the door, thinking of the potential it held for my family. But my dad was right: I'd be too vulnerable staying there alone, and I'd have to until Gene completed his two-month lease. Time was pressing upon me like someone breathing down my neck. I had one month to find a home before the baby arrived, and I knew my chances of succeeding in that were slim. I had one remaining offer, and I hoped it would arrive just when I needed it.

I got back to the refuge and Lisa let me in.

"Well, how's you?"

"Ok."

"Saw you got an offer."

"Yeah, I don't know if I'm going to take it."

"Why not?"

"My dad doesn't think it seems safe."

"Does your dad know you only get three offers?"

I nodded my head.

"Hopefully the third one is ok."

"If it isn't, you're going to have to get a private rental."

"I know. If I don't get it soon I might anyway. I have to have my own house before the baby comes."

"Well, you don't have to, but I understand why you'd want to."

"Yeah, I can't live here with a baby."

"Well, I'm sure we could make certain things easier for you."

"Thanks."

I was decided: I just wanted my own home with Gene in it, and once I was there, everything would be ok.

I took Hope to the playroom for a while and watched her playing with the toys. I didn't have much left inside to enable me to play enthusiastically with her. I showed interest in the toys she played with and stared at the sun-stained blinds. The layout of the room almost made it feel like I was in a friend's house, but when I read the instructions and health and safety regulations, I remembered I wasn't anywhere I could truly relax.

It comforted me a little that Hope seemed relaxed there; she knew her way around the room and knew exactly what she wanted to play with. *CBeebies* chattered in the background and I tried to listen to the positivity of the presenters' voices, wishing life was as simple as they conveyed it to be. The repetition of the same shows and the same characters told me on some level that life carried on, even though it didn't feel like mine was worth continuing.

■■■

Gene and I had another argument. He had got angry when I didn't answer my phone quickly enough. He'd accused me of being with someone else, and because I had sighed rather than immediately denied it, he believed I had cheated on him. We hadn't spoken in almost a full day when Gene phoned me to discuss how the birth would play out. He told me I had to ring him the minute I went into labour and he would make his way to the hospital. He would be there for Alice, but not for me, he said. I had lost his support when I'd decided to keep his daughter from him and "mess around with other dudes." I hadn't, but when Gene believed I'd done something, it was as true as if I'd done it. He was going to punish me in my most weakened state, and I didn't know what to do.

I went for a walk around the town. I needed to get some sea air, to clear my head. The refuge was becoming oppressive; I had to get out soon. I strolled around every street of the town, pushing Hope while she napped. It was getting hot outside; warm enough that I could stay out for as long as I wanted to, to escape the refuge, to pretend I had a different life. I walked from the beach, to the playground, to a café, to every shop that lined the street, to a fast-food place. It was after-dark before I returned home. I only did it when the last shops started closing and there was nowhere else to go.

When I got back to the refuge, I had a new bedroom. The staff had already let themselves into my last one and moved all my belongings. Nothing felt reliable anymore; everything was in perpetual motion. Change was no longer something I feared; it was just to be expected.

A new family had arrived that day and the workers had had to make room for them. My old room had two sets of bunkbeds in it that would accommodate four children, so Hope and I were moved into a small, side room. It felt a little cosier even though everything we owned was crammed in. Hope didn't seem the least bit bothered by our relocation, which unsettled me. She had grown too used to change too; I couldn't help wondering if constant transition was bad for a baby. She was just over one and she'd been uprooted nearly as many times as I had in my twenty-seven years. She wasn't even fazed by it. She played happily with her toys, exploring the new cupboards as hiding places and watching *Peppa Pig* on the TV above our heads. The theme tune soothed me a bit; Hope's routines were for my benefit as much as for hers. They were the only constants in my life.

Lana knocked and poked her head around the door.

"How are you getting on?"

"I'm just putting things away."

"Sorry we had to move you – I know it's a lot smaller."

"It's ok."

"At least you'll be close to your babies," she smiled.

I hoped she was right and that would still be the case days or weeks from that time. I wished I could keep Alice cocooned in my belly forever, where I knew Gene couldn't reach her and social services couldn't remove her from me, but time was ticking down with terrible swiftness. And after our last conversation, I had a feeling, accompanied by nausea, that Gene and I were as far away as we'd ever been from working everything out. We were meant to be working together against the agencies that kept us apart, but we were working against one another on top of that.

I knew Gene badly wanted to be at the birth, so I hoped he would rethink the conditions he had laid down. I couldn't allow him into the room if I knew he wasn't there for me as much as for the baby. I was the one enduring the labour pains and I was the one that would be there with him for hours until the baby appeared. I needed to know that he wouldn't create a rumpus in the labour ward. I needed to know he wouldn't embarrass me in front of the midwives or start talking down to me when I was in the late stages of labour. I needed to know that he wouldn't turn cold on me the minute our baby was born or walk out of the hospital with her while I was in too drugged a state to intervene. I had to be able to trust Gene to allow him to see me in such a vulnerable state again, and I wasn't sure if I could.

I phoned Gene back after I got Hope to bed. I had decided to hold off until he made the first move, but I knew deep down that I needed him more than he needed me and if I wanted things to be resolved, I had to be the one to initiate it. I couldn't come up with an apology, but maybe if I explained my point of view to Gene, he'd understand and agree to attend the birth on my terms. Maybe I was being unreasonable. Maybe I was dictating how the birth of our child should go. But the workers kept telling me that that was the role of the mother: to decide upon a birth plan. I didn't think that included deciding whether the father could be present, but they seemed to think otherwise.

"I don't know if I should have Gene or my mum at the birth."

"That's up to you, but do you think it's a good idea to have Gene there?" asked Lisa.

"I always assumed he would be there."

"Well, we have seen no change in his behaviour since you left. If anything, he's been more controlling since you got here."

"What do you mean?"

"He gets you to come into town pregnant with Hope, so he can guilt you into giving him money."

"It's so he can see Hope."

"He hasn't even tried to arrange contact."

"We see each other anyway."

"And you suffer abuse so he can do it."

I never really thought of Gene's behaviour as abuse; more that he happened to be disgruntled about living alone that day, or agitated about his lack of money, or resentful because I'd kept his child from him. They were all valid reasons for his responses. Like Gene always said: he had the right to be upset. His upset just felt a lot to me like violent rage.

I thought about the last time I'd seen him when he'd made a scene in town. He'd described himself as "upset" that time.

"Why are you angry with me?" I'd asked him after twenty minutes of silence and a refusal to hug me back.

"I'm not angry – I'm upset. I got the fucking right to be upset, don't I? Go on – tell me I don't," he taunted me.

I wouldn't dare do that; it was asking for trouble.

"Don't I have the right to be upset too?" I asked.

"For fucking what? You don't got the right to shit. You lost the right to feel upset when you walked out of the house. I can't believe you walked out while I was at work. You kissed me goodbye and told me you'd see me later. You knew you were fucking lying to me."

I looked at the ground; I had nothing to use in self-defence and I knew I'd have to make it up to him somehow. Hopefully if I had him at the birth, seeing his second daughter being born would be momentous enough to wipe his memory of all slights committed by me.

I returned to the present moment and looked Lisa in the face.

"I think I'm going to have Gene at the birth."

"Ok, as long as you feel safe with him there. If you do, make sure the hospital staff know you're in a refuge before he arrives."

I was tired of having to inform every professional that I lived in a refuge. I felt like *Hester Prynne*, but instead of a scarlet letter, I carried a temporary address that had to be written on everything that mattered. Everyone seemed to know what that address meant without me telling them.

I'd had an appointment at the doctor's surgery a while before, and as he'd been printing off the prescription for my Seroquel, he'd made a point of telling me that where I was staying was no place for a child. How he knew that without visiting it, I had no idea, but I took it as a signal that I had to get out before the baby came.

∎∎

That week I made another visit to the doctor. I needed to ask them to support my claim for one of my sickness benefits. It was up for renewal, and it couldn't have happened at a worse moment. My mental health was in a sad state, I was a month away from giving birth and I didn't have a home of my own.

Sadly, the GP didn't seem moved by my circumstances. She bombarded me with questions, demanding to know why I was claiming benefits. She scrolled through my entire medical history as if she didn't believe what I was saying.

"How long have you been on this benefit for?"

"Since 2012."

I looked around the room. It was decorated with family photos: photos displaying her own sons' academic achievements, and plaques that revealed her own.

"Do you have a degree?"

"Yeah, in French."

"Have you used it?"

"I did after uni, but things have gone downhill since then."

"Where did you study?"

"Glasgow."

"Why did you come home?"

"Because I was too unwell to stay there."

"You know," she said, leaning across her desk, her silver, engraved ballpoint hanging loosely between her fingers. "You can't just sit around doing nothing forever."

She gave me a pretend smile: one that hurt me more than a thousand scowls.

"I'm about to give birth, I have Bipolar Disorder and I'm living in a refuge."

"Well, you're wasting your life."

She scribbled her signature on the page in front of her.

"Try and get off them," she said, pushing the paper across the desk to me.

"Thanks," I said, walking from her office. I felt so beaten down I didn't know how I was still walking.

I got back to the refuge and I phoned Gene for support. Every professional that was meant to support me pushed me back into his arms and strengthened my reliance upon him for emotional help. Gene, as always, said the words I needed to hear. He gave me my fix, until the next time he kicked me.

Chapter Twenty-Two

"You didn't even let me go with you to find out the sex of our fucking daughter."

"I wanted you to come."

"Well, then why did you stop me? Fucking bullshit, man. You can't take that shit back."

"I was afraid you'd make a scene like at the first scan."

Gene and I were talking on the phone. Otherwise, I wouldn't have had the bravery to be so honest with him, for fear of him publicly firing off. I stood up less and less to Gene these days. His temper was more explosive than it had ever been. It had been unpredictable and violent in the house, but now there were no constraints on it; he had nothing left to lose. Part of Gene had always reigned his rage in, when he knew he'd pushed it too far, he'd make me promises again. But Gene had become less afraid to freely speak his mind; he no longer risked driving me out of the house – I had already left. But he still had me right where he wanted me.

"That wasn't my fucking fault – you were the one that started shit at that appointment. And you get to decide I don't see my fucking daughter? She ain't just yours. And if you try and keep her from me, you'll be fucking sorry."

"I'm not going to try and keep her from you."

"You already have. She barely fucking knows me."

"That isn't true. I meet up with you several times a week."

"I should have her on weekends."

"Well, I told you if you want to arrange that, you just have to contact social services."

Gene did a sour cackle.

"What the fuck? You should be dropping her round here and picking her up."

"I'm not allowed."

"Says who?"

"The workers. Because I'm in a refuge, if you want to see her unsupervised you have to organise it with social services."

"She's my fucking daughter."

"We're in a refuge."

"And whose fault is that?"

"I don't know," I started to cry. I couldn't be sure, but it suddenly felt like it was entirely mine.

"You listen too much to what other people tell you to think. You're weak-minded."

I couldn't even disagree, I knew Gene was right. My mind did feel weak; like it was falling apart as we spoke, physically breaking apart from all the stress placed on it.

"I don't want to do the wrong thing and lose Hope."

"You know, you could have lost Hope by now if I'd made the phone call. I've got all the recordings, the videos, the pictures – I could have her taken away in a minute."

I knew I'd better try to soothe Gene's temper; if I didn't, I might lose my daughter for good. Gene enraged was like an unhappy drug dealer; if you didn't cool him down quickly, he might kill you. Or so it felt to me. But I was prone to being melodramatic, so I was likely overplaying the situation in my mind.

"I'll bring her to see you more often."

"I want to see her every fucking day I ain't working."

"Ok."

I knew that meant a large proportion of life's days.

"Call social services and sort this shit out. Find out what we got to do so we can be under the one roof."

"Ok."

I felt sick thinking of lifting the phone to them, but I had to if I wanted to stave off Gene's hungry temper.

"Call me as soon as you're done."

"Ok."

"Hey? I love you."

"I love you," I said, crying.

"We'll get this shit sorted and we'll be a family again."

That was still exactly what I wanted.

"Hey?"

"Yeah?"

"What date are you due?"

"The 16th July."

"Right. Tell me the minute you're in labour."

"You're coming to the birth?"

"Fucking right I'm coming. I missed the scan, I ain't missing my fucking daughter being born too."

We'd discussed names before I'd left, settling on Alice for a girl. It was the name of Gene's Gram; his favourite relative.

"Are you still calling her Alice?"

"Yeah."

"Savoyard or your name?"

"Savoyard."

"Good. Make sure I'm on the birth certificate too."

"Gene?" I asked, tentatively.

"What, babe?"

"Are you going to be angry at the birth?"

"What the fuck kind of a question is that? I'll help. I ain't going for you though."

"Why do you keep saying that?"

"Because you need to hear it. I'm going for my fucking daughter. Make sure you know that. I ain't there for you."

"How can you say that to me?"

"You've left me out of everything else."

"Well, can't you say you're there for me too?"

"I'd be lying."

"Well, I don't want you there if you aren't there for me too."

"You're a selfish twat."

I hung up the phone. We were back to square one.

Chapter Twenty-Three

I lay in bed, dreaming about the ways I could end my life: jumping into the waves that hid the lethally sharp rocks beneath them, overdosing on my medication, jumping into traffic. But I had a baby growing inside me and whether I lived or not wasn't my choice to make. I was carrying a life that was important even if mine wasn't. I closed my eyes instead, turning out the light and praying that I would die naturally in my sleep instead.

I was only weeks away from giving birth and I needed a sign of hope. I had to take finding a house into my own hands; I could no longer entrust the Housing Executive with it. I'd find somewhere within my budget; somewhere where I didn't have to combat damp or re-plaster the walls. If I didn't like how the place was decorated, Gene could always take care of that once he moved in. I still wasn't going to tell him I was finding a house of my own; if I did, he'd want to know where it was, and if he knew where it was, he might come over. It seemed a ridiculous thought to have: that I couldn't face the thought of Gene knowing where I lived, but that I wanted him to move in with me. Those two opposing considerations battled one another in a maddening struggle in my mind. Neither of the options felt achievable: I couldn't keep Gene away, but I couldn't allow him to draw too near to me either. If I kept him at arm's length, but within my sights, I could hold onto the hope I had for reconciliation without committing myself to a life of punishment. When Gene proved once and for all that things would be different, I'd take the leap and let him move in.

I searched for houses in Belfast. I was finished with the town I had stayed in. It had been a pleasant getaway, outside the refuge at least, but not a place where I planned to become a permanent fixture. Hope would grow up in the town we had originally intended to live in and everything would be as it should have been: no money worries, no conflict, no abuse.

I settled on a perfectly ordinary-looking house: one where I could afford the rent, but that wasn't too far away from our first home. When I pictured Gene and me together, I could still only imagine us in that house. I imagined the algae removed from the decking, potted plants shooting up when Hope would have her first playhouse. We would have barbecues in the summer and laugh over stories we shared. We'd scoff at how we'd used to behave, in the past, before I'd been properly medicated and before Gene had got used to ehis new job in a new country. It was years behind us and we sat contentedly together, with our realised dreams the rope that tightened our bond.

In my mind, I walked indoors to the kitchen where I cooked the dinner I knew Gene would love. He loved my cottage pie every time I made it now; I had got the proportions just right. I didn't make amateur cooking mistakes anymore. Hope followed me inside and swung a leg over the pink painted saddle of her rocking horse: the one Daddy finished to make Mummy happy. I didn't have to worry about Gene taking Hope from me; I was perfectly stable on new medication and we were happier than I'd even known possible.

I snapped out of my daydream and filled up with anxiety when I had to face up to reality again. Moving house when I was eight months pregnant was the last thing I felt like doing, but I'd move into a skip if it meant escaping the refuge before the baby came. Everything in the house was so regimented; we had to fill out risk assessments if we stubbed a toe, the rules were glued to every wall, I'd been told off for walking too quickly up the stairs, I was growing weary of the weekly room searches. I had no corner in the world that felt like it belonged to me, and the workers noted down my every movement. I resented their heavy notebook that was filled with titbits from the lives of every resident, as if our right to privacy had been entirely removed. They were tight on confidentiality, but within the walls of their office, I knew everything was discussed. I had a week left to wait before I could move into the new house. I spent that time packing up my room. Everything was waiting in boxes long before it was going to be transported. I had slight reservations about the house, but I crushed those feelings before they had a chance to turn into thoughts. I had no time to look around; if I wanted to have a home of my own to bring the baby back to, I'd have to act quickly. There was no time to procrastinate over the small print.

The house was a mid-terrace: beige and bleak looking. It had small windows that let in little light. The road had a dreary feel to it; there were no potted plants and no efforts to dress the street up. Everything was uniform and functional. The houses were old ones, dating from a century before. It didn't look like much work had been done to the place since, but I could make it look nice. It wasn't damp, so, any other problems, I could work with. It was already furnished, so I didn't have to worry about that, at least. The letterbox was taped shut with duct tape which I found a bit disconcerting. The landlord said the last residents had got fed up with the volume of flyers delivered.

I told the workers I was leaving and slipped out without much in the way of congratulations. I knew they thought I'd made another impulsive decision, but I was eight months pregnant, so they understood the decision I'd made. I found it hard to feel much of an attachment to the people I'd lived with for four months; they were still adversaries to my marriage. If they'd told me before I'd arrived that I couldn't return home without social services intervention, I never would have left home. And I still resented them for that. They helped me, but also controlled my actions; it was a set-up I had grown used to in life. It only reinforced my belief that I couldn't trust another human being. Everything offered in kindness was undermined by the action that followed it. Threats sounded the same to me, whether they were coming from Gene or from the refuge workers. Pure goodness didn't exist in this world; it was up to me to choose the lesser of two evils, and I knew that was Gene.

Ok, Gene had his bad moments, but overall, he adored me, he protected me, he created distance between me and untrustworthy characters. None of that could be debated. I needed that level of protection in my life; I was an easy target, and if there wasn't someone looking out for me, I knew I wouldn't last long. I would make my new house as homely as it could be and by the time I'd finished, right before the baby was due, Gene would offer the sincere promise of change I knew he was capable of. He'd realise how much he valued his family: more than being right, more than missing work, more than controlling everything. My heart told me that Gene loved us too much to ever risk losing us for good. But I didn't know then that hearts are less reliable than heads.

Chapter Twenty-Four

I got unpacked in the new house, but it didn't feel like home. It was uncannily quiet. Music wasn't enough to fill the void. Living in the refuge had felt like living in a different realm, where in some way, real life couldn't touch you. Everything felt temporary with refuge living. I'd thought I'd hated that, but permanence was something that now terrified me. With permanence, came the need to make final decisions, and I wasn't ready to make any of them. So, I didn't tell Gene I'd moved into my own house. I continued meeting up with him as I had when I'd been in the hostel and pretended to walk the old way to my train, before turning back to go to the bus stop. My bus stop was the one next to Gene's now. I couldn't tell him that, so I waited long enough to let his bus leave and then sneaked back to get a later bus. I knew it was a ridiculous way to behave. How could I repair my relationship with my husband if I couldn't even be open with him? That was when I realised, I didn't trust Gene. I needed him, but I didn't trust him. That feeling was only reinforced by the subsequent meetings we had in town.

I met up with Gene at our usual spot. He'd got there first. I preferred when he arrived first, because I had time to prepare myself for the surge of fear that came when he caught sight of me. If he arrived second, he got to surprise me, and I no longer liked surprises; I'd learnt they were never anything good.

"Hey," Gene said, without stopping walking.

I walked beside him, wherever he was taking me to.

"Babe, I need you to swing by the ATM and loan me some money."

"How much?"

"A hundred."

"What for?"

"Babe, I ain't ate in a fucking week. I can't even afford to buy toilet paper for the house and it's my turn."

"I don't know if I can afford it."

"So, I'll just starve."

"No, I don't want you to starve. Why don't I come with you to the shop and help you pick up what you need?"

Gene shook his head.

"I ain't carrying that shit home from the center. If you get me the money, I'll swing by the store on my way home."

"Why a hundred?"

"Babe, I got to eat, got to pay my phone and I owe a dude I live with a pack of smokes."

"Fine."

I languidly pulled my debit card from my purse, hoping that in the process, it would strike Gene that he was asking a lot of me. He still hadn't given me a penny for food for Hope, for baby items, for the double pram we'd ordered together before I'd left. I was due to pick it up and I knew he wouldn't be footing the bill. I'd just paid a deposit, first month's rent and filled an oil tank; my bank balance wasn't exactly soaring. But I couldn't let Gene go hungry. Even if I managed to say no now, I knew he'd wear me down. I'd rather starve than let Gene go without. I still loved him more than I loved myself. I handed him the money and he pocketed it in one swift movement. At least I knew he'd be spending it on items for basic living; he wasn't using it for anything inessential.

"Thanks, babe. Man, I'm hungry, can we get something to eat?"

"Where do you want to go?"

"Want to grab a burger?"

We walked to the closest food chain and Gene waited with me in the queue. I withdrew my purse from my bag without question; that was the way of the world: Gene suffered, and I paid up.

"What would you like?"

"You know what I get, babe."

"Ok."

"Hey, get me a coffee too. Oh, and don't forget the ice."

I placed the order, hesitating over the details. My confidence levels had dipped so badly I could barely look the server in the face. I was questioning my every word, the volume of my voice, the extra items I'd inevitably failed to mention. I stood like a zombified version of myself, robotically reaching for my bank card. I wouldn't dare ask Gene to cover it; I knew he needed every penny I'd given him. I punched my pin into the machine and gathered up our items on the tray.

"Don't forget napkins, babe, and straws, and salt. I'll grab some ketchup."

Gene waited for me to select a table and then chose one for us anyway. We sat down together, and I saw the reflection of our family in the mirrors that tiled the walls. We could have been mistaken for a conventional family: eating together on a regular lunch date, chatting about nothing remarkable, but nothing traumatic either.

Gene took a few large bites from his burger, mopping sauce from his mouth.

"Is your burger good?"

"It's alright. Tastes like a fucking burger."

"How about your coffee?"

"I ain't tried it yet. Hey, hand me the ice, would you, babe?"

I took a few uncomfortable bites from my own. I felt guilty eating in front of Gene like I was rubbing in the fact that food wasn't a luxury for me.

"After this, I want to go to the toy store, get Hope something."

"Can you afford to?"

"I want to get my daughter something."

"Sorry."

"You can come with me and she can take it home with her. Hey, did you like the puppy daddy got you to play with?" he cooed.

Her eyes brightened when she looked at him, but she rarely smiled anymore. She looked at him with a strange, faint kind of recognition; like she'd once known him but struggled to place where or when. I wondered why, since he did feature in her life; albeit in friendly rather than a fatherly role. Gene shone some of his attention on her and she seemed to bloom in front of him like a springtime plant. He gave her short bursts of his attention, and then withdrew it completely, so the moments he gave to her seemed more precious than if they'd flowed continuously.

Hope was shoved back into the pram, so we could perform the tour of the city that Gene wanted to make. He always had an itinerary of where he wanted to go to, and we needed to check all items off the list before he could relax. Town wasn't a place for a baby; there were no playgrounds, no soft play cafes, nowhere for Hope to stretch out and crawl around. I knew our trips into Belfast were boring for Hope, but it was the easiest, and safest meeting point.

I followed Gene to the toy store. He perused the aisles, looking for a toy that sang songs and lit up; Gene always wanted toys that were flashy, and in your face; nothing basic. He found a toy karaoke machine, with a microphone and keyboard attached to it. I mentally subtracted twenty-five pounds from the cash I had given him and wondered how long he'd make the rest last. Based on experience, it would last a day or two and then Gene would need more. At least he still had his job, or so I thought.

Chapter Twenty-Five

"How's work going?"

"I quit, babe."

"What? Why?"

"There wasn't shit left to do there. It was costing me more money to get there than I was making."

"Well, how will you live?"

"I'll get another job, babe."

"Doing what?"

"I don't know. Hey – when you get home, look up painting jobs for me."

"Have you been looking?"

"Not yet. I ain't had time. You're better at that stuff than me."

I felt ill with panic. What if Gene didn't find another job? What if I had to fund him forever? Or worse, what if he lost his visa because of it? What if he had to return to America? The thought alone was unbearable; I'd have to find him another job.

A week passed, and none of the painters Gene called were looking for help. Everyone seemed to have gone into business themselves, and they were loath to share out their workload with anyone else. Without a work van or even a license, Gene was at a marked disadvantage. No one was going to hire him if he couldn't even transport a ladder. We had to look elsewhere.

"What else could you work as?"

"Anything, babe – stacking shelves, maintenance, manual labour."

I applied for every job that fitted that description. One cropped up, and Gene was offered an interview, but it was five miles from where he lived and there was no bus in that direction. I hoped he would take it anyway. All he needed, was something to financially tide him over, until a local job presented itself. It was in a hotel; Gene would work as a caretaker and help with any maintenance jobs that needed done. I hoped it would involve as little human contact as Gene desired. He just needed something minimum wage: something that would allow him to cover his small rent payment and afford food without having to rely on me to fund him.

Luck was on my side that day; Gene agreed to attend the interview. He decided to get the bus as far as it would take him and walk the remainder of the way.

"I'll get up early and walk there if I got to. We want the same things, babe. All I've ever wanted is you and our babies. I'll do what I got to do but promise me one thing?"

"What?"

"Don't lie to me. If you don't want to be with me, fucking tell me. Don't make me wait around for no reason. Because I'll go back to America if you've no intention of us being together."

"I do want to be together."

And I meant that statement with all my heart.

Chapter Twenty-Six

Gene was a week into his new job and things were going well; he was going every day, at least. The pay wasn't what Gene considered to be adequate, but he had few enough expenses to make it workable. I think on some level, he still blamed me for finding him a job that was beneath him. Gene should have been in a managerial role: one where he got to voice his opinions and make sure the work was done to his high standards. That's what he'd trained me to believe anyway.

"Do you like it there?"

"I don't fucking hate it. The journey fucking sucks."

"Sorry."

"It's alright – I'll find something else."

"Are you going to stay there long?"

"Until I find something else."

It was starting to feel like the "something else" Gene strove to find was nothing more than a mirage.

"What do you have to do?"

"Just maintenance work, babe. I don't know how to answer that."

I always wondered why Gene struggled so much to answer what I thought were direct questions. It gave me the sense that I was phrasing things in a needlessly complicated way, or that I took too much time asking inane questions for his liking.

"How long does it take to get there?"

"Couple of hours."

"Do you not get the bus into town anymore?"

"I can't afford that shit."

I thought about asking where the money I'd given him had gone, and how his tax rebate had drained away so quickly. But I knew that all that would do was incite his rage. You had to act inoffensive, but not uncaring with Gene. The only thing he hated more than when you caused offence was when you didn't react at all. No reaction was worse than a bad one. I'd learnt that by then, but it still hadn't registered with me why that might be the case.

"When do you get paid?"

"Next week. I'll just have to starve until then, I guess."

I thought about offering Gene money, but I knew he'd ask me for it anyway. If I could stall for a couple of days and wait for him to ask me first, I could figure out a budget to fit around it. If I paired back in every area, I could help Gene and still get by. I had already bought all the baby items I'd need. I'd had to repurchase them since I'd lost all Hope's hand-me-downs in the abandoned house. I'd been thinking of items that were important to me since I'd sent the key back. I knew they wouldn't still be sitting there. Even if they had been, I didn't have the audacity to phone the agency and beg them to let me into the house to get them. I'd left Hope's ultrasound pictures in a book I'd put them in to keep them pressed flat. I'd left the first little dress Gene had ever bought her in Flint: the one he'd got the day I'd told him I was pregnant. I'd left my original Kindle behind and my camera filled with all my pre-Gene photos. I'd left jewellery behind that my late grandmother had left me, and other inexpensive items that couldn't be replaced by any amount of money.

"What do you want to do?"

"Want to get me a coffee?"

I nodded and started pushing the pram in the direction of what had become Gene's and my coffee place. We walked in and sat down. I knew the staff by sight, but I'd never exchanged more than a coffee order with them. I still felt like they knew us intimately; they'd witnessed enough of our heated exchanges.

I got Gene's coffee: largest available size, black, cup of ice on the side and carried it to the table.

"Babe, would you get a highchair? My shoulder is fucking killing me."

"Ok."

I felt resentful that he asked me to get it on top of everything else, but I tried to suppress my reaction; I couldn't say anything negative without looking like I didn't care about Gene's pain. I dragged the chair over, struggling to carry it with my enlarged belly. I only had a couple of weeks to go and I was sure I wasn't meant to be carrying anything bulky, but no one else was going to carry the burden. I set the highchair down, untangled the straps and transferred Hope to it, digging in the nappy bag for her snacks and the wipes. Finally, I sat down. Gene had already half-finished his coffee.

"I got to ask you a favour, baby."

"What?"

"I got to borrow some money. Once I get paid, that ain't going to be an issue no more."

"How much?"

"Sixty bucks."

"Ok. Can I give it to you in a few days?"

"I need it today, baby."

"Well, I might need a few days to get it."

Gene gave me a look like he didn't believe me. He knew I was always careful with money and never went into the red.

"I need it today, babe. I got to pay a bill in the house."

"I thought your bills were included?"

"The electricity is – not the heating, babe."

"Well, can your landlord wait for it?"

"No, he's already asked me for it several times. Says he's coming round later for it."

"Ok."

"I'll walk with you to the cash machine after this, babe. I promise I won't ask you again. Once I get paid, everything will be alright."

I nodded, appreciatively. I was so grateful to Gene for telling me the words I longed to hear: that I wouldn't be solely responsible for our survival, that everything would become less strenuous, that we would finally have the happiness we'd had in Flint.

"I promise you baby – we'll be together. You're my whole world."

Gene's voice cracked, and his eyes filled with tears. There was something about the way he talked when he cried that reminded me of a toddler with a grazed knee and it was so heart-breaking I'd do anything to make it stop; even if it brought about my own undoing. I feared that I was stronger than Gene underneath it all. I was fragile, but I also knew my own mind and how close to suicide I was. Not knowing where Gene's upper stress limits lay filled me with the fear that taking his own life was a constant possibility. I could never let that happen. If it ever did, it would be something I couldn't survive.

"It's a nice day out," said Gene.

He seemed to be in good form again: his usual relaxed, unruffled self, without the angry edge. We smiled at each other, squinting to make eye contact through the sun that set our faces aglow, and I wasn't afraid anymore.

Chapter Twenty-Seven

"Hey, I saw you, walking around," said Gene, taking a sip from the coffee I'd just bought him.

"What?"

I tried to sound unflustered, but knew I wasn't putting on good front. Hopefully he'd attribute my anxiety to my mental health.

"I'm just fucking with you: I don't know where the fuck you live, babe."

"Oh."

I pretended to laugh, my heart still racing so fast it thumped like a stampede of springbok.

"I don't know why you won't just tell me where you live."

"I can't."

"Do you think I'm going to show up at the door? I ain't going to do that," Gene smirked.

I knew he thought I was being silly; I thought I was too, but something intuitive prevented me giving myself away.

"Is the town you live in nice?" he asked. It wasn't like him to express such a pleasant interest in something. It made me wary.

"Yeah, I like it."

"Where's it close to?"

"The sea."

"Everywhere in this fucking country is close to the sea."

"I never thought about it like that before."

"So, you ain't never going to tell me where you live?"

"I don't know," I said, looking down at the foam pattern on the top of my latte. My eyes traced its shapes and I tried to avoid further aggravating Gene.

Avoiding looking Gene in the face when you were withholding information from him was the best tack to take. If you made eye contact with him, his eyes seemed to read whatever you were thinking without you having to disclose it. I believed he could read my thoughts; Gene was all-knowing. Even if I didn't tell him where I lived, I suspected he somehow knew. He always knew the wrong people who had the right answers to any question he had to ask.

"You know, I know where you live anyway?"

"You do?" I said, searching his eyes and trying to stay calm.

I felt like bolting for the door with Hope before he had a chance to kidnap us. If he'd wanted to, he could have done it. I knew that, but simultaneously, I believed that he'd never do that to me. It was just my paranoia talking.

"I have a rough idea."

"How did you find out?"

Gene shrugged. "It's a small place – it ain't hard to figure that shit out."

I tried to remember if I'd ever made any allusion to the place that would have given away its location. Although we'd spoken hundreds of times since I'd left, I didn't believe I had. I'd been so careful not to. Someone must have told him, or Gene must have followed me without me knowing. I knew it was something he could do if he felt like it. It wasn't a question of whether Gene was capable of it; it was a question of whether he cared enough to bother.

"Where do I live then?"

"Nah, it don't matter."

"No – tell me," I needed to know how much danger I was in.

He said the name of a town.

Every muscle in my body seemed to seize up. He was wrong, but he wasn't far from being right either. I was grateful I wasn't in the refuge anymore.

"Who told you where I lived?"

"I don't fucking know, babe. I just guessed."

There was a glimmer in his eye that suggested it hadn't just been a random guess; someone was supplying him with information about my whereabouts, and it was only a matter of time until he found me in my new house. We lived only streets away from each other, and Gene liked to walk; often and far. Surely, he would stumble upon me before too long? I'd have to come up with a plausible excuse for why I was in the area. A friend that lived there? He wouldn't believe that. He knew I had no friends. An appointment? He knew my social worker was performing home visits. I'd come up with something that night. Worrying about it while I was with Gene just looked ultra-suspicious.

"Is that where the shelter is at?" Gene asked, smiling and leaning in.

"No, I don't live anywhere near there."

I took a sip from my coffee and refused to meet his eyes with my own.

Chapter Twenty-Eight

I didn't see Gene again before the birth; not intentionally at least. Once he got his bill paid, he returned to his volatile self: the person I'd grown more used to than the original Gene I'd loved. Maybe I loved him as deeply; I'd certainly do whatever I could to dampen his rage. If I kept him happy, the old Gene would come back to stay. He still visited from time to time, but never stayed long-term.

We'd had another argument about how the birth would play out. I still hadn't completed my birth plan and hadn't stated definitively who my birth partner would be. I was still equally torn between Gene and my mum. If Gene came, I'd feel happier. If my mum came, I'd feel safer. Choosing between those two outcomes was a lot more problematic than I would have imagined it to be. Happiness had always come first for me; even if it meant creating problems later. But I was getting more and more used to the peace I had when Gene wasn't with me; I still found the uneventful achingly dull, but I had caught a glimpse of what living without fear might be like. I knew the cocoon of the refuge wasn't a true reflection of life; it was an artificial mode of existence. I never felt wholly safe in it: not from residents' habits, not from social services, not from risk assessments, but when I was there, Gene couldn't harm me, at least not in person anyway. Now that I was living in a house of my own, there was no real protection in place.

The workers had offered to put a protection plan together before I'd left. They'd offered to alert the police to my circumstances and to the identity of my abuser, so if an emergency call was ever placed, they'd prioritise the call. I didn't want to draw attention to myself like that. More importantly, I didn't want to admit to the police that Gene might be a danger to me. I'd just downplay it all, keep to myself and stay secretive about my whereabouts and everything would work out ok. The police had already been informed of the times Gene had grabbed me by the throat, no thanks to my social worker. But that had been reported months before, and there was no recent evidence that he wasn't a changed man.

I had a worker assigned to my file who also did home visits. She called by my new house to meet Hope and me. I wanted to be as candid about everything as I had been with the refuge workers I'd known, but I couldn't afford to confide in anyone else. Her file would stay blank as far as new incidents were concerned. No matter what Gene did to me, I would remain loyal this time. We would rebuild our dream of a family and this time we wouldn't allow anyone's prying noses to poke into our problems.

The lady made a smiling entrance and made herself comfortable on my sofa.

"Aoife, nice to meet you. I'm Sara."

"Hi, nice to meet you."

I wouldn't look her in the face; I couldn't bring myself to get to know one more person; or more precisely, for them to get to know me.

"How are you settling in? Your house looks lovely."

She looked at me keenly, like she expected me to be happy with my new circumstances. The house was furnished, with a few of my knick-knacks on display, but it was far from the ideal I'd had in mind when I'd stood at the church pulpit.

"Ok."

I looked at the TV screen, wishing I could tell her the meeting was over and it was time to go home. Hope babbled to her and she seemed to make conversation much more easily with her than with me. She took her clipboard from her handbag: a symbolic gesture I shrank away from. She was going to put my personal details to paper and then file them with all the other sad human stories she kept in her office cabinet.

"Do you still see your ex-husband?"

I wondered why the workers hadn't communicated any of my history to her. It was like starting from scratch and the second time round, I knew better than to share too eagerly.

"Yeah, we meet up for coffee."

"Does he come to the house?" she leaned forward in her seat with what I perceived to be a gasp.

"No, he's never been."

"Does he know where you live?"

"No."

"Good."

Gene and I weren't getting along, and the last time I'd spoken to him, I'd left with a bitter taste in my mouth and in my soul, but I still hated hearing someone else implying he was a danger to me. I was able to keep my wits about me and assess when I was in real danger. With Gene, it was a different kind of danger. He was still my husband, so the situation couldn't compare to one involving a stranger.

I hurried through her questions, giving the bare minimum as answers. She announced that she'd be calling out once fortnightly, but I wouldn't be offering any information than I'd already given. I felt like telling her she was wasting her time and to sign me off, but a quiet voice inside told me not to do that.

I closed the door behind her and the house was deathly quiet. Her company was almost preferable to being alone. I was no longer used to living in a house with no noise about it. In the refuge, there was constant sound: cycles of laundry, TVs blaring, laughter in the halls. Maybe a home of my own was over-rated; I wasn't yet ready to face my thoughts alone. Every time I had a negative thought in the refuge, I could talk to one of the workers, and they knew me well by then. Phoning the helpline or ringing my new key worker didn't feel as safe to me. I turned on my music and decided to get Hope and me ready and get out of the place.

I packed Hope into the pram and set off to explore the new area: it was only a mile or two from where we'd lived before, but I didn't know a thing about it. The footpaths were dirty, covered in cigarette butts and dog poo. The residents of the street seemed to take less pride in maintaining their doorsteps than in my last street. It felt more like Flint, but I felt in much more danger than I had then, and I couldn't quite put my finger on the reason for that. Maybe it was walking alone in a new area; just myself, my baby and my bump. There was no one beside me offering the protection Gene did. But I was as terrified of bumping into him as I was of bumping into a random attacker. My line of thinking made no sense. I was in a state of perpetual confusion; suspended between longing for my partner and the terror that he produced in me.

I scouted out the new facilities in our area. There were several charity shops I'd never visited before. I knew one of them was good; Gene had told me about it. It was one of his local ones too. I walked into the shop, trying to avoid drawing attention to myself when the pram rattled through the door. I scanned the room for danger. No one I knew was there. But I was sure they could sense what was wrong with me. I was paranoid, and no one could be trusted. They were all watching me with wary eyes, judging me from afar. I thought they could hear my thoughts; that they heard them aloud like they were projected across the room by loudspeaker. But I was just acting "crazy" again.

I looked around as quickly as I could. I wanted to put in the days as quickly as possible, but they dragged slower than a music sheet of nothing but rests. I'd grown used to the town I'd been living in. So much so that I didn't know how to start over. I had found ways to fill my time in the refuge. I hadn't been happy; hardly content, but I'd been able to put in the day in little ways. Now time was empty and there was a blank space in my head: one that allowed it to fill up with unwanted thoughts. I thought about suicide, about self-harm, about hospitalisation, and there was no light entertainment in the air to keep those thoughts in check. I was too far into my pregnancy to venture further afield. I walked the same circuit each day: the library, the supermarket, the charity shops. There were no parks, no greenery, no sea to speak health into my thoughts.

One day I was walking down the same street, and I saw Gene. He was walking along the street at the end of mine: twenty feet from me. I froze on the spot, waiting for him to turn to me. Gene didn't commit human errors; not even the slightest one, like failing to spot someone in the street. He always noticed everything, all the time. My mind raced: how was I going to explain what I was doing there? Would he follow me home? Would he insist I let him into the house? Would something bad happen?

But Gene was my husband; the person who knew me better than anyone else, the only person capable of making me feel at home in this strange world. How could I react so fearfully about him? He was in his music zone; he was wearing the headphones I'd got him for Christmas. They must have blocked out all sound around him, and for some reason, he didn't turn his head to meet my gaze. I wanted to run away, but in equal measure, I wanted to run up to him and embrace him. I was so happy to see his perfect face. I wanted the comfort of one of his rough bear hugs, for him to reassure me that I could make it on my own in my new house. I couldn't speak, I couldn't move, I couldn't react; I just stood until Gene was in the distance and it was too late to catch him. Then I turned away and walked home.

Chapter Twenty-Nine

Things began to kick off in my street. The twelfth of July was approaching, and the neighbours were getting ready for the usual festivities, but in my fragile state, the sounds were enough to invite hallucinations into the room. The parties started with afternoon drinking, rowdy laughter and yells; they ended with street fights, doors being pounded and the sound of glass shattering. I couldn't tell if they were beating my door down, but I could hear them doing it. Whether it was really taking place, or my mind was playing tricks on me, I couldn't tell. But I was too terrified to sleep. I lay in bed, my eyes glued to the door, waiting for Gene to break in, waiting for one of the neighbours to kick my door in, waiting for death, and in a way, praying for it too.

The noises carried on throughout the night. I knew I had to get out of the house. But, how? I had just signed a one-year lease, filled the oil tank, moved all my belongings. Moving wasn't an option, or so I thought until I spoke to my mental health social worker. She rang me the next morning, as if my fear had travelled to her on the air waves.

"How are you?"

"Not good."

"What's wrong?"

"I don't know if this house isn't safe or if I'm imagining it."

"What's happening?"

"Drunk partying in the street, fighting and breaking things. Gene is also living down the road from me."

"That wouldn't help you with everything you've been through."

"I don't even know what's happening and what's in my head."

"Do you want to come in for an appointment and discuss what we can do?"

"Yes please."

I met her that day in the clinic. I assumed she'd think I was over-reacting, but she looked at me with sincere concern. I followed her into the office and sat beside her; no desk between us. Maybe she was trustworthy, and I'd branded her the opposite for reporting Gene to the police. I knew she had a "duty of care." I'd heard those words more times in the last year than I'd heard my own name. But some part of me couldn't forgive her for making the abuse that occurred between Gene and me official. It had gone from hearsay to making an appearance on a police report; one that would be tucked away somewhere forever; probably never to be read again, but existing nonetheless.

"Do you think you should move out?"

"I don't know where I would go. It took me so long to find my own house and now I'm there, I hate it."

"Well, sometimes the things we think are right for us aren't when we get them."

"I don't have anywhere to go anyway."

"Could you go back to the refuge?"

"I doubt it. Nothing has happened."

"Well, you're living close to your abuser."

"But he doesn't know that."

"It's not going to take him long to find out."

I hated the fact she made Gene sound like a villain. I wanted to storm out of her office, "cussing her out" as Gene would say, but I needed her help. And Gene wasn't exactly offering me everything I'd dreamed of on a plate. I stifled my reaction.

"I thought I hated living there, but I felt safer there than I do now."

"It's because you're protected there. No one knows where you live, and the police are on standby if anything happens."

I felt ridiculous for feeling so much at risk, but I simultaneously regretted not requesting my house be flagged on their system. If anything had kicked off, they would have been straight on the scene, but I couldn't betray Gene like that. I'd already betrayed him in every way conceivable. If I had done that, I would have been painting Gene as the attacker and myself as the victim, and that would have been lying. Our relationship wasn't that straightforward. Despite all the self-doubt I felt, I had to get back to safety, so I allowed my social worker to take charge of the situation. There was a room available in the refuge and the workers would welcome me back that day. My dream of having a family home to come home to with my newborn no longer existed, so it was no use playing house somewhere that was only a building. At least in the refuge, I'd have emotional support and childcare; two things I would have been lost without. I had less luck with my landlord; he wasn't pleased with my decision. When there's money on the line, people tend to be less understanding, but I couldn't afford to waste time worrying about that, so I let him keep my deposit and got my things moved out of there before he could bin them.

My parents helped me move back into the refuge. They were less unhappy about it than I'd imagined them being. The workers moved my room to the ground floor: a single bedroom smaller than the last one but with an adjoining bathroom, and more importantly, no flights of stairs. I had no idea how I would manage with two babies in that house. I still had to carry Hope most of the time. Even simple tasks like strapping them into the double buggy would require preparation; I'd have to transfer them in relays. When I pictured myself having two babies, I didn't ever picture bliss. I pictured myself struggling to the point of suicide. The workers acted like it would only require a simple readjustment, that it wouldn't be much different to what I was already doing. From my perspective, I was only barely managing, and I didn't have faith in my ability to do it on my own. Gene didn't help me develop any confidence in that area.

"We got to get this shit sorted. Line up some viewings, babe."

"I'm about to give birth."

"That's why I'm telling you to do it. You can't look after them two babies on your own."

On one level, I knew he was right; on another, his comment propelled me into proving him wrong. I'd show him I wasn't as incompetent as he believed me to be. Maybe then, he would finally have the respect for me I so badly craved.

"Make sure you tell me the minute you're in labour."

I went quiet.

"I need time to get to the hospital. Make sure you do it."

"I don't know."

"What don't you know?"

"Are you going to be nasty to me when I'm in labour?"

"I'll help."

"With the baby or with me?"

"Both."

"So, are you saying you'll be there for me?"

"No – I told you – the baby is the only reason I'm there. I ain't there for you – don't mean I won't help. But don't be misled about why I'm there."

"Why can't you just say you'll be there for me, so I feel supported?"

"You didn't let me come to any of the scans. You've prevented me being involved. I hardly see my daughter because of you."

"That isn't because of me."

"It is only because of you. You could have dropped her over here, but you chose not to."

"I didn't have a choice."

"Yes you did, and you fucking chose to keep her from me. I'll never forgive you for that."

"Never" seemed as final as a signature on our divorce papers. Gene and I could get back together, we could have more children, we could get a new home, but he would still never forgive me. That word gave me a feeling of strife. I could never relax so long as I knew Gene wouldn't forgive me. If we got back together, I'd forgive him for every one of my injuries, but I needed to know that would be something that was mutually granted. Until Gene showed me that he was prepared to start over, I couldn't make the slightest move towards him.

"I'll talk to you about the birth when you tell me you'll be there for me too."

"That's a threat."

"It's not – I just can't be that vulnerable when I know someone is in the room who doesn't want to be there for me."

"Well – I ain't lying to you."

I hung up the phone. I disconnected over half our calls. Frustration wasn't a word strong enough to convey how misunderstood I felt by Gene. It was strange that he could make me feel like he intuitively understood every one of my thoughts, irrational or not, but when he wanted to, he could make me feel equally unheard, cut off, disregarded. The workers told me I could have him at the birth if I wanted, but it had to be on my terms. I disagreed with their suggestion that I control events, but I knew I had to feel safe, or I couldn't allow him to enter that room.

Chapter Thirty

A week later, I went into labour. I made the phone call to my birth partner; the one I'd been dreading making. I'd been tussling day and night with my two options. I couldn't have both. If Gene was there, my mum would refuse to be there. If my mum was there, Gene would refuse with equal stubbornness. I had to arrive at a final decision, whether I wanted to or not.

The car arrived to transport me to the hospital and the workers passed me my hospital bag. I stepped into the car and almost hoped the rush hour would work against me getting there in time. My last birth had been so quick, I hoped the second might come even more hastily, preventing me from having a birth partner. I willed the contractions to build in intensity and frequency, but my body wasn't listening.

I got to the hospital, in pain and eager to find a bed. The nurse took my green folder from me and escorted me to a free bed. I waited alone behind the drawn curtain, waiting for my birth partner to arrive. I was getting panicky. I needed something to ease the pain; not in my belly – in my mind. The nurse gave me some gas and air, and I tried not to get worked up about everything; not knowing how the birth would pan out worried me less than not knowing how life would. I took slow and steady breaths from it and tried to slow my racing thoughts. Anxiety was growing inside me and transmuting into sickness. I vomited in the styrofoam container on the bedside table. The starched bedsheets felt uncomfortably taut beneath me, like a constrictive grip that threatened me with its ever-increasing pressure. I was in a hospital gown: one that left me on open view. I waited with only my worry as company until the bed curtain drew back.

"Hello, love."

My mum was in front of me with a bag of goodies: magazines, sweets, toiletries. She was prepared for a week's stay. It touched me: the things she'd remembered were things I hadn't even thought to pack for myself. She pulled a chair towards the bed and sat down. "How are you feeling?"

"Really anxious."

"Ok, just try and stay calm. It will all be over soon."

I hoped she was right; not just about the birth but about every kind of discomfort present in my life. She held my hand while I lay and breathed gas and air, staring at the ceiling. The lights were glaringly bright and the constant sounds of others' agitation around me were only serving to increase my own.

"Just try and relax, love."

My mum knew I was tense. She went to find a tea machine to get us both a warm drink. I was getting light contractions and I knew it was time to tell Gene. With my mum outside the ward, I knew it was the right time to make the phone call. She wouldn't have stopped me making it; but she wouldn't have encouraged it either. I picked up the phone, going to my recent calls. Gene was still always top of the list. It had been excruciating talking to him before I'd been brought in. I'd wanted to invite him to join me at the hospital, but fear prevented me doing it. I'd still had time to think about it, right up until I went into labour. But the time was here: the one for surety.

I clicked on Gene's name and the call connected. I listened, unable to breathe as each ring told me he wasn't there. The phone rang eight times and I disconnected it. I told myself he mustn't care enough to be there, or he would have been waiting for the moment, his finger resting on the answer button. Maybe that was too simple an excuse to make, but it helped me make my decision. I set my phone out of my reach and turned my attention back to my breathing. I was advancing towards active labour and I needed to stay calm and redirect my energy into my body. I would worry about Gene and his reactions later. I knew he'd punish me for not persisting with my phone calls until he answered, but I wasn't in any state to spend time considering that.

My mum returned to the bed, both hands holding cups of tea.

"Are you ok?" she asked.

I was writhing in pain. She propped me up with a pillow and fed some tea into my mouth. I replaced the cup with the mask and tried to breath rhythmically. A few tears made their way down my cheeks. They were for Gene, but I hoped my mum would ascribe them to labour pain. My waters broke, and the nurse got me a birthing ball. I tried to go into a calm zone; one where I connected with my body's natural reflexes. I wished I could go to that place at other times too, to disconnect myself from the constant emotional pain.

Everything moved so quickly there wasn't time to consider the enormity of it. There was a baby in the room, but I couldn't hold her because I was so worn out. I could feel myself slipping in and out of consciousness. I could see my new baby, but I couldn't reach her. All strength had left my body. My mum rocked her instead and I could hear her talking to her soothingly. It soothed me as much as it did Alice.

An hour or so later, I was feeling more alive and holding my newborn in my arms. The experience didn't feel as real as it had the first time round. Nothing about it felt magical, but that didn't lessen the love I felt for her. I dreaded my mum's exit. She had sat up since the night before and I could tell she needed a night's sleep, but I knew once she left, I'd be up all night, tending to my baby and reaching for my phone. Gene was sitting just a mile and a half from the hospital, and he had no idea that he had a new child.

The nurse moved me into a private room and wheeled Alice in beside me. My dad had been minding Hope the whole time and my mum would be occupied with that now too. I knew they'd bring her to meet Alice, but I was in hospital for three days and I knew I'd spend most of that time alone, unless Gene came. He was still allowed all the access he wanted when it came to visiting hours. He was the father, whether he'd been present for the birth or not. I looked across at my child and felt sorry for her. Her sister had had her father witness her birth and hold her in the days that followed. Alice hadn't even met him yet, and that was my fault.

The nurse brought me toast and tea and my mum took her opportunity to leave, while everything was winding down for the night. I watched the door close behind her and got my phone out of my handbag. I had forty-eight missed calls and eighteen messages. Gene hadn't been in the building, but he'd known I was in labour. He'd called me every name under the sun, cursing me for excluding him from such a precious moment.

It was the middle of the night and I was unsure if he'd still be awake. I tried ringing him and he didn't answer, so I sent him a message instead.

"Alice was born at 8pm. You're welcome to come up to the hospital any time you like. We're waiting to see you. I'm sorry for everything. I want you to see your daughter."

I got no response; Gene must have already been asleep.

Chapter Thirty-One

The next day was the loneliest of my life. The birth was over, the drugs had worn off and I was left with the demands of a newborn, my post-pregnancy emotions and still no word from Gene. My family were coming to visit me that afternoon. They were bringing Hope to meet her new sister. I just had to keep going until that moment. They might only visit for twenty minutes, but at least it would break up the stark silence. The nurse made her rounds, leaving me to my own devices since I was a second-time mother. I was glad to not be prodded at but would have talked to a cardboard cut-out had one been present.

I gave up on breastfeeding much quicker than I had with Hope. I didn't have the support or emotional resilience left to keep it up. I fed my one day old her bottle of formula and felt like I'd failed her on so many levels. She seemed much more content than I supposed her to be. I guess she wasn't clock-watching like I was. I checked my inbox every few minutes, but I hadn't missed a message from Gene. I sent him another message. Nothing. I looked at the blank TV screen and couldn't bear to turn it on. I just sat alone with my disappointment and my tears. After a while, when Alice was napping, I got up and went to the bathroom to cool my cheeks with a cold cloth. I applied my make-up and changed my clothes. I looked almost presentable. Maybe everyone would be fooled into thinking I was coping.

I heard joyous laughter outside my door and animated conversation. The handle pressed downwards, but the visitors continued their catch-up on the other side. I waited, holding Alice and feeling like I was under siege. How many people had come at once? Would they expect me to be excited about the whole affair? Did I have to pretend to be less traumatised than I was? Did I have to make forced conversation through forced smiles?

I watched the door handle until it clicked fully downwards. The door screeched open and my family and Pete walked in. I wondered if Gene might arrive at the same moment. Part of me hoped he wouldn't. If he was going to come at all, I hoped it wouldn't coincide with the visit from my family. I knew they couldn't sit together in the same room without hostile discomfort surfacing. I prayed he'd come as soon as they left and sit next to Alice and me, never leaving our sides again. I needed Gene more than ever, but he wasn't there. Even if he wasn't in body, I knew we were still mentally connected. Our souls were so interknitted it was like being caught up in a twisted net.

"Hello, love," my parents called cheerily. Pete and Poppy followed them into the room. There were more people than chairs and I told them to sit on the bed. Hospitality helped hold together the whole sham.

I sat upright in bed. Alice was still lying in her hospital cot.

"Aw," everyone cooed. "Look at your baby sister, Hope."

They picked up Alice and passed her to me. I held my baby on my other baby's lap and saw their sisterly bond begin to bud. My mum produced her camera and took some photos. I tried to smile. In the photos I saw months later, I almost was.

Poppy smiled at me. "You don't look like you just had a baby."

"Thanks."

Her compliment was kind, but no compliment, no matter how grand, would have compensated for unhappy I was feeling. Everyone took turns holding the baby. I kept waiting for Gene to appear in the doorway, but he didn't. I was in the same maternity unit I'd stayed in when I'd had Hope. Everything was flashing back to me. I could see Gene in the rooms like a widow's ghostly imaginings. I could see him sitting in the armchair next to me, slouched back, his foot propped on the other knee, his legs jiggling. I could see him cup Alice's head in his hand like he had done with Hope and speak beautiful words to her. I could see him carrying coffee to the room in cardboard cup holders, bags of Chinese food with plastic utensils and forty napkins.

"Everything will be alright, baby. You'll be out of here soon. We'll get you home and you'll be ok."

I squeezed my eyes as tight as two pincers, holding back the deluge of tears that wanted to break through.

Pete and Poppy smiled at me and held hands.

"We have some news we wanted to tell you," said Pete.

"Yeah?"

"We're engaged," said Poppy.

"Is that your ring?"

"Yeah," she blushed, showing me the jewel; the kind that had still never made its way to my finger.

"When did you get engaged?"

"This week."

I feigned a smile with all the strength I could muster.

It was official: everyone was happy but me.

Chapter Thirty-Two

Three days after I gave birth, I was signed out of hospital. Everyone was happy with my mental state; everyone apart from the person living with it. I was staying at my parents' house; they'd arranged to pick me up from the maternity unit. The refuge had offered to let me stay for longer than usual; typically, we were only allowed one overnight stay with friends or family a week. But I didn't see the use in staying longer; I was alone and there was no point in trying to convince myself I wasn't. I'd always have to return to the refuge with a newborn, so it was better to face it down before I got too comfortable in a warm home.

I smiled when I saw Hope. We hadn't seen each other in two days; not since the time my family visited the hospital. It was the longest period we'd been apart for, and I wasn't used to not having her company. She didn't talk yet; no more than monosyllables. But having her in a room comforted me; she was the one constant in my life those last five months. Hope, Alice and I were a new kind of family, incomplete, but one I'd have to get used to having. For the time being, at least. Gene and I would still get back together. Once he saw his new daughter, I knew he'd feel motivated to repair our rift.

He hadn't come to the hospital. I waited day and night for him to come, but he had better things to do, I guess. Or maybe he just couldn't think of anything worse to do than to meet the daughter whose birth he had missed. Or to face the person who was responsible for that fact. I knew I should have tried harder to reach him. I should have rung his phone right up until I was pushing. But there was no reversing the events that had passed. I'd regret them for the rest of my life; I already knew that, but there was nothing I could do to change them. Another thing Gene would have to forgive me for; I hoped his heart was big enough to enable him to do that.

My parents drove me home and I sat in the backseat between my two children. Seeing them side by side outside the context of a hospital visit made my future seem impossible. How would I look after two children alone? I had no home, I had no car, no job and no prospects.

The world had never looked bleaker to me, but everything felt numb. I couldn't take any negative action against my life; I just couldn't make positive plans either. I was stuck in that car seat, dazed and disoriented. I said a word to no one; I knew they were talking amongst themselves, but I wasn't part of it anyway. I was excluded from everything; the only loner in the vast world.

I took my baby to the spare bedroom: the one that used to be mine. It still had the same paint I'd chosen as a teenager and some of the same furniture, but all the items that had marked it as mine were long gone; most of them lost in 2 Belmont Place. I tried to remember how it had felt to be a child in that house; what sort of person I could have blossomed into that had died before fully flowering. It was useless; that person was no longer part of my reality. The world was a terror-inducing place. The naïve outlook I must have had had been obliterated by facing up to the truth of living. I lay down on the cold double bed; the one that Gene and I had shared when he'd first come to Northern Ireland. The sheets were freezing, and you could tell a body hadn't touched them in months. At least at night, Hope would be sleeping next to me, warming the spot that should have been Gene's. She looked more and more like him; when we lay with the silhouettes made by lamplight, I could see him coming back to life in her. He was only ten miles away from where my parents lived, but that day it felt like he was gone. Leaving the house on the 11th February hadn't been a single event; it was like waking up every day, surprised to find that the person you'd loved most had died while you were sleeping. Every morning when I woke up, I had a feeling of horror when I realised all over again that Gene wasn't beside me in the bed; that he wasn't allowed to be beside me in a house, that he wasn't even allowed to know where I lived.

I tried to get some rest while Alice took a nap, but I was too agitated. I couldn't even rest my limbs. I lay, staring at the ceiling and feeling my body twitching like it was on a high, but without the accompanying feeling of elation. I knew I should be sleeping while Alice was, storing up on energy until she next fell asleep, but I couldn't force myself to mimic her; there was too much on my mind.

Two days later, I went "home." The workers were waiting to greet me at the entrance. They'd seen me coming on the security camera before I'd even reached the door. They were eager to see the baby; there hadn't been a newborn baby in the house in a long time. It seemed that people who had only been strangers to me months before had got more pleasure from my pregnancy than I had. They'd seen the ultrasound photos, found out the baby's sex, performed a countdown, notifying me each day of how long I had to go to my due date. I knew it was a welcome delivery of good news, but I wasn't the appropriate person to deliver it. I tried to smile at everyone, avoiding getting involved in a long discussion and walking as hastily as I could with two babies in my arms to get behind my locked bedroom door. I didn't want to talk to anyone. As far as I was concerned, they could all fuck off. They were the ones that had encouraged the dissolution of my marriage. I was feeling bereaved more than blissful, and I needed to hide away, holed up in my room with my children and my regret.

From that moment, I was ultra-protective of my children. I saw the residents and the workers in the refuge as enemies that were trying to take custody of my children away. They had the power to do it too; all they had to do was fill out one too many risk assessments, make a comment to social services, a negative remark to the health visitor, and my girls would be gone. I had feared losing Hope when I'd first had her, but I'd known that Gene would slaughter anyone that tried to come near us. Now, I was alone, defending my own corner and trying to do it in a way that didn't raise concerns about my own mental state. It was a fine line to tiptoe along: act too protective and risk being diagnosed delusional, be too lax and lose my children to the wolves that hid in every corner. I didn't want to be near a soul; and I made sure I stayed emotionally distant from everyone.

I was still getting daily midwife visits, even though I was in the refuge. My room was like a walk-in wardrobe with baby items distributed everywhere, but she was complimentary about it. I could tell she was trying to make the best of a bad situation, and her false positivity only irritated me. No one was my ally and I just wanted to dispense with the niceties and send her on her way. She was an extra worry; one that didn't help me an ounce and was just another box to be checked. I was already checking so many in the hostel, a couple more was enough to send me over the edge.

"This room is so handy, isn't it?" she beamed, shuffling herself into a comfortable position on my mattress. There were no chairs in the room and other than the floor, perching on the bed was the only option.

"I guess, yeah. There are a lot of stairs here. It's easier when I'm carrying the girls."

"It's a lot homelier than I expected," she said, looking at the bits and pieces I'd used to try and add a little personality to the room.

"That's lovely," she said, pointing to the deer that read "World's Best Mum."

"Who got you that?"

"My husband."

She grimaced and rolled her eyes, as if she expected me to give a complicit roll of my own. I loathed her for it. How dare she suggest it was less thoughtful simply because it came from my husband? She was well-aware of my situation; it had been broadcasted through my whole medical file and to every department involved. I guessed it was her bit of gossip to get her through the dull work week; something to talk about until Friday rolled around. I felt like telling her to get off my bed and to get away from me, but I had to put on airs for the sake of my kids. Even if she was my foe, I had to put on pretend politeness, so I could keep custody of my children. Everyone was a threat.

"Are you breastfeeding?"

"Not really. I'm bottle feeding but haven't completely stopped."

"You should probably pick one and stick to it, so she doesn't get confused."

"Yeah."

I looked at every object in the room; at everything that didn't have a face that could watch me back.

"Seems like you're doing great, she's obviously very settled. Well done, I'll be out tomorrow again."

"Do you know what time?"

She shook her head. "We just come when we come; that's the way of the job."

I felt like telling her I was glad my time was as precious as her own, but I refrained from doing so. What did I have to do with my time anyway? My world was suddenly smaller and more claustrophobic. I thought about Gene and tried not to cry until she walked out the door.

"Well, I'll leave you to enjoy your baby."

She gave me a matronly rub on the arm and the door banged shut behind her. I was alone again, and I was drowning in my own mind. No one seemed to hear my last gasps for air.

Chapter Thirty-Three

Two weeks after Alice was born, I got the train to a station midway between Gene and me. Gene had agreed to meet me there. He'd finally phoned me, telling me his silent treatment was my well-deserved punishment for excluding him from the birth. I guess it was little to have to endure in exchange for causing him to miss such a historic moment for our family. I couldn't be upset with him when I heard his voice. Gene was the oxygen and my cannister was dangerously empty. I wasn't ready to tell him my exact location yet, so I agreed to meet him in the closest town. I hurried to him on the bus. It was a difficult trip to make; my first since having two children: my maiden voyage with the double pram. My anxiety was compounded by the fact the pram didn't fit on the bus. The bus driver had to open the emergency doors to let me on board. I struggled to keep the pram out of the gangway and neighbouring travellers glared at me. I wished I could have told them how much of an impact their unhappy looks made on me. I was already a bruise of a woman. They wouldn't have understood anyway; real empathy only comes from personal hurts and I could tell by their attitudes, they'd experienced little.

Twenty minutes later, I disembarked with my two babies. It was strange pushing them into the bus station. I felt twice as exposed as when I'd met Gene pregnant. With both babies in the external world, I realised how vulnerable we all were; but I was just being unreasonable. My post-pregnancy hormones were affecting my every thought; I knew my mental health was terrible but telling someone with the power to treat it wasn't an option; I couldn't own up to being unwell with two babies so reliant on me.

I stood inside the train station, looking back over my shoulder, then quickly to the left and right and to the front. I wanted to see Gene before he saw me. I wanted to know what mood was coming at me, to assess whether I needed to run, beg for forgiveness or collapse into his arms. I waited for what felt like an age, but what could have been only minutes. Finally, I saw Gene descend last, as always, from a train on one of the platforms. He stood out amidst all the other people who looked grey to me. He was colourful, charismatic and mysterious, even to me, who had known every detail of him.

He walked towards me in his heroic way; slow paced but determined. It made my heart pause its beating. He had that same look he'd had in Chicago, like he was hunting me down, but for a good use. Being used up by Gene was better than being squandered by anyone else anyway. His hair hung in his face and he smiled through it at me, taking me in a firm embrace. I smelled his scent as memorably as the first time we'd ever met. He smelled of that delicious mix of smoke and something unquantifiable that comforted me. I could detect that smell amidst five hundred others; it was the smell of home. I longed for him even though I was in his arms. He may have had me pressed against him, but there was still an impenetrable barrier between us. All the agencies worked to keep us apart, but we'd break through their barricade and show them how wrong they were.

"Man, I missed you," said Gene.

I started crying, shivering against his warm chest.

"It'll be ok, baby. Everything will be ok, I promise."

He peeled himself back from me slowly and strolled over to the pram. He tilted the hood back, so he could see his new daughter.

"She's tiny," he said.

"Where do you want to go?"

"Some place where I can sit and hold her. Is there somewhere we can take Hope?"

"Soft play?"

"Yeah, I don't care. I just want to hold her."

Gene followed me, only because he didn't know where we were going. I paid us in and released Hope to play in her padded playground. She looked gleeful. It was the only time I remembered seeing that look in her eyes when Gene and I took her out. I stayed near her, chasing her up the stairs to the slide and climbing into the ball pit together. I could see Gene sitting across the room with Alice. He stared at her with what could have been called tenderness, completely transfixed by her. I wondered if it was love for her that I saw in her eyes or merely curiosity. A new child to add to the Savoyard clan; another being to prove his power over women. I hated myself for thinking that, so I blocked the thought. Gene sat staring at Alice for the entire duration of our play session. An hour and a half later, we walked back towards the town.

"I want to stop and get the girls something," said Gene.

"Ok."

Gene ran into a charity shop and came out with a couple of cuddly toys. He perched one on each side of the pram next to its designated child. I continued pushing the pram towards the town centre. It was easier to do it without a heavy midsection.

"Hey, you hungry?" Gene asked. "What time is it?"

I checked my phone. "It's 5."

"Fuck, it's 5 already? We better get Hope something to eat."

"Where do you want to go?"

"Anywhere. Is that Chinese any good?" he asked, pointing to the restaurant beside us.

"I don't know. I've never been."

"Let's just fucking go."

Gene opened the door and I edged my way inside with the buggy, hoping the owners would save any disparaging looks they had for someone better able to handle them. Gene chose a table and the waiter brought us a highchair. Gene sat down while I got Alice out of the pram and ordered some boiled water to heat her bottle. He picked up the menu and scanned it in one quick eye movement.

"Man, this place is pricey."

I knew I'd be the one paying for it.

"Let's just stay. By the time we find somewhere else, Alice will be crying for a bottle."

The waiter returned with our hot water and his notepad.

"Are you ready to order?"

"Get me sweet and sour chicken, egg fried rice, a Coke."

"I'll have the same. Thanks," I said.

"This place is alright, man. At least there ain't a ton of fucking people here," said Gene. He still hadn't taken his jacket off and his leg was moving so much he looked ready to take off. There were some pretend orchids and a water fountain. Something about the ambience they were aiming for was incompatible with Gene's presence. It seemed too tranquil and easily disrupted. I hoped nothing would kick off. But thankfully, Gene didn't seem to be in that kind of a mood. Maybe meeting his new daughter had softened him towards me again. It didn't stop him dishing out his orders though.

"Put a bib on Hope, would you, babe? And ask the dude when he comes back to get me another Coke."

I nodded, checking the temperature of the formula and feeding it to our daughter one-handed while I dug in the nappy bag for a bib with the other.

The food arrived along with Gene's second drink. Everything was running smoothly, thank God. I didn't need anything small to contaminate our day. It was the purest kind of peace I'd felt with Gene since the beginning. He smiled at me across the table and I ate while I fed our baby.

"You're beautiful, baby."

"I love you."

"I love you too. Did you get your housing offer yet?"

"No, not yet."

"You got one left, right?"

I nodded.

"Well, make sure you take it – it don't matter what it's like – I can fix it up for us. We just need a cheap place to stay and then we can be together."

"Ok."

"Let me know as soon as you get it."

"I will."

"How much will the rent be?"

"I'm not sure – a couple of hundred a month?"

"Man, that's way less than we been paying."

"I know."

"Gene?"

I couldn't help myself asking the question I wanted to know the answer to, no matter how it affected the mood of our dinner date.

"What, babe?"

He moved his eyes slowly upwards, like he sensed it wasn't going to be a question he wanted to hear.

"Does it ever bother you that I'm in a refuge?"

"Why would it bother me?"

"Because I don't have a house."

"Well, whose fault is that? You're the one that left. Nobody made you do that but you. Well – except for your parents maybe. But you don't got to do everything people tell you to."

"I don't."

"Yes you do – you listen to every motherfucker – everyone but me anyway."

"I don't mean to."

"But you do. I'm your fucking husband, but you listen to motherfuckers you don't even know over me."

"I'm sorry."

"Well stop fucking doing it. You can't trust none of those motherfuckers."

"I know."

And I knew with conviction that he was right. If it wasn't for Gene, I'd be entirely alone in the world. He was the only one who understood how frightening it was to be alone with your mental state. I dreaded returning to the refuge; being asked a series of questions about my day, having my details noted in the book, bathing Hope in the communal bath with its circle of grime, sleeping on my rubber mattress. I wanted to up and leave, without ever returning; to leave everything I owned behind and cut my losses. I'd done it before; I could do it again. But could I rely on Gene to be there when I took the leap? I knew I could rely on his words; he was always gifted at saying the right things at the right moment, but would he follow through? Until I was sure that he could do the practical things he promised me, I had to stay where I was, like it or not.

"I don't want to fight with you, baby – I love you."

"I love you too."

I paid the bill and listened to Gene talking about how good the food was and how overpriced it was. I hoped the waiters only overheard the complimentary bits. Gene was good at giving compliments with a bitter aftertaste. His compliments always came paired with a comment that negated them. Despite his comments about the prices, Gene was back in good form. The conversation we'd had had been brushed aside, like it had never happened.

I packed up the baby items and Gene strapped Alice into the pram. Life was so much easier with two pairs of hands. I imagined for a moment having the married life I'd expected; one where we each took our fair share of the responsibility. But it was pointless wasting time fantasising about that; it just wasn't in Gene's character. You had to accept the person you loved as they were; not how you hoped they would be, or how they'd promised you they'd be.

We walked at a leisurely pace while Gene lit his post-dinner smoke.

"What are you going to do tonight?" I asked.

Gene shrugged. "Sit in my fucking room, watch TV. There ain't nothing else to do, right?"

"Yeah."

"What are you going to do? Who are you meeting after you leave me?" he asked with a sarcastic undertone.

"No one," I sighed. "I'm just going back to the hostel. Going to give the girls a bath and tidy the room."

"Right."

"You got TV there?"

"Yeah."

"Cable?"

"No."

"Me neither."

"Do you get bored?" I asked.

Gene took a drag on his cigarette and answered a tight "no" with the smoke still in his lungs. He exhaled.

"Not really, babe. I'm used to it: being by myself. Ain't got nothing better to do than wait around for you anyway, do I?"

"I don't want you waiting around for me."

Gene snorted with laughter.

"Been waiting around for you for six months,"

"I've been waiting for you to."

"No you haven't. You ain't got no intention of getting back with me."

"That isn't true."

"Yes, it is."

I started to get teary. The argument was minimal compared to most of our public ones, but I didn't have the strength to deal with it two weeks post-partum.

"If you want to be together, you got to do something about it. Set up marriage counselling. You've been telling me you'd do that since before you left and you still ain't done it."

Had I? I couldn't remember reaching an agreement about that, but I knew it was time to do something. If we proved to social services how seriously we took our familial problems and showed them the work we were prepared to put into fixing them, they'd know we belonged together. I had nothing more than I'd had the day that I'd walked into the refuge: no house, no independence, no peace. I decided to find out about marriage counselling the following morning. I knew it would have to be me that did it; I had to prove to Gene that I was serious about correcting the situation I'd brought upon us. I was worn down enough by then to adopt his perspective of what had happened between us. Truth and facts didn't matter; being happy was more important.

Gene walked me the ten minutes to the train station. My train departed from a different platform than his and he wanted to see me safely onto it. Or maybe he wanted to find out the general direction I was going in. Either way, I wasn't prepared to insist we separate at the entrance. I couldn't afford to piss him off. If I kept Gene calm, I was safe wherever I was going to anyway.

As luck would have it, one of the residents from the refuge was waiting on the same platform. I'd known she worked in that town but hadn't considered the possibility of us bumping into one another. In a town of thousands, what was the likelihood of bumping into the only person you knew that had any connection to the place? Fate was a cruel joker at times. It was an awkward introduction to be presented with; I couldn't tell Gene where I knew her from, but I knew he'd figure it out anyway. Gene was no fool.

"Hi," I smiled. "This is Gene."

I knew I was blushing; she was well-aware of who Gene was, and I knew she'd judge me for meeting up with him. She'd probably report it to the workers and they could laugh together about how weak-willed I was – always giving in to my supposedly abusive husband's requests to meet up.

"This is Christine."

She nodded and gave me a pursed-lip smile.

"Nice to meet you."

Gene grunted and smiled to himself; not at her. It was a look of his I was well used to; it made you think he was making a mockery of you in his mind; turning you into a joke he only had with himself.

We stood in silence for a few moments while Gene continued to smirk.

"Were you just working?" I asked.

"Yes," she smiled.

I couldn't do it again; I couldn't hold up the pretence that Gene was just a bit shy, a bit socially awkward, that he needed to be guided through the conversation. I knew Christine knew the truth; if not from my lips, from where I happened to be living.

I couldn't think of anything to say and my lip started to tremble. I'd never known trembling lips were a possible effect of crying until meeting Gene. I'd always thought it was something invented for effect in cartoons. But the pain I lived with Gene was a special kind;

one that made you tremble in every one of your body parts, in every nook of your soul.

Tears started spilling onto my face.

"Are you ok?" Christine mouthed, looking at me with empathetic eyes.

I nodded, knowing I wasn't a bit convincing, but it was the last thread left of my denial, and if I let that break, the whole disaster would be visible to me. I couldn't cope with that. So, I kept telling myself, I was as ok as a person could be. I still couldn't get my tears under control. Gene was getting aggravated; the furrow in his brow was deepening and he looked at me out of the sides of his eyes. Christine moved towards me and hugged me. I couldn't respond, but I let her hold my body. I was numb but being comforted was better than being abused. She held me for a few seconds, and I knew Gene would be angry, but I couldn't bring myself to pull away.

"Thanks," I said.

"Come here," said Gene, nudging his head in the direction he wanted me to walk in.

I followed him to the end of the platform, far enough away that he knew Christine wouldn't hear us.

"I know what the fuck you're trying to do."

"What?" I said, wiping a last tear from my cheek.

"You're trying to make yourself look like the victim. She might fall for your bullshit, but I don't. You can try to make it look like you're innocent, but I know what you really are."

Another tear made its way down the path drawn by the last.

"I'm not trying to do anything. I'm upset. You embarrassed me again. Why can't you just be nice to people?"

"I don't give a shit about what that motherfucker thinks of me."

"I know you don't, but you don't have to do this to me."

"You shouldn't care what she thinks either."

"You make me look bad."

"And you don't? You've convinced everyone I'm a fucking dick, when it's you who does the shit."

"I don't."

I said "I don't" because I had to attempt to defend myself, no matter how frail the attempt, but I believed everything about myself that Gene told me. I was manipulative; I was the one that had left, that had broken up our family, and here I was, trying to illicit sympathy from strangers. I left Gene looking like the bad guy, but he wasn't. It wasn't that simple. Yes, he had embarrassed me, but perhaps he was justified in doing so.

"I'm sorry."

"You can't do this shit – crying in front of people, making me look like a dick."

"I won't do it again."

I hoped I could get my emotions in check enough to follow through on that, or at least that we wouldn't bump into anyone else we knew.

"Baby, I love you. Let's not ruin today."

"I love you too."

"Is that your train?"

I turned to look at the train pulling in, the name of the town I was staying in in clear print on the front. Gene knew where I was going. I felt cold all over, with a flu-like chill. There was no turning back; the protective barrier was down. At least he didn't know the street name or house number I was staying in. I made myself a promise to never tell him that. I wasn't allowed to anyway. Doing so would be breaking confidentiality and putting the other women at risk. Gene walked away to get his own train before mine left. I waved to him, but he didn't see me; he had already moved onto the next thing. After the train began moving, Christine moved into the seat beside me. We were two of the few people on the board. One less thing to stress about; one less way to feel like I was occupying more space in life than I deserved. She placed her hand on my shoulder and I tried not to cry.

"You shouldn't let him treat you like that."

"Like what?"

"He was horrible to you."

I didn't think Gene had been; I thought he'd been unfriendly towards her, but horrible towards me? He had been in a reasonably good mood that day. I was flummoxed by what she said. She just didn't know him. She'd seen too little to gauge what passed between us. She didn't understand the dynamic of the relationship. She didn't know Gene well enough to judge him. I wanted her support but felt contempt for it at the same time; her support for me undermined Gene, and that was something I never wanted to do. I was on his side to the death, whether he believed it or not.

The twenty-minute journey extended to eternity. I just wanted to get back, lock myself inside my room and stay close to my only true friend: denial. I didn't recognise it as such at that point; I just knew I needed to believe the best, or I couldn't continue living. Life was an immense disappointment, but its potential for improvement was my lifeline. Things would get better once Gene and I had our own home, once I was away from the prying eyes of everyone in the refuge and every agency that got themselves involved in our family.

Speaking of unwanted visitors, the midwife stopped coming. Her visits were replaced by less frequent ones by the health visitor. She came bounding into the house one day, like she was delighted to be there and expected a carpet roll-out and a china tea cup as a welcome. She had equally bouncy hair; less curly than mine, but more obtrusive. She was rotund and looked like a warm person; I no longer trusted appearances. I was used to midwives being pushy types, with a few too many opinions on things that were none of their business, so I expected the worst. But she kept challenging my cynicism with her smiles. I still couldn't trust her, so I put the appointments in, saying the right things, doing the right things, amenably arranging future appointments.

"Well, how are you getting on with two?"

"Ok. Alice is crying a lot after feeds."

I'd been struggling to get her settled. Feeding Alice a bottle was a time-consuming task; one that resulted in her writhing in discomfort and crying herself into a frenzy. I just needed a bit of advice. I suspected it might be Lactose Intolerance that was the culprit. It ran in our family; I'd had issues with it myself as a baby.

"I should maybe mention that I'm Lactose Intolerant."

"Ok, maybe we should try switching milk and see if it makes a difference."

"Ok."

"I'm glad you told me that – helps us to narrow it down quicker," she smiled. I felt like I was under the shining light of her approval, but I knew now not to make myself too comfortable there. It could shift at any moment; that was what life was like.

"I'll give you a note to take to the doctor and then I'll come out in a couple of weeks. Ring me if there are any issues."

"I will."

She smiled favourably and walked out the door in her bustling way; she went busily on her way to get herself involved in someone else's business. I stayed behind in the playroom: our meeting point, after she left and let Hope play with the toys while I fed Alice.

The doctor gave me a script for a new kind of formula and our problems were radically reduced. Alice seemed more settled and I felt like a less incompetent mother. I knew I was still far from perfect, but the watchful eye of every agency and every worker was like a constant reminder that my children could be taken from me with one misstep. I kept to myself and met Gene in private.

Things were spiralling out of control in my own head. I couldn't place my finger on what had set me off; maybe it was the birth, the hormonal changes, the lack of support. Something needed to happen, or I'd give up on life entirely. I started smoking again. Cigarettes were the only form of control I had. I couldn't attempt suicide with two children in my care, I couldn't harm myself with everyone watching me, but smoking was a socially acceptable method of self-harm, an outlet for my anxiety. When the girls were asleep, I stood outside, under the fire escape, breathing fumes into my own body. Nearly every resident of the refuge was a regular smoker. I knew why; they needed a way to decompress. Everything was so high pressure indoors, every incident reported, every person cautioned on the most minor of offences: an item that didn't pass room checks, a broken curfew, a missed chore. I was beginning to loathe everything it represented; the failure of my marriage most of all.

The letter about my third housing offer was nowhere to be seen. Usually they took a couple of months to appear; I'd seen it happen to every lady that lived there, but my life wasn't as predictable. The house was changing; the people that had lived there when I'd arrived were moving on to new lives. The whole house was replaced with new women; myself the only original member from era. Sarah was leaving and with her departure, I lost some of my strength to resist Gene's orders. She had always been a quiet warning in my ear, a bit of perspective on what was happening to me, a non-judgemental observer. Now I had no one to run things by; the workers weren't objective in their observations - it was their job not to be.

The new house of women was more volatile. The previous one had been filled with thirty-somethings and upwards, people with a bit more wisdom and a bit less energy. This lot were full of impulsivity and unwise choices. I felt less safe there. The only resident that remained behind from when I'd entered the place was the one that had driven me out of my kitchen. She had increased her bullying tactics when the staff weren't around. But because everyone was reporting it, they couldn't do much about it. They didn't want to appear to victimise an individual, so it continued. She frequently removed my washing from the clothes horse before it had sufficiently dried. She replaced it with her own. She was too pushy with my children, talking to them but refusing to say a word to me. She seemed to have begun a campaign, honing in on weak points of every member of the house. I didn't want to stay there until Christmas. That was where I drew the line; if I didn't have a housing offer by the end of October, I'd take matters into my own hands. Gene and I would have the perfect Christmas I had dreamt of. I knew Christmas didn't matter to Gene, but he knew it did to me, so he'd have a second chance to help me make it special. With our romance renewed, I knew everything would fall into place anyway.

Chapter Thirty-Four

My mental health was rapidly declining and chain smoking was doing little to alleviate it. I put the girls down for their nap and took the baby monitor downstairs, using up every minute I could puffing away. The thing I'd complained about Gene doing too much, I'd started doing myself. I needed a coping mechanism; the only other one I had was Gene, and I couldn't reach him in the way I needed to. I couldn't curl up in his arms and beg him to take me home. We couldn't lock the door behind us and be alone together, with something unlike peace, but that I needed just as much. I'd thought that peace was the thing my life was lacking, but I hadn't known that leaving my home would disrupt it even more. Had I known that leaving would be as stressful as staying, I never would have decided to do it. For the rest of my life, I would blame myself for falling prey to an impulse that didn't show me the full picture of what my life would become.

I hoped no one would join me for a smoke. I didn't have the energy for conversation. I just needed to stand alone with my pain and my fantasies of life being different. If only I hadn't listened to my parents that day. Were they there for me the way Gene had been? If only I'd had the courage to walk out of the refuge while we still had our family home. If only I hadn't listened to the threats of the agencies that surrounded me, I could still be happy, I could only vaguely remember what happiness felt like. Getting up for the day was like waking to my own personalised version of hell. Had I been asked what the worst thing that could happen to me would be, I couldn't even have dreamt up what life had become. Losing the love of my life, my home and my vision of what my family could be; that was the ultimate loss. Terminal illness would have disappointed me less; at least an end to the suffering would have been in sight. I only knew I was alive by the breaths I took and the pain I felt every living moment of every day. And no one understood, except perhaps Gene. The workers got to clock out at 10pm, or whatever time their shift lasted to, return to their cosy homes with their families waiting for them to have a cup of tea and watch the telly. I never got to escape.

One night a week I'd go to my parents' house to stay over. That wasn't a holiday; it was like someone pressing the pause button on the torture device that never stopped and I knew it would start up again as soon as I left. The pain of losing Gene travelled with me even into the doors of their home; there was no place of retreat.

I wondered if Gene suffered as greatly every minute of every day as I did. The thought that he might offered me no comfort; it only doubled the amount of suffering happening in my world. I prayed we would get things "straightened out," as Gene would have said. But day followed day followed day, until months were advancing too quickly for me to bear. The longer that passed, the less likely it felt that Gene and I would reunite. He was growing comfortable in his bedsit, not making any effort to move elsewhere, or save the money to pay for any more than what he had. I was suspended in refuge-living; I'd forgotten how to exist in the real world. I knew I wanted out of this new captivity, but I'd lost all coping skills for life on "the outside."

Sarah and I had even referred to the outside world as that. We joked about it together; how it made it sound like we were imprisoned, and how, sometimes, it didn't feel much different than if we had been. But since Sarah moved into her own home, the laughter had stopped. There was no one to lighten the mood, and I couldn't handle the atmosphere's heaviness.

I was sleeping less and less. Noises in the house were disturbing me; everything felt enhanced, in a negative way. The lights were distressingly bright, the sounds were upsettingly loud, my housemates were suddenly menacing; the staff included. I was seeing things. Not full-blown hallucinations; more like the faint outlines of what could easily become them. Life was moving too quickly, but with a negative voiceover. I couldn't keep up with the pace of my racing thoughts, or the content of them that infected me with such despair. My smoking doubled and tripled, until I fed on cigarettes. They were my go-to solution for life becoming unmanageable; cigarettes and ringing Gene. I knew it was unhealthy, in theory, to have such great reliance on him. The workers had told me that so many times. They'd been gently encouraging me to break contact with him for months, and I still hadn't managed to reduce it one iota. It was like facing the thought of withdrawing from a drug, knowing how horrific it would be before you even attempted to do it, then taking twice the amount to ease the pain of that thought, on top of everything else.

"I don't know what to do," I cried to Gene on the phone. I was sitting on the bedroom floor, the room swirling around me, my emotions blinding me so much I couldn't see an inch in front of me.

"Baby, you got to do something."

"What?"

"I don't know – paint, draw, make something – anything to slow your mind down."

"I can't. I can't."

I was beyond the point of turning myself back. I was losing my vocabulary, and my ability to manage basic tasks. I knew I still had to do them, for my children's sake, and I would do them, robotically, for that reason. But my mind was as far gone as it had ever been.

"Ok. Meet me."

I knew meeting Gene would help my mind, but I couldn't conceive of how I was going to make it to another town. Gene would have to come to me. I was going to have to allow him access to my town. If I didn't, I might not survive beyond that day.

"Can you meet me in my town?"

"Where is it?"

I told him the name of it. He hadn't heard of it, and I wished, in a way, as soon as I said it that he still hadn't.

"Ok, just tell me how to get there and I will."

"You have to get the train. Do you have any money?"

"No, babe, I ain't got none."

"Ok, I'll send you some."

I would pay whatever I had to, to get Gene's special kind of therapy.

"Ok, hey, could you send me an extra ten? I'm out of smokes."

"Ok."

"Send it now baby and I'll run and get it."

"Ok."

I transferred the money to Gene's personal account. I had disabled our joint account weeks before, after the unpaid electricity bill incident. Keeping the account active was too much of a risk.

I sent Gene the money and waited for him to phone to tell me he'd got it and was on his way. When I got the phone call I'd been waiting for, I set out for the train station. I was partly excited to show him around my new town, partly apprehensive about having him know where it was. The two feelings fought a battle inside me, neither of them ever appearing to win.

I watched Gene get off the train. He didn't skip off in his usual way; he held onto the rail and lowered himself onto the platform, limping towards me. His foot must have got worse. Maybe he hadn't been taking his medication. I hoped he wouldn't ask me to get him more. He stopped in front of me, extending an arm and wrapping it around me in a half-hug.

"Hey, baby. Man, my fucking foot is killing me. I can barely walk. I got to do something about this shit."

I didn't ask about Gene's referral; that would have been like putting your eye to the barrel of a gun to check if anything was coming out of it.

"Where do you want to go?" I asked.

"I don't know this town, babe. Is there somewhere we can get coffee? I'd kill for a cup of coffee, man. I ain't had none in days."

"How come?"

"I ain't had the money to get none. There's some instant sitting in the house. I thought about taking it, but I don't steal, man. I mean, I used to, but that was when I was a fucking asshole."

"Why did you stop?"

"I didn't feel right about that shit."

"What did you steal?"

"Just food and shit. I'd starve before I'd steal now."

Gene was such an honest character; he'd never do anything immoral. Gene had told me how much he despised stealing before. He thought it was abhorrent, so I knew he'd never do something so disgraceful himself. We were the same; we may have had cultural differences, but our core values were alike. Like Gene always says, we want the same things.

"There's a coffee shop across the road."

"Let's go there, man. I ain't walking far with this fucking foot."

"Do you like it here so far?"

"Looks the same as everywhere else."

"Would you mind living here?"

"I'll live wherever you are. The place don't matter."

"It's next to the sea."

"I like that about it – reminds me of when I was a kid, being beside the lake."

I smiled at Gene and he smiled at me, and I was filled with hope again. I noticed that my mind had settled since being with Gene. He was the cure to the mental cancer that was eating me alive. If I stayed close to him, I could survive; I could even thrive.

"I'll get a highchair while you get the coffee, babe."

"Thanks."

"You're welcome. Eh, just an americano, babe. Large. See if they got any ice."

I nodded as I walked away; I knew the drill. I ordered our drinks and carried them to the table. Hope was on Gene's knee and he was talking to her animatedly.

"Here, baby," he said, holding her up like a binbag. "Take her and strap her into the highchair. My fucking hand is killing me."

"Ok."

"Hey," he said, connecting eyes with me and doing a sideways smile. "Thanks for the coffee, baby."

"That's ok."

I got Hope settled in her chair with snacks and sat down to join Gene for a coffee. Alice had fallen asleep in the pram; I was disappointed she wouldn't get to see her dad, but relieved to only have one child to occupy, so we could talk.

"You heard anything yet about a house?"

"No."

"We'll give it another month and then we'll start looking for places if we still ain't heard nothing."

"Ok."

"What will you do about work if you move here?"

"I'll find another job, babe. That ain't hard to do."

Gene took a confident slurp from his coffee and looked around the room.

"This place is alright, man. At least the coffee's decent. I'm guessing it's expensive though. You got Burger King here?"

"Yeah."

"We can just go there next time. Is it far away?"

"Ten minutes."

"Yeah, I couldn't have made it there with my fucking foot. Hey, after we leave here, can we swing by the grocery store? Could you get me something for dinner, baby?"

I hesitated. I was started to feel used for money.

"I ain't eaten in almost a week, babe. I know you don't know what that's like, but it ain't fun."

"Ok, why don't you pick up some things that will last longer – like dried food and cans?"

"I ain't cooking in that fucking kitchen. It's fucking filthy. I'll just pick up some hotdogs, some buns, maybe some turkey breast and I'll make sandwiches."

"Ok."

That sounded manageable for my budget. As long as Gene wasn't starving, I was happy. He was right; I had no idea what it felt like to go a week without food; I was just an overgrown spoilt rich kid. I thought about fasting out of respect for Gene; to show him I didn't just empathise with his pain; I had felt it myself. But I knew Gene wouldn't respect me for it. He only respected his own suffering.

I followed Gene into the shop and made suggestions as we walked around: offers, things I thought he might like, food that would last beyond that day. He turned it all down. My ideas were never as good as Gene's. I decided not to make any more contemptable suggestions. Gene picked up some deli meats, reduced because they expired that day, some bread, some crisps: his essentials. I followed him to the tills and he let me take over at that point. He stood sheepishly behind me, as if I was paying for my own food.

"Thank you," he said, grinning at the cashier. He took the packed bag from their hand and threw a few pennies in the charity collection container. Even when Gene was down to his last pennies, he was generous with them.

"Thanks, baby," he said, as we walked away from the tills. "I'm so fucking hungry; can't wait to eat this."

"Do you want me to get you lunch now?"

"Nah, babe. I can't walk around no more – my fucking foot, man. Want to walk me to the train?"

"Ok."

I didn't want Gene to go but didn't know how to ask him to stay with his foot in such bad shape. I walked beside him, pushing the pram and dreading returning "home." The painful emptiness that stayed inside me when Gene wasn't there was coming back like the hollow rumble of an unfed tummy. I walked Gene as far as I could without getting on the train. His train was already waiting, ready to go. I was sad we wouldn't get another half hour together. I'd hoped he'd just missed one, so we could sit on the ice-cold metallic benches, chatting about nothing for a little while longer. Gene seemed happy to see it. He gave me a kiss.

"I'll call you when I get home."

"Ok."

He peered under the pram hood and said goodbye to the girls. I wondered if Alice had the slightest inkling who he was.

"Hey," said Gene, squeezing my shoulder. "Everything will be ok. Just don't tell them motherfuckers much. That's the mistake you made: telling people too much."

"I know."

"They think they can control you now. Only you can stop them doing that."

"Thanks."

Gene turned away, got on the train, and disappeared into the distance.

Chapter Thirty-Five

My care was transferred from the Belfast team to a new one. I was upset by the change; I'd got used to my team. There wasn't much they could do, but they were caring and encouraging at least. I had had one difficult psychiatrist when I'd first been diagnosed with Bipolar Disorder. She hadn't been a good listener and hadn't believed a word of mine she'd heard. I'd been relieved to part ways with her when Gene and I got our house in Belfast, and I was worried about having a similar experience with my new team. At least with that team, my social worker had been supportive enough to offset the psychiatrist's destructive moves. I hadn't considered how things might be when both were in league together.

I met my new social worker a couple of weeks after having Alice. I'd been put back on Home Treatment as a precaution, but even with daily visits, no one had picked up on my deteriorating state. I was discharged and transferred to "community" care. That was just a euphemism for having a monthly appointment if you were lucky. I'd heard good reports from Home Treatment about my new social worker. According to them, he was older, witty and good fun; I took courage from that and hoped we'd be on the same page.

The day I met him I instantly disliked him. He wasn't witty; he was smarmy and cruel. He was the type to diminish your problems, to tell you your mental illness could be cured by pulling yourself together: the last person that should be in his profession. I was fearful. I knew I was in bad mental territory, and the last thing I needed was someone that wouldn't take me seriously and who would work against my attempts to get help. I sensed he would be that kind of a guy. But then again, my senses weren't always trustworthy. Gene had told me that constantly, or as he liked to put it "your perceptions are all wrong."

The guy's name was Allen and I knew he disliked me as much as I disliked him. Why, I couldn't be sure. Sometimes my dress sense rubbed people up the wrong way; if they liked you to be conventional, it made them uncomfortable. Maybe it was the fact that I had children. Maybe it was the fact I was staying in a refuge;

maybe he was putting his wife through the same wringer that the workers believed I'd just been through. I knew he was a bully. I was getting used to being around them; I seemed to meet them at every turn.

"Well, Aoife," he said, without extending a hand or bothering to shift from his spot on the sofa.

I sat down opposite him and tried to be superficially friendly; I'd better give him the benefit of the doubt, in case I was wrong. I'd been wrong about enough people's motivations that I couldn't trust myself to arrive at the correct conclusion anymore.

"So, you have two children?

"Yes."

"Are you trying to get your own house?"

"Yeah, I'm waiting on an offer coming through."

"Well, that's what we need to focus on: you getting a house."

I decided to bring up the fact that my mental health felt to me like a more pressing concern.

"I want to get my own house, but I wanted to talk to you about my condition."

"What about it?"

"I'm not coping well at the minute."

"You look like you're coping fine to me – looking after two kids on your own, you've just had a baby without any psychosis, you've been discharged by Home Treatment."

I wanted to tell him that they'd missed something glaringly obvious, but I decided against it. They were all fiercely defensive of one another. The world of mental health services was a corrupt one.

"I haven't been feeling good myself though."

"Right, well what is it that you want us to do?"

"I think my medication needs changed."

"Well, are you a psychiatrist?"

"No, but I know how I feel."

He smirked and did a shrug.

"Isn't Anita your health visitor?"

"Yeah."

"We work in the same building. I'll have a chat with her and see what is best to do."

I wondered what she could possibly have to offer in the way of mental health treatment, but I'd let him tick whatever boxes he had to if it meant getting proper help.

"So, how have you been feeling?"

"My moods have been changing violently, I've had hallucinations, I feel paranoid, like people are out to get me."

"A lot of that could be to do with living here. That's why I say we should try and move you along into your own house."

"Yeah, but that isn't the main problem."

I knew he didn't believe me, so there was no use in arguing the point with him. He knew how it felt to be inside my head better than I did; he was the professional.

"Ok, so you find out about your house and I'll see what I can do."

"Thanks," I said.

"Here is my card. If there is an emergency, you know to go to A&E?"

"Yeah."

"Ok, I'll come and see you in two weeks, see how things are then."

I felt like clinging to his leg and begging him not to leave. Two weeks in bad mental health was like two years when you were feeling normal. He had no idea how much of a battle it would be to keep myself alive for another two weeks with no additional support. I didn't even know how I'd last to the end of the day. I returned to my room and bawled into my pillow until I had to collect Hope from the creche. Then, to calm myself down, I picked up the phone to Gene.

"Yeah, baby?"

"I can't do this."

"Do what, baby?"

"Live. It's too hard. There's no help."

"Slow down, baby. What happened?"

"My new social worker is a dick."

"Ok, what'd he do?"

"He wouldn't arrange for me to see the psychiatrist and he isn't coming back for two weeks."

"Did you tell him how you've been feeling?"

"Yeah."

"What the fuck, man? What is wrong with them people? Every time you see them, you come away worse. Then I got to pick up the pieces."

"He thinks I'm fine."

"You aren't, babe."

"Can you see it?"

"Yeah, things ain't been good."

It was like striving to be understood in a language you didn't speak, then having the person repeat back to you what they thought you'd said and the entire meaning had been changed. With Gene I never felt that way; where my mental health was concerned. He was the only person that understood.

"Don't let him away with that – ring him tomorrow if you ain't good. You got to make these people do their job right. They ain't going to try if you leave them alone."

I knew Gene was right. I would phone him, and he would have to do something to help.

Chapter Thirty-Six

I told the refuge workers that I wasn't well. They already knew before I'd finished the first sentence.

"We know there is a crisis," said Anne, pragmatically.

"How do you know?"

"We know you. You haven't been yourself lately."

Lisa sat next to her, nodding her head.

"You have an appointment with the health visitor tomorrow, don't you?"

I nodded, tensing inside.

"Want me to sit in on the meeting with you? We can tell her how things have been?"

"Ok, thanks."

I was relieved someone was willing to accompany me and act like a buffer between myself and the health visitor if any communication difficulties arose. I seemed to have such bad luck getting across what I was trying to say to every professional with whom I crossed paths. The next day, Lisa buzzed the health visitor into the building. She was just there to carry out her routine checks on Alice. I decided to be honest with her about my mental health when she asked how I'd been feeling. Lisa would back me up and make sure there were no misunderstandings between us.

"How are you?"

"Not good."

"Why not good?"

Lisa nodded encouragingly at me.

"My head isn't good. I've been struggling with my moods."

"What's happening?"

"I seem to be going back and forth between feeling very high and very low."

"Ok, I don't see it having an effect on the children, so as far as I'm concerned, I don't need to do anything. They seem happy and well-adjusted – that's all I'm worried about."

"Yeah, they are."

Lisa cut in. "Aoife has been doing great managing two kids. They have everything they could ever need, but she hasn't been well herself. She was wondering if you could advise her on what to do? "It's not my department, so I wouldn't know what to suggest, but I think she should talk to her mental health team about it if it's causing her distress."

"Ok, so you need to get in touch with your social worker," Lisa said to me.

"I'm sorry I can't do more to help you. It's not my remit. All I'm here for is the girls."

I wondered if she was just slacking off and trying to avoid getting any extra work dropped in her lap, but at least she had faith in my parenting. That boosted my confidence levels, even if it didn't help my illness. In the end, I still had no one to turn to; just Gene.

■■

I was alone in a house filled with strangers. No one was a friend. Things were becoming too emotionally heightened for me to cope with. My parents were away; they'd gone to England for a few days to visit my sister and Pete. They lived in England by then; Poppy had moved there to join him since his career was established over there. My parents hadn't left the country since I'd gone into the refuge, and I was suddenly terrified by their absence. I went to their house every Saturday and stayed overnight. I didn't know how to get by without that sitting like an exit at the end of the week.

I woke up the day after they left, and I couldn't speak. By that I don't mean that I couldn't think of anything to say; I physically couldn't speak. Most of my vocabulary had disappeared and I couldn't construct an intelligible sentence. My verbs and nouns seemed to be there, but all the filler words that made them make sense were gone.

I phoned the social worker. Maybe if he witnessed my symptoms, he'd know I needed my medication adjusted and arrange a meeting with the psychiatrist. The hope of that was the only thing keeping me alive. The phone rang and went straight to voicemail. He mustn't have been on duty yet. I checked the time: 9.45am. Maybe he didn't start work until 10. I'd try again then. The next time I phoned, the same happened. I left a voice message; I'd leave it to him to contact me.

An hour later the phone rang. I picked up, almost gasping in despair.

"Aoife, did you ring me?"

"Yeah."

"What's wrong?"

"… don't know. Can't … can't speak."

"What do you mean."

"Can't find…. Words. Gone."

He paused; more of an impatient pause than a reflective one.

"What do you want me to do?"

"Don't know," I cried. And I didn't; I just knew I needed help.

"Ok, I'll get back to you soon."

Later that day, he arranged an appointment; not with the doctor, but with himself. He wasn't going to grant me access to the specialist; I hadn't proved myself enough to him yet. He was going to come back to the refuge to assess my symptoms in person, I supposed. I waited anxiously for his arrival. Once he got there, he would see what was happening to me and I'd get the help I needed.

In the meantime, I phoned my parents. I knew I was interrupting their holiday, but I was too unwell to be able to control that. I just needed someone I trusted to calm me down. I put the girls down for their nap and went outside with my smoke. The phone rang a couple of times and my mum answered. There was the sound of busyness in the background, and I knew she wouldn't be happy to hear from me. I needed to hear from her.

"Yes?"

"Can't speak. Words missing. Need help."

"What do you want me to do?"

"Help."

"I'm in England, what are we meant to do? Come home? We can't do that."

"Help," I sobbed. I couldn't find the words in my mind to say anything else.

"Aoife. We're visiting you sister."

I hung up on her. I was desperately angry. Part of me felt unentitled to feel that way, but the people I needed most weren't around when I needed them. I picked up the phone to Gene. He was right; he was the only person I could trust, the only person that was there whenever I needed him, any time of the day or night. I didn't remember ever phoning Gene and him not answering, unless he was angry with me. And that was my own fault. Gene was right about everyone, right about everything; the conditions attached to being with him seemed insignificant in the face of mental disturbance. I needed a carer, and Gene was the only person willing to take up that post. I'd have to pay him to do it; pay for his groceries, for his transport, pay for his cigarettes, but that was a small sacrifice to make for his constant care. Otherwise, I was alone in the world, and I was going to die. I thought about dropping the kids into the creche, going to bed with my full box of Seroquel, I thought about stepping onto the train platform at the perfect moment, about submerging myself in the stormy sea. If I didn't stay with Gene, those were my only options. I could only keep myself alive and care for my kids with his support, whatever I had to endure in exchange for that.

"Gene?"

"Yeah, babe."

"Can't speak. No words."

"What's happening, baby?"

"Words, gone. Parents... gone."

"Ok, just calm down, baby. It'll be ok. You just need to try and get your emotions down. I think your brain is short circuiting or something. It's probably because you're so stressed out."

"Yeah."

"I'm here for you, baby. I'm always here for you. Them people ain't never there when you need them. I'm so fucking angry with them."

"Yeah."

"I'm here for you, baby. I'm always here. I can meet you every day if you need me to."

Gene calmed me down enough that my speech came back. He was right: he was always there for me. Gene would even put me before his work, before his commitments and obligations. There was no one else who would make such sacrifices for me. My family wouldn't even make room for me in their holiday. I suddenly felt incredibly bitter towards them. They'd talked me into leaving Gene that day and I hadn't wanted to, hadn't been ready to. They'd implied they would fill his shoes where support was concerned if I left. And they'd gone away for leisure while I was living in a refuge. Gene was right about them: they were selfish people that had intentionally broken up our marriage; just like Gene had warned me they would one day do. I had to get out of the mess and get home to Gene.

Later that day, the social worker arrived. My words had returned to me, but my sanity hadn't. He walked into the building with an air of entitlement; like he had more right to be in the place than any of the women did. By his side, was the Health Visitor. She gave me a sly smile and the manager led them upstairs to wait in the living room while I deposited the girls in the creche.

They were sitting side by side on the sofa when I walked in. I sat on the opposite side of the room, feeling cornered and alone.

"Well, I'll tell you why we're here," said Allen, leaning towards me, a strange smile on his face.

"Ok."

"We've decided to make a referral to social services."

"What? Why?"

"We have to – you're telling us you aren't well."

"What does that have to do with my kids? I'm taking good care of them."

"It has to be affecting them."

"It isn't."

"There's no way it's not," said Allen, still smirking at me.

I looked at the Anita.

"You told me you thought I was doing a good job."

"You were having lots of difficulties with feeding."

"Alice is Lactose Intolerant. How is that anything to do with my parenting?"

"The staff have had to give you a lot of support with feeding."

"Did the staff say that?"

It wasn't true. I'd allowed one of the child workers to give me advice on how to wind a baby with colic; she had had one herself. Would she really have told them that? I'd thought she'd just wanted to help.

"Yes."

I didn't know whether to think that the staff had betrayed me, or whether she was lying to suit whatever agenda she had. I couldn't understand how I'd seen her only days before and she'd said I was coping well with my children, and now, suddenly, she thought I was a threat to their wellbeing.

"We don't think you should move out of the refuge yet."

"What if I get a housing offer?"

"We think you should defer it – explain to them that we've recommended you stay here."

"I thought you said it was important I got my own house?" I said to Allen.

"Well, we didn't know about your mental state then - you'll need help to look after the girls."

I started crying uncontrollably. I couldn't hold back or keep the mask I wore for public view on anymore.

"I love those girls. I take good care of them, all by myself. I don't need anyone's help to look after them, nor do I ask for it. You've turned me asking for help with my mental health into an issue about my children when it has nothing to do with them."

My condition seemed to have worsened since I'd entered the room. Not only was I not getting help; I was now afraid of losing my children. I wanted to beg them to withdraw the referral, but I knew it would be a fruitless fight. They already had their minds made up. I knew they were colleagues, and probably friends, and that only heightened my feelings of paranoia. I wasn't paranoid for no reason; there was a conspiracy against me and everyone was in on it: the social worker, the health visitor, the refuge workers. With all the professionals and their reports working against me, I had no hope of proving them wrong.

The two professionals before me looked at me blankly. My speech didn't draw the slightest sympathy from them. I guessed they were both incapable of it; if they'd ever had it, their jobs had wiped it out of them. I despised them, thinking of them returning to their own conventional homes, where they could sit around, with the families they took for granted, without an ounce of regret for what they'd done during their working hours. As far as I was concerned, they had destroyed what was left of my life to destroy. I didn't know if I would lose or keep my children, or have interference from the authorities, but either way, they had extinguished the last of my faith in myself.

Chapter Thirty-Seven

"Those motherfuckers did what?" Gene asked, the pitch of his voice rising. It rarely did that, so I knew even he was surprised.

"They're just doing that so they don't got to do shit about your mental health. You know they're punishing you for asking for help, right?"

"It feels like that."

"That's because it's how it is. Don't let them motherfuckers get you down. You're a great mom. You don't got nothing to worry about."

"They don't seem to think so."

"Fuck them assholes. They don't know you. Can't the staff stand up for you?"

"They seem to have taken their side."

"Bunch of fucking pussy motherfuckers. I told you not to trust them people. I hope you ain't told them nothing they can use against you."

I hoped I hadn't too, and I feared that I had.

"Listen, baby. We'll get you help. We don't need them motherfuckers."

"How? I tried ringing my parents but they're on holiday."

"Wait a minute – they're on holiday, when you just had a baby?"

"Yeah."

"Man, you got to start listening to me about these people, babe. None of them give a fuck about you. Even my ma wouldn't do that shit, and my ma's a fucking cunt."

"Yeah."

"I mean it, babe – I don't know nobody that would treat their daughter like that. Your parents are worse than mine."

"How?"

"Mine are drunks and drug addicts, but at least they don't pretend to be good people. Yours just don't want people thinking nothing bad about them, but they don't do what they say they'll do – it's all for show."

"I don't know."

I didn't have the strength left in me to battle anymore; to figure out who wished me well and who wanted to bring me down. Gene seemed to be the only one fighting my corner, so I decided to try to trust him again. I'd tried to trust my family instead, but where were they when I was in such a dangerous place?

"I want to die."

"Don't say that, baby."

"I do – I can't do this anymore. Everything is always so hard – I can't keep going."

"You can – you're the strongest person I know."

"Because I look after the girls? Apparently, I can't even do that properly."

"That ain't what I meant, babe."

"What did you mean?"

"Most motherfuckers would be dead by now, right?"

I still don't know if he meant by that that I'd lived with more mental turmoil than most could withstand or if I'd managed to live despite his efforts to drive me to the grave.

"I need to go to hospital."

"Can they adjust your meds?"

"I don't know, I think so."

"I'll go with you."

"Ok."

Usually I would have argued against it and insisted I was able to go by myself, but I was beyond that point. I couldn't pretend with strangers, I couldn't pretend with Gene, I couldn't even pretend to myself that I was alright anymore.

Chapter Thirty-Eight

Gene and I walked into the Accident & Emergency waiting room. It had been a long journey with an unwell head, but we made it and I relaxed a little. I looked at the waiting times on the screen: four hours: standard for Northern Ireland. We sat down on the hard metal seats and Gene helped himself to the snacks in the vending machine.
"Do you want some, babe?"
"Just a coffee, please. Are you getting one?"
"I guess, if that's all there is. It's probably terrible though."
He filled two cups and brought them over. The girls were both still asleep thanks to the vibrations of the bus and the walk. I hoped they'd sleep for a good while; long enough so they wouldn't wind up with bad-tempered boredom. There was a play room to the side of the waiting area. We'd take them there when they came around. Gene and I got to be alone for a valuable minute, even in an unromantic setting with far too many companions for comfort.
"Man, this place is slow. How do they get away with this shit?"
"I guess they're always busy."
"It ain't like this in America."
"You're paying for healthcare."
"I'd rather pay for decent healthcare than put up with this shit."
"Yeah, me too."
Gene surveyed the room, his foot propped on the other leg, sipping his coffee the slowest I'd ever seen him drink before.
"None of these motherfuckers look like there's shit wrong with them."
I had my head in my hands to try and stop the spinning.
"You ok, babe?"
I shook my head.
Gene pulled me towards him, kissing me on top of the head.
"We'll get you help soon, baby. Just try and relax. Calm your mind down – it ain't nothing but an illusion."
"I'm scared."
"I know, baby. It's the worst feeling in the world. I been there, I fucking know."

"How do you get through it?"

"Ain't much you can do but wait for it to pass."

I started crying, tears pressing down my face like the pressure mounting in my mind. The people waiting around us were taking on other forms: like ghosts of the people they used to be. They were all dead to me now; I was in another realm. It was like looking without being allowed to touch; I couldn't feel my hands, couldn't feel the seat beneath me, couldn't hear the multitude of strangers' words that rose up around me in a deafening din.

"Baby, you'll see the doctor soon. Want to take the girls to the playroom?"

Hope was stirring and looked anxious to get out of the pram.

"Ok."

I finished my coffee and handed it to Gene. He put the cup in the bin for me and took my arm to steady me. I knew in that moment that he was the person I wanted by my bedside in my last moments. I couldn't believe I had betrayed him by excluding him from the birth of our daughter. And in spite of that, he was still the only person there when I needed someone.

We took the girls into the play area and it revived them, like they could sense new toys were nearby. I sat on one of the kids' chairs. It reminded me of the ones in the refuge; the ones I'd sat on tens of times having a quiet word about Gene with the child workers while they helped me with the girls. He was right: I had blackened his name to every listening ear. I didn't know how he had it in him to forgive me for that. He wouldn't let me forget it of course, but he appeared to have forgiven me that day. I needed to be clearer about where my loyalty lay. I couldn't continue to meet up with Gene, return shell-shocked to the refuge and expect the workers to listen to my anguish. I needed to keep schtum and keep Gene's and my bad moments as close to my heart as the private moments between us that I cherished.

"Look what Daddy's got for you," Gene sang to Alice.

She lay on his knee, looking tinier than usual and much more vulnerable. I couldn't help hoping his mood would stay as bright as it currently was.

Gene waved a Scooby Doo toy he'd found in the room in her face and talked about every episode he planned to watch with her once we were living together. I felt my gut tighten like the ribbon knot around a present. Was that a gift that he was truly offering to us, or was it a gift I'd struggle to untie for the rest of my life, only to finally open it and find dust inside?

I was being illogical again; I couldn't allow myself to trust my tangential thinking. I knew when I wasn't well, I was prone to disappearing into my dream world; the one where I came up with implausibly negative scenarios. If I didn't adopt a more positive attitude, I was going to perish, sooner rather than later.

We sat in that confined room for an age, the girls getting fed up with the toys that missed every component essential for proper play. I was growing weary and ready to give up and start the long journey home when the door burst open and a doctor said.

"You aren't Mrs Savoyard, are you?"

"Yes."

"We're ready to see you."

I looked to Gene, expecting him to jump up to accompany me. I thought he'd want to have as much input as I did, but he stayed in his seat.

"I'll stay with the girls, baby. It'll be easier for you."

I felt hugely uncomfortable with that. What if he took his opportunity to run out the hospital doors while I was otherwise occupied? What if I never saw my daughters again? What if he told social services he'd had to take care of them while I went to hospital, because I wasn't able to? I had no choice but to trust him. There was no one else there to help and the doctor was waiting for me to follow him out the door.

"Ok," I said. "I won't be long."

"Just take whatever time you need."

I didn't know whether to thank Gene or ask him to promise to not take the girls while I was away. I couldn't make such a ridiculous remark in front of the doctor, or they'd think I needed to be locked up rather than treated. I just needed to get medication, get "home" and look after my children. I was doing it for them as much as for myself.

I walked into the unwelcoming ward and the doctor drew the curtain around me. I wondered what its purpose was when your illness was mental; everyone could hear your every word through the thin fabric anyway.

"Well, what can we do for you?"

"I have Bipolar Disorder and I'm not getting any help," I started to cry.

"Ok, what way are you feeling?"

"Like I'm going crazy. I don't think my medication is working since I had my baby."

"You're not going crazy. Don't you have a key worker?"

"Yes, but all he did was refer me to social services – he won't let me see the psychiatrist."

"Ok. Well - the problem is that because you're already attending mental health services, we can't really do anything."

"But he isn't helping me."

"If you were new to services, we could call the crisis team and they could visit. But if you aren't well, you need to talk to your social worker about being put on Home Treatment."

"They just took me off Home Treatment. I'm here because I can't get help from anyone. I just need my medication adjusted."

"We can't do that."

"So, what can you do?"

"Well, are you suicidal?"

"I'm having thoughts."

"Are you going to act on them?"

I wanted to say I might, but I knew if I did, it would seal my fate with social services, so I shook my head.

"Are you going to hurt anyone else?"

"No, but I'd never do that no matter how ill I am."

"Well, come back when you're going to harm yourself or someone else. If you have control of the thoughts that's the main thing."

I wanted to grab their sleeve and plead with them, telling them the truth, but I couldn't – I had two kids I couldn't lose. They meant more to me than my own health did.

I walked out of the room and stormed down the corridor, crying and shouting before I got to Gene.

"Baby, keep your voice down."

"I can't," I bawled.

"You got to, you can't do this in here."

"There is no help, there's nowhere to turn. They all just lie – it doesn't exist. I want to die."

Gene grabbed me by the arm and pulled me, along with the pram out the automatic door. I knew everyone in the room was watching, but there was nothing I could do about that.

We got outside to the footpath, where the noise of the traffic and sirens drowned out my howls.

"This is exactly how you cannot act in public."

"I can't help it – I want to die."

"You're going to have to help it – or you're going to lose the girls. You can't do this shit here."

"But there's no help."

"I know, baby, I know, it's fucked."

Gene pulled me towards him and wrapped me in a firm embrace. I cried all over his brown leather jacket; the one he loved so dearly, and he didn't even care.

"I'm sorry I'm wrecking your jacket," I tried to compose myself a little.

"It don't matter, baby, wreck it as much as you want."

"I love you," I said, raising my lips to meet his.

"I love you too, baby. Things are going to be ok – I know it don't feel like it, but you got to trust me on this."

"Ok."

"Once we're living together, I'm going to tell these motherfuckers to go fuck themselves."

I wished I could encourage him to do that. I thought of mental health services and how it appeared to exist before you tried to access it; then, when you touched it, you found out it was merely a hospital cut-out with nothing but a blank wall behind it. And there was no way to prove it or change it. No one would believe me, and everyone was complicit in it. I didn't know how much longer I could keep going without help.

Chapter Thirty-Nine

I was in the common area, keeping myself to myself. The bully was passing between her own kitchen and the one adjoining mine. The workers had moved me to a different one. I felt like she was trying to intimidate me, so I kept quiet and got on with preparing dinner as quickly as I could. Hope sat in the high chair at the entrance to my kitchen. The bully squeezed past her and took some cling film from one of my drawers without asking. Something about it reminded me of Gene peeing in the garden drain.

The kitchen door burst open, with a loud greeting of "hello" from one of the workers. She was called Beth and had been off sick for most of my time in the house. I didn't know her well and she was still making her mind up about me; I knew we didn't click, but I still made an effort to get to know her.

"Hello," I said as she passed by. She was on her way to the back door for her smoke break.

"Hello," she sang. She always seemed bright and breezy; but never formed a deeper connection with anyone. Maybe that was what enabled her to do her job.

"Honey, you're always so quiet within yourself. If you're not talking, she's not going to be talking," she said.

"Hope? She's one. I talk to her all the time."

"Her speech hasn't come on much. If her mummy is quiet, she's going to be quiet too. You just need to chat, chat, chat non-stop."

I couldn't help wondering if that was what had got her where she'd planned to go: the inability to ever shut up.

I nodded, gritting my teeth and turned back to the dinner pan, making a few statements to Hope on principal. I'd never allow her to see me not talking to Hope from then on, even if I had to force the incessant talking. The worker went out the back door and the bully leered at me. She was pleased with herself. Any criticism, whether "constructive" or not was a point on her side of the kitchen.

Later that day, I had a knock on my bedroom door. It was Ciara. She wanted to schedule in time for me to spend with Hope in the playroom. I'd used the playroom unofficially many times, but they needed to record on a chart the exact times I was checking in and out, so they could pass on to the health visitor how much time I was spending interacting with my child. I had no privacy anymore. If I'd been jailed, the freedom I would have had there would have been immense in comparison. I signed up for a few hours that week. They'd be checking in with me to ensure I was following through on what I'd agreed to do. They knew I took Hope out every day: to the park, for dinner, to the play café. But as they said, because I was out, and they weren't with me, they couldn't testify to the fact that I was spending time appropriately with my daughter. They couldn't trust me to tell them the truth.

I complained to Lisa about it: about how I felt monitored, how my independence had vanished, how it felt like the workers had turned on me. She acted distantly understanding but reiterated the facts: they were backing up the health visitor and helping me build evidence that I was a good mother. I didn't understand why seeing me with my happy children, day in, day out wasn't enough proof of that. It was official: I was a terrible mother. I deserved to have my children removed from my care.

Chapter Forty

The social worker was due to arrive. Not my own, but the one that had received the referral. I was a million miles beyond anxious, on my way to hopelessness. Gene had advised me to record the meeting. I had to agree; it was necessary to do that. How else could I prove what I'd really said when they tried to use my words against me, the ones that they had invented?

I walked into the creche. The social worker had specified that she wanted to see me with my kids, probably to scrutinise my parenting and corroborate the others' observations. I couldn't sleep the night before; I kept falling into a shallow sleep and being awoken by nightmares of my children being removed from my care. I had enough problems to worry about without being able to cope with that one thrown into the mix.

Thankfully, the lady arrived promptly the next morning: 9am on the dot. The workers alerted me to her arrival and I descended the staircase to greet her. I turned on my voice recorder, just to be on the safe side. I couldn't trust anyone anymore, especially when it involved my children. Even the refuge workers who had burst with pride about my parenting had turned on me. I remembered the manager and me having a private chat once when I'd been doubting myself as a mother. She'd told me she'd met a lot of good parents and a lot of bad ones. She'd said if a great mum got an A, she'd have given me an A star. She seemed to have forgotten that conversation since the health visitor and the social worker had voiced their concerns. I thought about the fact the workers had told them I was struggling with feeding Alice and anger surged up inside me, but there was nowhere it could go, so I choked it back down and left it to fester inside with all the other injustices that bred contempt in me.

I opened the door to the play room tentatively and tried to appear as calm as I could. The lady jumped up from her seat with a smile and extended a hand to me. She seemed immensely more approachable than my own team.

"You must be Aoife," she smiled.

"Yes, nice to meet you," I said.

"I'm Erin. Lovely to meet you."
I sat down on a chair opposite her, still holding Alice and flicking my eyes back and forth between her and Hope, who was playing with the dolls house, oblivious of what was going on.
"I have to be honest with you –
"Yeah?"
"When I saw the report, the first thing I thought was – would you give the girl a break? You've got enough on your plate without this."
"Thank you," I said, with more gratitude than I could convey.
"I'll tell you the points that were raised in the report and then we can discuss them."
"Ok, thanks."
I chatted intermittently to Hope and winded Alice who was crying a little and still struggling with colic.
The lady looked at me with compassion rather than judgement.
"So, the health visitor was the one who sent the report about the children. It says it was discussed with her and your social worker."
I nodded.
"It says that your daughter's speech hasn't developed, and they say you aren't talking enough. The refuge workers agree that in the communal areas you don't. But I know you aren't in your natural environment or living with ordinary circumstances. You probably don't feel relaxed enough to talk to your children the way you would in your own home."
She was so perceptive I couldn't believe it. I'd thought that was something that didn't exist in this world, where everyone twisted your words and your actions to illustrate their untruthful points.
"Thank you. You're right – I can't relax in the communal areas, or I'm busy trying to cook. There is a lady who starts talking to my children. If I talk to them, she cuts in and it makes me really uncomfortable."
I understand that, and no one knows what happens behind the closed door of your room.
I nodded.
"Your children seem content and like they are thriving to me. I have no concerns. Once you're in your own house, things will be different. Another point the health visitor raised was that you needed a lot of support from the refuge workers to care for your children and she worried you wouldn't manage in a house of your own."
"That isn't true."

I accepted help when offered, but never sought it out. I didn't even ask my family to babysit, never mind bother the workers with requests for help.

"I know she says this, but it's not what I'm seeing," said Erin. "You've settled your baby by yourself today, and you're interacting normally with the girls."

"Thanks, I just asked for help with my mental health and I feel like they turned it into an issue about my kids. I didn't understand, because a few days earlier, the health visitor told me she had no concerns."

"Well – I have none. I'm going to close and write that in the report. You can still contact us if you need any support, but I'll leave that up to you."

"Thank you."

If I couldn't have Gene, or a house of my own, the only other thing that mattered to me was having my babies with me without worrying that someone might take custody away from me.

"Do you hope to get your own house soon?"

"Hopefully, I'm waiting for my offer."

"The report says you still hope to reunite with your husband – is that right?"

"Yeah, but I'm afraid to, in case it causes problems with social services."

"Well, as long as you keep us updated along the way and we make a protection plan, we can work with you and your family."

"Thank you."

"Maybe you should look into marriage counselling, or anger management classes for your husband. We want to work with families, not split them up."

"I appreciate that. Thank you for being so understanding."

"No problem, I'm going to let you go, you've got your hands full."

"Thanks," I smiled. I pressed my hand into hers and let her out.

I sank back into my seat and let out a sigh. Everyone else might be out to get me, but one professional was on my side. I knew there would be a post-meeting review, but at least one person would be standing up for me when I wasn't there. She might have been the only person who believed I wasn't fundamentally a bad person, my husband included.

Chapter Forty-One

I didn't get any help with my mental health, but after the inter-departmental meeting, the social services case was closed. After the additional stress of that, it almost felt like I'd got what I'd initially asked for. From then on, I'd have to manage my mental health alone. I couldn't be honest about it; I was now well-acquainted with the risks of doing that. Suffering alone was what I was used to, with Gene's help, at least. If Gene was nearby, one way or another, I'd keep going. I was grateful he had remained in the country despite the fact I had moved out. He always talked about how he should have gone back to America, but the thought of that made me feel panic-stricken. Gene was still my life-raft, even though I was regularly told that he'd put me in a refuge. Still, no one understood the complexities of our case. I was at fault as much as he was, just in different ways they couldn't grasp. Gene had lived with me; he knew me inside out; no one could challenge the truths he'd told me about myself and convince me they weren't true.

I'd never met someone as smart as Gene before. If anyone questioned him, they just couldn't begin to comprehend the vast well inside him where he gathered all his knowledge about people. He could read people like open books even when they still had their security seal in place. He instinctively knew what people were thinking. No one understood my mental anguish like Gene. No one understood my thinking process like Gene. No one understood what I needed like Gene.

The workers were sharing a new way of living with me, and I didn't like it one bit. Everything in their world was too ambiguous, too open to interpretation, too wishy-washy. They taught me what relationships should look like: both partners working, both partners responsible for their own happiness, both partners leading separate lives. Gene and I were much more intense than their model couple; we needed each other all the time, we didn't enjoy being apart, we entirely affected each other's moods. That to me, felt more like real romance; more like something I wished to attain. Their version of love seemed to me like an over-diluted drink that lacked flavour. Ok,

Gene and I had a turbulent relationship, but at least we were passionate about each other, at least we'd die for one another; at least we'd rather spend our time together than dividing it in so many ways we each only got a small segment of each other. They could reiterate the same points to me, day in, day out, but they could never win me round to their way of thinking. Gene had chiselled himself too deeply into the circuits in my brain; anything less than Gene felt superficial and feeble. Once I left the refuge, I knew I'd return to my old ways and that Gene and I would prove their modern version of love to be as flimsy as it was. Our love was powerful, extreme and unruly. I believed there wasn't a love like it in the world, and so did Gene.

■■

My third and final housing offer arrived. I had changed my area of choice to the town I was living in, and I'd been offered an apartment on the outskirts of it. Two miles from the town, it wasn't exactly convenient, especially without the use of a car, but I was desperate to get out of the refuge, to escape the watchful eyes I believed were keeping a tally of all my actions for a future social services referral. I went to look at the flat the day I got the letter, just to see where it was located and what size it was. It looked very cramped for familial living. It was the size of our half of the house in Flint. I told Gene it was smaller than I'd imagined. He told me to make sure I took it anyway. All we needed was somewhere to stay with low rent, and we'd be on our way to getting our dream.

My dad offered to look at the flat with me, to make sure there were no major issues with it, and that the area was safe. I didn't care much about either factor; by then, the back seat of a friend's car would have been preferable to the hostel. I knew I'd have a quick look and agree to take it; we were just going through the formalities for my dad's peace of mind.

We met with the building's caretaker for the grand tour. He unlocked the chains that covered the door. There were metal shutters covering the windows, so you couldn't imagine how it would look with someone living there. The caretaker said it wasn't an indication of the safety of the area; it was just one of their regulations, to keep vacant flats secure.

I walked into the tight hall and wondered where I'd store the pram, or how I'd get it through the doorway. The hall looked dark and dank, but the rooms of the flat were bright and fresh; just smaller than I'd envisaged. There was a small living room, a box room-sized kitchen and bathroom and two single bedrooms. We would make it work, even if we were living on top of each other. Anything would feel luxurious compared with all living in one bedroom. A lot of work needed done to the place, but at least Gene was skilled at that sort of thing. In his capable hands, I knew everything would be alright. I followed the caretaker outside to see the garden. Each flat had its own strip of grass; they were aligned like stripes, no fences between them. I'd take the girls to the playground instead. Perhaps by then, Gene would be happy to come with us.

"What do you think?" I asked my dad.

He shrugged. "Seems alright."

That was what I thought too; it seemed alright; no great potential, just basic.

"We'll talk about it after, sure," said my dad. "Thanks for showing us around," he nodded to the caretaker. "Are you about here much?"

"I'm always around fixing bits and pieces."

"Is it a safe area?"

"It seems safe enough, but I only see it in daylight. In darkness, it could be another story, but as far as I know, it's fine."

My dad nodded. "Ok, thanks for taking the time to show us round. How long does she have to think it over?"

"I'd get back to them quickly. There are a lot of people on the waiting list that would snap this place up if they had the chance."

My dad drove us back into the town centre. I looked out the window at the surrounding area. It was barren; all that existed there was a drive-thru diner and a supermarket. In the Winter, I knew I wasn't likely to venture further than that. With a double pram, my options were limited, and it was on top of a rather steep hill. I thought about the flat; I brought up no strong emotions, for nor against it. I was looking for a permanent station, and it felt like a landing pad, but it was hard to imagine it looking homely with unpainted walls, cables hanging out of every wall and not an appliance in sight.

"Well, what are you going to do?" asked my dad. We arrived back in the town and passed the shops, the seafront and the local facilities. I felt more connected to civilisation again, and I realised, I didn't want the flat. There was nothing much I could fault about it, but it just wasn't the place I envisioned myself living. I'd be isolated; even stranded out there. That was the last thing I needed for my mental health. I knew the refuge workers would be stunned if I turned my final housing offer down. I wondered if anyone had had the audacity to do that before. It just didn't fit into the loosely held idea in my head of where I saw myself going. Gene would be angry, the professionals would think I had lost the plot, but I had to do what felt right to me, or rather, listen to what didn't feel right.

"I'm not going to take it," I said, with the first sign of self-assurance I'd displayed in years.

My dad nodded.

"I liked it."

"Yeah, I thought it was alright. Needed a lot of work done to it – but it was in good enough shape."

"I just don't think I want to be so far away from the town. I don't think it'd be good for my mental health being stuck there."

"Well, if that's what you think, love, just look for a private rental." I knew I was mad to consider it, but I had an instinctive feeling in my gut, and for once, I couldn't ignore it.

Chapter Forty-Two

"You do realise this is your last offer?"

"Yes."

"Do you realise the significance of turning down a third offer?"

"I think so."

"You'll be removed from the housing list for a year before you can reapply."

"Ok."

"Ok, Aoife, if that's what you want to do, that's up to you – but you'll have to start looking for a house now and aim to move out in the next few weeks."

"That's ok."

The worker smiled at me. "I understand why you want to live in town instead."

"I just can't see myself coping when I'm that remote and don't have a car."

"That sounds sensible to me. If you want to run any of the locations past me, work away. I know the parts of this town that are ok and the parts you'd want to avoid."

I'd been living on one of the to-avoid streets for months and hadn't noticed much in the way of danger, but I was staying in a place that cocooned me from it too. I knew my own home wouldn't have a direct dial to emergency services, CCTV in operation and reinforced glass.

Gene wasn't happy that I'd turned down my offer.

"Why did you turn it down? We could have fixed it up – it was cheap, that's all that matters."

"I'll find somewhere else."

"Not for 200 a month."

"No, but I'll find somewhere reasonable."

"I don't care where we live so long as we're together – just find somewhere, babe – and quick."

It was the beginning of October and I'd left our home eight months earlier. Despite all that had come to pass in that time, it was hard to believe that I'd left almost a year earlier. I was running out of time to find a house, and I had to hurry up if I wanted to leave the refuge before the Christmas season set in. I'd spent so long in that house it had become normality to me, but I couldn't bear to spend Christmas there; I just wanted a home of my own, a Christmas tree to put my children's gifts under and a kitchen of my own to cook in. More than that, I'd lived in the refuge for too long and if I stayed on, I feared I'd never adapt to regular life again.

I looked at houses, but I did it without Gene. Part of me was still too afraid to tell him their location, in case I ended up signing a lease for one of them and he knew where it was. He might show up after dark and wreak his revenge. Maybe he was waiting until I was staying somewhere without tight security; maybe then he'd take the girls from me, when no one was looking and there was no crowd to slow his escape. Gene told me he loved me with everything in him, but something told me he hated me with everything in him too. His loving half would dart in front of a bus to push me out of its path, but his hateful side would shove me under it, or at least coerce me into jumping in front of it myself. I could never be sure of Gene: what his mood would be, what he was capable of, when the evil stranger would reappear and if he'd choose to stick around. Could I chance it? Could I put all our lives on the line in the hope that Gene's promises were true and that we'd finally be happy, not just a portion of the time, but every day? How did I know he wouldn't punish me for the rest of my life for my wrongdoings? I knew he resented me for them; he reminded me often enough. And I knew that I deserved his resentment. No other wife I'd heard of had behaved as atrociously towards their husband as I had. I'd promised I'd never leave him, and I'd committed the ultimate betrayal.

The second house I viewed was the one I was going to take; I knew it as soon as I walked through the door. I could visualise Hope and Alice playing there, it was safe and contained for young children and it was affordable. I walked straight from the house to the agency to submit my application form. I was worried I wouldn't get it; my rental history wasn't impressive, and my current address was a hostel. The manager had offered to provide me with a good reference, but I doubted that would be enough to convince the agent that I'd be a reliable tenant. If they decided to check my previous address out and rang the agency for the details, I knew I'd be in trouble. The agency didn't know my reasons for leaving; they just knew I'd upped and left one day, neglecting to take my belongings with me. I'd been a joint tenant on the lease, so when Gene hadn't paid the rent for the couple of months before he was asked to leave, as far as they were concerned, I hadn't either. I'd likely cost them cleaning fees, not to mention any additional damage caused by Gene. I was probably one of the worst tenants they'd ever had, at least from their restricted viewpoint.

Thankfully, the new agency's checks were less rigorous than I'd expected. The house had just been put up for rent, and I was the first to apply. I got it. In two weeks, I'd be living in my own house, hopefully never having to set foot in a refuge again. The house was unfurnished, but I'd expected to move into one that was on the housing list anyway. I'd buy the basics and Gene and I could gather items we both liked once he was living there too. I still didn't tell my parents I'd decided he would join me later; if I did, they never would have signed as guarantor. Without a guarantor, I'd be homeless forever.

I packed up everything I owned in the refuge and sat waiting for my moving day to arrive. Everything was changing in the house. More rules were being broken by the current line-up and it seemed like a good time to leave. I'd miss the refuge workers, in a funny way. They'd become a second family to me, and I wasn't allowed to keep in touch with them after I left. We could discreetly acknowledge each other if we crossed paths in the street, but we couldn't seek each other out. You could still phone the house after leaving to update them on how things were going, but they told me most women stopped calling after a few weeks; they'd moved onto their new lives. I assumed I'd keep in touch. Bad connection or not, I'd had some unexpected laughs and memorable conversations while I'd been there. They'd lived with me every day for nine months; they knew me as well as anyone did.

"Will you miss us when you leave?" Lana asked.

"Yeah, but I can't wait to get out," I smiled.

"You've been here a long time. I remember when you first came here."

"You do?"

"Yeah, you were like a different woman."

I couldn't see much change in myself, but it's hard to recognise change in yourself.

"I can't remember that day very clearly – it was all a blur."

"You've done well."

"I still wish I hadn't come."

"I know – just make sure if you let him move in, you keep your name on the house. If it's your house and things get out of control, at least you won't lose your home again. You can just tell him to leave."

I nodded, but knew if it came to it, Gene would never leave, no matter whose name was or wasn't on the lease.

"Why do you think I'm different now?"

"You looked terrified when you got here – you couldn't even talk to us or look anyone in the eye. Now you smile and joke around."

"I guess."

I didn't notice that I felt inordinately happy compared with when I'd arrived, but she must have been right. If I was more positive and felt more capable than when I'd arrived, it was only because relations had improved between Gene and me.

"Did you think I would go back?"

"Yeah, but I think it's better you get your own house and have your say over who lives there."

"Do you think I did the right thing?"

"Coming here? 100% When a woman comes through that door, I'm amazed by them. It's the bravest thing they can do."

"Really? I thought you'd think we're pathetic."

"Why would I think that?"

"Our lives are a mess."

"Leaving is a huge step. Most people couldn't do it."

"I always thought of it as weakness."

She shook her head forcefully. "It's anything but."

"I'll miss some things about living here."

"Yeah, it's good craic sometimes."

"It'll be weird living alone."

"You'll be fine. You'll get used to it again."

I had my final meeting, to close my file in the refuge. I'd still have a worker in the women's centre to give me support. I'd agreed to attend the group counselling programme to keep learning about what a healthy relationship looked like. Maybe if they could change my mindset, I'd find one someday.

"Well, Aoife," Beth pronounced. "You've done a great job."

She was full of praise but wasn't as perceptive as she needed to be. She took the attitude that once you decided to leave, you were done and dusted with your rehabilitation and on to better things.

"I have?"

"Yes, when you arrived here, you didn't even recognise that you were being abused."

"Yeah." I silently wondered if my attitude had changed at all when it came to that point.

"You're a great wee mummy, and I know you'll be just fine when you leave here."

"Thanks."

"You're going to have a good life."

"How do you know that?"

"I just do."

I wondered if things were ever that simple. Wasn't life a constant ebb and flow of good and bad experiences? Did things ever resolve themselves once and for all? I'd used to think that way and this was where it had landed me: in a homeless shelter for abused women. Did I still believe that everything would be alright in the end? I now knew that hardship was a constant component of life, and that tainted my fanciful view of it somewhat. I smiled sadly, thinking about the person I'd used to be, before Gene, before the refuge, before motherhood. I'd been pure, naïve and well-meaning. I'd seen the best in people when there wasn't even a hint of goodness to be found. I'd had so many aspirations, so much faith that life would work itself out for the good. That was all gone.

A couple of days later, I moved out. I said goodbye to the workers, with hugs and promises to keep in touch. I gave them leaving presents and it felt much like my school send-off when it was time to go to university. They were like proud parents, sending me off to better things. I moved into my new house with the help of my parents and a small van. I didn't need a moving lorry; I didn't own enough items to fill one. We unpacked most of the items. I had a blow-up bed I'd borrowed from my parents, just like Gene when he'd moved to Flint. I knew what he'd felt like now, moving to a new house with nothing to fill it with. At least I had a fridge and a bathroom sink. He was right; I still knew nothing of hardship. I sat down on the wooden floor of the living room, taking a breather. I owned one chair: a wicker one that my parents had brought round from their house. I used to use it in my old bedroom while I worked at my desk on homework and studied for a brighter future. I didn't use those books anymore. I had a first-class degree in French, but I might as well have left secondary school when I'd got fed up with it.

I didn't have the means to use it, nor the emotional endurance. I was a mother now, but not in the way I'd hoped. I was juggling family life alone and that was the most I could cope with. I felt like an absolute failure. I'd thought I'd work as a translator, or an interpreter, or a teacher. But life hadn't followed the planned path I'd mapped in my mind. I had to accept where I was: starting from scratch on benefits, two children under two reliant upon me, no promising career. I couldn't face the thought of such desperate failure, so keeping my hope for Gene and me alive was what kept me trudging along. Repairing my marriage was all I had to look forward to.

"Well, you've got your own house now," smiled my mum. "Congratulations."

I couldn't understand why I was being congratulated on such sorrowful circumstances. I didn't feel a trace of joy inside me. I had never wanted to have my own home; it was the last thing on life's wish list.

"Let's get something to eat," said my dad. "I'll get Chinese."

"Thanks," I smiled. I hoped I had enough cutlery and plates to feed everyone on. All but one of us would have to eat on the floor.

I remembered my mum visiting 2 Belmont Place and saying how house proud I was. I thought about all the items we'd bought for our family home the first time round. It was less than two years earlier, and I'd spent hundreds on crockery, kitchen equipment, Christmas decorations, cushions, throws. They were all in the nearest skip now, or, they'd likely made it to the landfill. I was buying everything when I'd already had everything in that home. I hadn't thought through the utter destruction that my leaving would bring about; not just to Gene and myself, but to our home and belongings. The worst feeling was knowing that the place you still considered home no longer existed. It had new tenants living in it now, ones that had made their own imprint on the place, getting rid of the last details that showed we'd ever lived there. I wanted to go to the house; to stand outside it and use its familiar front to help me cling to the dream I wasn't yet ready to discard. The problem was that the house had become so much more than a building. It had become a symbol of the life I could have had if I hadn't made the mistake of leaving. I replayed that day in my head to a sickening degree, always imagining I'd chosen not to follow my mum's advice. We could have been happy in that house, if I had just tried harder, if I hadn't abandoned Gene so easily. So many beautiful and distressing moments had occurred in that structure. I couldn't face the thought of other families making new memories there. It was our house: mine and Gene's, whether we lived there or not. It had risen in my mind to the level of a heavenly abode, one I had no hope of entering, but I constantly strove to reach in my mind.

It was at that time that I tried to recreate our old life. I'd lost so many items in the move and they'd all become precious to me, even if they'd been relatively meaningless to me when I'd lived there. I wanted to repurchase all of them. If I did, maybe I could pretend none of the last year had happened. Maybe it would bring a feeling of home to my new house. It was so much more aesthetically pleasing than the last house, but it would never be that house, and so, I had to do with it what I could. I used the pots and pans Gene and I had cooked with; my dad had lifted everything practical he could fit into his car from the downstairs of the house. I had the pot that Gene used for deep frying; it had a ring inside it that remained from the hot oil. I had the slotted spoon he used for fishing out fries. I didn't have a use for it, but I kept it anyway. It was like having a piece of my real home in the new house. I looked out for clothes I'd had that I'd lost in the house; I replaced the missing ones with similar patterns and styles. I looked out for décor that resembled the kind Gene had liked. I also bought things I knew Gene would have discouraged me from buying. I was conflicted about whether home meant having the freedom to choose what I liked or replicating the items that had last made me feel at home. The objects I found that were the same as those that Gene and I had owned made me feel a strange mixture of comfort and terror; just like Gene.

Gene knew I'd moved out of the hostel. He seemed to sense it the day it happened, just like I sensed he had left his job. He decided to stop going around the time I moved; he couldn't keep up the five-mile walk, and the work was wearing him out. They had underpaid him in his last pay check and had refused to correct it; enough was enough. I panicked when I found out, as I always did when Gene did something wayward, but he assured me he'd find something else. That job hadn't been the answer anyway; it had barely provided him with enough to pay the bills. He started on part time hours, with the promise that they would increase the longer he stayed, but there was no sign of that happening. Gene couldn't settle for poor treatment, so he had to take a stand. That's what he kept telling me. He couldn't just let people disrespect him and walk all over him. If he sacrificed his self-respect for the sake of a job, he would have nothing left. If a job challenged his values, it wasn't the right job for him. I had to understand that, even if it meant he starved to death.

"I'll just eat hotdogs, babe. The landlord is pretty cool here – if I'm late with the rent by a month he won't mind."

I was terrified that Gene had misread the situation and assumed he was more lenient than he was. If Gene got kicked out of the bedsit, he'd literally be living on the street. Where else was he going to find with such affordable rent and no need for a guarantor? Meanwhile, I was selfishly settled in a new home, with no trouble getting a guarantor. I'd promised my mum I wouldn't allow Gene to move in, but she'd understand if he did - I'd had to do what was right for my family. The girls needed their dad, and I needed my husband. I was running out of steam to survive alone.

I'd put in a request for a new health visitor, and a new social worker. I had decided to adopt Gene's policy; if something wasn't working for me, I'd cut myself free from it. He'd inspired me in so many healthy ways. My new social worker was a bit lacking in passion and in personality, but anything was preferable to the wolf that had been unleashed upon me the last time round. The health visitor acted sorry to see me go; she claimed she had wanted to see me living in my new home; the one she had worked to prevent me finding. I would never forget what those two individuals had done to me and my girls; it had left a permanent scar on my heart. I knew more than ever that I needed Gene's mighty hand protecting me from all the evil that might befall me. It was lurking behind every corner I turned in life.

I still didn't tell Gene where the house was. I didn't want him to know its location until we had okayed it with social services. I'd decided to do everything by the books. I would do exactly what the one trustworthy social worker had advised me, including them in every step. Then, we wouldn't fall upon any new and unwanted surprises.

I continued meeting Gene in my town. I wouldn't tell him even the general direction of my address; he thought I was displaying a ridiculous level of paranoia, but I had to protect our family, no matter what. Part of me was still afraid to tell him where we lived, in case he kicked the door down, or worse. I knew that it was just my mind, blowing things out of proportion, but I couldn't turn down the sick feeling in the pit of my stomach.

I walked to the train station; ten minutes in which to consider turning back. I couldn't. I felt compelled to see Gene, even though the thought of it made me ill with worry. What mood would he be in today? How much money would he need? How many people might witness one of our public outbursts? I tried to push those questions to the back of my mind, keeping my love for him at the foreground; that, and my hope for our relationship.

I approached the entrance to the station and contemplated turning back one last time, but I powered through it. I had to; Gene had come all the way from Belfast, using the money I'd sent him to get there. He could have used it for something else, but he'd chosen to spend it on seeing me. I walked up the steps to his platform, my heart in my throat. The cool currents the trains brought with them when they drew into the station blew my hair upwards and chilled me to the bone. I stood alone on the platform. It was a weekday morning and all other foot traffic was moving towards Belfast. Gene's train pulled in and he lumbered off it. He seemed to be the only passenger; everyone else must have been in work.

He limped along the platform, like a stage for the performance of his aches and pains. I'd come to suspect that he might have been putting them on, or at least, turning them up for my sake. If he looked in too much pain to work, I couldn't fault him for not going, or for asking me for money, or for making me buy his medication. Maybe I was just letting my negative worldview colour my opinion of him and his actions.

"Hey, baby," he said, giving me a smile, askew.

"How's your foot?" I asked, through gritted teeth. I resented asking about it and tried to avoid it for as long as I could without looking uncaring. I knew a lengthy conversation about it would follow, during which Gene would extol the benefits of opium.

"Fucking agony, man. I ain't taken no meds today."

"How come?"

"Didn't have no money to do it. Hey, babe, can we swing by the pharmacy? You can run in and get me some Co-codamol."

"Ok," I said, trying with everything in me not to roll my eyes.

How had I become so insensitive and unsympathetic? I used to feel Gene's pain like it was my own, but now his pain was something I prayed would pass without causing us any more problems. Gene walked with all his weight on his other foot, stopping every few feet to grimace and groan.

"This is fucking insane, man. If I don't get on a proper pain regimen soon, I ain't going to be able to walk. I can barely hold my fucking daughters with this hand."

He opened and closed his hand several times for effect, or perhaps to just loosen it up a bit. I loathed myself for thinking such unfeeling thoughts. Gene was right: I was like his half-sister – just a cold bitch who laughed at his pain.

We arrived at the door to the pharmacy.

"I'll wait here, babe. I'll stand with the stroller."

"Ok, do you not want to come in?"

"Why the fuck would I do that? It don't make no fucking sense."

I hesitated for a moment.

"Baby, I'm not going to take the girls. If I was going to do that, I'd have done it already. It only would have took one phone call to SS."

He said SS like social services was something he was privy to; like a close friend whose name he had affectionately abbreviated.

"Fine, I'll get them."

"Thank you, baby." He smiled at me again.

I kept my eyes on Gene from behind the glass door. I spoke to the pharmacist, with my gaze still fixed on Gene. I knew it probably made me look like a suspicious character, but I had to prepare myself to run if Gene bolted to the station with the pram. If he got the girls on the train before I reached it, he could take them anywhere, and I would never know where they had gone to. I knew if that happened, I'd receive little support from social services to get them back. I had voluntarily met up with Gene and allowed unsupervised contact. They were his daughters too; he was as much within his rights to take them as I was. As the queue slowly edged its way forwards, I hated myself for putting myself and my daughters at risk. It had seemed like an irrational thought on the way to the station, but now that Gene was there in body and his mood seemed susceptible to sudden change if he didn't get what he wanted, I realised the risk was real. I just had to get his medication and get through the morning without saying the wrong thing and I'd get my girls safely home to our house. I could do that; all it took was a little bit of acting and tongue-biting, and I wouldn't say anything to offend him. Thankfully, I knew what Gene's triggers were; I just needed to keep my opinions to myself and let him do the things I didn't want him to: swearing profusely in front of the girls, ordering me around, getting me to pay with things. Saying nothing wasn't so hard, was it? But why had I never managed to say nothing in the house? I'd told myself so many times that all I had to do was avoid behaving the way I did, and things wouldn't get out of hand. But they always somehow did anyway.

I reached the till, asked for the tablets and flung the exact change at the pharmacist. I knew what her questions would be, and the order in which they would come at me. I automatically answered, trying to appear nonchalant as I could. Then I walked out the door. Gene was still standing in the spot I'd left him in; maybe he was right – maybe I had to trust him. Something told me I shouldn't, but he'd stayed true to his word, and the girls seemed relaxed.

I peered under the pram hood, and they both gave me a smile. They looked so small and fragile there, like two little china dolls. If I lost them, I'd never survive it. I knew I needed to stop taking the risk, but I didn't know how to survive without Gene. I imagined life without him for a moment, and I was paralysed by fear. I could barely make it through an hour of my life without lifting the phone to him. He was the only reason I hadn't committed suicide yet. He had been the only listening ear when I'd been in my darkest days in the refuge. I remembered him accompanying me to the hospital and I knew that if he wasn't around, no one else would have volunteered to do the same. Danger, or none, I was stuck where I was.

I had just met my new worker the day before. She had reinforced the points I'd had drilled into me in the refuge: abusers don't change, there are no excuses for abuse, I am a capable woman who is able to cut contact. I ticked the boxes on her list of questions but had no intention on following through on any of her advice. She didn't understand how enmeshed my life was with Gene's. She didn't understand how my mental illness affected me. She made striking out on my own sound simple, when it was anything but.

Gene leaned in and gave me a kiss and I pushed all the points she had tried to drive home to the back of my mind. I'd heard them every day for almost a year, and I was no closer to receiving them. My mum said I needed help: the same level of support I'd had in the refuge. My family were aware of the fact I still met up with Gene, but they didn't think it was a sensible decision. I knew they thought it was foolhardy, but I also knew they couldn't comprehend the level of my dependency on him. Without Gene, my children would have no mother. He was the one working away in the background, keeping the whole show together. I was tired of being congratulated on my achievements: looking after the girls alone, finding my own house, staying stable. None of it was truly happening; it was all an illusion for the outside world. Only Gene knew my true mental state.

"Hey, babe," he said, "Let's go get a cup of coffee and I can take these."

"Ok. Where do you want to go to?"

"I don't care – let's just go to Burger King or somewhere. You can get Hope some chicken nuggets."

"Ok."

I pushed the pram in the direction of my house, hoping Gene wouldn't somehow sense we were nearing it. He seemed to know everything about me without me telling him. Could he read what I was thinking? I tried not to think anything significant just in case he could. He probably knew people who could inform him of my whereabouts anyway. I didn't know how they amassed their information, but Gene had a way of sniffing out what he needed to know.

"So, are you going to tell me where you live?" he asked.

His question seemed to confirm my worries.

"Not yet," I said.

"What are you so afraid of? Do you think I'm going to show up at the door?" he laughed. "I ain't going to do that."

"Yeah."

"Well?"

"I want to run everything by social services first."

"So, arrange a meeting with them. I've been telling you to do that for months."

"Ok."

"Seriously, call them up and tell them we're getting back together – there ain't nothing they can do about that. You give power to people that they don't have."

"Yeah."

"Stop being such a fucking coward."

"I'm not," I pleaded, suspecting he was right.

"Set up marriage counselling too."

"Where?"

"Anywhere, I don't give a shit."

"Who will mind the girls?"

"We'll take them with us, it ain't a big fucking deal. You just make it one because you don't want to go."

"That isn't true."

"Well, prove it then. If you want me, you got to prove it, because you ain't done nothing you've said you were going to do."

"I'm sorry."

I resolved to research marriage counselling as soon as I got home that day. I didn't know what had held me back from arranging it so far. I was afraid that once I was in a room with Gene and a counsellor, I'd suddenly be the responsible one for all our problems. But Gene and I weren't different; that's what he always told me: "we're the same, you and me."

Chapter Forty-Three

I phoned the only marriage counsellor I'd heard of. It hadn't been something I had ever hoped or planned to go to, so my knowledge of where to find one was severely limited. They had a twelve-week waiting list for an initial consultation, followed by a further wait until they could squeeze you in for regular sessions. We couldn't afford to wait around any longer. It was coming up to Christmas time and the thought of Gene and me having to meet up in a coffee shop if we wanted to see each other sounded bleak. Hopefully, if social services knew we had lined up marriage counselling or had had a session or two, they'd lighten up a little with their rules for us meeting.

I came across a local counselling service run in a church. I knew Gene would protest about going; he hated organised religion and I knew he'd expect them to try to convert us to Christianity while we were there. I was reluctant to attend in a church too; I was worried Gene would make an unsuitable remark and we'd be ejected from its doors.

I phoned up to find out how it worked. The lady I spoke to was extremely approachable. She wanted to know our circumstances but didn't give any appearance of judging them. Maybe we would get further with a service that wanted to preserve marriage at any price, rather than contemporary counselling that didn't view divorce as a failure. I arranged an appointment for the beginning of the new year. I hoped Gene would be willing to go with me.

I phoned social services immediately after. I wanted to confirm with them that we were going to attend counselling and get their consent to get back together. I didn't know it wouldn't be that straightforward. They said we would have to complete the counselling programme first and meet with them to discuss the terms of our reconciliation. I'd do anything to get my family back together; I hoped Gene was as committed to that aim as I was. He was terrible at biting his tongue, but he did have an awareness of what was and wasn't appropriate to verbalise. If he knew our family was under threat, I hoped he'd say and do all the right things. With a police report filed, evidence of my residency in the refuge and Gene's lack of employment, I worried that they wouldn't be on our side.

The phone rang, and Gene picked up.

"Yeah, babe."

"What are you doing?"

"I'm laying watching TV – ain't got nothing else to do."

"Are you looking for a job?"

"Don't start, babe. I don't want to fight with you."

"I'm not fighting. I rang a marriage counsellor to set up an appointment."

"And?"

"We start at the beginning of January."

"Cool, where is it?"

"Not far from me."

"Ok. How much is it?"

"Free."

"What's the catch?"

"It's in a church. Is that a problem?"

"No, I'll fucking go anywhere if it means I get my family back."

I smiled. I knew he'd even cross the sea again for me if he had to.

Chapter Forty-Four

Christmas without Gene was cruel. It didn't equal the cruelty of my episode with social services, but I'd believed Gene and I would be back together by Christmas. I wanted Hope's second Christmas to destroy the disappointment of the first. I'd never noticed before how much of an occasion for couples Christmas was. Everywhere I looked, there were lovers holding hands, buying joint presents for their kids, going on festive outings together. I took the girls to the Christmas market with my parents and tried not to mope so much I ruined the mood of the day. I wanted to invite Gene, but there was no way they would go if he was there. I had to work to keep everyone happy at Christmas and mentioning Gene's name to my dad was enough to send him into a depressive slump. My family didn't feel whole; without Gene, the main component was still missing. I thought about all the couples who unthinkingly invited their parents and their partners to their Christmas dinners. They didn't know how lucky they were to have that as an option. I wished I'd appreciated our previous Christmas more. At least I'd been allowed to have Gene and my parents in the same room for the exchanging of presents and the brewing of coffee. I would spend my Christmas Day at my parents' house. Social services would never allow Gene to come around anyway, even if I had persuaded my family. Everyone hated Gene; he was right – I was the only one that loved him unconditionally.

I packed the girls' presents and stocking fillers into the boot of my dad's car. Gene hadn't given me a present for them, but it wasn't his fault – he could barely afford to feed himself. I wished I could feel at home in my own house, but the thought of laying out the girls' Christmas presents alone after-dark was more than I could bear. I needed to get away for a few days, to have the distraction of others' company rather than fretting over my own let-downs.

My dad drove me to his house; my parents generously shared their Christmas with me, but I couldn't help resenting the fact that the family was composed of couples other than me. I was the only one without the person I loved most by my side. I watched Poppy and

Pete cuddling in the one armchair and felt hopelessness growing back inside me. I'd always had a lot of hope stored up inside, but its volume had become so diminished I struggled to find it anymore. I prayed Christmas would pass quickly and cursed commercial occasions for emphasising my pain.

My parents laid out their presents for the girls alongside mine and I looked at my own pathetic pile, feeling it was yet another disappointment I had presented my girls with. I was a useless mother: I couldn't provide them with anything that someone else couldn't do better. I imagined myself removed from the world, a couple stepping in to take up my parenting duties. It seemed like an option that the girls would find more fulfilling. At least if I was out of the picture, they would have a chance at conventional happiness. But I knew I needed to stop being so negative: Gene and I were going to go to counselling and everything would get resolved.

The turkey was carved, the tree taken down and reality resumed once more. For once, I was glad the celebrations were over. They'd been nothing to me but a moment of mourning.

■■■

January was as dreary and uninviting as always, but I put my faith into the upcoming appointment at the church. Once we went there, everything would seem rosier. The day of the appointment, I met Gene nearby. We walked the mile to the church, me pushing the pram, Gene limping.

"We're going to be late," I said, quickening my pace.

"Babe, would you slow down? I can't walk no faster with this fucking foot."

"Ok, but what if he sends us away?"

"He won't, babe. You worry too much about everything."

I hoped Gene's cock-eyed optimism would be right this time.

We arrived and luckily the guy who was taking the session had been held up. He looked at me with surprise; he hadn't known we were bringing our children with us. We had no choice; my parents wouldn't mind them whilst I attempted to repair my marriage, and I didn't know of a babysitter to call. The man didn't seem put off by it; he asked the secretary to bring him a basket of toys and allowed the girls to play at our feet.

"Thanks, man. We have trouble getting babysitters," said Gene.

"No problem, sometimes it's hard to find someone you're happy leaving your children with. Especially when they're so young."

"Thanks, man," beamed Gene.

The counsellor gave him a look of approval and I sensed that they were going to get along well. I hoped he would stay even-handed with his advice and not mark me as the reason for all our issues. I knew Gene's stories sounded bad, taken out of context, at least. He had lost his family, his home and was staying in a bedsit he could barely afford, surrounded by a variety of unsavoury characters who only spoke to him when it was his turn to refill the toilet paper supply, or when they needed to bum a smoke, or vice versa.

"I'm Stephen, what are your names?"

"I'm Gene."

"I'm Aoife, nice to meet you,"

I smiled and then looked away. I knew I needed to keep my eyes on Hope and Alice; if they got up to mischief it would be my job to sort it out.

"Well, why don't you start by telling me what you'd like to get from counselling?"

"We want to get back together," said Gene.

"Are you separated?"

"Well, we're together, but we ain't living together."

"Ok, since when?" the man pencilled something onto his pad.

"Since last February."

"Ok, so what happened?"

"She left," said Gene, pinning me in the air with his thumb.

"Ok, I think maybe we should avoid making it sound like we are blaming each other," said Stephen.

"Sorry, man. My wife left last February, wasn't it, babe?"

"Yeah, it was."

"And why did you leave?"

"We weren't getting along," said Gene.

"Well, do you want to give me some examples?"

"Well, we have bad arguments, I mean *bad* arguments," said Gene. "We don't know how to manage conflict properly. We need someone to teach us how to do it."

"Ok, well, I think I can help with that, but you'll have to be prepared to both put in the work."

I nodded. I felt like questioning him on how I could have made the unworkable work. I felt like explaining to him what I'd learnt through the women's shelter: that there's no reasoning with abuse, that you were wrong even when you did what you thought was right, but I wanted to fix our relationship, so I kept quiet and nodded earnestly.

"What first drew you to Aoife?" Stephen asked.

"She's super smart, man. Smarter than I'll ever be. She's beautiful. I knew she'd be a good mom."

"And do you still feel that way about her?"

"Yeah, man. She's the love of my life."

Gene did his secretive smile at me and I smiled back.

"And what drew you to Gene?" he asked me.

"He's intelligent, really funny, he understands me more than anyone I've ever met."

"So, you are with each other for good reasons, but something has just gone wrong."

"What way do you talk to Aoife? Are you loving towards her?"

"Yeah, sometimes, man. That's the problem – I tell her how much I love her and call her baby – then we start arguing and she ain't baby no more."

"What do you call her then?"

"Uh, I can't say it in here," laughed Gene.

Stephen did a little laugh and then became serious again.

"So, you name-call when you're arguing?"

"Yeah, all the time."

"Ok, so you want help to stop doing that?"

"What do you do in arguments, Aoife?"

I was too ashamed to own up to everything that I'd done, so I hesitated and held back for a minute.

"I go from zero to one hundred when we argue. I don't know why it happens, but I'm fine one minute - the next I can't calm myself down. I start screaming at Gene and run away."

"What do you think causes that?"

"I think it's because I think Gene is criticising me."

"Are you?" he asked Gene.

"Probably, but I don't mean to. I think she' s criticising me and then I act like an asshole. Sorry – I shouldn't have said that in here, but it's true."

I was surprised by how transparent Gene was being. I'd expected it to be almost impossible for the counsellor to draw any admission of fault from him. But here he was, opening up to him like I'd always wanted him to do to me. I couldn't remember Gene ever owning up to anything close to full fault for one of our fights, but he seemed happy to do it with the counsellor.

"I'm going to give you some worksheets to take home and fill out."

"You're giving us homework?" Gene smirked.

"In a way – yes. It's a questionnaire about your partner – to help us work out what you need help with and what you know and don't know about each other."

"Alright."

"I'm going to arrange another appointment with you and we can discuss what you've been working on."

I flipped through the stapled worksheet. There were pages of questions; I couldn't imagine Gene ever sitting down to spend time doing something like that. But maybe I needed to stop making assumptions about him. That's what he always said: I assumed I knew what he was thinking. There was so much I needed to correct in my own behaviour that I hadn't ever sat down to properly think through. Maybe Gene had been right about marriage counselling all along.

"I'm going to book you in for two weeks from now if that suits?"

"Yeah, man."

"Is it ok we'll have the kids with us?" I asked.

"Of course, you've just been happy to play, haven't you?" he smiled at them. They had pulled out every toy and moved onto the pamphlets and business cards he had set out on the coffee table beside us.

"Hey, that ain't yours," said Gene, kindly.

He took the paper from Hope and Alice's hands and put it tidily away. It was the first time I'd seen Gene tidy up after himself, or our kids, in a public place. Maybe he was changing after all.

We walked back into the town.

"Well, what did you think?" I asked, pushing the pram and squinting to see through the rain. It was pelting down; a day to be indoors. I thought about the house and wished I could invite Gene inside. I pictured us sitting over coffees in the kitchen, talking in the most relaxed manner we had since I'd left. Then I pictured Gene passing comment on how I'd decorated the place, how my coffee didn't taste right and him taking charge of my laptop to play his own music. I felt a surge of sickness in my stomach. It was as much a relief as a disappointment that he couldn't come over.

"It was a waste of time, man. He didn't say nothing we don't already know."

"He was nice."

"Yeah he was nice, but he don't got nothing to teach us we couldn't figure out ourselves."

"So, are you not going back?"

"I'll go back. We're just doing this so social services get off our backs."

I nodded, but part of me was disappointed that he didn't want to attend for the improvement of our relationship too. I knew we had things to learn about handling conflict, and if Gene wasn't willing to work at it like I was, things would slip back into what they'd been before.

"What are you going to do now?"

"I got to get some food, babe. Can you come with me to the store and get me something for dinner? I ain't ate in days, I feel fucking weak."

"Ok."

I followed Gene round the shop while he filled his basket: bread, hotdogs, sandwich meat.

"Man, them are pricey for Doritos. We'll swing by B&M after this and I'll pick some up there instead – save us some money."

"Ok. Why don't you get some tins of food - so they last longer? Don't you need something healthy?"

"I just want to eat hotdogs, babe. I ain't cooking in that fucking kitchen. I'd probably get food poisoning if I used it."

"How do you make your hotdogs?"

"In the microwave."

"Oh, ok."

Gene loaded his basketful onto the conveyor belt and I paid the shop assistant. It was only ten pounds, but I was getting annoyed with the fact Gene seemed to expect it from me, and that he never tired of asking me, or experienced any embarrassment doing it. I felt guilty for thinking such thoughts; how could I be such a selfish, callous person? I had what I needed: food, a comfortable home, enough money for more than the basics. Why did I resent sharing it with Gene? Wasn't that what you were meant to do with your partner? Give them everything they needed without unwarranted questioning?

"Ok, babe. Let's go to B&M."

I put my card away, but kept it handy, knowing it would get swiped a few more times before the day was out.

Gene got his *Doritos*, and all was right with the world again. He pulled me towards him and planted a kiss on my forehead.

"I love you baby. Want to get something to eat?"

"Ok, where do you want to go?"

"Burger King? Man, I'm hungry."

"Ok."

I pushed the pram the couple of miles to the food court. I was weary; my load hadn't changed a bit. Whether I lived with Gene, in the refuge or in my own home, something weighed me down, and I couldn't place my finger on what it was. But my mum always said that's what it was like having young children: it was just a stressful time for everyone, so I tried to believe that.

"I'll get a table while you get this," said Gene.

I left the pram beside him and he picked Hope up, grabbing the nearest highchair and strapping her in.

"Beautiful Hope and Alice. Did you miss Daddy?"

It seemed to be the first time he'd noticed her all day; but maybe that was just because we were in a more relaxed setting.

I ordered Gene's burger. I never needed to ask what he wanted; it was always the same thing, in the same composition, with the same expectations. I got myself a coffee and a snack and some chicken nuggets for Hope. I felt guilty that the girls had been cooped up in the pram for so long. But there wasn't a great deal we could do about that. With poor weather, our options were limited: no parks, no walks by the sea, no journeys further afield. I doubted Gene would be willing to do that even with the sun beating down, but it was still a pleasant image to aim towards in my mind's eye.

I carried the tray to the table.

"Did you get ice, babe?"

"No, sorry, I knew I forgot something."

"Get it, babe."

"I can't, the guy is busy cleaning up."

There only appeared to be one server working and he was in the process of clearing several tables and looked closed to questions.

"So fucking what? Interrupt him."

"I can't."

"Yes, you can, you're just too afraid of people."

"I don't want to be rude."

"It ain't rude. What's rude is leaving me sitting here with coffee I can't drink because you won't ask one fucking question."

"I'm sorry – I'll ask after."

"Fine, I'll fucking do it."

Gene got up from his seat like he was bursting through a wall. He shoved his chair backwards and it screeched painfully on the shined floor.

"You don't have to get angry."

"I'm not – I'm just sick of coming last."

"You don't."

"Yes, I fucking do."

Gene stormed off to get his ice. I didn't start eating my food; I felt like doing so before he'd been looked after would be a display of disrespect. Hope was casually prodding the chicken nuggets on her tray. I took Alice out of the pram and cushioned her on my arm. She'd be looking for a bottle soon. I'd remembered to ask for the boiled water to heat it, but not her daddy's ice. Maybe Gene was right: he always did come last.

He came back to the table.

"You got it?"

"Yeah, I got it."

He sat down in a manner that somehow felt violent. I leaned backwards a little. I tried not to do it noticeably, so he wouldn't react more explosively, thinking I was avoiding him.

"I don't get why you wouldn't just get it," he grumbled.

His voice carried all over the restaurant. Thankfully, we were the only ones there and the server seemed too occupied to notice what we were talking about.

"I'm tired of you giving me orders."

"I don't."

"It feels like that to me."

"That's because you over-react to everything. I just asked you to get me ice and you made it into a huge issue."

"It was because of the way you ask."

"I just asked you."

"You could say please or thanks. You just say "get me…" It makes me feel like shit."

"I don't order you around. I just asked you to do one thing, because you forgot."

"I've got too much to remember."

"It ain't that much, babe – a cup of ice?"

My emotions were quickly outgrowing their available space inside my body. The lid was about to blow off, and I didn't know how to keep it in place.

"You treat me like crap," I said, my voice growing in volume.

"Would you keep quiet? Everyone is going to see how crazy you are."

"No one is about."

"So, you don't got to control your fucking self? Everyone knows what you're like – your mom, your dad, your cunt of a sister."

"Stop."

I didn't want to cry, on principal. I didn't want Gene to know he could affect my emotions so greatly, but I couldn't hold it back.

"Stop fucking crying. You just do it to get sympathy – to make people think you're the victim."

"I don't –

I couldn't speak clearly anymore; my voice was vanishing, crushed beneath Gene's larger one.

"You're such a good fucking actor. You should win an Academy Award."

"You treat me like shit."

"I don't do shit – you do it to yourself. You're a miserable bitch who can't get along with anyone. Even your own fucking family talk about it."

"What do they say?"

"That you're always creating drama, that you fall out with everyone – everyone knows what you are."

I got up from the table. I suddenly wished there was a sea between Gene and me. I needed to get away from him, but wherever I went to, I knew he'd follow me. I'd have to walk around with him taunting me until he calmed down enough to get his train home. I knew I'd have to apologise, or he'd never let me go home, and if I tried to, he would follow me there. That was the main thing I needed to ensure: that Gene didn't find out my address: it was my one sanctuary. I suddenly desperately wanted to be in the place I'd been so reluctant to consider home.

I put the girls coats back on and strapped them into the pram.

"Where the fuck are you going?"

"I need to get out of here."

"Where to?"

"I don't know." I just needed to get out into the air. The room was stiflingly close.

I pulled my own coat on and emptied the tray on the table into the bin. Even if Gene was tormenting me, I still refused to adopt his policy where not cleaning up after yourself was concerned. If I didn't have manners and I didn't have kindness, I had nothing of importance left in me. I'd already abandoned all my original values and opinions for Gene. I refused to let him take the last of my goodness. He laughed at me, like I was pitiful and didn't even know how to storm off properly. I pushed the pram and walked at a quick pace. Gene stayed by my side, whispering cruel nothings in my ear. "You're a worthless bitch. Everyone knows it. I'm going to make sure the girls know the truth about you. You're the worst person I've ever met. You're a coward, a spoiled little girl."

I tried to blank out what Gene was saying, but his words were feeding right into my softest spots; the private places where I kept every doubt I had about myself and my decency. I thought back to when I'd been a teenager and I'd been bullied in school; they had said similar things to me and it brought it all back to me. They hadn't known Gene and Gene hadn't known them. The only common denominator was me. The things he said about me must have been true.

I walked as quickly as I could, trying to get away from Gene. He kept pace with me, continuing the outpour of insults. I stopped, disentangling his bag of groceries from the pram.

"Here," I said, shoving it into his arms, "Take this."

"I don't fucking want that."

"Take it, I'm going home."

"It's fucking garbage, throw it in the trash."

"I just got you all of that."

"I know, I fucking know that. There you go again – trying to make me feel like a piece of fucking shit."

Gene started to walk away from me. I wanted to claw my way out of my body and my life. I pulled items from the bag, hurling them in Gene's direction. I turned to walk away; a confused man handed me one of the items that had been lying on the ground. I guess he thought I'd dropped them or was trying to make me feel better about the situation at hand.

"You're one crazy motherfucker," I heard Gene shout behind me.

"I hate you," I cried, running away.

I pushed the pram at top speed, trying to get home before Gene had a chance to follow me. I looked back over my shoulder every few feet, to make sure he wasn't there. If he found out where I lived, there would be nowhere to escape to when things kicked off next time round. I hated Gene so much I wished I could never see him again and be ok with that. But I couldn't; I needed Gene for my survival, so we'd be seeing each other again. But that moment, I had to get as far away from him as I could. He was the evil stranger and I wanted nothing to do with him until normal Gene made his reappearance. I resolved to put my phone away, to not make the ritual arriving-home phone call that I always made after we left each other. It was hard to resist the urge to do it; it was so engrained in me. I'd been conditioned to call Gene no matter what was happening; whether I was joyful, distraught or enraged, he was my go-to person. I needed him to comfort me even when he was the one that had upset me; that was how much I was hooked on him. I picked up my phone, thinking about ringing him so he'd calm me down, but I knew he'd make me apologise. I knew I owed him an apology for throwing food at him in the street; I had behaved like someone deranged, but I had felt provoked, whether my reaction had been out of proportion to the provocation or not. I didn't want to apologise, but I had to; I couldn't survive the evening without talking to Gene. He was the only company I had in that lonely house, the only way I passed my evenings, the only thing keeping me going through the long days. That night I apologised to Gene. I finally got up the courage to endure the scolding I'd receive when he picked up the phone.

"You better be ringing to fucking apologise."

"I'm sorry."

"For what?"

"For acting crazy?"

"You were acting like a raving lunatic – throwing food at me in the street. Everyone saw it."

"Who did?"

"A hundred people probably."

"I'm sorry I lost it."

"You got to learn how to control your fucking self."

"I know, I'm sorry."

"If you do that shit to me again, you'll be fucking sorry. I could have called social services and you'd never see the girls again."

"Don't say that."

"It's the fucking truth."

"I apologised."

"Ok, talk about something fucking else."

My mind was blanker than an untouched canvas.

"I don't know what to say."

"Fucking think of something."

"Did you get something for dinner?"

"What the fuck do you think? What kind of a retarded question is that?"

"Ok. My head is off," I started crying. "I need you to calm me down."

I stepped outside and lit a cigarette. I stared at the view that kept me company through every crisis that caused me to smoke there.

"You got to figure out how to control your head. You let how you feel dictate everything."

I couldn't argue with him; as always, he was right.

Gene seemed to give a version of the truth that was entirely true but that omitted nine tenths of the full picture, so you couldn't tell him he was wrong, but everything was unfairly taken out of context. I didn't understand that enough at that point to offer it as a defence. Had I done that, Gene would have knocked it down with one of his more leakproof arguments anyway. No matter what I said, or didn't say, I couldn't win. That's what it felt like to me; maybe I was misinterpreting the whole situation. My brain was more muddled than a jigsaw in transit. I couldn't begin to see out of the mess to identify what was happening, or why I felt the way I did.

Chapter Forty-Five

I met Gene for our second session of marriage counselling. He'd done his homework on the train there. We'd had to answer questions to see how much we knew about each other. I failed to see what relevance that had to our communication difficulties but completed the exercises with care anyway.

It asked me about Gene's tastes, his favourite things about our relationship, his fears. I thought I knew most of them. He'd taught me about those things, repeating them the way an actor repeats lines when rehearsing for the big night. I knew every fact for a questionnaire about Gene, but I still didn't know what secrets he kept stowed away in his soul. Gene understood everything about me, but there remained things I feared Gene would never tell me about himself, no matter how close we got. I wondered if any of his ex-partners had ever managed to extract the secrets I wanted so much to hear.

We walked up to the church in the rain. It was all uphill, which seemed to sour the mood even more than it was in its natural state.

"Fucking wind and rain, man, I hate this shit."

"Me too."

"Maybe we should just fucking skip it."

"No, we can't do that. It's only our second session."

"This weather is fucked."

"We have to go."

"Stop acting so fucking controlling. You don't get to make decisions for me."

"I'm not trying to – I'm just worried if we don't go now, he won't have us back."

"You worry for no fucking reason. He'll fit us in."

"How do you know? What if he takes us off the list? Where will we go to instead?"

"Fine I'll fucking go if it means I don't got to listen to you bitching about it."

"You don't care."

"I just came all the way here on the train with no money and my foot is fucking killing me – don't tell me I don't fucking care. I'll fucking go. After I got to swing by the pharmacy."

"You're still taking those?"

"Stop fucking jumping to conclusions about shit. A guy I live with asked me to get him some while I was out."

"He takes them too?"

"Yeah, I think he's got a problem."

"Why?"

"He takes boxes of the shit every day. He don't know what he's doing."

"Does he take more than you?"

"Babe, I ain't addicted to the shit – I just take them now and again for my fucking foot. This guy has to travel all over because none of the pharmacies will even sell them to him. Now, that's an addict."

"Ok, but is he paying for them?"

"He gave me five bucks to get them for him."

"I'm not going in."

"What?"

"I'm not going to go in – they'll turn me away. They know me now."

"So, let me get this straight - you're going to let me go back without the meds I said I'd get? He's going to be fucking mad. You'd put me in that situation?"

"I don't believe anything you're saying – I think they're for you."

"You don't fucking believe me?"

"No."

"You're the one that twists the fucking truth – telling me you're finding us a house, telling me you're coming home, telling me I get to see my fucking daughter being born."

"I didn't lie – you were scaring me."

"Fucking bullshit, man. I ain't heard nothing as ridiculous as that in my whole life, and I've heard some ridiculous shit."

"I'm away."

"Fine, go – you were the one that said the dude wouldn't have us back."

"He won't."

"Well then put crazy away. Keep fucking walking."

I walked ahead of Gene with the pram. I hoped that putting some distance between us would calm me down before I had to appear normal in front of the counsellor, and that Gene's bad mood would somehow be carried away by the breeze. Gene stormed over to me, taking the pram from me and walked ahead of me. It felt like a threat to take Hope and Alice away, but my emotions were making everything seem amplified again.

We sat down in the cramped room, like nothing had happened, Hope and Alice at our feet. They made a beeline for all the objects in the room they weren't supposed to touch. I had a feeling the session would be a challenge; not just emotionally, but when it came to entertaining our children, and the amount of material we'd get covered with them there.

"How are you both?" smiled Stephen, sitting down.

He sat facing us in an armchair, smiling fondly at the children. He was the antithesis to Gene. He wore a V-necked jumper and his trousers hung at his ankles when he sat down. I expected him to judge Gene by his appearance alone, but they seemed to get along well. I still worried he would pick a side and that it would be Gene's. Gene was much better at working people than I was. They always fell prey to his charm. I knew that charm would be turned off the minute we walked out the door, but that was just because Gene knew he could be his natural self with me. I knew I should take that as a compliment, but sometimes I wished Gene would still make the same level of effort for me that he did with certain strangers. Gene was very selective about who he chose to be friendly to, and once he'd used up his friendly resources, he'd be ratty with anyone who came close to him for the rest of the week. I was jealous of the counsellor; he got the best of Gene that week, and I'd probably get the worst as compensation for his energy expended.

"Good, thanks," I tried to smile.

"Alright, man. This weather sucks," said Gene, shaking the raindrops off his hat and putting it back onto his head.

"Do you have far to come?"

"I live in Belfast. She lives nearby," he signalled to me with a jerk of his thumb.

"Try and use Aoife's name when you're talking about her."

"Alright, why?"

"She might feel less important if you refer to her as "she.""

It made a nice change to have someone stand up to Gene for me, no matter how minor their complaint. Maybe my hyper-sensitivities weren't all completely irrational. An objective outsider had noticed one of them too.

"How did you get on with the worksheets?" Stephen asked.

"Alright, man. I believe I got all the correct answers to your questions."

"Well, let's run through them. You go first," he said to me.

"I put that Gene's favourite things to do are to go shopping, listen to music and watch TV."

"Sounds about right," smirked Gene.

"What did you put for Aoife?"

"Crafts, reading, vintage shopping."

I nodded.

"What was your favourite gift that Gene ever got you?"

"I put the trinkets he brought me when he first arrived in Northern Ireland."

"Huh," said Gene.

"What's wrong?"

"Nothing, I just thought you'd put the girls. I thought you'd say they were the best thing I ever gave you."

For a moment, I wanted to say that he was right and that he had given them to me, in every sense of the word, but I bit my tongue. It was easier to feel brave to fully speak my mind with a third party in attendance, but I had to remember that he wouldn't be there for the walk home afterwards.

"I didn't think of that," I said. "That's what it is, I guess."

Gene looked satisfied that he was right.

"What was your favourite gift Aoife got you?"

"The clock."

"I didn't think you liked the clock."

"Why?"

"You didn't really react when I gave it to you."

"It's my favourite thing you ever got me, baby. I brought it with me when I left."

"Oh, yeah, you left the drawing I did of you in the house when you left, but I collected it when I cleared out the house. Remind me to give it to you."

Gene nodded. I was a little hurt he'd forgotten to take it, considering how effusive he'd been about it when I'd presented it to him.

The simple questions seemed to prod at more complex pain I couldn't explain. Maybe that was the point of the test: to unearth the real issues. But I didn't have any more clarity about how to begin to address them. Gene and I had so many causes of resentment between us and we'd only known each other for three years. If someone had lived with us and been able to coordinate every conversation we had, perhaps we would have been able to crush every incompatibility. I couldn't understand why every discussion we had felt like he we were sidestepping each other, understanding each other, but being unable to make our lifestyle choices match up.

"What are your similarities?" Stephen interrupted my line of thinking.

"We got the same values," said Gene.

I tried not to raise my eyebrow in his direction. He had promised me that we had before we'd got married, but any of the ones we'd supposedly shared seemed to have vanished since Gene's visa had been approved.

"How so?"

"Well, she don't sleep around and I don't sleep around. We're the same in that way."

I wondered if our sexual habits were enough to substantiate that our values were the same.

"Ok?" Stephen seemed to be thinking the same thought I was.

"Well, most people go out drinking every night, hooking up with different people all the time. We don't do that – we want the same thing – to be together and be happy."

I couldn't argue with that, but was it truly possible? Doubts sprang up inside my minds like an overgrown garden you couldn't keep on top of.

"How about you, Aoife? In what ways do you think you and Gene are similar?"

"We understand each other."

"What do you mean?"

"The way our minds work – they're similar – he's the only person that can calm me down."

"Yeah – she has Bipolar Disorder. Most people don't get it, but I get it."

"And how do you know what to say to help?"

"I just do."

"So, the basis is there for a good relationship – you just need a bit of help communicating."

"Yeah."

I didn't agree nor disagree; I didn't think it could be summed up as simply as that.

"Is there anything you think you need to change about yourself to be able to have a successful marriage?"

"Uh," said Gene. "I kind of have this thing where I have to control everything."

I looked at him, astounded. He'd never admitted such a thing to me before; this was enormous progress. If I could get Gene to see that he'd been trying to control me, it would be easier to convince him to stop doing it than if he didn't even recognise it as an issue. I'd thought it was a quality Gene didn't see in himself, but apparently, I had been wrong, or he'd had a massive revelation in recent days.

"Why do you think you do?" asked Stephen, leaning back in his chair, like he was getting comfortable for a time-consuming topic.

"I don't know, dude. I don't mean to but I'm insecure I guess."

"Do you think that is a good way to handle it?"

"Probably not, but I don't know no different."

Our time was up, and we walked out of the session together, Gene pushing the pram.

"Thanks, man. See you next time."

"Did you find that useful?" I asked, when we got far enough away for honest discussion.

"I guess."

"I was really surprised at what you said."

"Which part?"

"The thing about how you have to control things. That's great that you noticed that and admitted to it."

"And I was waiting for you to say the same fucking thing, but you didn't, did you?"

"What do you mean?"

"You got to control everything too. It ain't just me, man. But you won't admit to shit. You're too afraid of looking bad."

"That's not true."

"Yes, it is."

"So, you didn't mean it?"

Gene just shook his head, not like a refusal, more like he couldn't comprehend the nonsense that was coming from my lips. I walked beside him in annoyed silence and he gave the pram back to me. At least he wasn't storming off with it; I was just thankful it was in my grasp.

"Let's go to the fucking store and get these meds."

"Ok."

I didn't want to have to be the one who went in, but I knew I wouldn't have a choice in the matter.

"Here," said Gene, handing me a fiver. "I'll wait with the girls."

"What will I say if they won't sell them to me?"

"Just make something up. Say they ain't for you."

"What if they say no?"

"They ain't going to say no. Would you stop fucking worrying and just get them?"

Gene was right; they didn't say no. But they did look at me with unnerving recognition. I sensed it was the last time they'd hand them over, and I knew it wouldn't be the last time I'd be expected to buy them.

"Here," I said, handing Gene the tablets and his change.

"Thanks, babe. Dave would have been salty if I hadn't got them."

"Yeah."

I didn't believe a word he said, but I didn't know why. Gene was such a blunt person you had to believe everything he said. If he wouldn't lie about how you looked in an outfit or how much he detested the dinner you'd just made, why would he lie about anything else?

"What are you going to do now?"

"Go home, I guess. Hey, when is Hope's birthday again?"

"12th March. You forgot?"

"You know I'm not good with dates, babe."

"Do you know when mine is?"

"Uh, June?"

"July."

"Oh. It ain't personal, babe – I just ain't good with numbers and stuff."

"Ok."

"That's in a week. What are we doing for Hope's birthday?" Gene asked.

"I hadn't really thought about it."

"You're spending it with your fucking folks, aren't you? Fucking bullshit, man. I don't even get to see my own fucking daughter on her birthday, again."

"We can do something."

"You aren't going there?"

"We're staying there that night, but we could do something ourselves during the day?"

"Like what?"

"Go for lunch and to soft play?"

"Alright, I guess. Tell me when to meet you and I'll be here. Hey?"

"Yeah?"

"I need you to give me some money."

"I can't, I'm sorry."

I thought about the counselling I was getting outside the hours I spent with Gene and how much they had reinforced the point that I needed to start disentangling myself from him financially. I was funding his lifestyle and he still hadn't contributed a penny to our children. Intellectually, I understood why they were against me doing that, but emotionally, I hadn't caught up. I was responsible for Gene. I had brought him to Northern Ireland. Without me, he'd still be living in America; maybe without a permanent roof over his head, but at least with knowledge of how life of the streets worked. Without my support, he'd have starved or been beaten to death. I had to keep paying to keep him safe. If anything happened to Gene, it would be all my fault.

"Babe, I'm fucking starving. Don't make me beg."

"Fine, but I can't give you much. How much do you need?"

"Fifty?"

"I'd hoped he would say twenty, because with Gene, there was no negotiating. Once he stated a figure, you were either giving him that amount or running for cover from the outburst when you didn't. I withdrew fifty pounds and Gene took it from my hand, pocketing it. I hoped he would use it for food. I had begun to doubt what he spent it on. If it wasn't used for food, I hoped that at least, it would be used for cigarettes, and nothing else.

"When will I see you again?" he asked.

"I don't know. I guess it depends on money."

"Yeah, why don't we just wait until Hope's birthday and save your money?"

"Ok."

"Call me when you get home."

"I will."

I walked away, with a mixture of sadness and relief. Even Gene's scent brought me comfort; it was the smell I associated with the greatest comfort of my life. It was the scent I had inhaled each time I'd been pressed to his chest after lying on the floor crying and being filmed. It was like a drug: it gave me my fix and destroyed me at the same time, bringing all the bad memories to the surface and signalling approaching danger. The churning in my stomach died down as Gene disappeared into the distance and out of sight.

I walked home to my own quiet house. The peace inside the doors had become more familiar to me. I'd learnt how to live alone again, but not how to survive day in-day out with no one to help me in my hours of wakefulness. Gene had everything I needed, and as long as I could see him, but keep a safe distance, everything would be alright. That night I had a smoke in silence outside. Gene had gone to bed early with a headache. I felt the cool night air pinching my cheeks and for a minute, I felt a hint of life about me again. Then, I heard the sound of impending danger carrying through the night: a couple's argument travelling to me through the air. The woman was screaming, and screaming, and screaming, and I could hear it ringing in my own heart, like a reminder of where I needed not to go.

Chapter Forty-Six

I walked into the women's centre and took a seat while I waited for my appointment. There were magazines, leaflets, posters everywhere, documenting episodes from my own life. I tried not to take them under my notice and focussed my attention on the coffee cup the workers had placed in my hands. I was waiting for a room to come free, and then I'd have a good chat with my key worker. I'd gone from daily support to fortnightly support, and I felt myself weakening with the infrequency of the appointments.

"Hi, Aoife," my worker smiled, poking her head around the door frame. "Want to come upstairs now?"

"Ok."

I followed her into a little box room with cushions, boxes of tissues and perfumed air. It felt as homely as a place like that could feel.

"Take a seat," said my worker, gesturing to me to sit down.

"How have things been going?" she asked, smiling serenely.

I couldn't help wondering what her private life was like. Was her marriage perfect? Was she in the right position to advise me on my own life choices? Did the happiness the organisation portrayed truly exist?

"Ok, I guess."

"Are you still meeting up with Gene?"

"Yes."

"Ok," she sighed. "And how has that been?"

"We're going to marriage counselling."

"Ok," she said, settling back into her seat.

"You don't think it's a good idea?"

"I think marriage counselling is a great idea, if there isn't abuse. But with abuse, I don't know if it would work."

"Why?"

"Because abuse is intentional."

"Ok."

I'd heard that statement hundreds of times, but I still struggled to apply it to Gene. Surely, he just struggled to control his behaviour due to his mental health? He was always telling me we wanted the same things: to be happy together and have our family. Shouldn't I believe him? After all, I knew him intimately. The worker in front of me had never met him. How could she know his true intentions without having even shaken his hand?

"So, you think it's a waste of time?"

"I didn't mean that. Just – be careful."

"What do you mean?"

"I would hate to think the marriage counsellor didn't see the full picture and was approaching counselling like it's a balanced relationship. Or that Gene manipulates him into thinking you're at fault."

"Yeah."

A quiet voice inside me told me she was right to be apprehensive, but that didn't fit with the perfect picture of what I hoped to attain through marriage counselling, so I chose not to listen to it.

"When did you last see Gene?"

"This week."

"Ok, do you think it might be a good idea to distance yourself from him for a while and see how you feel?"

"I can't."

"You just don't think you can, but you've shown everyone you're very strong."

"I can't. The only reason I survived the refuge was because Gene was talking to me the whole time."

"Well, I don't know what else I can say. You've heard all before really, haven't you?"

I nodded.

"I am listening, I just don't know how to act on it. I don't know how to live without him."

"Well, you need to protect yourself. Can you at least limit contact and try to stop sending him money?"

"I can say no on the phone, but once we meet in person, I know I'm not leaving until he gets the money he needs."

"Why, what are you worried will happen?"

"That he'll take the girls."

"Do you think he would?"

"I don't know."

"Does he threaten to often?"

"Sometimes."

"Why do you let him see them?"

"They're his children. I took them away from him."

"Do you believe that?"

"Yeah, that's what he says."

"Does that make it true?"

"I don't know. But if I didn't meet up with him, he could have them taken off me."

Although I gave that as the reason for meeting Gene, my heart knew it wasn't the only reason. The main reason was because I hoped things would change and that we would finally be the happy family I'd believed we would be. The other reason was that I depended on him for my stability more than I did on my Seroquel or any medical professional. He was the only person I could trust, who knew when I was well and knew when it was being blown out of proportion by my team, who knew when I was crazy and knew when they were minimising it. If I didn't have Gene there to stand up for me, I would have been locked up months before, my children put into care. It was a catch 22: if I didn't see Gene, the girls might end up in care: if I did see Gene and something kicked off, they could end up in care too. I suspected the first scenario was more probable than the second, so continuing contact with Gene always won out.

I mentally left the room for a few moments, wishing I could find a way out of this life; a way to commit suicide without it having a negative impact on my girls. It was the only solution. I was tied to Gene forever: miserable with him, miserable without him. I was entrenched in misery no matter which way I turned. There was no positive path to take. I sometimes wondered if I had unknowingly died from an overdose and that I was trapped in hellish eternity without even realising it. How every day played out was a worse hell than I ever could have imagined before it became my life. Tears slipped down my cheeks and I reached for the tissue box on the coffee table.

"Are you ok?" Jennifer asked.

I shook my head. I wasn't looking for her to offer me any consolation or a series of platitudes. I knew that I was stuck in the spot I was in forever. Even if the worst happened and Gene died, I would still be stuck, mourning him forever and replaying our failed romance in my head in the sequence it should have followed. "If only" was my most common thought, and if that occurred, it would continue until my last breath.

"Well, what would help?"

"I don't know."

"You can talk to me about it. It's confidential."

"I've heard that lots of times and it rarely is."

"Ok. You're signed up for the freedom programme in September. How do you feel about that?"

"I don't know. I hope it works."

"I think you understand everything on an intellectual level, but your head and your heart are in different places."

I nodded, screwing up my face as I cried and wiping my eyes with a tissue.

"I don't know how to make it stop."

"The only way to make it stop is to walk away."

"I can't."

"You'll only know that if you try. Why don't you try taking a break for a week or two and see how you manage? The helpline is 24/7. Just try ringing us instead of him."

I nodded and tried to acquire a smiling face again. I knew I couldn't do it, but I'd try my best.

A few hours after I left the appointment, I phoned Gene. He was "salty" I'd gone silent for so long. Gene didn't like you to go quiet at all, but if you did, you had to check-out beforehand with a plausible excuse. Going quiet with no explanation was the worst kind of offence.

"Who have you been fucking?"

"What? No one."

"Well, you fucking disappear for hours on end without even a text – what the fuck am I supposed to think?"

"That I'm busy."

"You're "busy"? Busy doing what?"

"I had a meeting."

"With the people from the shelter?"

"Yeah."

"Ohhh," Gene said, smarmily, "what were you saying about me?"

"Nothing."

"Right. I know you been talking shit about me. That's alright, you don't got to tell me."

"I haven't."

"Aoife, I know you have. You don't got to lie to me."

"I'm confused."

"You're always confused. You talk to them people and you get more confused because they try to turn you against me."

"I don't want them to."

"But you let them. It's because you don't know your own mind –
you got to get other people to tell you what to think."

"I don't."

"Ha."

"I'm sorry."

"Whatever. You fucking vanish for hours and then come back,
crying to me "oh, my head, it's all messed up, help me." And you
expect me to be right there. Fucking bullshit, man."

"That isn't why I talk to you."

"All we talk about is your fucking messed up head. We never talk
about nothing else."

"Well, what do you want to talk about?"

Gene didn't reply.

"Every time I try to talk about another topic, you shut it down. If I
talk about anything of general interest, you make fun of it or don't
answer me," I said.

"Maybe I'm not interested in what you're saying."

"Then I can't win."

"You're a lunatic. Here comes crazy again, I was wondering when
she was going to make her fucking appearance."

I started crying.

"Please, can we just stop fighting? I don't want to fight with you. I
love you. I don't even know how the arguments start."

"They start because you love to argue."

"No, I don't. That makes no sense."

"Every time we're getting along, you got to fucking ruin it with your
bullshit."

"Well, let's stop fighting. We can talk about something else."

"I don't got nothing to say."

"Well, what am I meant to do?"

"You figure it out."

"Why can't you just tell me?"

"You're a smart girl – you figure it out. I shouldn't have to tell you."

"My head is spinning."

"That ain't my fault."

"I didn't say it was."

I hung up on Gene. My emotions were slamming against their roof
and if I didn't end the call, they were going to explode through it and

land on top of him. I wasn't stable enough to be able to manage another argument. I put my phone away for the rest of the evening. Maybe the workers were right. Maybe Gene wasn't good for me. Every time I spoke to him, my head seemed to go off more. He righted me when someone else had destabilised me and destabilised me when things were going almost right. I was stuck in a cycle. Not the cycle of violence, like the workers said, but a cycle of my own. The workers had explained the cycle of violence to me fifty times. There is a period of elation: the honeymoon period, followed by tension building and walking on eggshells and ending with the explosion, before returning to the first stage again. It often stretched out over weeks or months. But mine were too frequent to fit into that box. All three stages occurred practically every day, sometimes multiple times a day. So, it wasn't the same; it couldn't be that. I'd come up with any excuse to make it not that, even if it was.

Chapter Forty-Seven

It was Hope's birthday and I'd already given her all her presents.
Gene couldn't afford a present. That didn't bother me; I didn't care
about material items. Anyway, he had helped me pick out my
presents from us. All I cared about was being a normal family and
celebrating our child's birthday together. I met Gene at the train
station and he suggested we walk to *Burger King* first to get a cup of
coffee.

"Should we just get one at the soft play place, so Hope doesn't miss
out on her birthday?"

"She's two years old, babe. She don't know what's happening. Also,
the coffee is probably fucking garbage there."

"Ok," twenty minutes wouldn't make a great deal of difference to
how the day panned out. I thought that even though I was aware of
the significance of a five second period in Gene's changing moods.
If Gene got the coffee he wanted, at least there was more chance of
him being in good form for soft play. I knew he'd rather shove
knives under his own nails than spend the morning at a place like
that, but he was playing along that day, doing what I wished he
would. I was grateful to him for that, for keeping the peace.

"That's good coffee for a dollar, man," said Gene.

He smiled at me and I laughed at how even after more than a year on
Northern Irish soil, he still spoke like he was an American living in
America.

I was in Gene's good graces, and the day was looking bright. The
sky was filled with soft puffs of white cloud, like dashes of icing on
top of the cake that would be our good day. I walked alongside
Gene. He rested his hand on top of mine while I pushed the pram. He
drank his coffee, made cheerful conversation and didn't mention his
foot once.

We got to soft play and got the last table left.

"It's fucking jammed in here, man."

"Yeah, I thought it would be quiet this early in the morning."

I'd been wrong, again. Gene didn't look happy to have to squeeze
into a corner table. Every table was booked with bags, few people

making use of the table tops. I was waiting for Gene to dislodge someone's coffee with his own and plonk himself down in their seat, but he just looked at them disparagingly instead. Maybe that was merely because they were human. Gene's mood was turning; I could sense it. One thing went wrong and the whole set came crashing down.

Hope ran in to play and Alice was sitting in the padded baby area, trying to eat a plastic ball. Gene down next to Alice and me.

"Watch Hope, babe."

"I can see her from here."

"There is some dude in there."

"He's the dad of that baby I think."

"You better keep an eye on Hope."

"Why?"

"We don't know that dude, and I can't see what he's doing from here. He could be a fucking child molester for all we know."

"I doubt it."

"Where would you hang out if you were a child molester?"

"I don't know, why would you even think of that?"

"Just go and watch her, babe."

I was getting irritated, wondering why it always fell to me to do all the running in our relationship. And all the running originated with Gene's orders: his choice of coffee, his fears for our children, his specifications for everything we did.

"Why can't you do it?" I asked.

Gene gave me a look that shut me up.

I followed Hope into the play area, wondering for a moment if Alice was any safer where she was sitting. I didn't like leaving her with Gene. I knew it didn't make sense. He was her father; the farthest person from a stranger to her, and yet, something tugged at my gut as I moved away from her. We spent most of the morning apart. I kept trying to take my opportunity to sit with Gene, but he didn't seem to want me to sit down. He kept spotting potential dangers and sending me to attend to them. I could see him sitting alone with Alice and wondered why he didn't want my company as much as I craved his.

A couple of hours later, we packed up to leave. As we were walking out of the soft play centre and Gene was talking to me, I bumped into a girl I knew: a girl that had lived in the refuge with me. I couldn't introduce her to Gene. I didn't want to either. I didn't want her to know I still saw the man she would have considered my "abuser." She didn't know the details of our relationship; she would just see him as a bully and view me as weak for spending my time with him.

"How are you?" I asked.

"I'm ok, thanks. I'm pregnant, how are you?"

"Congratulations. I'm fine thanks, just out for Hope's birthday."

"What age is she? Happy birthday, wee woman," she smiled at Hope.

"She's two. When are you due?"

"Not for months. I only just found out."

Gene cut in.

"I'm going to the bathroom," he said, sourly, and slunk off.

"Is that him?" she asked.

I nodded and looked away.

"Yeah, I kind of figured it out."

"Is it that obvious?"

She nodded. "Take care of yourself," she said, touching my arm.

"You too."

I waited outside the toilets for Gene to emerge, filled with fright. What would he say when he came back? What had I done to upset him? He had been talking to me normally only moments before and now he was fuming. I couldn't work out what it was that I had done. Every second felt like the countdown to my own death. I thought about running away before it was too late. But it was pointless; I couldn't stay away from Gene for good, and that was the only way to avoid my punishment. I would have to wait where I was and deal with whatever came at me. Gene walked out in silence, his feet making up for the lack of sound. His soles kicked his aggression into the tiles and I felt a horrible tingle in my stomach, like bad butterflies.

"What'd I do?"

"You fucking know."

"Tell me what I did."

Are you being fucking serious?"

"Yeah, I don't know."

"You're a regular genius, aren't you? I was talking to you and you cut me off to talk to that girl."

"I'm sorry, I didn't realise."

"You interrupted me while I was talking and just started talking to her instead."

"Well, I didn't expect to bump into her – I thought it would be rude not to."

"You didn't mind being rude to me."

"I didn't mean to be, I just stopped to talk to her."

"I always come fucking last. You could have listened what I had to say and then talked to her."

"But she would have thought I was blanking her."

"So, you cut me off instead?"

"I can't do that with someone I barely know."

"So, you can do it to me? This just shows what I have to say ain't important, man."

"It doesn't. I didn't have time to think. I just stopped to say hello to someone I knew. I was listening to you."

"Oh really? What was I saying when you interrupted me?"

"I can't remember."

"You can't remember? You were listening real good, weren't you?"

"Gene, I can't remember now."

I was too stressed to remember who I was, never mind what had just been discussed. I knew it was something trivial, like what we should have for lunch, or what Gene thought of soft play, but I should have realised what a grave error it would be to interrupt Gene, no matter what he was talking about."

"I'm sorry, can we just forget about it?"

"No, I ain't forgetting shit. Nothing I have to say is important."

"It is, I'm sorry. Let's not ruin Hope's birthday."

"I ain't the one ruining it."

"I didn't do anything."

"You didn't do anything?"

"No."

"So, you don't get what you did wrong?"

"I don't get why it's such a big deal. It was an accident."

Gene's voice became filled with malice.

"Yeah, poor little innocent Aoife. You never do any fucking thing on purpose."

"I didn't."

I started crying. I badly wanted the day to be good, but I sensed there was no coming back from this. Maybe if I got Gene lunch, his mood would improve. I'd pay him back for the injury caused to his ego.

"Stop fucking crying. You always got to look like the victim, don't you?"

"I'm not trying to look like anything. I just want to have a nice day on our daughter's birthday."

"Well, whose fault is this?"

"Please, let's stop fighting for Hope."

"I ain't the one fighting."

"Do you want to get lunch?"

I balled up a tissue and tried to dry my eyes as subtly as I could in the middle of a busy Saturday street.

"I'll sit with you, but I ain't fucking eating."

"Where do you want to go?"

Gene shrugged. "Don't make no difference to me."

"Chinese buffet?"

"I don't give a fuck."

I withdrew the cash needed to pay for lunch and walked quietly next to Gene. I tried to emit calm rather than petulance, but Gene thought I was sulking anyway.

"Why ain't you talking?"

"It's been half an hour since that happened and you're still arguing with me."

"I'm upset."

"You're angry."

"I'm upset."

"You seem angry."

"Your perceptions are fucked. Just because you think something don't make it right. You interpret things wrong. I'm upset you disrespected me."

"I didn't mean to."

"You did."

"I'm sorry. Please, let's just stop this. Let's just get along."

"I'm coming for lunch with you, ain't I?"

I wondered how that was enough to indicate I'd received Gene's forgiveness.

We sat down at a table and I got highchairs for both girls. Gene sat beside me, keeping his jacket on and looking like he was about to run out the door.

"You can go up first," I said, sitting down.

"I ain't fucking eating."

"Why?"

"I don't want none."

265

"Why not? Are you not hungry?"

"Yeah, but I don't want nothing."

"Why, if you're hungry?"

"Because I don't want to have to sit and listen to you bitching about how you have to pay for everything. It ain't worth it, man – I'll go without."

"I don't want you to. I want you to eat with us. It's our daughter's birthday."

After several minutes more coaxing, Gene finally got up and filled his plate. I joined him a few minutes later with my own food and the girls'.

"How's your food?"

Gene shrugged. "Alright I guess."

The tension suddenly slackened, and the day was almost normal again. Relief passed over me like a pair of strangling hands loosening their grip.

"I got to go after this, babe."

"Ok, where are you going to?"

"Just got some shit I got to do in the house."

"Ok."

"When are you going to your folks?"

"At 5."

"What are you doing there?"

"My mum is making a birthday dinner."

"Right."

"Are you annoyed you can't come?"

"It don't matter. How I feel – it don't matter. Never does."

"That isn't true."

"Ya'll will have a better time without me there. You can all laugh at me while I'm not around."

"Why would we do that? I wish you could come."

"I ain't invited – that's alright. Just make sure my daughter knows that's not my fault. Make sure you tell her Daddy loves her."

"I will."

I felt as tense as before but with upset rather than fear. I could never get the balance between us right. I paid for our meal and we walked out of the restaurant. I walked Gene back to the train station.

"You want to stand with me while I have a smoke?"

I nodded and took one too.

"Make sure them people don't take over our daughter's birthday.

Make sure they know their place."

"Ok."

"I'm serious, babe. You got to stand up to them people."

"Why?"

"What do you mean, why?" You fucking know why. Don't ask ridiculous questions."

"Sorry."

"Ok, babe. I got to get my train."

"Gene?"

"Yeah?"

"You know we have marriage counselling on Tuesday?"

"Oh man, do we?"

"You don't want to go?"

"No, it's not that – I just forgot."

"I love you."

"I love you. Bye, babe."

I watched Gene walk into the station, up the stairs, out the door and out of our lives again, and I felt such sad relief.

Chapter Forty-Eight

"I need help," I said to my new mental health social worker.

She was kind, but ineffectual. The resources were lacking for her to carry out her job properly. I knew, at best, she might stick me back on Home Treatment, but something needed to shift. I was losing control of my mind like a car with locked steering, and there was nowhere to turn for help; nowhere but Gene.

"I'll see if I can get Home Treatment involved. You were involved with them before, weren't you?"

"A few times, yeah."

"Ok, I'll see what I can do."

"How do you feel?"

"Like the sandcastles I've built up in my mind are sliding down all at once."

"What are the sandcastles?"

"My sanity."

She looked at me blankly, like I was talking in riddles rather than metaphors.

I knew Gene would understand how I was feeling without me even having to struggle to locate the correct description. Trying to get anyone else to comprehend was extra work and a waste of energy I didn't have to squander. Once she left, I decided to phone Gene and get proper help.

Everything was becoming so overwhelming I couldn't see the day I was in as a single unit. All I could see were the thousands of potential days ahead that would make up my life and every one of them that I would struggle to stay alive to complete.

"Yeah, babe?"

"I can't cope."

"What's wrong, babe?"

"My head. Everything is racing."

"Ok, just relax, babe. I'm here. I'll look after you."

"Thanks. I don't know what to do."

"You just got to do something, babe – anything. Get the girls in the stroller and walk. Get out of the house. Distract yourself."

"I can't."

"You got to try. Why don't you paint?"

"I can't do that when the girls are awake."

"Sure you can. Just do it on the counter where they can't reach."

I knew the practicalities of that weren't the issue; it was the fear of focussing my attention on anything other than the girls and being labelled a bad mother again.

"I'm worried about anyone saying I'm a bad mum again."

"You're in your own house. No one is watching you."

It felt like they were. For the paranoia I felt, there may as well have been cameras attached to every wall.

I travelled back to the refuge in my mind and relived all the feelings I'd had there when the social services referral came about. I hadn't been spending enough time with my children. We were constantly in the same room as each other, but, according to them, they didn't have enough varied activities. I took them out too often, turned the TV on too much, didn't check-in to the playroom often enough for monitored play. I couldn't relax in my own home; not just that day, but ever again.

"Every time I call, the TV is on, babe."

"What? I hardly use it."

"Are you kidding me? It's on every fucking time I'm talking to you."

"You were the one that told me to let them watch TV."

"All the time?"

I couldn't understand what was happening to me. I'd spent hours telling Gene how stressed out I was that the girls hadn't got enough activity in our one room in the refuge, how the TV had been one more than I'd wanted it to be, and he had always reassured me that I barely used it. He had recommended I use it more. Gene was always lauding the educational benefits of TV viewing for children, and here he was, accusing me of over-using it. My world jolted and flipped upside down. I felt like a tiny figure on the great globe, hanging upside-down and trying not to let go of the small piece of land that was the only thing securing my position in the world. My mind was falling apart, and I hung up the phone.

I needed to do something, or I was going to die. I could hear my phone insistently ringing on the kitchen counter. I didn't answer it; Gene's shouting would only make me feel worse. I bundled the girls up in their coats, grabbed my packet of cigarettes and pushed the pram out the door. I went straight to the seafront at a march. The wind pushed me back with every step I took, like it was willing me not to do exactly what I wanted to. I wouldn't do it anyway; not with the girls there. I felt like throwing myself into the sea and being done with it all, but I couldn't abandon my girls like that, leaving them alone on the footpath for a stranger to find; God knows who. I just needed a plan of action, I needed to stop sitting around, waiting for things to get better when I knew they never would. I pulled my hood up and the wind blew it down; the rain started and that only exacerbated the feeling that there was no alternative.

I watched the sea slamming into the rocks and wished it was doing that to my body too. Anything was preferable to this so-called life. I stopped to light my cigarette, the wind blowing my lighter out with each strike. Things couldn't get any worse than they were; even the elements were raging against me. I needed to talk to someone and I knew it couldn't be Gene. I picked up the phone to my mum.

"I need help."

"What's wrong?"

"I don't know."

"I'm out at the minute – what do you want me to do?"

"I don't know – I need help."

"Do you want me to come down there? I can't do that at the minute."

I started crying and hung up. I was alone in the world. No one loved me. No one cared if I died; least of all me.

Chapter Forty-Nine

I had a plan. I would ask my mum to babysit the girls, pretend I was going to an appointment and end my life instead. I wasn't entirely sure how I would carry it out; probably an overdose, or a last leap into the sea, but I'd do it when the girls weren't there to witness it. They would go into care; I knew my parents wouldn't take them. It would be too much of a demand on them. They had their own lives. Everyone had their own lives; everyone but me. My life was over. It had ended the day I'd left Gene; I'd just been biding time, waiting for things to get better, but they weren't. They never would. I was stuck in an awful loop that would continue until I reached my natural death. I didn't have the strength left in me to endure life until that time. It had been a year and a month since I'd left Gene, and it had felt longer than the other twenty-seven years before I'd left. I wasn't alive anyway. I was breathing, walking around, speaking, but it was all just a façade; I was dead inside and there was no reviving me. If my emotional pain had been physical, I would have died a thousand times over by now.

My phone rang: Gene. We had marriage counselling that day, but I knew he wouldn't make it. He'd been edging his way towards cancelling for the last week. I answered anyway.

"Yeah?"

"Hey, babe. How are you?"

"Not good."

"What's up, baby?"

"I want to die."

"Don't say that, baby. What would me and the girls do without you? If you die, I'll die too."

"No, I don't want you to."

"I just need to make sure I do it right. If it doesn't work, I'll lose the girls and be stuck here without them."

"I'll meet you, baby. Meet me at the train station in an hour."

"I don't know if I can."

"Just meet me there. All you got to do is get ready and walk to the station – that's all. Start with putting clothes on – just one thing at a time. You can do it, baby. When I meet you, everything will be ok. I'll look after you."

"Ok, I'll try."

"I'll message you when I'm on the train."

Gene was the only person who could save my life. I had to get to him. I got ready as quickly as I could with my mind a jumble. Everything was a struggle: putting toast in the toaster, pulling clothes on, packing the nappy bag. I couldn't think clearly, couldn't remember anything, didn't know how to do the most basic of tasks anymore. I buttered the girls' toast, dripping tears onto the counter next to it, and trying to hide it from them. When I turned around, I put on a pretend smile and acted like everything was our version of normal.

An hour later, I met Gene at the train station.

"How are you now, babe?"

"Not good."

"I know, baby," Gene pulled me towards him and kissed me on top of the head.

"You got to fight back, don't let your fucking head win."

"I can't."

"You can. You're fucking strong, you'll be ok."

I tried to trust what Gene told me, but my mind was in fierce disagreement with him.

"Are we still going to marriage counselling?" I asked.

"Why don't you call them and cancel, babe? You ain't feeling well anyway."

"I want to go."

"Why?"

"So we can get back together."

"One week ain't going to make much difference."

"Please."

"I ain't feeling good neither, babe."

"Well, can we still go?"

"Let me get this straight – you're going to make me walk all the way up there when I'm not feeling well just because you're scared to cancel?"

"I'm not scared to cancel."

"Ha! You're scared of everything."

"I'm not. I just don't want to miss one."

"One session ain't going to make no difference."

"How do you know?"

"I just fucking know. Now, call him before it's too late and reschedule."

"What if he won't have us back?"

"He can't take us off the list because we're sick."

I didn't think Gene seemed sick. It looked to me like he had a case of the "can't be bothereds," but I knew stating that would only reduce the chance of us attending. I picked up the phone and dialled the number.

"Hello?"

"Hi, we had an appointment today at 11, but Gene is sick. Could we reschedule?"

"No problem, will I book you in for next Wednesday at 12?"

"Yes please. Thanks."

"See you then."

"Bye."

She was right: she would be seeing me then, but she wouldn't be seeing Gene.

"Babe, did you call SS yet? What did they say we got to do?"

"No, they said we had to finish marriage counselling first."

"I think we should go see them."

"What?"

I'd never thought of intentionally setting foot inside their building. I'd worried if I had, they would come up with a reason to take my children away from me, so I gave them a wide berth.

"We got to sit them down and tell them how it's going to be."

I couldn't understand how Gene could be so confident when it came to addressing them; he didn't fear them one bit. I was terrified to even look them in the eye; they had a power that filled me with terror every time I gave it any thought. Gene wasn't worried about losing his daughters; as far as he was concerned, he already had.

"Where are they in this town?"

"Beside the doctor's surgery."

"We can walk up there now and talk to them."

"I thought you weren't feeling well?"

"Babe, would you stop?"

"Ok, we can go but what are we going to say to them?"

"We're going to tell them how it's going to be – that we're a family and we're moving in together again. There ain't nothing they can do about it."

"We can't phrase it like that."

"Yes, we can, stop being so fucking afraid. They can't do shit."

"You don't know that."

"I do, I seen it hundreds of times in America."

I wondered for a moment if Gene meant in his own personal life. I doubted this was his first experience with social services. Maybe he did know more about it than I did. But perhaps American social services were less hard-line than the Northern Irish squad.

We started walking up the hill to their department. My body was telling me to turn back with every step that I took. What would Gene say to them? Would they decide I was an unfit mother and take my children away? Would they narrow the conditions of our involvement, objecting to us even meeting up in a public place until they had reassessed our case? It felt like we were asking for trouble by going. The dust had settled, in a new place than before, but I was reluctant to voluntarily shake it up again. Every time things were peaceful, Gene chose to disturb them again.

We approached the building and saw several office workers standing outside enjoying their smoke breaks. They glanced at us with suspicion, like they knew one of us was an abuser. I wondered if they could tell which one; if they could tell me which one. Gene produced a smoke too and stood outside, inhaling and exhaling with no sign of hurry about him. I wanted to get it over and done with, so we would know the outcome of inserting a hand into the raging lion's mouth. Gene was unperturbed as always. No circumstance seemed severe enough to ruffle his feathers. What I didn't know then was that Gene didn't fear anything because he didn't have anything to lose; nothing irreplaceable at least. If one family had to be scrapped, he could move elsewhere and start from scratch. He'd done it before, multiple times. It was no big deal.

"Alright, I'm ready," said Gene, putting his extinguished cigarette into his "pants" pocket.

My stomach sank. The building was anything but welcoming. The windows had metal grills on them, posters in every window about how to report a case of child abuse. I wanted to run, run and never look back. But I couldn't leave Gene. Even if I left him for that hour, I'd be back later that day. I couldn't stay away from him, even if it was outlaid that I had to. That was what terrified me. If it came to a choice between seeing Gene and keeping my girls, could I stay away from Gene for good? I hoped the love I had for my girls would be enough of a protective factor if that situation came about, but I was addicted to Gene more than any drug addict was addicted to their fix. Theoretically, I could talk about cutting contact, but if I wasn't with Gene, I was speaking to him on the phone, or thinking about him, or funding him. My ill health was worse than I'd ever realised before; and not just because of my mental illness. It was the worst case of love sickness - the sickest of loves.

We walked into the lobby and up to the receptionist. Gene stepped back and let me do the talking.

"Hello, we were just wondering if it would be possible to speak to a family social worker?"

"Do you have an appointment?"

"No, we were just hoping we could speak to someone for a few minutes."

"I'll see what I can do. Take a seat."

She gestured to the empty waiting area. Apparently, we were the only fools to present ourselves at their feet. I hoped I'd know the right things to say if a social worker joined us. I hadn't planned for this; I hadn't had time to weigh the weight of my words. It had all been Gene's idea, but now that we were in the building, it was up to me to improvise.

A loud, gruff lady burst through the door.

"Hello," she said, "What can I do for you?"

"We just wanted to talk to someone about our relationship."

"Ok?"

"We want to live together again."

"Do you have a case with us?"

"Not at the minute."

"What were the circumstances of your separation?"

"I was living in a refuge."

"No," she said, no hesitation. "You can't just move in together. We need to oversee it."

"Ok."

"Have you spoken to anyone about this before?"

"Yes, I had a social worker briefly after our daughter was born."

"What did she say you would have to do if you wish to reconcile?"

"Attend marriage counselling."

"Have you done that?"

"We're attending it at the moment."

"Well, you'll have to complete it first. I'll get someone to give you a call later. But under no circumstances are you to move back in together in the meantime."

Gene didn't say a word. He'd been put in his place, at least until we got out of the building and he had command of the conversation again.

"Fucking bullshit, man."

"What is?"

"Them people think they can tell us what to do."

"They can."

"We could just move in together you know. Ain't nothing they can do about it."

"That's not true."

"Aoife, you give these people too much power."

"I have to – they can take my kids away from me. I'm not risking that."

"No, they can't."

"They can."

"No, they fucking can't."

I couldn't help wondering how Gene had so much confidence and faith in the fact they would never work against us. From where I was standing, it seemed clear that they could, and would, if we crossed them.

"We just have to finish marriage counselling."

Gene looked irked. I could tell that he thought the whole process was pointless. He'd been happy to use my failure to arrange marriage counselling as a crop to whip me with, until I'd organised it. Now that we were finally attending it, Gene seemed to have lost enthusiasm for it. Gene's dreams were more useful as fantasies than realities. I could live more happily in one of the dreams he wove into a story than I ever could when he tried to make it a reality. That was a hard realisation to arrive at. Every one of my days had been spent working towards achieving the flawless marriage I'd thought existed at an immeasurable point in the future. But did it exist, or was it only illusory? I'd only know if I kept trying. If I stopped trying, I'd eliminate every chance of it becoming real. I couldn't cope with being the one responsible for that. I had to have put in every effort to restore our relationship, even if it was only a fruit machine when I reached the endpoint: costing me more than I was ever refunded in coins won.

I was losing strength; the only thing keeping me going was my hope for the appointment the next week. We had nine sessions left. That equated to three more months apart. Once we completed them, we could move in together. No one could stop us. Three more months of endurance; that was all that life demanded of me. My hope was the fuel that kept me running.

Chapter Fifty

The following Wednesday, I set out to marriage counselling. Gene and I had had an argument, and I had no idea if he was accompanying me to the appointment or not. Time would tell. I couldn't remember what the argument had been about: probably money, or my cowardly behaviour. I prayed he would show up at the door when I got there, but when I arrived, there was still no sign of him.

"Hello Aoife, is Gene on his way?"

"I don't know if he's coming today," I said, sheepishly.

"Oh?"

"We had an argument. He might come, but he hasn't messaged me."

"OK, well, we can start, and he can join us when he arrives."

Stephen seemed convinced that Gene would arrive, but he still didn't know the full story; of that day, or of our marriage. He had been sold Gene's dream version of events, just like I had. I pitied him a little, for the false hope he held on to. Somehow, I could identify his as false, but not my own.

"Well, is there anything you would like to discuss before Gene arrives?"

"What like?"

"Any issues you feel you can't discuss when he is here."

"Well, yes."

"Ok, feel free."

"I've been told our relationship is abusive."

"By whom?"

"I lived in a refuge for almost a year."

"OK, I didn't know that."

"Yeah, I don't think Gene is going to come today, on principal. He'll think it's my fault he missed it."

"Right, how is it your fault?"

"Because I argued with him before he was due to come."

"He still could have come if he wanted to work through your issues."

"So, you think he doesn't?"

"It doesn't seem that way. I don't know much about your

relationship – only the little that you've shared with me so far. You're quiet in the sessions – I haven't heard much of your side of the story. Want to tell me yours from the beginning?"

"Ok. I met Gene online. He lived in America, but he couldn't leave. He had unpaid child support for other children."

"How many children?"

"Three, but he only told me about two of them."

"Had he been married before?"

"Twice, but he only told me about one of the times."

I sensed that Stephen was emotionally backing away from me. Anyone that knew the truths of our relationship tended to recoil a little, but I usually put it down to them being judgemental. They just didn't know Gene on a personal level. They were judging him based on his credentials without giving him a chance to show them who he was. That was what I had done: I had given Gene the chance to teach me who he was instead of deciding who he was based on his history. But Gene had jigged his history to create the character he wanted me to get to know. He hadn't been straightforward with me; I had to acknowledge that. He had masked parts of who he was, of who he had been before I'd met him.

"I didn't know that. So, how long have you known each other?"

"Three years."

"And how long had you known each other before you got married?"

"We'd been speaking for seven months on the phone, but we'd only met in person eleven days before."

"So, you didn't really know each other?"

"It felt like we did. He understood me more than anyone I'd ever met before. I have a mental illness and he was the one person who got me. He still is."

"Ok, but how long were you married before things took a turn for the worse?"

"Well, right after we got married, Gene grabbed me by the throat once, but he promised it would never happen again."

"And did it?"

"Yes, but only a couple of times. The reason I left was because I felt like he was controlling me."

"And was he?"

"He was phoning me all the time, telling me what to wear, who I could see, and he was isolating me from my family."

"That sounds like emotional abuse."

"That's what I've been told."

"In the refuge?"

"Yeah."

"Well, it's up to you what you do. If you want to continue with marriage counselling, that's your choice. All I can tell you is my impression of it. It seems like you had what was basically a holiday romance, got married and then he immediately started treating you badly, once he knew you weren't going anywhere. It didn't stay good for long."

"Ok."

"Do you think that's what happened?"

"I don't want to."

"I'll let you think about what you want to do. If you want to come back, just give me a ring. But what I had suggested might not work if your relationship has been abusive."

"Ok," I said, walking out of the room and away from the one person who seemed to have supported our getting back together. He had only done so because he hadn't known the real story. Gene and I were alone in the world again; the only ones that believed in us. I still couldn't let go of the hope that was slipping out of my hands, but that I clung to for dear life.

Chapter Fifty-One

The next time I saw Gene, he tried his best to kill that hope. He announced that his rent was due; his landlord had told him to pay up or get out. I'd assumed he was up-to-date with his payments. He just didn't want to admit to me that he'd fallen behind. The workers were right: there was no end to the cycle of financial problems. I bailed Gene out, he got into more debt, I bailed him out of more debt, he got into even more. They'd told me the only way to put a stop to it was to stop paying, but did I have the strength to do that? Gene's problems were my problems even more than they were his, because I cared about consequences. I cared about what happened to him even when he didn't. I'd put myself into financial hardship just to help him out of his.

"How much do you owe?" I asked, my stomach scrunching as I said the sentence.

"Eight hundred."

"Isn't your rent two hundred a month?"

"I ain't been able to pay for months, babe."

"Why didn't you tell me?"

"I knew you'd give me shit because I walked out of that last job, but it wasn't right for me – I had to."

"When do you need it by?"

"Tomorrow."

"What'd your landlord say?"

"That I got to pay it or find somewhere else to live."

"And he's going to kick you out tomorrow?"

"He told me this a while ago, but I was too scared to tell you. I was afraid of how you were going to react. I tried to find a way to pay it, but I couldn't. You're my last option."

That was an awful lot of pressure to suddenly be under, especially since I had had no time to prepare myself for the revelation, or to prepare my bank account for its sudden balance plunge.

"Gene, I don't know if I can afford this. You are always asking me for money."

"I don't fucking ask – you just give it to me."

"That's not true."

"Name the last time I asked you for money."

I couldn't remember, nor was I going to list the times even if I did.

"Ok, I'll give it to you."

"Great, thank you, baby. I'll meet you near your place tomorrow."

"OK, where will we meet?"

"I'll meet you outside the bank and come with you. Will you recognise me? I'll wear a red rose in my lapel," Gene laughed.

He had turned his humour on again now that he'd got what he needed. I was no less drawn in by his charm than the first time he'd asked me for money, or rather, implied that he needed it and told me I was his last resort. That was Gene's cop out: half the time when he asked me for money, he didn't phrase it like a question; he phrased it like a statement and left it up to me to feel the guilt and decide to help him. With death, homelessness and starvation the only other options, it was an easy decision to make. It didn't feel like a choice to me, but Gene always told me it was. He said I liked to help him and then throw it in his face; to remind him of the countless times I had paid up for him.

I was having doubts about handing over the money. I could have used it towards a car, a holiday, clothes for the girls for a year or two. But without it, I'd still be able to meet our basic needs. I couldn't leave Gene living on the street while the money was sitting doing nothing in my bank account. The bills were paid, we had everything we required, and I had money left over; keeping it when Gene was in his current position would just be self-indulgence.

I would save every penny I could in the year that followed and get it back. Then, I'd use it for a treat for myself and the girls, once Gene was financially stable. It would enable him to focus his attention on finding a permanent job. I had to do what I could to keep him in the country. I knew if Gene ended up homeless, he'd go back to America. He knew America's streets better and had a better chance of survival living rough there than in Belfast. If he had no place of address, he'd lose his visa anyway. It was unimaginably dangerous to our marriage.

The next morning, I woke early and got ready to meet Gene. I'd agreed to meet him at 9am: the minute the bank opened. He wanted to get the money to his landlord as early as possible, to show him he took his tenancy very seriously. He couldn't risk further pissing his landlord off and being evicted the following month. He'd be timely with his payment, friendly and respectful, and all would be well.

I walked up the hill towards the bank. There was a bench outside, and somehow, I knew Gene would be there first that morning. If there was a transfer taking place in his direction, he was much more punctual than usual. Sure enough, I saw his large form and his long hair from blocks away. He was sitting slumped on a bench, his back to me, his earphones probably plugged in. From behind, I always thought Gene was severely depressed, but once I reached his front side, I always found that he was just absorbed in his music.

Gene turned around in his seat and saw me coming. He got up and strolled towards me, lingering on every step, like he couldn't be bothered advancing towards me; that was my job. I approached him and hugged him, against his belly, smelling the pungent odour of tobacco. He must have changed his smokes; probably to something cheaper. He leaned in and kissed me right on my pink lipstick.

"You ready, baby?"

"I don't know if I can do this," I said, looking away, and hoping the crowd around me would act as a buffer between myself and Gene's rage.

"What? You told me you were going to give me the money. I told my landlord I'd pay him today because of you."

"It's a lot of money, Gene. I don't know if I can afford it."

"Listen, let's go and sit down somewhere, you can get breakfast and we'll talk it over."

I knew to Gene that "talk it over" translated to "talk you round," and I was reluctant to go along with it, but there was nowhere else to go. I was with him; he was watching me with a hunter's eye, and I wasn't going anywhere, not without an emptied wallet, at least.

"Let's go to that place on the corner. You can get pancakes or something."

Gene slung his arm around my shoulder as I pushed the pram. "Would that make you happy, baby?"

I nodded, but I knew that it would take a hell of a lot more than that to retrieve the happiness I had lost what felt like so long ago. We walked to the nearest café and sat down.

"Do you want something to eat?" I asked Gene, tentatively. I couldn't help feeling like I was allowing myself to be used if I offered to pay when Gene had just asked me to lend him eight hundred pounds.

"No, babe. Just get me a coffee. Get something for you and the girls though."

The waiter appeared, took our orders and turned to leave. I wanted to beg him not to leave us unattended. I dreaded the conversation that would follow his departure from our table.

"Baby," said Gene, leaning across the table and taking my hand in his own, hynotising me with his eyes. "You got to help me. You're my only option."

"Can you get your landlord to wait another month until you get a job?"

"Baby – even if I got a job, I'd still be months behind on the rent."

"Why didn't you tell me you were behind?"

"Because I knew you'd act like this. You love making me feel like shit."

"I don't. Why would I love that?"

"I don't fucking know – you tell me. Listen – this is the last fucking time I ask you for money. Once I pay this, I'll have nothing. But I'd rather starve than ask you for a penny."

"Why?"

"Do you know how much of a piece of shit I feel for asking you this?"

"No."

"It don't feel fucking good, and you only make me feel worse."

"I'm sorry, I don't mean to. I'm just stressed out."

"You're always stressed out – that's just the way you are. Even when there's nothing to be fucking stressed about."

"Stop swearing at me."

"I'm not swearing at you – I'm just fucking swearing, and I'll swear all the fuck I like. You fucking swear."

"I know, but it's the way you do it – it makes me edgy."

"Everything makes you edgy."

"That's not true."

"It is – and you know it. It's your head fucking with you – you can't help that shit. But don't blame me for it."

My head was spinning, and I could barely remember my own identity, never mind my account number to withdraw the money.

"Here come your pancakes, babe. Eat up and we'll go get this shit done."

I didn't realise that I had agreed to it again, but I'd better not challenge Gene if I didn't want a scene in the restaurant. It was filled to capacity, and the last thing I needed was another public embarrassment. In a town as small as that one, I'd be running into every witness on an almost daily basis afterwards. I wanted everyone who saw Gene to think well of him. That way, if we needed anyone to vouch for the fact that we were a normally functioning couple, I could easily find someone to corroborate it.

I ate my pancakes in silence, drawing out each bite for as long as Gene would allow me to. I needed time to think, and it was hard to think of an exit plan when Gene was right in front of me. I had the sense that I needed to run as fast and as far as I could when Gene next turned his head. But the girls were strapped into two highchairs; doing so would be impossible. I finished eating, still trying to figure out how to postpone withdrawing the money without angering Gene. We got to the steps of the bank and Gene sent me inside. I made it to the swivel door and turned back, joining Gene outside again.

"Did you forget something?" he asked.

"No, I'm sorry, I can't do this."

"What the fuck do you mean, you can't do this?"

"I can't do it."

"Sure you can – you just turn around, walk into the bank and withdraw the money, babe."

"I can't afford it."

"Yes, you can, you're just being a selfish bitch."

His name-calling only made me more resolute about not handing over the money. He would have to steal the card from my purse if he was going to do it or hold a gun to my back while I talked to the cashier. But this wasn't a thriller; this was my life, and overly-dramatic situations like that don't happen in real life. We would have a reasonable discussion in calm tones and we'd sort it all out.

"Go inside and get the money now, babe. I got to pay Richard today."

"I can't. I'm sorry. Here," I said, sliding a tenner out of my purse. "Take this."

"What the fuck am I meant to do with that?" asked Gene. His nostrils were flared, and his forehead was forked again.

"Use it to get the train home and something to eat. I'm sorry for wasting your time."

Gene smacked the money out of my hand and it landed beneath us on the street. I guess even money didn't mean as much to him as he made out it did. It wasn't about the money; it was about something else – something he'd been trying to attain all along and had never managed to fully get: my obedience. A tear slid down my cheek and landed on the ground.

Gene roughly unbuckled Alice from the pram.

"What are you doing?"

"I'm fucking taking her."

"No, Gene. No!" I yelled. "Give her back, please."

Gene stormed off, Alice's head poking over his shoulder, her eyes looking into mine for what might be the last time I ever saw them.

"Where are you going?" I yelled.

I couldn't afford to care how many people were watching us anymore, or what they might think of my behaviour. I was going to lose my baby, for good, and that was the only thing I could see or hear.

"Gene!"

Gene kept walking, speeding up his pace. I ran with the pram, trying to catch up with him so I could calm him down and convince him to return Alice to me. I caught up with him and reached for his arm.

"Stop grabbing me!" yelled Gene.

I noticed many pairs of eyes on us and worried they'd think I was attacking him.

"You're grabbing me when I'm holding a baby."

"I'm not," I shouted. "I'm just trying to get her back. Please, I just want to hold my baby."

"You ain't getting her," said Gene, his lips straight and his voice even-toned. There was a sinister undertone to his words, like a sarcastic comment said through a grin.

He took off again, walking as fast as he could. I trailed along behind him with Hope still in the pram. She looked more worried than Alice did. At two years old, she was more aware of what was happening, and of my distress than her sister was. Alice seemed to think it was a fun game; just one of Daddy's jokes.

I caught up with Gene again and reached for Alice.

"Please, let me hold her."

"No, stop fucking grabbing me. You're going to make me drop her," he said, with emphasis.

"Stop acting crazy."

"I'm not, I just want to see my baby."

"She ain't just yours. She's my daughter and I ain't handing her over."

"You want to stay with Daddy, don't you?" he said to Alice.

He smiled, and she smiled back, not realising his smile was menacing.

"Gene, you can't do this. You're taking her because I wouldn't give you money?"

"That ain't why I'm taking her," Gene smiled into Alice's eyes. "I just want to see my daughter."

"When will you give her back?"

"You ain't getting her. I told you that. You want to keep my fucking daughters from me for over a year? See how you fucking like it."

"I didn't."

"You did – and you know what you are. You can pretend to other people you don't – but you know and when the girls are older, they'll know too. I'll make sure of that."

Gene stormed off again, in the opposite direction this time.

"If I give you the money, can you give me my baby back?" I yelled behind him.

He ignored me and kept walking too quickly for me to keep up.

I ran faster and grabbed Gene's arm. I reached for Alice, but Gene held her as high up as he could, so I had no hope of reaching her. Every time my hand almost reached her, he jerked her away and held her over his head again, like a toy in one of his favourite games.

"Gene," I cried, "Please."

I could barely talk; just yell and beg and bawl.

"Someone is going to call the cops and they're going to take you away, you crazy bitch." He raised the volume of his voice. "Stop grabbing me when I'm holding a baby. You're going to make me drop her. You're going to hurt her."

"I'm not – I just want to hold her."

I could feel all eyes on me. Everyone in my new town knew I was crazy now too; there was no escaping it. My reputation followed me wherever I went.

I followed Gene as he strode up and down the same street tens of times. Even if I couldn't reach Alice, I had to stay with him. I couldn't trust him enough to let him out of my sight. I didn't know what he might do; I knew he was capable of almost anything if it would sufficiently punish me for my mistreatment of him. He got to the bridge over the water and wove his way around it. It had several levels and only one entrance and exit. I couldn't see through my own tears to figure out how to get onto it. I could see Gene with my daughter, but I couldn't get anywhere near him. I'd lost the game; it was finally ending, and Gene was going to get exactly what he'd been aiming for all along: full destruction of Aoife. If he couldn't replace her thoughts with his own, her desires with his own, her values with his own, he'd destroy what was left of her as retribution. And what was the only way left to destroy me? To take my daughters away from me. Gene knew it was my worst fear. He'd listened for hours on the phone while I explored every worry about that scenario cropping up. He had extoled my mothering capabilities and slated social services hundreds of times. He knew I was a good mother, so they couldn't take my kids away. I hadn't realised that the person to do that would be my confidante; the one I had confided all my fears to all along. He knew me, he knew how much my children meant to me and so, he knew the final way to bring me down.

While I tried to work out how to reach Gene on the bridge, he made his escape and headed towards *Main Street* again. He charged up the hill with our daughter over his shoulder. I raced as fast as I could up the hill with the pram, trying to catch him. A man paused with his daughter by his side, to ask if I was ok. Even with Gene physically removing my child from me, I couldn't own up to the truth. I nodded through my tears and turned away from him. I knew where Gene was going to: the train station. If there happened to be a train waiting on the platform, he'd step onto it and I'd never see him or my daughter again. I had to beat him to it. I ran to the station, bumping into passers-by as I went. I couldn't even see their faces anymore; they were merely impediments, lifeless forms to whom I meant nothing.

I lost sight of Gene. The street was too busy to keep up with him, and no one understood how critical it was that I reach him. They were busy hurrying to the shops as much as I was hurrying to recover my lost child. Things like this didn't happen in Northern Ireland; they happened in American dramas with plots so exaggerated they were never believable. But here I was, living inside one, with hundreds of viewers with their noses pressed to the screen. I got into the train station and into the lift. I couldn't leave the pram behind; I had to take Hope with me. As the worn-out lift made its sluggish ascent, I hoped it wouldn't make me a minute too late. I heard a train starting and pulling out of the station as the doors opened. I looked at the destination on the display: Belfast. Gene was on the train and I was too late; my daughter was gone for good. I'd managed to keep my first-born, despite Gene convincing me on numerous occasions that he would take her from me. And now I had sacrificed my second daughter to him. All the visits with Gene that had beforehand, felt necessary for my mental state, suddenly seemed trivial in the face of losing one of my precious children. I didn't know what to do. Even if I waited for the next train, I wouldn't know where he had gone to next. I could go to his house, but would anyone let me in? And what then? Would he hold Hope hostage too? I ran out of the station, propelled along by despair rather than the adrenaline that had rushed through me only moments before. I cried as I walked, anything but discreetly. I didn't care if anyone saw. I had nothing to hide anymore. I was a ruined person; just an empty, broken wreck.

"Are you ok, love?" asked a middle-aged woman, placing her hand on my arm.

"No," I admitted, for what felt like the first time, to myself or to anyone else.

"What's wrong?"

"My husband took my daughter – because I wouldn't give him money."

"Call the police," she said to her friend.

The lady dialled the emergency services before I had time to argue with them. The thing I had dreaded all along had occurred: Gene had been reported to the police, because of me. I couldn't cope with that thought any more than the thought I had lost my child: I had destroyed my family in one action. Those two women suddenly became my adversaries and I backed away from them.

I walked back towards the station, checking it for a second time, just in case Gene hadn't got onto the train. Maybe he wouldn't do that to me. Maybe he was just trying to frighten me, so I knew how it would feel if he had to go back to America. Maybe he was just desperate and didn't know how else to behave.

That second, I saw Gene storm out the side door of the station. He still had Alice in his arms, and she no longer looked in good humour. Even she realised this wasn't a joke. I wanted Alice, and she wanted me, and the only thing standing between our bond was my so-called husband who I still loved more than I loved myself.

"Gene," I yelled, chasing him down the street.

I wanted to warn him that the police had been called, so we could make a hasty exit before they pulled up and put our problems on paper forever. If they took a report, social services would be informed, and Gene and I would have no hope of getting back together. We would be a fractured family for good, and my heart would be even more fragmented.

I couldn't catch up with Gene in time. A siren whirred, and I pretended I didn't know it was for me. The car seemed to have identified me: it wasn't hard to put two and two together. I was walking along with a double buggy, holding only one child, probably looking dishevelled and distressed. I still refused to look at them. I kept walking, hoping they'd take the hint and go back to the station. I didn't want or need their help.

"Excuse me," shouted the policeman.

It was too late. I couldn't ignore him any longer. I turned around slowly and tried to avoid looking him in the eye.

"Yes?"

"Did your husband take your baby?"

"Yeah. We just had an argument."

"Ok, where is he now?"

As he asked the question, Gene strolled back towards us, looking rather nonchalant. His rage had subsided, and he was ready for answering police questions, or rather, for lying in response to them.

"Hello, we received a phone call from someone anonymous."

"Ok, what about?"

"They said you took this lady's baby because she wouldn't give you money."

Gene glared at me; I knew it was for breaking the pact; for telling the truth to anyone other than Gene. I was irrepressibly shaking, and there was nothing I could do to stop it. I was shivering even though it was May, and a sunny day at that.

"Do you want to sit down?" asked the policeman.

I felt gratitude for his tenderness, but I just wished Gene had been the one to offer me one. He was always the one that comforted me after he had created the chaos, and I didn't like anyone else to step into his role.

The policeman moved towards me with his notepad, and his female co-worker took Gene aside to make notes about his side of the story. I didn't want to say anything, but I was so upset I could no longer hold back. It was like trying to piece together the same cracked jug that had already been glued fifty times, and now there were too many chips missing to make it look like it wasn't broken.

"I was in a refuge," I said under my breath.

"Ok," said the policeman, writing that on his pad.

"I know you don't want to tell me about this, but I have to pass this on to social services."

"Why?"

"Because a third party reported it. You were causing a public disturbance, so out of respect to the observer, we have to take it seriously."

"Ok."

I couldn't say much else, and I could hear Gene in the background, joking with the policewoman and informing her that I was "Type 2 Bipolar." She seemed taken in by him and likely attributed the disturbance to my unstable mental state.

The policeman moved beside her and spoke to Gene.

"What started the argument?"

"I asked her for money for rent."

"Ok, well, why did you do that?"

"I can't afford it. If I don't pay my rent, I lose my visa and I end up back in America. I want us to stay together."

"Do you want to stay together too?" the lady asked me."

I nodded.

"Well, can you lend him the money this once?"

"It's not just once," I mumbled, but I doubted she heard me.

"I been trying to get a job, man, but I can't find one. It's hard finding employment when I ain't from here. I ain't got none of ya'll's qualifications, and nobody wants to hire me because I ain't from here."

The policewoman looked at him compassionately.

"Well, I'm sure you'll work things out," she said. "We'll let you go. Just try not to have any more arguments in the street. You'll get in trouble for disturbing the peace."

Gene winked at them and gave them his sideways smile.

"Thank you," he said, waving over his shoulder to them as we walked away, hand in hand.

We got a few metres down the road and Gene became serious again.

"You're going to have to give me that money, babe."

"I know."

"Ok, I'll wait here. You run and get it."

I walked into the bank, this time with no hesitation in my step. It was worth paying the money to get home in one piece, without having to talk to any more police officers.

"Could I withdraw eight hundred pounds, please?" I asked the cashier, handing her my passport and providing her with my account details.

She looked at me inquisitively, like she was wondering what I could need that much cash for, but she didn't say anything. She counted the notes out, and as I watched her do it, I realised how much sacrifice it had taken to save those hundreds of pounds, and how great a fraction of our savings it accounted for. I felt pained to part with it, despite the fact it was nothing but material wealth. The emotional wealth I'd be gaining in exchange for it would make it worthwhile. Gene would be happy, he would still have a roof over his head and his visa wouldn't be in jeopardy. It was the right thing to do, even though it felt wrong.

I walked outside and handed Gene the wad of cash. He took it from my fingers, without an ounce of visible regret or a second thought. He pulled me towards him.

"Thank you, baby. I promise you – everything will be ok."

Gene walked me a few metres downhill, in the direction of my house – the house of which, thankfully, he still didn't know the location.

"I better go and pay Richard, babe."

He took his phone out of his pocket and held the screen up to his face.

"I got missed calls from him. I'd better hurry before he gets salty. I'll call you, babe."

I walked the rest of the way home alone, and I had never before experienced the same kind of beautiful relief combined with severe shock. I could barely breathe, I couldn't look back, I couldn't imagine seeing Gene again after such a debacle, I couldn't imagine never talking to him again. I'd decide what to do about it when I got home.

That afternoon, my dad, Poppy and Pete were coming for lunch. I had to calm myself down and focus on making everyone a servable lunch. Maybe if I put extra effort into the food I served and the smile I applied when they rang the doorbell, no one would notice anything amiss. I struggled to assemble the sandwiches. All feeling had gone out of my hands. My brain had slowed to a halt and all I could feel was fear thick as fog and internal numbness to match the bodily numbness.

The doorbell rang, and I tried my utmost to smile. I answered the door, and everyone sang their hellos and exchanged their hugs. I couldn't feel a thing. I wasn't human anymore. All the human heart I'd once had had been bashed out of me, and I couldn't tell you exactly why or how. My mind was a mass of confusion, and there was no returning to my former self and the possibilities that had followed me through my early life. I wasn't yet twenty-nine, but I had the experience of a ninety-year old, not to mention the fatigue and disenchantment with life.

I served out the sandwiches, amazed I'd managed to assemble them at all, and sat down at the end seat at the table. I crumpled over, exhausted, using my own hands to prop my head up.

"Are you ok, love?"

My face screwed up and I knew I couldn't lie. I shook my head.

"What happened?"

"Gene took Alice today, until I gave him money."

"How much?" asked my dad, livid.

"Eight hundred."

"You gave him eight hundred pounds?" he asked.

"Yeah."

"I can't believe you gave him more money. Are you stupid?"

"Wait a minute," Pete jumped in. "Aoife has just been through something traumatic. That isn't helpful."

"Thanks," I whispered. "I'm going outside for a smoke."

I stood outside, breathing a little of the day's stress out of my lungs. I hoped someone would join me; namely, Pete, but no one came. They wanted to give me my space. I stubbed out my cigarette and went back inside, more composed, and ready for small talk.

"So, what happened? Are you ok? That sounds awful," said Pete.

"Gene needed money for his rent. It's my fault really – I said I'd meet him, so he got the train here, and when he arrived, I wouldn't give him the money."

"So, he took Alice?"

"Yeah he carried her all over town. If I tried to get her, he shouted that I was trying to grab him when he was holding a baby."

Everyone shook their heads and stared at the table top. I knew the tablecloth wasn't that interesting; no one knew the right thing to say.

"So, he kidnapped Alice until you gave him money? You know that's extortion?" said Pete.

"I don't know," I shook my head. "He needed the money, or he wouldn't have had anywhere to live."

"So, he's behind on rent again? Love, he's never going to get out of debt," said my dad.

Part of me knew that, but I was too troubled to get into such a discussion. It would only draw more negativity out of the well inside me that was spilling over. My family made vague conversation for the rest of the lunch hour and then left me alone once more with my thoughts.

I picked up my phone. I had nowhere else to turn now that everyone had left. I had missed calls from Gene, but I decided to ignore them. I'd call him in a day or two when things had settled down again. I was too traumatised to hear his voice again. Every time I thought of him, I just thought of my daughter's head bobbing over his shoulder and the feeling of losing her forever. I picked her up and smothered her with kisses; I was so grateful to have her back, I could barely even be sad about what had taken place. Tomorrow would be a new day, and Gene and I could start over. I'd always promised I loved him unconditionally, and it was true. He might do things in this life with which I didn't agree, or that filled me with despair, but that didn't threaten my love for him. It was sturdier than any manmade, or God-created structure, and it would never wane, no matter what happened.

Chapter Fifty-Two

For two days, I didn't contact Gene. I needed time to make sense of what had happened to us. A large part of my discomfort came from the police involvement. I'd never had any type of involvement with the police; as a bystander, or as an aggressor. They had made me feel like I belonged to the latter category; a co-conspirator in the disturbance of public peace.

I finally picked up my phone to call Gene. It was his birthday, and I needed to wish him a happy birthday, however limited our contact with one another had been. He hadn't made great efforts to contact me either. I had had two missed calls from him and an email stating that he needed to run something by me, or he'd have to make the decision himself. Whatever it was could wait until everything had cooled down. I didn't want to jump from one disagreement to another. Gene ran every decision past me; the trivial ones, at least. Which flavour of popcorn should he get today? Should he walk into town or get the bus? Should he get hotdogs or ham for dinner? I knew it would be nothing urgent, no matter what it was.

When I called Gene, he sounded distant; like we didn't know each other as well as we did. He was probably still feeling aggrieved after the events of a few days before. After all, I had contributed to the police being called out, by sharing our secrets with a stranger.

"Hey."

"Did you pay the rent?"

"Did you get my email?"

"Yeah, what was it?"

"It's kind of late now."

"Well, I was in shock after the other day. I needed a couple of days to calm down."

"I tried calling you."

"Yeah, I saw you rang a couple of times."

"I'm in America."

I went silent for what felt like an hour.

"What?!"

"I'm back in America."

"What?"

I couldn't comprehend what Gene was saying to me. Surely, he had to be joking? I'd given him the money to pay his rent in the end, so he had had no need to leave.

"You should have answered your fucking phone the other day."

"I didn't know that was what you meant."

"Well, you didn't answer me for three fucking days."

"So, you go to America? I don't believe you. I know you're just trying to upset me."

My one real fear was coming to life before me.

"I ain't lying."

"Prove it. I don't believe you."

Gene hung up on me. I wondered what that was meant to prove until I received a message from him: a photograph. It was the "fuck-you" man on his middle finger, the finger held up to me, in front of an American socket. My heart seemed to fall out of my body. It had been dead for a long time anyway, so it was just like ridding my body of the extra weight.

My brain asked itself a million questions. Was Gene telling the truth? Had he edited a photo to make it look like he was in America? Did he use the money I gave him to go home without telling me? Was he still sitting in his house, just a few miles away, laughing at how gullible I was? I'd believed so many of his lies before. What made this one any different? He was just trying to wreak his revenge for the week before, for me handing over the money so unwillingly. He wanted me to know what I had risked in delaying giving it to him.

But no, Gene was in America. But maybe he would come back, or maybe I could go there. The situation was still reparable, as far as I was concerned.

• •

Months passed, and Gene and I remained in sporadic contact with one another. Sometimes Gene vanished for months at a time and then reappeared, like not a moment had elapsed, like he was testing my faithfulness to him.

I stayed for months in the town where I'd lived in the refuge, waiting for my lease to come to an end. I intended to move as soon as it expired. I would move back to the same area that Gene and I had lived in. I would buy all the items we had originally owned together and recreate the life we had had there. If I lived where we used to be together, I could bring the relationship that continued in my imagination back to life, almost convincingly. I couldn't bear to accept that Gene was three thousand miles away, all over again. I found a flat, just around the corner from our old house. It didn't resemble the house in the slightest, but it was within feet of Belmont Place's familiar front door. I walked past the house every single day, staring at it from afar, trying not to arouse suspicion in the current occupants. The bedroom window was still permanently wide open, just like Gene had preferred it to be. The house looked the same, minus the cigarette butts peppering the driveway and the lamp that used to light the hall window, that had now been replaced with a vase that wasn't our taste. I loathed the new occupant for changing our home. I wished it could forever remain in the state it had been in when I'd left, so I could soothe and torment myself each time I walked past it. Seeing the facade of the house made me feel like I was almost home, but not quite. I could never walk through its door again, no matter how painfully I wanted to. I imagined asking the current residents if it was ok if I looked around, to reassure myself that things had happened as they had, that I had been justified in my decision to leave, that I hadn't imagined the entire thing. I knew if I could just see the inside of one of the rooms, it would bring every memory back to me like it had happened only hours earlier. But I never could. I couldn't even look at the photos of the rooms I'd taken on my phone; my phone had wiped its memory of most of the photos I'd taken in the last year. That life was long gone, and there was nothing to be done about it. So, I kept walking up the hill, in the direction of the shops we used to visit together, never forgetting to look back over my shoulder at Hope's bedroom window. I could still see the bookcase next to the window; the one where I had kept the lamp Gene hadn't allowed me to display in our bedroom. I remembered looking at that window from the other side, feeling like a caged animal; one that was going to never feel the tang of fresh air in my lungs again. I thought of myself facing that mirror, trying to recognise the image in it and sobbing silently, so Gene wouldn't accuse me of playing the victim again. That window was just enough of a reminder to keep me half-heartedly edging towards my future. One day, I bumped into our next-door neighbour from 2 Belmont Place, coming out of the post office as he was going in. He didn't say hello, but he gave me a strange smirk; like he was the last person left to know the truth about the deranged character that had lived inside that house. I still see him sometimes, out walking his dogs, and every time I do, I get horrific flashbacks.

I finished the freedom programme. I found it neither useful or useless; they didn't understand the full story of my marriage. Their rules were too general to apply to an individual life. My key worker, Jennifer, was getting fed up with me; I could feel it in the air at our appointments the way I could sense it when Gene was in foul form. "We're just going in circles here," she said to me one day.

I took what she said to heart and never phoned her again. She didn't believe in me anymore than I believed in myself. She thought I was mentally stuck in the relationship forever, and maybe she was right. As for my original *Kindle*, the one that contained all that works that had defined me before I met Gene, it was stolen by one of the cleaners who cleared out 2 Belmont Place. Not long after it had been emptied, I signed into my account online and found that it had been renamed as "Joan's Kindle." I can only surmise that is what happened to it – I had left it behind in the house, inside one of the binbags. It's quite fitting really; that my literary identity was wiped out and replaced with someone else's.

I never got my music back. Gene never brought his external hard drive into town to allow me to transfer it to my computer. I didn't force the issue; I had enough other things to worry about. Maybe my dad was right; sometimes, you just have to cut your losses, even if it's like cutting off a part of yourself.

I started to date someone, but I still loved Gene with my whole being. I knew Gene would consider it to be the ultimate betrayal. I was tired of being stuck in limbo; waiting until my death bed was rolled out for a final chance at reconciliation with Gene. He was the one, the only one I'd ever wanted or needed, but if he'd wanted to be with me, he would have stayed in Northern Ireland. I told myself I had to force myself to move on with my life, but I couldn't. I had to be honest with Gene. I had to tell him that I had betrayed him. We were still married, and I had cheated him. I hoped that he would forgive me. He had always told me that if I cheated on him, that would be the one thing he could never forgive. Honesty was more important to me than acceptance. I lifted the phone.

"Gene?"

"Yeah?"

"I have to tell you something."
"How fucking many?"
"How many what?"
"How many dudes?"
"One."
"Whore."
"I was trying to move on. You don't even talk to me anymore."
"So, you're saying what you did is right?"
"No, I hate myself for it."
"You cheated on me."
"I was always faithful when we were together."
"Are you my wife?"
"What?"
"Are you my fucking wife?"
"Yes."
"Then you're a whore."
"I'm sorry – please forgive me. I love you."
"You're only telling me this because you want to hurt me."
"That's not true. I wanted to be honest with you. It was a mistake."
Gene hung up on me, but I kept ringing him. I wasn't going to give
up on him, no matter what he called me, no matter how many times
he rejected my apology, no matter how much he destroyed me. He
was the one, and my last chance at happiness. Finally, he answered.
"Yeah?"
"I love you."
"You do?"
"I'm so sorry – I only want to be with you."
"Well, prove it – move here for me."
"Where are you living?"
"In a trailer park, with Rain."
"Are you working?"
Gene exhaled his smoke. "No, I mean – I'm babysitting for Rain.
She and Dean split. She's on her own with three kids now."
He said it like it was an unimaginably difficult situation to be in; one
that required empathetic friends that were willing to put themselves
out for additional support.
"Does she pay you?"
"The government does – forty dollars every two weeks."
"How do you live on that?"
"I don't – it covers my smokes."

"Well, what do you eat?"

Gene refused to answer me.

"I'm just trying to work out what we would live on."

"We'll figure it out."

Doubts screamed loudly inside my mind again.

"I have the picture I drew of you. You left it in the house. Do you want me to send it to you?"

"You can burn that shit – it's garbage. Are you coming here, or what?"

"I don't know."

"Eh, babe, I got something I got to tell you."

"Yeah." My heart hit its overused pause button.

"I got warrants again."

"What? How?"

"Driving without a license."

"You drove without a license?"

"I had to."

"Why?"

"To get to a job interview."

I knew Gene was lying, but I wasn't prepared to argue with him about it when we had just made up.

"Anyway, I got to pay two hundred dollars by next week or I'm going to jail."

"For how long?"

"Six months."

"For driving without a license?"

"Yup. I told Rain I didn't want to ask you for the money, but you're the only person I know I can ask. I told her I wasn't going to ask you, but she talked me into it."

I remembered an allegory I'd heard in the refuge for abuse. It played out in my mind, like something had begun to click.

"You walk down the street. There is a pothole. You don't see it – you fall into it. You walk down the street again, you forget about the pothole, you fall into it. You walk down the same street, you remember the pothole, you try to step around it, but you slip into it again. You walk down a different street."

It was time to walk down a different street, whether I was ready to or not. I wasn't going to give Gene the money. I wasn't going to offer to bail him out, and I'd see through his actions whether he still wanted to be with me as much as I wanted to be with him.

"I don't have the money – I'm sorry."

"I guess I'm going to jail."

"I'm sorry, I wish I could help."

"I won't be allowed my phone in there – I'll call you in six months when I get out."

Gene hung up on me.

■■

Six months passed. I still don't know whether Gene made it to jail or not; maybe he was just making the whole story up to punish me for my lack of support. During that time, I had regularly sent Gene photos of the girls, updates on what they'd been doing and messages reminding him how much I loved him. Finally, one day, when I'd stopped expecting him to reply, he did.

"What do you want?"

"I love you."

"Call me."

I phoned Gene and every sad strand of my soul stilled as I waited for the sound of his voice.

"Hey."

"Gene – why won't you speak to me?"

"What's the point – you ain't coming here."

"Why do you say that.?"

"It's all just a fantasy, man. You ain't got no intention of coming here. I waited for you in Belfast – for a year and a half. You kept telling me we were getting back together, and we never did. You told me you'd find us a house and you never did. I'm just a fool."

"You aren't. I love you. I need your help if I'm going to move there."

"What do you mean?"

"I need you to come and help me over there. I have too much to bring, I have to sell all my stuff, I have to bring both girls – it's too much to do alone."

Gene didn't offer to help.

"You ain't coming – just say it."

I think he just wanted me to say it to make it ok for him to abandon us.

"It's not that."

"It is. I'm fucking history."

"Don't say that."

301

"It's true – I ain't got no reason to live no more – I don't want to."

"Don't say that – I love you so much."

"You're the love of my life," said Gene.

"You're the love of my life," I sobbed.

"Even if you meet someone else and get married, I never will. I'll love you until I'm in a box in the ground," he cried.

"I don't want to meet someone else – I love you. I just want you. I always did."

"I'm done. Go and find happiness, my girl."

"No, I can't be happy without you – I need you."

"You'll be alright – once I'm gone. I wish I'd done this more violently, so you could enjoy the pictures as I do it."

Gene hung up and I never heard from him again. I don't know if he's alive, or if he's not. Every day I hope the fact I haven't heard about his death through his family or on the news means that he's still living another day and sleeping another night. Even three thousand miles apart and with no contact, my love for him endures. What comforts me, is thinking of us, just two souls under the one enormous blanket of the same sky, its stars the symbols of our unrealised fantasies. I hold onto hope; no longer for Gene and me, but for the unknown yet to unfold up ahead. The little chink of light that is my hope has yet to be extinguished. I keep placing one foot in front of the other; my art, my girls, my faith in fate working things out driving me forwards. I live in a new house in a different neighbourhood now; I try to avoid our old house. I have the final divorce papers stowed away in my room, in case I ever need them. I hope that someday I meet someone who makes me see what everyone else saw was wrong with our love. I don't know what the future holds; for me, or for Gene, but I hope, for us both, it's life. Every time I walk down a street and see a figure in the distance, in an outfit of all white – resembling painter's whites, the flashbacks hit me: I see Gene storming towards me, sickness fills me up, my heart races. They get closer, until I can see the outline of their features and I know for sure that it isn't Gene. That's when the devastating disappointment sets in, and I wish to God that it was. But once they pass me, I'm filled with that beautiful relief again. Now, to me, that's the closest thing to bliss. And because of that feeling, I know for sure, I didn't imagine the abuse.

22329909R00180

Printed in Great Britain
by Amazon